TAXMAN

John Ginos

Fulton Books, Inc.
Meadville, PA

Published by Fulton Books 2021

TAXMAN is a work of fiction. All incidents, dialogue and characters with the exception of some well-known historical events and figures, are products of the author's imagination and are not to be construed as real.

Where real-life historical persons appear, the situations, incidents, and dialogues concerning those persons are fictional and are not intended to depict actual events or to change the fictional nature of the work.

ISBN 978-1-63710-521-4 (paperback)
ISBN 978-1-63710-523-8 (hardcover)
ISBN 978-1-63710-522-1 (digital)

Printed in the United States of America

I dedicate my debut novel to my lovely mother, R. Jean Ginos (1930–2012). Your enthusiastic passion for reading and writing has been a lifelong inspiration for me, as well as your other children, grandchildren, and great-grandchildren.

Contents

Prologue 7

Chapter 1: The Beginning 11
Chapter 2: Los Angeles Stress 1995 35
Chapter 3: Inside the Workplace 51
Chapter 4: March Madness 73
Chapter 5: Final Four 95
Chapter 6: Gray May 116
Chapter 7: June Gloom 135
Chapter 8: Hotel California 161
Chapter 9: Summer Heat 193
Chapter 10: Game Plan 213
Chapter 11: Working the Plan 240
Chapter 12: Battle Lines 260
Chapter 13: Deadly Intentions 281
Chapter 14: Solo Aggression 310
Chapter 15: Republican Convention 1996 325
Chapter 16: Presidential Election 1996 341
Chapter 17: Congressional Oversight and Hearing 1997 358
Chapter 18: End Game 376

Epilogue 401
Author's Notes and Acknowledgments 405

Prologue

Nothing in this world can be said to be
certain except *death and taxes*.

—Benjamin Franklin

As he bursts through the door, he is startled, staring directly into the barrel of a Glock 19 9mm handgun, suppressor attached, pointed at his face in a double-handed grip by a former soldier wearing surgical gloves. The man is clearly ready to end his life in an instant if his next move isn't done in a submissive attitude.

He immediately stops in his tracks, throws up his hands, and exclaims, "Whoa, easy T! It's just me!"

"Being ex-military, you should know better than busting in here," his partner retorts and slowly lowers his weapon but doesn't completely relax to a noncombative posture. "What's happening with the subject?"

"He's out cold. Time to move!"

"Let's check it out," the armed man says as he shoves the weapon into his waistband and grabs the gym bag next to him on the floor, at the base of the closet in the bedroom.

They proceed to the living area, where the subject is lying unconscious on his side on the floor a few feet away from the arm-chair but in front of the coffee table.

"You sure he won't wake while we are doing this?"

"Not a chance. I used enough to knock out a horse! He's a big dude. No sense on taking any chances."

"Yeah, let's be quick and precise."

T opens his bag and pulls out another pair of surgical gloves, handing them to his partner along with a surgical mask. They both apply masks, and T, the obvious leader of the operation, methodically rolls up the victim's sleeve.

As he removes a syringe from the bag, his partner asks, "Tell me again why we are offing this guy. For some kind of IRS tax issues?"

"Too late to question things, man. Concentrate. This is worth a lot of money for my client and will allow us to follow our plan to get out of this shit."

"Just seems like a real straight shooter. A death sentence might be a little extreme, don't you think?"

"We are not being paid to overthink this. We just need to make sure our tracks are covered. We complete this, see the rest of the job through, get paid, and we're done! Now quit talking, and let's finish this."

"Okay, good. I really don't like this dude you're working for. Sooner or later, I have a strong feeling he'll screw you too."

Without another word, the partner tightens a rubber surgical hose around the victim's upper arm with a knot. As the vein in the crook of the victim's left elbow bulges, the leader inserts a two-inch needle into the vein and slams a "Hot Dose" mixture of heroin and battery acid into his bloodstream.

They take the victim's right hand and place his fingers onto the syringe, making sure that his prints will be the only ones detectable. They empty the glass of booze on the coffee table down the sink and replace it with a quarter full of the same, but uncontaminated, beverage.

Next, they remove his billfold and confiscate the $225 cash it contains, tossing it into the bag while leaving the wallet on the floor next to his body. They remove their masks and all evidence of either of their existence in the room, and the partner takes off his toupee, glasses, and gloves, tossing them into the bag.

"Where's the girl?" asks the leader.

"Just outside in the hallway, making sure the coast is clear."

"Is she still unrecognizable? Looking like the woman who checked into this room?"

"Oh, yeah. Cas is real good with makeup, and that wig makes her look like an entirely different person."

"Call her and make sure we are clear to leave."

The partner pulls out his cellphone, makes the call, and hangs up. "Good to go," he says to T.

After shutting the door behind him, the leader removes his surgical gloves and shoves them into his pocket. With the gym bag in tow, the three of them move quickly toward the stairwell.

It is 9:15 p.m. as they enter the parking garage. They get into two separate cars—the leader in one, the partner and the woman in the other.

The leader places a quick call to his boss as he drives away. "It's done," he says and then hangs up.

And with his two words, a life is gone just like that.

CHAPTER ONE

The Beginning

Jordan Duncan was born on August 15, 1969, in San Diego, California (coincidentally, the first day of the Woodstock Festival on the other side of the country), to parents, Edward Duncan and Gabriela Esposito-Duncan. Sadly, Jordan's father was killed in action in Vietnam on December 1969. He never knew his father and was raised by his mother as an only child.

> I'm the one
> I found the birthday of the sun
> But all things change
> And I think it's the birthday of the rain
> —Sung by Melanie at Woodstock (8/15/1969)

Jordan's parents met and dated in high school. They married after graduating, both at the age of eighteen years old.

Gabriela was five feet eight inches tall, slender, and had long athletic legs. Her brown hair is parted in the middle and cascades down her back nearly to the waist. Dark-brown eyes are esthetically set on an attractive sculpted face, which features a thin longish nose, full lips, and a beautiful complexion of olive-toned skin.

She was born in San Diego shortly after her parents, Antonio and Gina Esposito, migrated to the US from Italy in the late 1940s following the end of the Second World War, along with her father's brother, Giordano. Tony managed an auto body shop and settled his family in Chula Vista, a small suburb of San Diego just north of the Mexican border.

Edward Duncan was the youngest of three children born to Bert and Emily Duncan in Chula Vista, California. Bert owned a Farmers Insurance franchise and was well known in the small community. Eddie became an exceptionally good athlete in his youth. He had an outgoing personality, quick wit, and was popular among his peers.

By the time he was in high school, Eddie became somewhat of a legend at Chula Vista High because of his success as the quarterback on the football team. He was 5'10" tall and weighed 165 lb., had straight sandy-blond hair that covered his ears, pale-blue eyes, and an Irish-looking round face.

It was during the spring of their junior year at CVHS that the popular Eddie Duncan met the shy Gabriela Esposito at track practice. Everyone in the school knew who Eddie was, but Gabriela was different from other girls. She didn't seem to notice or be overly impressed with Eddie's athletic accomplishments. She trained hard and was quite successful in her own right, running the 440 and 880 on the girls' track team. Edward noticed her almost-perfect stride and couldn't help but admire her long athletic legs as she ran.

He thought keeping pace with her while running the longer distances she incorporated into her training might help improve his stamina and maintain top speed in the sprints that he ran. She was surprised but agreed to his request that they train together. Though they had different backgrounds and personalities, the two of them became good friends and started to see each other socially. They became almost inseparable during their senior year. Much to the astonishment and dismay of other girls, Eddie asked Gabriela to be his date to the senior prom.

They were in love. Their goals and aspirations for the future included each other. Edward's dream was to go to UCLA. He had gone on a recruiting trip to the Westwood campus and knew that was where he wanted to play college football. Unfortunately, the coaching staff at UCLA were concerned about Edward's lack of height. They had just accomplished a shocking upset of number 1 ranked

Michigan State in the Rose Bowl and were led by All-American junior quarterback Gary Beban. They advised him to play a year at a local junior college, and they would reevaluate his scholarship potential at that time.

Sadly, Eddie graduated high school in 1967, the year of the highest number of draftees into the US Army for the Vietnam War. Edward Duncan was drafted in the late summer of 1967 to join the over five hundred thousand US troops in Vietnam. He and Gabriela decided to get married before he reported for duty. Without the blessing of either of their parents, they eloped to Las Vegas one weekend and got married with no regrets. He excelled in basic training and was asked if he would like to become part of the 101st Airborne Division. Eddie thought it might delay and possibly minimize his actual combat time in Vietnam, so he agreed. He was very wrong!

The circumstances of Eddie's untimely death left a hollow feeling in Gabriela's heart. She had to work and try to fill the role of parenting solo. As much as she did her very best to ensure Jordan didn't want for love or the necessities of life, she knew that she couldn't replace a father figure in his life. It broke her heart, but that was the hand she was dealt when her husband died in 'Nam.

She continued to run, mostly in the mornings, to try to keep her sanity and her figure. When Jordan was an infant, she pushed him in the stroller as she ran. When he was a toddler, he would ride his bike next to her as she ran, trying his best to keep pace. By eleven, he felt he was old enough to run with her, and he struggled to keep up. It wasn't until he was in high school that he could match his mother's steady pace. This morning ritual kept them closely connected in spirit and mutual respect. It was rare that either of them missed a day.

Genetically, Jordan was blessed with his mother's olive complexion and his father's pale-blue eyes, wavy light-brown hair, and a nice smile. Jordan inherited both his parents' athleticism. He excelled in football, basketball, and baseball in youth sports in San Diego County. In 1982, as a twelve year old, he played on the South Bay (Chula Vista) Little League all-star team that advanced to the Western Regional Championship game played in San Bernardino, California.

Throughout his adolescence, Jordan was rather socially reclusive, even though he was developing into a very handsome athletic kid. He always felt different and somewhat embarrassed by the fact that he didn't have a dad like the other kids. Of course, his athletic talent helped him gain confidence, and the many coaches that he encountered growing up were able to teach him discipline and guidance from the male perspective. The rebel in him came out more in the classroom and his reluctance to participate in any religious youth camps or gatherings. His mother, being a full-blooded Italian, was brought up in a strict Catholic home, and she tried to instill that culture in their home and encouraged him to be involved in the local Catholic parish. Jordan did not gravitate at all to the local priesthood leadership. Gabriela didn't push it, as he was a good kid and stayed out of trouble. She encouraged and supported him in his athletic pursuits as it consumed most of his time outside of school.

In 1983, Jordan at thirteen was attending junior high school, and Gabriela was managing an Italian restaurant in Old Town San Diego owned by her uncle, Giordano. She met an investment banker from the East Coast named Phillip Conley. He came to San Diego for business and was quite charming, and they started dating whenever he came to town. The following year, he proposed, and they married when Jordan was fourteen. It was just after his freshman year in high school. Phil insisted his new family move to New Jersey. The move across the country was met with much resistance from Jordan. He was just coming into his own as a teenager and a high school student/athlete. He was developing a love for the ocean, learning to surf with his buddies at Imperial Beach, and was beginning to get over his social awkwardness.

Animosity began to build between Jordan and Phil. He remained close to his mom, and their love was mutually unconditional. However, her marriage to Phil had driven a wedge between them metaphorically speaking. Jordan didn't trust Phillip Conley and his motivation in marrying Gabriela. He refused to go to New Jersey and wanted to stay in SoCal, even if it meant living with his paternal grandparents. Gabriela's parents had moved back to Italy to tend to her sick grandmother.

Gabriela always had a rather frosty relationship with Eddie's parents, as they had been against the marriage in the first place. They were shocked and outwardly disappointed when they found out that Gabriela was with child while Edward was still in the army. They were devastated by his sudden tragic death. They cut off contact with Gabriela and her newborn son, their own grandson. But Jordan suggested that Gabriela contact them and ask if he could reside with them for the next three years while he finished high school. She didn't have the heart to tell him that it was not an option, and she insisted that they stay together as a family. Phil had suggested that they put him in a private boarding school in Southern California. Gabriela, to her credit, flat out refused to consider that option. She was a lot stronger in her relationship with Phil than what many believed.

In the late summer of 1984, the newly formed family moved to Short Hills, New Jersey, an upscale community in the northeast section of the state that served mainly as a suburb to the wealthy Wall Street executives that commuted across the Hudson River to work in New York City.

Fortunately, Jordan met a new friend almost immediately. Ironically, their first encounter did not start out on a positive note. It was summer in New Jersey, and he had never experienced the humid, muggy conditions of the northeast summers. Each day he rode his bike around town, sweating and inwardly cursing this awful new environment he was forced to endure, desperately looking to find a game or sport in which he could participate. One day, as he rode through Taylor Park on Main Street, he saw some guys playing basketball. An aspect he noticed and liked about New Jersey was how green it was during the summer. After all, it is called the Garden State. This basketball court was surrounded by grass and large oak trees just outside the twelve-feet wire fencing that encompassed the court. He watched for a bit until the game ended and asked if he could participate in the next game.

Alvin Bockman Jr., who was the biggest kid on the court and the obvious ringleader, smirked at this new unknown kid and asked sarcastically, "Who are you going to run with? I don't see any team with you!"

Jordan, being a typical nonconfrontational, laid-back Californian, simply said, "I'll run with whoever. Doesn't matter to me."

One of the other kids chimed in, "Whoa! Sounds pretty cocky, Li'l Al. Who you gonna run with this hotshot?"

"You for one, Rizzo and Hoagie. Me, Gambo, G-dog, and Teddy Ballgame will take it out!" replied Al.

"What!" the kid with the smart mouth, who Jordan later learned was named Miles Jackson, said. "Y'all gonna punk us!"

"Shut up and D up, Jacks," instructed Alvin.

So they ran four on four, full court. Game to eleven by ones, with two points for a shot made behind the three-point line. Jordan was familiar with the setup, as they ran the same street ball in Cali. It was hot and humid, and Jordan was not used to this stifling condition. He quickly realized that he was faster than the others on the court.

Jordan was not a type A, alpha dog, whatsoever. On the other hand, this dude they called Lil Al (Jordan assumed it was the kind of scenario where the big fat kid was called Tiny in a diametrically opposed manner) was definitely the alpha dog on these courts with this group of kids.

Jackson, who was the only black kid on the court, was right when he assessed that Lil Al had kept the best players for himself. After Al's team scored the first five points and Jordan's teammates were obviously mentally and physically ready to concede defeat, Jordan's fierce competitiveness kicked in. He drained a long shot behind the arc (two points), stole the ball on the next possession, and went all the way for a layup. They double-teamed Gambo, forcing a bad shot, which Rizzo rebounded. Jordan brought the ball up court and passed it to Jacks, who hit another two-pointer. Suddenly, they were tied five all.

Jordan then witnessed Lil Al's competitiveness as he became very physical and resembled a football player playing basketball. He bullied his way inside to score on the next three possessions. However, Jordan's teammates, following his lead, were now more engaged. They spread out on the court and passed the ball to the open man.

One of them, the kid they called Hoagie, had a rather good shot if not contested.

The teams traded a couple more baskets, and it came down to a ten-ten game, with Lil Al's team having the ball.

"Gotta win by two!" shouted Jacks.

"No shit," responded Al.

They fed Al the ball on the low post, with everyone clearing out. Jordan was now on Al, even though he gave up nearly half a foot in height and more than fifty pounds in weight. He tried to use as much leverage as he could to keep Al from backing him down to the hoop for an easy layup. As Al kept pounding his girth into him, Jordan realized it was a useless endeavor to try to muscle him away from the basket. With a quick sidestep just as Al was dipping his shoulder and lunging into Jordan, he was suddenly gone. Lil Al stumbled to the asphalt and lost control of the ball. Jordan scooped it up and started a fast break the other way.

He caught the eye of Hoagie and nodded toward the right corner of the court on their offensive end. Jordan drove the lane, and three guys converged on him, with Al still trying to catch up from the backcourt. Jordan dished the ball to Hoagie, who was all alone in the corner, just behind the three-point line. Hoagie caught the pass and, without hesitation, gathered himself and launched a high-arcing shot. Nothing but net!

"Game!" shouted Jackson as he ran over and bear-hugged Hoagie, who had a somewhat shocked but greatly satisfied expression on his face.

"Dang it! Why would you guys leave the three open?" yelled Al.

Jacks high-fived Rizzo and then Jordan. "Where you from, man. What school you go to?"

"I just moved here. Guess I'll be going to Milford," Jordan replied.

"Do you play football?" asked Miles.

"Sure." Jordan responded.

"Cool, 'cause that's our sport. We hoop for fun," Jacks added.

Gambo shouted, "Let's run it back. That was so friggin' lucky. I can't believe it! Since when does Paul Hoage hit a game winner? Hell, he never even tries a game winner!"

Lil Al wiped the sweat off his face as he finished gulping down a Gatorade he had stashed under the bench adjacent to the court. He looked at his group of teammates surrounding him. They were anxiously waiting for his instructions as to what to do next. They did not know if he wanted to kick the crap out of this new kid or get his revenge on the court and run it back.

"Nope. Dude ran circles around us! I gave him our two weakest players plus ball hog Jacks, and he still kicked butt, fair and square." He walked over to Jordan, who quite frankly did not know what to expect. He had braced himself for the worst but also held his ground. The big guy extended his hand, and Jordan took it. "Alvin Bockman. Welcome to Short Hills."

"Jordan Duncan. Nice to meet you, and thanks for the run."

That was the beginning of a friendship that would set in motion an extraordinary high school experience and establish a long-lasting relationship based on the foundation of trust, confidence, and mutual respect.

Jordan found out that Little Al was not a diametrical reference. His father, Alvin Bockman Sr., was literally Big Al, as he measured 6'7" and just over 300 lb.! He played football at Penn State in the mid to late '60s, was part of the Nittany Lion undefeated team in 1968, Honorable Mention All-American, and was drafted into the NFL. Al Bockman played defensive end for the New York Jets for six years until a torn ACL and MCL in his left knee essentially ended his career. He coached the defensive line at Penn State for a few years, then decided he wanted to run his own program and applied for the football head coach position at Milford High School in Short Hills, New Jersey. He later also became the athletic director at the school and taught US history. He became the closest thing to a mentor that Jordan had ever experienced.

Little Al and Jordan became best friends during the next three years. Though their personalities were definitely dissimilar and they continually argued over East Coast / West Coast biased opinions, their friendship was based on mutual respect and a little envy on both sides. Jordan admired the way Al could speak to adults, peers, girls, authoritative figures, and...well, just about anyone. His confidence, quick mind, and wit seemed to know no bounds. On the other hand, Al admired Jordan's naturally cool demeanor, his athletic skills, and...damn it, his good looks! They encouraged each other, they competed against each other, they challenged each other to become better, but they *always* had each other's back!

The high school experience reached its apex in the fall of their senior year during the 1986 football season. Jordan came to love the fall season in New Jersey, the way the leaves changed colors, how the air cooled to a crisp invigorating temperature, and that football was played every Saturday! Big Al had prepared this particular class (with it being his son's senior year) to the highest performance level of any of his previous teams.

It was difficult to compete in the competitive field of high school football in New Jersey in a small upper-class community like Short Hills. Parents had other aspirations for their kids. Academic success or excellence in the arts were the focus rather than risking injury and devoting so much time to a barbaric sport like football. However, Al recognized talent, and he was dedicated to teaching these boys to become men with discipline and commitment to achieve greatness in a team environment. With this approach and his genuine care for the kids, the parents were onboard with their precious offspring being groomed under the tutelage of such a successful and educated man as Alvin Bockman Sr.

When Jordan Duncan arrived in Short Hills and showed up at football practice in 1984, Big Al felt as though he had found the last piece of the puzzle for their championship run. He had been grooming this group of youngsters since Little Al was playing Pop Warner football. His desire was to build an aggressive stalwart defensive unit that would create havoc for the opposition, causing miscues and opportunities for his conservative offense.

Al Jr. was the leader of the group and anchored the defensive line for obvious reasons. He was the biggest among them. By the beginning of his senior year, he was 6'5" and weighed 265 lb. and had thick jet-black hair that hung almost to his shoulder, dark eyes under eyebrows that resembled dark caterpillars, a broad nose, and a perpetual five o'clock shadow that gave him quite an intimidating appearance. He was the smartest, the most articulate, and he was the coach's son!

As a senior, Jordan stood at 6 ft. and was 175 lbs. with almost no body fat. He excelled at the free safety position on defense. He had thoroughly enjoyed being the leading receiver on offense in his junior year teaming with the shy and introverted but blessed with a rocket arm quarterback, Paul Hoage. Coach Bockman wanted him to focus solely on defense for their title run and declined his wish to play both offense and defense.

The 1986 season was magical as the Millburn Millers went undefeated and won the state championship, led by a stifling defense that allowed an average of just under seven points a game and posted five shutouts. Jordan was named first team All-State at safety, Salvatore Gambadoro was also first team All-State at linebacker, Alvin was second team at nose tackle. Jordan and Little Al went on a recruiting trip to Penn State (Happy Valley, PA) and were offered scholarships. Gambo accepted a full scholarship to Rutgers University, and Ted Balcolm (Teddy Ballgame) signed a letter of intent to play at the University of North Carolina on scholarship. Jordan, Little Al, and Big Al all watched on TV in delight as Penn State defeated Miami in the Fiesta Bowl on January 2, 1987, to win the NCAA National Championship!

In 1985, when Jordan was fifteen, Gabriela gave birth to a beautiful baby girl, Teresa. Teri, as she was affectionately called, became Phil's pride and joy. Gabriela continued to enthusiastically follow Jordan's high school football career, never missing a game. Overweight and unathletic, Phil rarely attended games until Jordan's senior year, when it became evident that the team was special and Jordan was one of its stars. It became an asset to proclaim that his "son" was a high school football star and being recruited by Penn State.

Lil Al routinely doled out nicknames to his social peers. It was considered a sort of rite of passage in their circle of friends to be tabbed with a nickname from Alvin Bockman. He began referring to Jordan Duncan as D-Can or sometimes simply JD. Al was, without doubt, the big man on campus, literally and figuratively.

As Jordan progressed through high school, he had matured physically and socially. However, there was a lingering uneasiness boiling within him emotionally as he tried to internally come to terms with his feelings about how he was left fatherless as an infant.

Jordan and Phil never developed anything more than a relationship of tolerance during his high school years. He felt as though everything Phil did was to better position himself in his standing with peers and rivals to ultimately create a persona of wealth and power. In short, he felt as though Gabriela was Phillip's trophy wife. It was evident that Jordan didn't like Phil and the feeling was mutual. Phil put up a front to Gabriela that he and Jordan were developing a friendship. He promised her that he would help finance Jordan's college education.

Always scheming, he approached Jordan after his junior year and proposed that if he could land a college scholarship (thus letting himself off the hook for college tuition), then Phil would purchase a new car of Jordan's choice. Phil knew he would probably be more inclined to want some sort of SUV than a hot, expensive sports car. His gamble paid off, as Jordan chose a blue 1986 Ford Bronco (Al referred to it as the *D-Can Buckin' Blu Bronco*). However, the caveat was that if Jordan, for whatever reason, did not maintain the scholarship, then he would have to make payments to Phil to keep the car.

Internally, Jordan's struggle to come to grips with what he perceived as his father's choice to become a hero for his country over coming home to his wife and child continued to fester. He did discover that he had developed an internal moral compass that guided him in decision-making. However, he consciously rejected others that tried to force their morals and beliefs onto him.

Alvin Bockman Sr., in addition to coaching football, taught US history and had an affinity for US military history. Jordan and Big Al studied the history of the Vietnam War. The senselessness of that war only frustrated Jordan more in regard to why his father chose to go back after his initial draft tour was up.

Edward Duncan had become an outstanding soldier in the 101st Airborne Division of the US Army after completing basic training. When he came home on an R&R in the late fall of 1968, before heading back to Vietnam, he made love to his beautiful wife, and unbeknownst at the time to either of them, she became pregnant. He promised he would be home when his tour was up the following year. He did come home shortly for the birth of his son in August of 1969.

However, Edward had shown great valor and bravery in the Battle of Hamburger Hill in May of 1969. The Army, as part of their efforts to keep more highly skilled experienced soldiers in Vietnam, requested that he reenlist for an additional six months for a special op. They offered him a benefits package similar to that of the enlisted soldiers. After much discussion between husband and wife, Eddie felt that he had an obligation to help fellow soldiers who had become like brothers to him but were facing increasingly more difficult circumstances in the war. He promised his wife that, in six months, it would definitely be over. He would be hers forevermore, and they would raise their beautiful son together. The additional benefits would help finance his education and allow them to one day purchase a home.

In December of 1969, in the jungle of Southeast Asia, Edward Duncan was killed in an ambush by Vietcong soldiers. As Jordan read about the battles and repeated mistakes made in the Vietnam War, he vowed that he would never take the hero's path.

The day before watching Penn State play Miami in the Fiesta Bowl on January 2, 1987, for the NCAA National Championship, Jordan was at home alone on New Year's Day. Phil, Gabriela, and baby Teresa had gone to New York City. Jordan tuned in to the Rose Bowl game played in Pasadena, California. There were over 103,000 fans packed into that famous stadium. It wasn't only the game per se, but the atmosphere, the grandiose setting of the occasion preceded by the Rose Bowl Parade, and most significantly, the near-perfect seventy-degree temperature and sunny skies of the greater Los Angeles basin had captured Jordan's attention.

He literally felt a warm tingling go up his spine and settle into his heart as he realized how much he missed being in Southern

California. He was homesick. He didn't mention any of this the next day as he watched Penn State win the National Championship.

Big Al could hardly contain himself. His excitement and sense of pride swelled as his alma mater and former coach, Joe Paterno, upset the highly favored Miami Hurricanes in an exhilarating game played in the Arizona desert.

Big Al kept repeating, "That could be you, boys, next year!"

When the National Letter of Intent Signing Day came in early February, Little Al came to pick Jordan up at his house to go down to the school and sign their letters of commitment to Penn State University in a ceremonial display. Jordan postponed his signing date and said, much to the surprise of both Little and Big Al, that he was offered a recruiting visit to UCLA and decided he was going to take them up on it. The main reason was to get a free trip to LA. Alvin Sr. didn't think that was very wise, but he could see that Jordan had made up his mind.

During the week of March 5–8, 1987, just prior to graduating from high school, Jordan flew to Los Angeles for an official recruiting visit to UCLA. The flight was on Thursday, March 5, nonstop but long. He found his heart pounding as the plane made its descent into LAX. He gazed out the window in amazement at the massive Pacific Ocean and shoreline. The sun was bright and many aqua-blue dots of swimming pools scanned the landscape below.

There was a group of three—two players and an assistant coach—waiting to pick him up at the baggage claim. Smiles and handshakes all around. Jordan stayed in the dorms on the UCLA campus. On Friday, he got a tour of the campus, had lunch at a fashionable LA café, and was told that they had tickets for him to attend the PAC 10 Basketball Tournament that night, which was being held at Pauley Pavillion on the UCLA campus.

The arena was famous for housing so many of the great UCLA legendary basketball teams of the past and the now-retired most famous coach of all-time, the "Wizard of Westwood," John Wooden. The place was electric that night as UCLA easily disposed of Arizona State 99–83. On Saturday, Jordan met with the coaches, including the head coach, Terry Donahue, and some players. UCLA had a brilliant sophomore quarterback named Troy Aikman and was trying to build its offense around his passing talents.

Jordan, who had suffered two concussions while playing safety in high school, asked Coach Donahue on a whim if it were possible for him to try out for a wide receiver position on the team rather than free safety. The coach, considering Jordan's athleticism and ability, thought it could work and offered him a scholarship to play wide receiver if Jordan would be willing to redshirt his freshman year. Jordan was thrilled at the prospect!

That afternoon, they took him to Santa Monica Beach, where they rode beach cruisers down the paved path to Venice Beach. The people, the energy, the laid-back atmosphere, the beachside shops, the sand, the surf, the palm trees, the basketball courts, Muscle Beach, Oceanfront Boardwalk… Jordan knew that this was where he wanted to go to college! At night, he was escorted back to Pauley Pavillion; actually got to shake hands with Coach Wooden, who was sitting courtside; and also met some of the UCLA cheerleaders. UCLA's basketball team won the PAC 10 Tournament that weekend, and Jordan flew back to cold Newark, New Jersey, airport. But was no longer despondent like the first time he flew into New Jersey three and a half years ago. Jordan was full of hope and excitement.

The dilemma he faced now was telling his mom, Little Al, and Big Al of his decision. He was going to college at UCLA. They would not be happy. He knew one person who would be ecstatic—Phillip Conley. Jordan would be moving across the country. He could only chuckle at the thought and irony of pleasing the person he least desired to make happy.

Gabriela was understanding, though sad, that Jordan would be so far away at college. But she knew inside that his heart had never really left Southern California. Besides, it had been Eddie's dream to play football at UCLA. Anytime her son showed character traits of his father, it generated warmth in her bosom. It occurred more often than she let anyone know, including Jordan. She generally would simply show the slightest of smiles during those moments. He would return for the summers (maybe), or perhaps it would be feasible for her to take Teri and go to LA occasionally and watch him play at UCLA.

Big Al was a little less understanding as he had pulled strings with Coach Paterno to get scholarships for both Jordan and Little Al. But Alvin Bockman Sr. had been an athlete himself and knew that when a kid set his mind and heart to something, a real competitor would follow his instincts and make it happen. He did understand that Jordan loved the West Coast, and he vowed to explain his decision to Coach Paterno.

Little Al was the most devastated of all. He and Jordan had truly become best friends, not just teammates on a state championship football team. They had shared things with each other that neither had shared with anyone else. They had talked about their innermost fears, dreams, and fantasies, and they were sure their friendship would last a lifetime.

Jordan assured Al that their friendship would endure and that they would stay in touch and meet up as often as they could. He invited Little Al to come experience the West Coast with him. Alvin Bockman Jr. had never been to California. They came to an agreement that this separation would not terminate their friendship.

After graduating from high school in May of 1987, Jordan spent the next couple of months with his buddies and family in New Jersey. In early August, just before his eighteenth birthday, he packed up his Bronco and made the drive across the country to Los Angeles. He enrolled at UCLA and began his college career.

On his first year, he redshirted as Coach Donahue had suggested, learning the offense and practicing without being eligible to play in games. He loved the SoCal lifestyle, enjoyed his classes, and met a girl that he started dating regularly. Leslie Monroe was also a freshman, a surfer chick from Huntington Beach. It was a beach town just down the coast in Orange County. It was about forty-five minutes away and had the moniker of Surf City and was where they held the annual national surfing championships.

Leslie was a pretty, blond-haired, brown-eyed, slender young lady that seemed to have a perpetual tan and white-toothed smile. She and Jordan met in an English 101 class and were instantly attracted to each other. She was intrigued about his experiences living on the East Coast, yet their bond was strengthened by each having Southern California roots and a love for the sunshine and beaches that dominated the California coastline. From Jordan's perspective, Leslie was always in a good mood, and he appreciated the positive energy he felt in her presence.

Jordan flew back to New Jersey at the end of classes for the summer of 1988. That would be the last summer he would spend in New Jersey. Upon returning to UCLA, he played backup wide receiver and on special teams during the fall of 1988. He really liked his teammates, the coaching staff, and his dorm brothers, and he was having a lot of fun hanging out with Leslie without them getting too serious in the relationship. Leslie liked that Jordan was on the football team, as she had been a high school cheerleader and enjoyed sports. They were dating each other exclusively, surfed together, cared for each other a lot, and there was no drama or pressure in this relationship. Jordan just didn't know how to fully commit to a long-term relationship, and Leslie felt that they were too young for that anyway.

Late in his freshman season playing football at Penn State, Al suffered a broken collarbone. Little Al had thoroughly enjoyed his time in Penn State and, in fact, he excelled in academics there. The coaching staff informed Alvin that they would like him to redshirt the following season. He decided to visit California with Jordan about a month before football practice was to begin in the fall of 1988. Jordan was excited to show his buddy what life was like on the West Coast.

It only took a couple of weeks before Little Al had formulated a plan. He was going to give up playing football, as he didn't find it nearly as enjoyable on the D-1 university level as it was in high school, where he'd been bigger, stronger, and could physically and mentally intimidate his opponents. He was going to return to Penn State for one more semester, cram in as many credits as he could, and then transfer to a Cal State school. He would go to school year-round and streamline his undergraduate degree so that he could enroll in law school after two more full years of college.

Jordan always admired Al's resiliency when he had a goal in mind. The tricky part would be informing Big Al of this plan. He did upon returning to New Jersey, and his dad was more supportive than Al Jr. had anticipated. As it turned out, all the talks and coaching experiences they shared through his youth and high school years about building character, integrity, accountability, and responsibility, whether it was playing football or whatever else he decided to do with his life, was truly what Alvin Sr. was all about. He loved his son, his family, and the players he coached, and he genuinely wanted them to succeed in life and become productive men of high character. He was extremely proud of Al Jr. for putting such an emphasis on his education.

It certainly didn't pass by Lil Al's attention that the girls in SoCal were drop-dead gorgeous and fun-loving! He enrolled at Cal State Los Angeles in January of 1989. Al received his bachelor's degree in English literature in just over another year. He was accepted at Loyola Law School in downtown Los Angeles, and he concentrated on sports and contract law. Alvin Bockman Jr. knew exactly what he wanted to do—become a sports agent and represent players in the National Football League. The college years in Los Angeles for both Jordan and Al were full of excitement, accomplishment, and a ton of fun. They lived together in a two-bedroom apartment in Brentwood, centrally located between UCLA, Cal State, Loyola, and the Santa Monica Beach. Even with the horrendous LA traffic, they were able to navigate their way around to maximize their good fortune of living in La La Land!

Leslie Monroe graduated from UCLA with a degree in communications in June 1991, which was one year ahead of Jordan, as he divided his class schedule to coincide with his redshirt year. Leslie decided that she wanted to see more of the world. She was to depart just before Jordan's last football season with a girlfriend to go tour Europe, and eventually she would land an assistant concierge job at a resort hotel in Paris, France.

Before leaving, however, on 8/15/1991, Leslie surprised Jordan on his twenty-second birthday and took him on an excursion in his Bronco down the Pacific Coast Highway to Dana Point, California, which is a small beach town just south of Laguna Beach in Orange County. Throughout their relationship, while attending UCLA, Jordan had taken time to become acquainted with Leslie's family in Huntington Beach and had even gone surfing several times with her father, Michael Monroe. Now a practicing dentist in HB, Mike had been an avid sixties surfer in the OC, when he met and surfed with the legendary Kory Edmunds. In the sixties, Edmunds was the first professional surfer. He was currently the premier designer of longboards at the Hobie Surf Shop in Dana Point.

As they parked in the lot in front of Hobie's and sat in the Bronco, Leslie turned to Jordan and said, "My dad likes you a lot, Jordan, and thinks that you are a really good surfer. However, he says that your aggressive style on your shortboard denies you the beauty of longboard surfing, which is entirely different. So he talked to his old friend Kory Edmunds, and Mr. Edmunds has a customized board for you as a gift from my father!"

Jordan was completely dumbfounded. He just stared at Leslie for a long moment, his mouth slightly agape. "I don't even know what to say, Leslie. That is *so* awesome!"

She grabbed his hand and quickly replied, "Well, let's go inside and see what he came up with." She flashed that gorgeous, spontaneously natural smile of hers, opened the Bronco door, and jumped out.

Kory was waiting just inside the workshop, which was adjacent to the retail section and accessible inside the store. Leslie made the introductions, and he presented Jordan with one of his autographed vintage surfboards as a gift from the Monroe family. Jordan was thrilled with both the board and for meeting the surfing legend. After Mr. Edmunds had shared some nuances about the features of his style board, he explained some differences in surfing a longboard as opposed to shortboard surfing.

Then out of the blue, Kory said, "Heck, why don't I just show you? You got time to surf now? Doheny is only a mile down the road."

Jordan quickly turned and looked at Leslie, who threw her arms up in the air and said enthusiastically, "Let's *go*!"

It was truly a highlight of Jordan's life—surfing the famous Doheny State Beach with the legendary surfing pro who recounted to them the good ole days when he surfed this beach that was referred to as Killer Dana for the huge waves it produced prior to the development of the adjacent Dana Point Harbor. Jordan relished in receiving surfing tips from Kory and having a blast with his fun-loving girlfriend.

As they were drying off at the Bronco and having just bid adieu with a cool bro hug from Kory, Jordan gazed at Leslie as she was drying her sun-glistened blond hair. She had stripped off her wetsuit down to her underwear and was mostly hidden to the public by the Bronco door. Jordan once again marveled at how truly beautiful Leslie was not only in her physical glory but within her sweet heart.

He pulled her in tight to his shirtless body and slowly kissed her passionately. He was going to miss her terribly, and he briefly wondered if he had given her enough attention and enough effort in the relationship during their UCLA experience. He would worry if this laid-back, happy-go-lucky California chick could stay golden in the harsh real world that she was about to face.

As they drove back up the coast, they joked, laughed, and listened to classic and punk rock, reminiscing the past four years. In anticipation of their evening, as they drove up the PCH through Laguna Beach, Crystal Cove, and Newport Beach, they rolled down the Bronco windows and sang aloud the lyrics along with Kurt Cobain on the Nirvana's *Bleach* CD!

That evening, they went to see Nirvana perform live at the Roxy Theatre in West Hollywood, wrapping up a perfect birthday! Jordan loved Leslie in a special way. She was his first real girlfriend, and he considered the Kory Edmunds surfboard a reminder of his relationship with her. Along with his *Buckin' Blu Bronco*, it became one of his prized possessions. He and Leslie had some great times together in college and vowed to stay friends as their lives went in different directions.

Al good naturally tried to convince and motivate Jordan that he would be his first client as a player agent in the NFL when he was drafted (he had already come up with a Nike endorsement slogan for his friend/client: "D-Can Just Do It"). Jordan knew it was more Al's pipe dream than his. Quite frankly, he was getting a little tired of the grind of playing football at such a high level. The time and dedication, the aches and pains of training, and trying to constantly improve were rigorous, but the reality was that he didn't feel that he had the skill set nor the pure love of the game to play at the professional level. He felt fortunate that he was able to play at UCLA on scholarship and was feeling good about contributing to the success of the team. However, he felt that he was neither a star nor a pro prospect.

His entire college football career was capsulated in a crowning moment of his senior season during their rival game with USC. The Bruins had not beaten the Trojans since Jordan had enrolled on campus. Once again, the nationally ranked Trojans were seemingly headed to victory over their crosstown rivals as they led by twenty points in the fourth quarter in Jordan's last game at the Rose Bowl. Spearheaded by a backup fifth-year senior quarterback who had been in the program for long as Jordan and with whom he had developed a great on-field rapport, the Bruins made a miraculous comeback. The two of them connected on several first down conversions, a touchdown completion that brought the Bruins within six points, and on the last play of the game, a beautifully thrown forty-eight-yard bomb into the back corner of the end zone that Jordan gathered in a step ahead of the defender as he was going to his knees.

UCLA won 38–37 by scoring 21 fourth-quarter points! In all, Jordan had 10 receptions for 162 yards and 2 touchdowns, including the game winner. It was by far the best game of his college career. Amazingly, as the final gun sounded, he was mobbed by teammates and a contingent of Bruin fans from the stands, none of whom were as important to Jordan as Gabriela, Teri, and Little Al, each of whom was in attendance.

A photographer had captured the moment with an incredible photo of Jordan making the catch just before going out of the back of the end zone. The concentration on his face, wide-eyed; the color of his blue eyes matching his pale-blue Bruin jersey; the visualization of his flexed arm muscles as he clutched the ball—the whole image was of such intense clarity and was captured at perfect timing that the shot was used for the cover of *Sports Illustrated*. It also was blown up, framed, and displayed in the hallway of Pauley Pavillion. It was among a collection of action photos that lined the walls, including superstar UCLA luminaries in their athletic accomplishments, such as Jackie Robinson, Rafer Johnson, Evelyn Ashford, Gail Goodrich, Gary Beban, Mel Farr, Lew Alcindor, Sidney Wicks, Bill Walton, Marques Johnson, Ann Meyers, Jackie Joyner-Kersey, Karch Kiraly, Kenny Easley, Troy Aikman, and others.

Jordan felt a little embarrassed that he was on this wall of fame but humbly realized it just happened to be the climactic moment in an outstanding comeback victory over the school's rival that was caught in a near-perfect photograph. Unbelievably, he was now known around UCLA alumni as something of a sports hero. It opened doors for him but, at the same time, drew more attention to him than he desired.

In June of 1992, Jordan graduated from UCLA with a bachelor's degree in economics. Gabriela, Teresa, and even Phil attended the commencement ceremony along with Alvin Bockman Jr. Afterward, the five of them went to dinner at Guido's on Santa Monica Boulevard to celebrate.

As they were enjoying dessert, Phil said to Jordan, "So what's next in the illustrious laid-back life of Jordan Duncan?"

Jordan, after a moment of awkward silence, replied, "Not really sure, Phil."

Phil offered, "Well, I guess I could pull some strings and get you into the investment banking industry. But you would have to start at the bottom and work your way up the ladder as I did."

Jordan and Gabriela both knew this was a total BS as Phil's father was a Wall Street banker and had spoonfed Phil into a nice well-arranged midmanagement position right out of college.

Phil continued, "No more easy street, pal. The football scholarship pandering doesn't exist in the real world—"

Jordan cut him off there by saying, "Thanks anyway, Phil, but I think I'm gonna go a different route and stay out here in LA."

Phil let out a little sarcastic snorting sound as he replied, "Of course, you are. Just milk your fifteen minutes of fame playing football at UCLA and hang out at the beach, surfing for as long as you can."

"Now, Phil, there is no need for that kind of talk," chimed in Gabriela. "Jordan has been highly successful in both athletics and academics. I'm sure he will do well at whatever he chooses."

"Yeah, Dad, I haven't seen *you* ever on the cover of *SI*!" retorted little Teri, who idolized Jordan. She was a pretty good budding soccer star in her own right, and in fact, she wanted to one day play soccer at UCLA.

Alvin, who was seated across the table from Phil, next to Jordan, couldn't help but snicker at that comment. If he had his way and if Gabriela and Teri weren't present, he'd reach across the table and punch Phil.

"Watch your mouth, little girl," warned Phil. "You and your mom live a pretty nice lifestyle thanks to me!"

"That's enough," stated Gabriela. "Let's allow these boys to celebrate Jordan's college graduation. We have an early flight tomorrow. I think we should head back to the hotel."

Jordan kissed both Gabriela and Teri goodbye and shook hands with Phil, thanking him for the dinner.

As he was walking toward his car, Alvin yelled out from behind, "Yo, JD, wait up!" As Al got within a few feet of Jordan standing in the parking lot, he had a rather angry look on his face as he said with authority, "Screw Phil! That pussy is so friggin' jealous of you, man, he can't even see straight!"

Jordan chuckled and replied, "Thanks, Al, but you know, as long as he doesn't abuse my mom or little sister, I really couldn't care less what Phil Conley says or thinks."

"Right on, man, because you know what?" replied Al. "I don't know one person that would choose to be Phillip Conley rather than Jordan Duncan!" He wrapped his huge right arm around Jordan's shoulder.

"I don't know about that, Little Al. Dude has made a lot of money."

"Dude, *we* are going to make a lot of money!" said Al. "And we're going to have a helluva lot of fun doing it and with a helluva lot more class than that jackass."

Jordan could only laugh out loud as he realized how good Al was at making him feel positive. There was nothing that Alvin Bockman Jr. didn't believe was possible with the right mindset and a proactive approach. Jordan had always kind of played second fiddle to Al socially and academically, and he didn't have any problem with that whatsoever.

"Thanks, Al. Catch up with ya later, buddy. I'm gonna head down to the beach and go for a little run."

During this "midnight run," a lingering thought that had resided in his brain for several years came to the forefront of his mind. If UCLA had offered his father a football scholarship right out of high school, chances were that he would have been deferred in the army draft. He never would have gone to Vietnam and would have lived happily with Gabriela… Then again, in that scenario, perhaps Jordan would never have been born, certainly not when he was. So he felt it was some kind of poetic justice that he received the UCLA scholarship, and it was paramount that he made the most of it. At that point, he had no clue how and when he would fulfill that goal. The truth was, he had no idea what type of career he wanted.

After a few weeks of surfing, chillin', and lackadaisically looking for work, Jordan was contacted by a gentleman by the name of David Jacobs. Mr. Jacobs happened to be a huge UCLA football booster and a longtime season ticket holder.

His first words to Jordan were "That was the most exhilarating moment in my life of watching college football when you caught that pass to beat SC."

Jordan was gracious in accepting the compliment but didn't really feel like talking about it anymore. David quickly changed the subject and surprised Jordan in knowing that he had a degree in economics. He asked about what type of work Jordan was searching for. Jordan couldn't articulate much of an answer, so David bailed him out by explaining the business he ran as a CPA. He perceived personality traits and potential in Jordan to excel in the tax resolution business. Jordan had no idea what that meant, but he accepted the invitation to meet for lunch the next day at Fromin's Deli in Sherman Oaks, which was just about a five-mile jaunt up the 405 from Brentwood.

Over lunch, which David generously paid for, he explained to Jordan that his company helped people that were experiencing tax debt collection pressure from the IRS. Recently, the IRS Collection Division had revived the dormant "offer in compromise" program, which allowed delinquent taxpayers to submit an offer to the IRS as a settlement to resolve their tax liabilities. David and his newly formed tax resolution business had been instrumental in bringing these delinquent taxpayers out of hiding, so to speak, and to the doorstep of the IRS to close cases in a win-win scenario.

The position David was offering to Jordan would start as a sales position meeting with potential clients, listening to their dilemma of tax problems, and explaining various solution opportunities while enticing them to retain the firm's services. If Jordan liked the work and demonstrated the skill set to succeed, David would set him up to complete the necessary steps in becoming an enrolled agent, able to represent clients in a "power of attorney" position to the Internal Revenue Service. Jordan liked the idea of helping the "underdog" and thought it could be a fulfilling type of profession. He accepted and began his working career at Jacobs and Goodman Tax Resolution in August of 1992, just before turning twenty-three years old.

To this point in Jordan's life, things have progressed fairly smoothly. Though he grew up without a father, he has enjoyed and reaped the benefits of a loving mother and little sister, a wealthy stepfather, a great group of friends, caring coaches, exceptional high school and college athletic experiences, a sweet and beautiful girlfriend, and a best friend whom he can always count on. He has earned a college degree, lives in sunny Southern California, loves driving his Bronco, and has a bitchin' surfboard that fits nicely on top and slices through waves like a warm knife through butter!

Life is going to become more complicated as he enters the real world of work, commerce, taxes, and the undeniable gray area that exists between them!

CHAPTER TWO

Los Angeles Stress 1995

Merging on to the I-10 east off Olympic Boulevard in Santa Monica can be kind of tricky as it is one of those left lane on-ramps. It is 9:25 a.m. on Monday, March 6, 1995. Jordan knows that it is just under fourteen miles from his beachfront Mariner Village apartment complex in Santa Monica to the Jacobs & Goodman Sherman Oaks office on Ventura Boulevard. Normally, his commute at this time (timing is everything when considering LA traffic) takes approximately twenty minutes. However, with the simplest of distractions, such as a fender bender lane closure due to construction on either the 10 or the 405 (which seems to be perpetual) or a rainy day (Angelenos are notoriously poor wet-road drivers), the commute can easily escalate to forty-five minutes to an hour and a half. Luckily, after nearly three years of this commute and almost a decade of living and driving in LA, Jordan has alternative routes when necessary—via side streets.

His level of success at work has earned him the prerogative to request no appointments with first-time new clients prior to 10:00 a.m., thus helping avoid wasted commuting time.

This particular morning, he has an interesting 10:00 a.m. appointment with a first-time client. Mr. and Mrs. Williamson are a referral from one of Jordan's b-ball playing buddies from the Venice Beach courts. Tio Williamson has become a regular running mate of Jordan's, as their games mesh nicely and they are almost identical in age and height. When he found out what Jordan does for a living, which was after months of running together on the VB courts, he seemed rather interested. After another month passed, Tio confided in Jordan that his parents were dealing with some IRS problems and that perhaps Jordan could help them. At first, Jordan wasn't sure if he meant giving them some pro bono advice, which he had no problem doing. However, when inquiring about their issues, which Tio reluctantly shared, he realized that their situation had recently become urgent, so he suggested they call his office and schedule an appointment.

The traffic on 10 wasn't bad, but as Jordan merges onto the 405, he can see the dreaded snaking line of red flashing brake lights going up the hill toward Sherman Oaks. He glances into the rearview mirror and notices the gray misty wall of fog receding back into the vast ocean from whence it came. An endless sky of brilliant azure blue with a few cotton balls of clouds off in the distance over the San Gabriel mountain range is on full display out the front windshield. Weather has taken an odd course this year to date in LA, where the usual consistent sixty- to eighty-degree temperatures hardly ever deviate.

Jordan recollects how, two weeks ago, Los Angeles experienced the warmest heat wave for February in the history of the city, where the temperature hit ninety-five degrees. It has since dropped thirty degrees as the high hasn't topped sixty-five in the past few days and is projected to stay in the mid to high sixties throughout the coming weeks. Jordan switches on the radio to listen to some music and relieve his stress over the delay on the freeway. A DJ is relaying the news.

Not a day goes by now without multiple updates on the O. J. Simpson trial, which started in January. Racial tension in LA escalated exponentially a few years back during the Rodney King arrest, brutal police beating, and subsequent riots in south central Los Angeles. Now with the double murder charges on OJ, the city is in the national spotlight once again for racially motivated crimes and indictments.

Jordan thought he lived in a kind of bubble down on the beach that isolated him from such violent activity until that bubble burst three weeks ago. Over President's Day weekend, there was a gang-related murder of three men in Santa Monica on Friday night, then a stabbing on the Santa Monica Pier on Saturday, followed by a shooting and stabbing on the Venice Beach Boardwalk on Sunday that witnesses said was initiated simply by one person bumping into another!

The tension in the City of Angels is thick as people seem to be wound extremely tight these days. He switches to sports talk radio, and the news isn't uplifting there either. The Major League Baseball players' strike continues, and spring training has been postponed and possibly cancelled. The strike started last August, resulting in the World Series being cancelled in 1994! On top of that, both the Los Angeles Rams and the Los Angeles Raiders have left LA after the 1994 season. The Raiders returned to Oakland, and the Rams ventured out to St. Louis, of all places, to play football. So with the racial tension at a fever pitch, there is social and emotional tension building as well.

As if the cumulative stress levels weren't already off the charts, LA is still feeling the figurative and literal aftershock of the Northridge earthquake that rocked the greater Los Angeles basin last year. Californians had been warned for nearly a century of the next "big one" since the devastating 7.9 San Francisco quake in 1906. In 1989, the Bay Bridge was cracked in half by a massive trembler that measured 6.9 on the Richter scale. Five years hence, SoCal was shaken up rather dramatically. Though the Northridge quake was not quite as strong as the others, measuring 6.7, it was followed by two aftershocks of 6.0, which were part of thousands of plate-shifting movements that lasted for weeks. This was by far the costliest earthquake in North American history as the damage was estimated at over $40 billion.

Some religious types are throwing around the apocalypse scenario. Personally, Jordan doesn't see the correlation between race, sports, weird weather, mother nature, and religion. Let the politicians and religious sects frame their theories and responses, but for the masses, life goes on, and they adjust accordingly.

But there is no doubt that people in Los Angeles are uptight and on shaky footing, and the laid-back happy-go-lucky attitude in

SoCal that Jordan loves about this region is being tested to its core during these turbulent times.

Already stressed to the max, imagine getting a notice from the Internal Revenue Service informing you that you owe back taxes and have mounds of penalties and interest piled on. They aim to collect. People are ready to explode!

Fact is, work is going great for Jordan. He enjoys what he does and feels quite accomplished in helping those in need resolve their tax problems. He is the number one producer of revenue for Jacobs & Goodman Tax Resolution.

His cell phone rings, and he quickly glances at his watch. It's nine fifty. "Hello, this is Jordan."

"Hello, Mr. Duncan, I just wanted to inform you that your ten o'clock appointment, the Williamsons, have arrived here in the lobby."

"Sunshine?" Yes, that is her real name. "What are you doing in the office on a Monday morning? Don't you have school?"

"Shhh, spring break," she whispers as though the clients can hear both ends of the conversation. "Vanessa took the week off to be with her kids," she continues quickly and discreetly.

"Okay, I'm about ten minutes out," Jordan replies. "Tell them that I am finishing up some things and will be out shortly to greet them. I'll come in the back door."

"Yes, Mr. Duncan. I will let them know," Sunshine declares confidently into the microphone of her headset.

He gets off at exit 63A and turns left on Sepulveda Boulevard. The light is green, and he takes the next left in a quarter of a mile onto Ventura Boulevard. It is 9:56 a.m. as he pulls into the underground parking garage. He parks, jogs up the two flights of stairs, slips through the backdoor, grabs his jacket from his office, and goes down the hallway to the lobby to greet the Williamsons.

He is genuinely interested to hear their tax story and what is going on with the IRS. Everyone is different, but it never ceases to amaze him how there is a common thread between them all. He is confident that he can help them find their way out of this dark abyss of owing back taxes before he even hears their story. It's just a matter of navigating them to the best possible solution and convincing them that he and his firm are the right team for the job. There is always a way!

Jordan enters the lobby with a warm but not too gregarious smile. He wants his clients to feel comfortable and at ease with him; however, he understands these are typically not happy times. He's wearing a brown tweed sports jacket and a long-sleeved Abercrombie & Fitch maroon and tan plaid shirt with a thin tie. He's in khaki slacks with brown loafers.

He reaches out to shake hands, first with Mr. Williamson and then his wife, as they stand to greet him. "Hello, I'm Jordan Duncan." They look to be in their early to midfifties.

Mrs. Williamson speaks first. "Irma Williamson, and this is my husband, Tyrone." Irma is a stout, curvaceous woman wearing a long forest-green skirt and a brown knit sweater top. With one-inch heels, she is eye to eye with the six-foot Jordan. She is at least two inches taller than Tyrone and must have twenty to thirty pounds on him. She wears her black hair a couple of inches above her shoulders and has bangs covering most of her forehead. She doesn't appear to have on much makeup, nor does she wear jewelry. She needs neither as she is a naturally attractive woman in a stoic manner with coffee-colored smooth skin.

Tyrone is of slight build and has the veins in his forearms and calloused palms of a man who has spent many years working with his hands. He's wearing an off-white button-up short-sleeved shirt. His pants are navy-blue cotton, and he's wearing scuffed-looking black wing-tipped shoes. He has short black hair, which is graying at the sides and receding from his forehead. His face features prominent high cheekbones and is a little more weathered than his wife's, with wrinkles on the corners of both eyes and the sides of his mouth. His upper lip sports a thin dark moustache.

Jordan recognizes instantly that Irma will be the one to carry the conversation, although that does not necessarily indicate that she is the sole decision maker in the family.

"Let's go into my office and have a chat. Can I get you some coffee or water?"

"No, thank you, Mr. Duncan. The sweet girl at the desk offered. We already drank enough coffee this morning before the drive. Any more and my nerves will be frazzled, and Ty will be visiting the boy's room more than he'd like."

Tyrone mumbles, "Mmm, hmm."

They follow Jordan down the hall and, at the end, take a left where his office is situated. It is between Marlin Goodman's much larger corner office, which he occupies maybe two days a week at most, and the office of the resident tax attorney, Karen Wallach, who never seems to leave. Across the hall from those three offices is the large "call center" office. It has several cubicles, each complete with phones, headsets, and personal computers. Closer to the front of that spacious office, another cubicle is set up for JoJo Montanez, the rather extroverted call center manager.

"Please have a seat." Jordan motions to the two leather-backed chairs sitting in front of his desk. He keeps a modest-looking office with a 4 x 6 ft. desktop that has drawers on one side and a file cabinet placed perpendicular on the other side. He has a high leather-back chair on wheels that he scoots around on a large thick plastic sheath that helps him maneuver from drawers to filing cabinet. There is a laptop computer on the desk. Behind Jordan on the wall hangs his college diploma from UCLA. Over his other shoulder hangs his framed Certification of Enrolled Agent, which was awarded from the Internal Revenue Service.

There is a table with some potted plants against the sidewall and a larger plant in the corner next to the window, which overlooks Ventura Boulevard and has white faux wood vertical blinds. On his desk, opposite the computer, is a plaque standing upright and faces the clients. It reads:

Internal Revenue Service:
"If You can't Dodge 'em, Ram 'em"

As the three of them sit down, Jordan says, "My objective today is to hear about your issues with the IRS in regards to your tax bill. Then I will explain how the collection system works within the IRS and how we might be able to help you resolve this problem. Does that sound reasonable?"

"Yes, sir," responds Irma.

Jordan smiles as he says, "I'm friends with your son Tio. So even though I know this is profoundly serious business, please, let's make it a little less formal. You can call me Jordan. I genuinely want to help you. I give you my word that I will be honest and straightforward with you. If we can help, I will explain to the best of my ability how we may proceed."

"Thank you, Jordan. And please call us Irma and Tyrone—or just Ty. We are a bit scared of the federal government and what they can do to us. Honestly, we just don't trust 'em," says Irma.

"Sadly, they give you good reason to not trust them," replies Jordan.

"But we will get more into that after you explain the details of your situation. If you don't mind, please share with me how the tax problem came about. And what is the latest correspondence that you have received from the IRS?" Before Irma can respond, Jordan looks at Tyrone and says, "We good, Tyrone?"

After a brief moment of silence as Tyrone looks straight into Jordan's eyes, he answers, "Tio say you got some game out on dem courts."

Jordan laughs and replies, "I really enjoy running with Tio. That son of yours can ball! You ever play hoops, Tyrone?"

"Oh, back in the day, I could get up and down a li'l bit. In fact, I used to ball on those same courts as you boys—back before they added that fancy main court with dem plexiglass backboards and that three-point line!" Tyrone's demeanor is much more upbeat now.

Quickly Irma cuts in, "Now, Ty, I'm sure Mr. Jordan don't have the time to go on 'bout all this ballin' nonsense back in the day."

Again, Jordan chuckles and says, "Actually, I'd love to hear more. Maybe we can grab a beer sometime in Venice and chat. So please tell me your story about why you are here today."

As Jordan suspected, it is Irma who scoots up to the edge of her chair and begins to share the details of why they are in his office today.

Irma shifts her weight a little and clears her throat. "Well, first thing I think you need to know, Jordan, is how we live. Tyrone and me have six children. Our oldest daughter, Trina, is thirty years old, and Lord only knows where she be living. Somewhere back east, I suppose. Our son Ty Junior is twenty-seven, and poor soul, he has some addiction problems. He is kinda in and out of our place. You know Tio. He's twenty-five, lives at home, but he is truly a godsend at times as he helps with the li'l ones when his daddy is in too much pain. He's always got that smile on his face—you know how he is."

"Yes, I do. A joy to be around, always the life of the party, and smart as a whip," Jordan interjects.

"Then we have Thomas, who is fifteen and in high school. I worry about him, but so far, he seems to be more like Tio than Ty Jr., thank the good Lord. We was blessed with twin girls, Tia and Tillie, when we was both in our forties. They are eleven now. Financially, it's a burden, but my daughters are true angels! Ain't that right, Tyrone?"

"Yes, um, true angels from heaven," Tyrone agrees.

"We don't live in but a tiny three-bedroom apartment on the southeast end of Venice," Irma proclaims. She continues, "Tyrone had a good union job with Caterpillar for about seven years as a heavy-equipment operator. In late summer 1991, he was rear-ended on the freeway comin' home from work, and it left him with constant pain in his back. He couldn't no longer work. 'Cause he was not hurt on the job, he could not get workers' comp. 'Cause they couldn't reach a deal, the union was left with no contract earlier that year, so he couldn't get disability pay neither."

"Tyrone had been there less than ten years, so he couldn't keep his benefits too long. They put him on what they called leave of absence with no pay. He was going to a chiropractor for therapy, but our insurance ran out. Then it became necessary for me to go find work, and Ty would stay home with the li'l ones. I found a job with a small cleaning outfit in Culver City. They had contracts to clean houses, and I was put on a crew. They hired me as an independent contractor, I believe is what they call it. So they pay me every other Friday, but they don't take out no taxes. Thank the Lord 'cause we need every penny just to pay the bills and eat."

"We was scared that we weren't gon' be able to pay rent from month to month. So we was trying to save whatever we could. We didn't file our taxes for the years 1991, '92, and '93. We didn't hear nothing from the IRS, so you know, no news is good news when you think you may owe money." Irma takes a deep breath and wipes the beads of perspiration that are forming on her forehead with her sleeve.

Jordan quickly reaches into his side drawer and pulls out a box of tissues that he has on hand to offer clients, generally for tears. Irma accepts the gesture and thanks him.

She continues her story. "Last June, everything seemed to happen at once. Caterpillar union workers went on strike 'cause of the bad working conditions, and the company let many employees go, including Ty, since he still weren't working no how. Same month, we get a letter from the IRS saying we owe back taxes of $23,000! We was shocked!"

Irma has a furrowed brow as she continues, "But seriously, I thought it must be some kind of mistake. Couldn't possibly be that much. We was trying to figure out what we could do next and if there was some kind of work Tyrone could do. Honestly, Jordan, we always thought eventually Ty would go back to his job at Caterpillar soon as his back would allow it and everything would be okay. I hate to say it, but we ignored them letters. They came 'bout every other month or so, and nobody contacted us about paying 'em." Again, she takes a deep breath, and she swallows hard.

Jordan quickly asks, "Would you like some water?"

"You know, I think I would."

Jordan immediately gets on the intercom and says, "Sunshine, would you please bring a couple of cups of water in for the Williamsons?"

"Sure thing. Right away," responds Sunshine.

After they each drink some water and Irma wipes her brow again as Tyrone gently rubs her shoulders with his right hand, Irma goes on with the story. "In January, we got this letter." She pulls out a folded letter from her purse, straightens it out, and hands it to Jordan. "Now that scared us, and that's when I think Tío heard me crying and asked, 'What's wrong?' I don't like to share my worries with my children, but he saw the letter and panicked."

She adds, "I think that is when he contacted you. Just two weeks ago, we got a message on our answering machine from someone at the IRS. They asked us to call 'em back as soon as possible. We was going to, but then we got a message from Tio to call your office. So that's where we at up to right now. Are we too late?"

"No," Jordan responds right away to try to ease their anxiety a bit. "However, action needs to be taken very quickly. So just to be clear—you have not spoken to anyone from the IRS as of now?"

"No, we have not," reiterates Irma.

"Okay, that is actually good." Jordan shifts from his listening mode, sitting back in his chair, taking in all of what was said very attentively, and now leaning forward. He begins speaking. "First, let me say thank you for sharing your story with me in such great detail. I know these are not easy things to talk about. However, transparency is absolutely necessary if I am going to be able to help you."

He continues, "I would like to start by explaining how the Collection Division of the IRS works, where you are currently in the process, and what you can expect moving forward."

"Oh, that would be good," Irma says as she seems to be a little relieved by having completed telling her difficult story. Tyrone nods.

"I will try not to bore you with details, but I think it is important for you to understand what you are dealing with. The Collection Division of the IRS is divided into three groups. First is the service center, which sends computer-generated notices of tax bills. If they don't get full payment of what they say you owe, you get assigned to the Automated Collection System—or the ACS for short. They follow up with phone calls to try to collect the taxes. If they still haven't collected all of what your case states that you owe, they assign your file or case to a revenue officer. This is a real live person in local districts—here would be the Los Angeles District. The revenue officer assigned to your case will want to make sure the government collects all that they possibly can from you to satisfy your proclaimed debt."

Jordan sees the fear in their eyes already starting to formulate. He continues, "Now before I go any further about how they will try to collect from you, let me explain how you ended up in collections in the first place. There is no tax debt to collect without a tax assessment. There are several ways a tax bill can be assessed, but let's just focus on what has transpired in your case."

He senses that he has their full attention. It is important to Jordan that he doesn't try to overplay the fear factor. Everyone knows that people are generally motivated into action by two main factors—benefits of something to gain or fear of something to lose. It has been well established that fear of loss seems to be the stronger motivator. Within this business, the IRS does an outstanding job of creating fear without much help from tax pros. Jordan has found that trying to accentuate the already existing fear can seem disingenuous. It is more effective to be extremely honest and forthright in explaining how the IRS operates and how he can help them find the best, quickest, and least costly solution to their problem.

"In your case, you did not file taxes for a three-year period, '91–'93. The IRS, however, receives income information from your employers for those years. For you, Tyrone, it would be a W-2 from Caterpillar, and for you, Irma, it is what they call a 1099 from the cleaning service. These are just the form numbers on the income-reporting systems. Now since the IRS doesn't possess the fastest nor most accurate computer systems, they are always a year or two behind in assessing taxes. With the income information, for the sake of time and to penalize you for not filing on time, the IRS generates a Substitution for Return on your behalf, simply referred to as an SFR. Believe me, they aren't doing you any favors with an SFR as they just take the income reported and file you as single, no dependents, and only allow for the standard deductions. Then they tack on penalties and interest, and voilà, that is how you get assessed an exorbitant amount of taxes due. They send that to the service center in the Collection Division and begin the computer-generated letters that you started receiving last summer. Any questions so far?" Jordan asks.

"So you sayin' they file our taxes as two single people with no kids?" inquires Irma.

Jordan nods. "Yep."

"That ain't right," quips Irma abruptly. Tyrone just shakes his head as he looks toward the floor.

"No, it's not, and we can fix that. But there are other solution options to consider that could possibly result in a better outcome for you."

"Let me continue with where you are now in the collection process and what you can expect. Okay?" Jordan asks.

"Yes, that would be helpful." Irma encourages him to continue.

"Right now, based on the fact that you received a phone call and you have received this letter, you are in the ACS."

"Is that good or bad?" inquires Irma.

"Personally, I don't like my clients in the ACS, and I try to get them out as soon as possible," Jordan states in a very matter-of-fact way.

"Uh-oh, we in trouble?" Irma is starting to get nervous.

"Let's talk about this letter, and I'll try to put it in perspective. Starting with the service center, after a tax assessment has been made, a series of letters are sent. They are called CP balance due notices, the first of which is a nonthreatening Notice of Federal Taxes Due. Then every five weeks, you get another letter. They are sequenced: CP 501, Reminder of Unpaid Tax; CP 502, Overdue Tax; CP 503, Urgent-Payment Required; and CP 504, Final Notice of Intent to Levy."

Jordan pauses and then continues, "Honestly, nothing really happens until you get the CP 504, which you just handed me today. This is the last letter you receive from the service center. They are just computer-generated so unless you mail in a payment, no collection activity is enforced. However, the CP 504 means that the IRS has given you ample thirty-day notice and warning that they will begin collection enforcement. They escalate your case to the ACS, and after thirty days, they have all the authority and power necessary to levy your bank accounts or garnish your wages without any further notice."

"Oh, my Lord!" exclaims Irma as she covers her mouth with her hand.

"That would just sink us and put us all out on the street. I would lose my babies. Oh, Jordan, please don't let that happen." Irma is now quite agitated. Tyrone is rubbing his chin as he silently looks on.

"We can stop that from happening. I'm just telling you where you are in the process. Being in the ACS is what I call the black hole of the Collection Division. The reason is that the ACS is made up of hundreds of clerical-type employees sitting at cubicles, soliciting taxpayers on the phone to pay the balance due. One of the difficulties in working out solutions with them is that no one individual is assigned to your case. Therefore, they enter notes into the computer. Any follow-up is with a different clerk, and believe me, a lot gets lost in the note transactions. It's like starting over with each call. The real scary part is that these ACS tax collectors are used to taxpayers being delinquent on payments. They have heard about every excuse possible, so they have become unsympathetic. Incredibly, since they receive the cases just after the thirty-day notice of intent to levy has expired, they have the power and authority to levy a bank account or garnish wages with simple strokes of the keypad at their fingertips!"

"What can we do, Mr. Jordan?" Irma pleads.

"Let me tell you how we operate at Jacobs & Goodman Tax Resolution. We essentially have a four-step process to resolve every tax problem." Jordan is ready to help relieve their stress. "First, I've noticed you looking at this plaque on my desk, Tyrone."

Tyrone nods and says, "Yeah, what's that mean?"

Jordan smiles and says, "I was on the freeway one day, sitting in traffic behind a pickup truck. There was a bumper sticker that read, 'If you can't Dodge it, Ram it.' I got to thinking how that aptly applies to dealing with the IRS. No one wants tax problems. We try to do our duty but pay as little as legally possible in taxes. So essentially we want to dodge or avoid the IRS to the best of our ability.

"However, if a problem arises, and they start chasing you for collection, it is never a good idea to ignore them or try to hide from them. As you have found out, they will find you, and time is never on your side. The 'no news is good news' theory doesn't work. Penalties and interest continue to accrue until the problem becomes enormous."

"So my approach, and that of Jacobs & Goodman, is to be aggressive and proactive. Ram them with resolutions. Their mission is to collect the most amount of taxes in the least amount of time. They want to 'feed the beast' and close cases as a revenue officer has explained it to me. We provide them with all the financial documents that will prove they are getting the most that they can expect to receive and justify closing the case. So I had this plaque made to signify that strategy."

"Mmm, hmm," mumbles Tyrone as he nods his head.

Irma adds, "So how you do that?"

"Back to our four steps," Jordan continues.

"First, we are going to relieve the pressure from you. We offer you protection from collection activity." He holds up the CP-504 letter in his hand. "By taking the power of attorney, dealing specifically and exclusively with your tax issues, you won't have to worry anymore about having your assets levied or seized as long as you stay in compliance with what we ask you to do, which is to provide financial information on a timely basis. The second step is to help you restore your financial stability. We are going to offer you a confidential analysis as we sift through your tax returns, income statements, assets, and liabilities.

"Third, we will officially represent you to the Collection Division of the IRS. You will never have to meet with or talk to them alone. That is why I said it is good that you haven't spoken to anyone from the IRS. If you talk to them, they will offer to help you fill out the necessary financial documents to proceed with collection activity. Having someone from the IRS help you is kind of like allowing the fox to watch the henhouse, if you know what I mean. They have ulterior motives, which are not in your best interest. We will explore all options with you and guarantee that we will find what is in your best interest.

"Last, we resolve your tax problem no matter how long it takes. There is not a time limit. We will see it through until we reach a resolution. The key to success is to legally and reasonably present your financial situation in a way that shows that you are as they say—'robbing Peter to pay Paul' just to make ends meet."

Irma places her hand on Jordan's forearm and says, "Honey, we darn near murdered Peter by now."

Jordan smiles and says, "There will be multiple options to explore. One would be to simply file your taxes properly for the years in question and set up a payment plan to pay them off. That will at least cut your debt in half, although interest continues to accrue. Another option would be to submit an offer in compromise to the IRS that could very possibly result in you paying much less."

Jordan concludes by saying, "Irma, Tyrone I am very confident in saying that we can protect you and resolve your tax problem so that you can get on with your lives."

They both nod, and Irma asks, "How much will this cost to have you represent us?"

Jordan doesn't hesitate in saying, "We require a retainer of $1,500 to take power of attorney and offer you immediate protection. We will also examine your tax returns and fill out the necessary financial documents. Everything we do with you is confidential, and we will consult with you, outlining all possible outcomes. If we simply prepare your returns, negotiate to abate some penalties, and work out the best possible installment agreement for you, your total fee will be around $2,000 depending on time spent, of which you will have already paid $1,500. If we submit an OIC, it will take much longer and require more forms and proof of documentation. The total fee could be as high as $4,500."

"Whew, that would just about do in ole Peter, God bless his soul," says Irma as she looks at Tyrone. "What do you think, Papa?"

"I don't think we have much of a choice." Tyrone looks Jordan in the eyes and says, "I trust the man. Tio say he good people, and he seems to know what he talks about."

Irma grabs Tyrone's hand, looks at Jordan, and says, "I agree. How soon you need the money?"

"We will file the POA the day you can pay the retainer in cash or money order or, if by check, the day it clears," exclaims Jordan.

"Well, we do have a little emergency money. I can give you $1,000 now. Can you meet us in Venice tonight or tomorrow morning for the rest so we don't have to make this trip again?" She reaches into her purse, pulls out ten $100 bills, and placed them in front of Jordan.

"Absolutely. I will have you sign the POA now, and we will file it this afternoon. I will drive down the hill and meet you in Venice outside of Gold's Gym at, say, five thirty?" Jordan asks, looking at Tyrone.

"I can do that," says Tyrone.

"Very good. Maybe then you will let me buy you that beer and tell me about your hoop-playin' days?" Jordan says with a smile.

Tyrone nods and smiles, and Irma just shakes her head. Jordan pulls out the power of attorney and a client agreement form and shows them where to sign. He gives them a receipt and explains the next steps in accumulating information. He advises Irma to expect a phone call from Tonja Farley, the office manager, who will start filling out the necessary financial documentation.

Jordan walks them to the lobby, shakes hands with both Irma and Tyrone, and reassures them that he will begin the process to protect them from collection activity. They thank him and walk out the door.

Sunshine smiles and says, "Sounds like you have some new clients."

"Yep. And they need the POA filed today. You know how to do that?"

"Of course. Give the file to Tonja, and she will have me process it."

Jordan laughs. "Listen to you being all professional like."

"So when are you going to teach me to surf? I'm out of school all week," Sunshine asks enthusiastically.

"Valley girls don't surf," says Jordan as he strolls down the hallway with a smile.

"Ughhh, I'm *not* a Valley girl!" exclaims Sunshine, her voice rising as Jordan disappears from her vision.

CHAPTER THREE

Inside the Workplace

At the Sherman Oaks office of Jacobs & Goodman Tax Resolution, if you turn right at the T in the hallway opposite from the direction of Jordan's office, you immediately encounter the copy room on the left. It houses the IBM copier, fax machine, paper shredder, and main computer printer with many file cabinets along the back wall that contain records of all the Jacobs & Goodman clients. Next to the copy room is an employee lounge with table, chairs, and a kitchen area. There is a refrigerator and a pantry full of food. Adjacent to the kitchen is an office set aside for the company's marketing guru, Brookes Peterson. Then you have the employee restrooms and a door to an exit stairwell at the end of the hall.

Across the hall from Brookes's office is the small office of Tonja Farley. She is the glue that holds this company together, as David has adequately described her main purpose. Her official title is office manager, but it is by design that her office is right next to the large corner office (which is complete with a sitting room, bar, and attached bathroom) of one David Jacobs. She is virtually indispensable to him. Often, he can be heard simply yelling out her name "Tonja!" as though he can't be bothered trying to figure out her intercom office line.

In the lobby, next to the reception desk is a door that opens to a conference room. There is a glass wall that views out into the lobby and reception area. The room contains a large table with enough chairs to seat fourteen people. On the opposite end of the room is a large whiteboard attached to the wall. The conference room is used for monthly sales meetings and serves as a general meeting room. When in town, Arthur Gipson utilizes the conference room as an impromptu office. Mr. Gipson is a retired IRS regional director who now functions as a tax consultant for both Jacobs & Goodman Tax Resolution as well as the parent company, Epstein, Levin & Ohlman CPA Tax Consultants.

As is customary, if Jordan doesn't have an immediate next appointment, he likes to go into Brookes's office and debrief concerning his new clients. Tonja will join them as she will be activating the client file that he has brought on.

Brookes Peterson generally leaves the door to his office open. Jordan always taps on it before entering in case he's on the phone. As he walks in, he plops himself down in one of the two guest chairs.

"Well," says Brookes, "do we have new clients?"

"We do," responds Jordan.

"Excellent. Let's get Tonja, and tell us tell about it."

Brookes is a good listener. He is the type of person who genuinely sees all situations in life as either learning or teaching opportunities. He is thirty years old, is married, and has two young children. His wife is a stay-at-home mom, and they practice the Mormon faith. He attended BYU in Utah, where he received a degree in communications with an emphasis in advertising. During college, he married, and upon graduating, they moved to SoCal, where both he and his wife grew up. He worked at the Orange County Register for a short period of time before realizing that he wanted to and was capable of operating his own advertising company. He has a level of maturity and business acumen beyond his years.

He was struggling with only a few clients when he answered an ad by David Jacobs, who needed a marketing specialist. His first meeting with David took place inside Fromin's Deli. It was January of 1992, and David explained that the IRS Collection Division was opening the doors to entertaining more offer in compromise submissions.

He detailed briefly what that meant for his business model and asked Brookes straight up, "How would you market that program as a business model?"

Brookes didn't hesitate in describing himself to David as a direct-response specialist. His method featured what he called the six *M*s of marketing: motive, market, message, medium, measure, and MAP (marketing advertising plan).

Though David was impressed with his confidence, he countered by stating that he felt he needed to focus on his and his partner's credentials as CPAs and tax experts as the main component to his marketing.

"With all due respect, Mr. Jacobs, I think you are missing the boat with that style of advertising. The masses are only interested in WIIFM: 'What's in it for me?'" Brookes continued quickly as he sensed David was not used to being told that he was wrong about anything. "As you have described the OIC program to me, I can envision creating newspaper ads declaring how delinquent taxpayers are settling their debts for pennies on the dollar with a new IRS program. We will generate urgency to act immediately! It's new, it's fresh, it's urgent, and we are the experts that they need."

David, who was ready to tell this young hotshot to get lost a couple of minutes ago, was now intrigued. There is something unique about this brash yet very wholesome young man that he gravitates to.

"What specifically can you do for me?" David inquired of Brookes.

"I will make your phones ring constantly. You will need to set up a call center to screen the calls. The screeners will need specific scripts to qualify the callers for this IRS program. They will then enthusiastically schedule appointments for those that qualify to meet with your tax experts. You will need multiple offices with tax experts to meet and sign up new clients."

Again, David paused before extending his hand. "You are my guy, Brookes Peterson. Let's work out the details on compensation, office space, budget, and time allocation."

Brookes didn't quite know how to react, but something told him that he could trust this squatty, older, crusty, entrepreneurial

Jewish CPA. "I believe in this project and in your vision for success, Mr. Jacobs," said Brookes as the two men shook hands.

"Please, from now on, call me David." That was the beginning of a solid, successful business relationship.

For the record, prior to David meeting and hiring Brookes to help him market his tax resolution business, almost all marketing activities in the industry was done by contacting tax lien recipients. The IRS has the right to inform the public on who owes taxes. This is done by recording a Notice of Federal Tax Lien at the county recorder's office. It was extremely time-consuming and not extraordinarily successful to obtain that list and send solicited letters to delinquent taxpayers.

Jacobs & Goodman Tax Resolution methods were literally a game changer in the industry as they began marketing—using primarily newspaper ads to promote the once-dormant procedure of offer in compromise to resolve tax debts most efficiently and effectively.

"See if Tonja is available," Jordan says to Brookes before detailing his meeting with the Williamsons.

Brookes punches her intercom line. "Do you have time to meet with Jordan and me in my office? He just signed up a new client couple and wants to debrief us."

"Give me one minute, and I'll be right over, unless DJ yells for me," Tonja responds.

"So real quick, Jordan, what was the key trigger to get them signed up on their first visit?" Brookes inquisitively asks while on the edge of his chair.

Jordan calmly pulls the CP 504 letter from the new file he has created and tosses it across the desk in a nonchalant manner. "The golden ticket," Jordan says with a smile.

"Ah yes. The IRS fear tactics at work," states Brookes. "How do you respond when they show you these letters? I mean, do you say, 'Oh my gosh, you are going to lose everything unless you hire us right now'?"

"Hahaha, not exactly. You just have to act cool, like you've seen thousands of these before. But it's important for them to realize that this is the tipping point of the IRS getting serious about enforcing collection. Up until they get this letter, everything from the IRS is just talk. Now they have self-empowerment to take whatever they want from you without any due process," Jordan explains.

"Wow, fascinating, isn't it? The way the tax system works." Brookes shakes his head.

Tonja bursts through the door, always going a hundred miles per hour through this office, just trying to keep up with her workload. "Hey, handsome, nice job!" She gives Jordan a high-five before sitting down next to him.

"Thanks," he replies as he drops the file on her lap.

"Why do you always refer to him as handsome, but I am always just Brookes or 'Hey, you'?" Brookes asks with a smile on his face.

"Well, my dear, you are a married, religious man with two children. I am a divorced, working mother of two kids who has no social life. So any flirting or fantasies that I may have at work will be reserved for this gorgeous single man next to me," Tonja responds as she winks at Jordan. "I think it is perfectly fine. Do you disagree?"

"Oh, no." Brookes raises his hands up defensively. "I was just wondering why he gets all your flirts. Now I know," he says with a big grin.

All three laugh. In actuality, the three of them work very well together, and though they don't discuss it, they each know that individually and as a team they are a major component to the success of J&G.

"So what do we have here?" Tonja inquires as she opens the file, which, at this point, only consists of a signed POA, client agreement, and some general personal information. It also includes the tax debt amount assessed of $23K.

"I'm thinking OIC," says Jordan. "They were SFR'd for three years, so the debt is obviously bloated. Midfifties, mister is out of work, semi-disabled. Missus is a 1099 house cleaner. They have three minors and two adult children living in a three-bedroom apartment. No assets to speak of."

"Gosh, I don't know how these people survive sometimes," Tonja says sympathetically while shaking her head.

"So it's a slam dunk OIC, huh?" Brookes states.

"Brookes, Brookes, Brookes, how many times do we tell you? With the IRS, there is no such thing as a slam dunk," Tonja counsels. She looks at Jordan. "Where are they now?"

"ACS. Got the CP 504 about forty-five days ago. Received their first call from ACS couple weeks ago but haven't talked to anyone. Voice messages."

"Okay, we have to get them out of ACS ASAP," Tonja instructs.

"No problem," Jordan replies.

She looks back at Brookes. "When you are submitting an OIC, first you want to make sure you get the client out of the ACS to negotiate directly with a revenue officer. Then it's a matter of which revenue officer [RO] gets the assignment. They are not all created equally, and they have a lot of latitude on how they want to collect." She then turns to Jordan. "By the way, just before I came in here, I was on the phone with Bobbi."

Bobbi Sinclair is the branch chief of revenue officers in the Los Angeles District office. She and Tonja have a good working relationship. She is tough but fair as she recognizes the win-win scenario of working with tax professionals. Jacobs & Goodman Tax Resolution is by far the leader of OIC submissions in LA County.

"She says Jack Arbuckle has his panties in a wad over one of your clients and needs to talk to you immediately. Apparently, he has left you messages."

"Let me guess—Alice Johnston?" Jordan says dryly.

"Yep. You'll call him?" inquires Tonja.

"Yeah, I'll call the jackass. By the way, all his calls have been this morning, and I was busy with clients."

Tonja shakes her head. "He is such a prick. Oh, sorry, Brookes."

Brookes laughs. "I get the gist of it."

Brookes, being Mormon, doesn't swear, drink, smoke, or participate in any other vices as far as Tonja and Jordan can tell. However, he never acts holier than thou or sanctimonious in any way. That is a reason why they trust him and enjoy his company. He always seems to be in a good mood and works hard, and he certainly keeps the phones ringing as he promised David three years ago!

Just then David pops his head in the door. "Sunshine tells me you signed up a new client today. How much?" Funny how when talking to Tonja about new clients, her first question is about the type of service Jordan anticipates from the new clients. With David, it's always first about the dollars generated.

"A $1,500 retainer, and I quoted them $4,500 for an OIC, which I think is very doable," answers Jordan.

"Excellent. Good job." David then turns to Brookes. "Ron Kessler is coming in later this afternoon, and I'd like to talk about the ads. You available to meet with us?"

Brookes knows that this isn't really a question. "Yes, absolutely. I will make myself available. What time?"

"Say, 3:00 p.m., my office?"

"I'll be there."

David looks at Tonja and says, not in a mean way, "I need you in my office now." He turns and leaves.

Tonja rolls her eyes at the other two, waves goodbye, and says, "See ya later, boys."

"Catch ya later, Brookes," Jordan says as he stands up.

"Okay, Jordan. Nice job. And I want to hear more when we can talk again."

Jordan proceeds to the copy room, where he fetches the file on Alice Johnston. He knows what's going on with the case before he calls her assigned RO, Jack Arbuckle. But he wants to review the history of the case prior to engaging in verbal battle with Arbuckle.

Revenue officers in the IRS Collection Division are somewhat of a rare breed of individuals. They are different from revenue agents, who work within the Examination Division and perform audits. To become an RA, one must have an accounting degree and be a CPA, tax attorney, or an enrolled agent. There are no such requirements to become an RO. Revenue agents are the true number crunchers within the IRS—the check and balance, if you will, that helps augment the self-assessment tax system that the US government has established. They perform random and some not-so-random audits. Revenue officers provide collection enforcement of said assessments. They clean up the messes of delinquent taxpayers that often are the result of gaps that are left after audits. There exists some dissention and resentment between the divisions.

As Jordan explained to the Williamsons, revenue officers are the last line of the collection process after the service center and the ACS. Their job description is simple—collect delinquent taxes.

The IRS, through the authority of the Department of Treasury's Internal Revenue Code (sanctioned by the US Congress), has given revenue officers a tremendous amount of power and latitude in the enforcement of tax collection. Unfortunately, that power goes to the head of some ROs. Jack Arbuckle in the Los Angeles District fits that description.

The priorities for a revenue officer are (1) to collect money and (2) to close cases. The good ones maximize both! Jack calls it "feeding the beast."

The top revenue officers turn over their case inventory every forty-five to ninety days. J&G has found that can work to the advantage of the tax pro and, subsequently, the taxpayer. It is imperative in Jordan's mind. Tonja is on the same page, although sometimes they struggle on that front with Karen Wallach to give the impression to the ROs that closing cases as quickly as possible is also the goal for J&G. Work with them in a cooperative manner, incorporating a win-win type of attitude. Who knows what Marlin Goodman does with his cases as he is seemingly on an island of his own? His only responsibility is to his senior partner, David Jacobs. Tonja goes way back with both David and Marlin and has learned not to clash with Marlin. There is no love lost between Marlin and Jordan. Marlin disdains the "golden boy" status that David bestows upon him. Jordan sees Marlin as arrogant and doesn't appreciate the way he treats the staff. He also suspects Marlin's reluctance to share specifics about his cases.

Jacobs & Goldman Tax Resolution LLC was created in 1991. David Jacobs, who ran operations on the West Coast of Epstein, Jacobs, Levin & Ohlman CPA Tax Consultants Inc., approached the CEO of the firm, Alexander Epstein. His plan was to expand the scope of their services. With multiple connections within the upper ranks of the IRS, Jacobs and Epstein had become privy to studies that were done apropos to delinquent tax accounts and the collection activity.

The amount of delinquent taxes on the Internal Revenue Service's (IRS) records was growing and so was the amount classified as "currently not collectible" (CNC). At the end of the fiscal year in the late '80s, IRS's inventory of individual and business delinquent accounts totaled $130.6 billion. IRS had classified as CNC, thereby suspending collection action on 40 percent of that inventory.

Most of the CNC amounts will never be collected. Because of the large amount of recorded CNC tax debt and the potential revenue losses, the chairman of the Subcommittee on Oversight, House Committee on Ways and Means, requested that GAO (US government's accountability office) examine whether IRS's CNC determinations were appropriate and whether IRS's efforts to monitor CNC accounts for future collection potential were adequate.

The study concluded that the IRS is losing the potential of collecting hundreds of millions of dollars because of its CNC determination, oversight, and monitoring processes. Their recommendation was that the commissioner of Internal Revenue Service should establish specific guidelines for determining taxpayers' ability to pay delinquent taxes.

Based on the ascertained taxpayers' collectability potential, they recommended the IRS should entertain legitimate offers to settle the tax debts. The mechanism for such a program already existed in the form of offers in compromise. If escalated in the proper manner, the expanded use of the offer in compromise program would be beneficial in three ways: (1) dramatically reduce the amount of CNC accounts on record; (2) encourage delinquent taxpayers to come forward to settle their debts, helping the Collection Division close a higher percentage of existing cases; and (3) generate a revenue stream for the IRS that is not currently being realized.

The entrepreneurial side of David Jacobs seized that opportunity to suggest opening an affiliate company, specializing in tax resolution for individual and business delinquent taxpayers. The market was ripe, and David had a potential client in mind to test a proof of concept of the new friendlier version of offer in compromise.

Ronald Kessler was a local construction contractor who had done the work on an expansion of David's Encino, California, home. Mr. Kessler, upon learning that Mr. Jacobs was a partner in a CPA tax consultant firm, confided in him that he had fallen behind on some taxes. Though he was making modest installment payments, with an exorbitant amount of penalties and interest tacked on, it seemed impossible for him to climb out of that debt and was on the verge of being classified CNC and put out of business. David suggested to Alexander Epstein and to a regional director of the IRS, Arthur Gibson, that the firm prepare an offer in compromise for Mr. Kessler that would represent his collectability potential over the foreseeable future.

The Internal Revenue Manual on OIC states that an offer must reflect "all that can be collected from the taxpayer's equity in assets and income, present and prospective."

In simple terms, the acceptable offer amount must represent the present value of the reasonable collection potential. To determine the future monthly payments into present value, the IRS considers what the taxpayer could pay over sixty months and then discounts the accumulation of those payments to present value.

The formality of submitting an offer in compromise on behalf of Ronald Kessler was executed, and after some negotiations on acceptable expenses and asset valuation, the offer was accepted by the IRS. Mr. Kessler settled for literally pennies on the dollar. He was delighted!

David Jacobs was commissioned by Alexander Epstein to be the president of the new affiliate company created in tax resolution, focusing primarily on taking power of attorney for their clients then submitting and negotiating settlements with the IRS through the new and improved version of the offer in compromise. David insisted that Marlin Goodman, his lifelong friend and colleague who was currently a CPA and junior partner at Epstein, Jacobs, Levin & Ohlman CPA Tax Consultants, come with him as a junior partner. Marlin also lived in the Los Angeles area. They established Jacobs & Goodman Tax Resolution LLC in October of 1991.

In February of 1992, the IRS issued a new Internal Revenue Manual outlining changes to the offer in compromise. District directors were charged with training their branch chiefs and revenue officers on the proper computations for acceptable offers. This kicked off the start of what would become the "golden age" of the offer in compromise program.

As pioneers of this new and improved OIC program and with their hotshot marketing guru in tow, Jacobs & Goodman Tax Resolutions business took off like a rocket. They started with one office in Sherman Oaks and set up, as per Brookes Peterson's suggestion, a call center that was under the direction of Tonja Farley. Tonja had worked at the E, J, L & O Tax Consultants as their Los Angeles division office manager. In fact, the only two people that David Jacobs had insisted come with him to start J&G Tax Resolution were Marlin and Tonja. David and Marlin were the tax managers who met face-to-face with clients.

Soon, it became necessary to have an office closer to downtown. With the lure of settlements for pennies on the dollar, many high-end, huge-liability clients came forth, and the firm decided to set up an executive suite in Beverly Hills. Marlin lived in Brentwood, so it made sense that he would be the one to sit with clients in Beverly Hills. Next came the Bay Area as Brookes convinced David that the *San Francisco Chronicle* had an extremely large subscription base, second only to the *LA Times* in California. They established an office in Burlingame, near the SF International Airport. They hired a very seasoned tax manager by the name of Sterling Frey, who was an enrolled agent that once worked as a revenue agent in the IRS Examination Division. He hired an office manager, Sally James, and a TDA (tax delinquency analyst, which is their formal name for a salesperson), Reed Franklin.

Since then, J&G has expanded to include executive office suites in Orange County, San Diego, Riverside, Rancho Cucamonga, San Jose, San Francisco, and Emeryville. There are currently six tax managers and six acting TDAs (Marlin, Jordan, and Tricia Sherman, who is a tax attorney in San Francisco, perform both TDA and tax manager functions). All leads and appointments set out of the Sherman Oaks call center.

They have submitted and had accepted hundreds of OICs from 1992 to 1995 and are by far the most aggressive and highest-producing tax resolution firm in CA and the nation when it comes to the implementation of the offer in compromise program. They are well known in the Collection Division of the IRS, particularly in the California districts as being professional and thorough in their OIC submissions. However, as Tonja had reminded Brookes, there are no "slam dunks" OICs, and all ROs are not created equal when it comes to their attitude and cooperation in processing and accepting offers.

And this circles back around to Jack Arbuckle! Jordan is not really sure how long Jack has been a revenue officer, but he has had several encounters with him over the past two-plus years.

During that period of time, Jordan has also worked with various other ROs in the LA District office, including the branch chief, Bobbi Sinclair. No doubt they each have their particular style and methods of processing OICs or installment agreements (IAs). Negotiating over financial statements, assets, and viable necessary living expenses are key components to attaining an accepted offer. Deadlines come into play, and taxpayer cooperation in providing the documentation is crucial. Most ROs are reasonable.

Jordan has determined that Jack is probably a paranoid man with extremely low self-esteem and carries a huge inferiority complex. Thus, Jack constantly tries to convince everyone that he has superior power and intellect over *all* delinquent taxpayers and most tax pros. Unfortunately, as stated, the IRS empowers the revenue officer with a scary amount of authority and leverage to inflict severe methods to collect past due taxes.

One of the most annoying and frustrating elements Jordan encounters time and again with Jack is his constant badgering. He happens to know that Jordan played football at UCLA, so he refers to Jordan sarcastically as Superstar. He has made it abundantly clear that he is a USC fan and goes out of his way to point out what a superior football program Southern Cal has over UCLA—as if that has anything to do with tax resolution. Jordan refuses to engage in that kind of argument. Jack also tries to use sports metaphors in his conversations about Jordan's cases.

For example: "It's the fourth quarter, two minutes left, and you have no timeouts left, Superstar. No Hail Marys gonna fly with me!" Then other times, he'll say things like "It's not a level playing field, Superstar. The Internal Revenue Service grants me power to fulfill their mission, which is to collect the tax, get the money, and feed the beast in whichever way I see fit!" He even went as far as once telling Jordan, "You know how you sports thugs like to hang motivational quotes on your locker room walls? Well, guess what sign I've hung over the door to our conference room. 'SEIZURE FEVER—CATCH IT!' That's right, Superstar. I am the king of property seizures in this town. Tell your clients that!"

Jordan got a big laugh from Tonja and Brookes when he shared that gem. Jack is a real piece of work.

Jordan's approach in most cases with Jack Arbuckle is to just ignore the BS and stick to the facts and data that are available. When all is said and done, it's just a numbers game. The kryptonite for any revenue officer is that if they reject an offer without a substantial reason, you can take it to appeals. That makes them look very bad to their superiors, especially during this golden age of OICs. On the other hand, it is tough to get an OIC overturned in appeals. It's definitely in everyone's best interest, especially the taxpayer, to do it right the first time and negotiate a fair settlement—most difficult with Jack for sure but doable.

Jordan picks up the phone and, with the Johnston file in front of him, dials Jack's direct line.

"Arbuckle here."

"Jordan Duncan, returning your call."

Jack seems neither surprised nor angry. "Well, the Superstar does return calls after all."

"What's up, Jack?" Jordan asks impatiently.

"What's up is that your loser client, the daycare lady, is late again on her IA, and I'm going to have to take some action," Jack retorts with a mixture of sarcasm and authority.

Jordan responds defensively, "I presume you're talking about Alice Johnston. It's only the sixth of the month. There is a ten-day grace period!"

"What do I look like? The pope? The service doesn't extend grace, especially to perpetual delinquents!" shouts Jack into the phone.

"Did she pay any of it?" inquires Jordan.

"Five hundred dollars and says she'll pay the balance by the 15th."

"So what's the problem?" Jordan says, sounding a little annoyed.

"The problem, Superstar, is that her IA is for $1,000 on the first of every month, and it is considered late by the sixth." Now Jack sounds annoyed.

"Look, Jack, I have a meeting with her next Monday the 13th [he doesn't actually have that scheduled as yet, but he needs to buy some time]. I will get the other $500 to you by the 15th. But I've been working the numbers and think we can flip this into an OIC."

Jack cuts him off, "No can do, Mr. Bruin. Too much equity in the house."

Jordan is quick on the response. "The house is only half hers. The rest belongs to the deadbeat ex-husband. It needs a lot of repairs. Anyway, like I said, I'm meeting with her next Monday. I'll get the balance of the IA for March. Then we will prepare the OIC forms before April 1 or make another installment payment."

"If you don't pay by the 15th and again the full amount on April 1, I'm shutting her down and seizing the property. I can't bother with this woman anymore. I have too many cases to close. Time to feed the beast, Superstar!"

"Thanks for the call, Jack. Talk to you next week." Jordan hangs up without waiting to hear another smart-assed response. He hits the intercom line for the front desk. "Sunshine, could you please get in touch with Alice Johnston today and schedule her for an appointment on next Monday, the 13th? She probably needs it to be in the afternoon. Tell her it is mandatory!"

"Will do. Do you have her file, or is it in the copy room?" Sunshine asks.

"I'll bring it to you." Jordan knows that it is going to take some creative maneuvering to save Alice this time.

Sunshine Kessler is the sixteen-year-old daughter of Ronald and Susan Kessler. As David Jacobs's prototype OIC client that helped launch this highly lucrative business venture, Ron Kessler has remained close to David. His story is featured in the "aditorials" (coined by Brookes to refer to the brilliantly designed newspaper ads that he writes like editorials). David considers the Kesslers like family, and he has a particular soft spot for Sunshine. He offered her a part-time job working in the office after school and in the summers.

Sunshine is a pretty girl with long blond hair and blue eyes—just what you would expect from a California girl named Sunshine! Her name has an interesting origin. Ron and Sue were SoCal high school sweethearts during the hippie movement in the sixties. The highlight of their youth was when they ventured back east in a VW van with some friends in the summer of '69 to attend the Woodstock concert in upper state New York. While enduring enormous crowds, lack of food, mind-blowing music, and drugs, they also had to deal with inclement weather. Mid-Sunday morning, as the rain subsided, the sun burst through the clouds. Susan swears still to this day that as she looked skyward into the brilliant sunlight, she saw the face of an angel appear. Ron has always silently wondered how drug-induced that vision might have been.

However, they subsequently married and were blessed with the birth of a baby girl nine years to the date, August 17, 1978, after that miraculous sunburst of an angelic vision experienced by Susan. Both felt inspired to name this wonderful bundle of joy Sunshine. She has fulfilled everything her parents had hoped for as she is truly the apple of their eyes. She is an extremely bright, happy girl that has many friends and much ambition. She also feels a closeness to Jordan as their birthdays are only two days apart and, in an abstract way, are connected to Woodstock. He was simply born the day Woodstock opened in 1969, and her parents were actually at the concert, where they experienced the inspiration for her name. Jordan thinks of it as a coincidence. He likes Sunshine as her energy seems to brighten up the office.

After getting the balance of fees and having a nice chat with Tyrone Williamson over a couple of beers and putting him at ease that the POA was filed on Monday, Jordan is meeting Tio at the Venice Beach courts on Wednesday at 5:30 p.m. along with Little Al. It should be interesting as these two friends of Jordan have never met each other.

Jordan likes to ride his bike down the path along the beach from his Santa Monica apartment to the Venice Beach courts. Wearing blue UCLA gym shorts and a gray sweatshirt, he has a backpack strapped to him, which carries his b-ball, T-shirt, and game shoes. You cannot wear the same Nikes biking or jogging that you play ball in. His running shoes are low-cut and lightweight. His b-ball shoes are black mid-high Air Jordans with reinforced insoles and a white with red trim Nike swoosh.

Just as he pulls up to the courts, his phone, which was in his backpack, rings. He recognizes Little Al's number. "Hey, where are you?"

"Be there in about ten minutes," Al responds. "Great news! Got Gambo an extension with the Niners," he says very enthusiastically.

"That is great."

"Yeah, in fact, I just got back from San Francisco, and I'm driving up from LAX now."

"Do you have your gear to hoop in?" asks Jordan.

"You know I always have a gym bag packed and ready," replies Al. "I'll tell you all about the contract after we play."

"Sounds good. I'll treat at Maroni's to celebrate," Jordan says with a smile on his face.

"Perfect!" Al loves the sausage dogs at Jody Maroni's Sausage Kingdom, which is a small sidewalk cafe on the Venice Boardwalk across from the b-ball courts.

Jordan almost always shows up a little early to stretch and shoot around before playing. As he begins his routine, Tio arrives on his bicycle. He has on a pair of old gray sweatpants cut off just below the knees, a black T-shirt, and old black canvas high-top Converse. His mid-high black Nike Air Jordans are tied together and slung over his shoulder. He has a basketball wedged between the seat and the back fender.

"Hey, Taxman, how you be? My folks be feelin' good after meetin' with you." He gets off his bike, and they go through their handshake routine and bro hug quickly.

"They seem like really good people, Tio. I'll help 'em out of their mess."

"I appreciate it, man. Hey, where's your buddy?" Tio asks as he looks around but doesn't see any other white dudes on the main court as Jordan is shooting on one end while a game of three on three is being played at the other end.

"On his way, be here in a few," answers Jordan.

Just then, Alvin Bockman comes jogging up in a business suit, carrying a gym bag. Without saying a word, Jordan points to the public restroom about fifty feet away. Al hurries over and reappears moments later in his navy-blue sweats that say "Penn State Football" on the thigh in white letters. He's wearing a white T-shirt with a navy-blue insignia of the Nittany Lion across the chest. White Nike high-tops adorn his feet.

Jordan has shed his sweatshirt and is now wearing a gray T-shirt with no sleeves. Even though the temperature is in the low sixties, once they start running, Jordan will not feel the chill in the air. His backpack is tied to his bike, which is locked to the bleachers.

Al has an outer bag covering his suit. "Should I run this back to my car? It's not far away," Al inquires.

"No, just lay it across my bike. It will be fine," Jordan assures him.

Al walks closer to Jordan and whispers, "This is a $2,000 suit, man."

"We're playing right in front of it, and it's still daylight. But if you want to be sure, pay one of these kids ten bucks to keep an eye on it," Jordan suggests.

"Good idea. Be right back." Al completes his transaction by giving two youngsters $10 now and a promise of $10 more when they finish. He hustles out onto the court, where Jordan and Tio are warming up.

"Tio, this is Al Bockman. Al, Tio Willamson." Jordan makes the introduction.

Al extends his hand, and Tio shakes it and says, "Whooee, you be a big boy. Whaddya go, 'bout 6'4", 285?"

"Try 6'5", 250—ala Charles Barkley!" Al responds confidently.

"Hahahaha!" Tio bends over laughing. "Bruh, you be Charles Barkley like my girlfriend be Halle Berry!" Tio can't help but continue to laugh.

Truth is, Li'l Al is a legit 6'5" but currently tips the scales at around 275.

"We gonna talk smack or play ball?" Al asks without a smile.

"Not sure your buddy could run full court just yet. Let's grab these brutha's over there and run threes half court," suggests Tio.

"Set it up. Let's hoop," says Jordan.

Ever since *White Men Can't Jump* premiered in 1992, with Wesley Snipes and Woody Harrelson featuring much of the film at the Venice Beach Courts, there has been an influx of hopeful hoopsters coming from all over the country to play on these infamous courts.

For the filming, they made significant improvements to the main court, putting in plexiglass backboards and three-point lines and even painted the courts blue. The outer courts (three of them) remain black asphalt. Unfortunately, for the local hardcore ballers, the influx of newbies include many of what they call Billy Hoyle wannabes—white guys dressed in baggy shorts and backward ball caps that want to play on the main court and measure their skills against superior players who are often former college and pro athletes.

It is annoying for the true players. So they are very selective now on who can match up on the main court. The general rules set by the Venice Beach Parks and Recreation declare that it is a first-come, first-serve system of playing time. However, on the main court, if you are an unknown, you are immediately sent to the outer courts and must "earn" your way to the main court. Winning team stays; losers move to a lesser court.

On nonsummertime weeknights, there is a lesser crowd, and often the premier players break up and play three on three half-court games on the main court. Such is the case tonight. Everyone on the court is athletic and can shoot. Al is definitely the anomaly, but his size advantage, excellent ability to use body leverage, and the familiarity that he and Jordan have on the court playing together is evident. Al sets some stonewall screens for Tio, which frees him up for wide-open jumpers or an open lane to the rim.

Tio at 6" and only 155 lb., has the ability to palm the ball, and with a vertical leap of 37 inches, can dunk easily. Tio incorporates a killer crossover dribble move that often leaves even the quickest defenders helpless in trying to stay in front of him. Jordan's jump shot is deadly accurate, and at 6'0", 180 lb., which is 5 lb. less than his football playing weight at UCLA, he remains in excellent physical condition. Jordan and Al have mastered the pick and roll, and Tio joins in on the fun.

They sweep through three different teams of three on three. The opponents suggest mixing things up and running five on five full court. Time and diminishing daylight prohibit that, but they all agree to meet Saturday morning to continue their competition.

Jordan, Little Al, and Tio walk over to Maroni's to grab a sandwich and beer—Jordan's treat. They walk the twenty yards back to the main court and sit in the bleachers to eat next to their bikes and stuff.

"Ya know, big guy, you more like Sir Charles than I would have ever guessed" Tio admits with a smile as he high-fives Al. "Of course, all 'below' the rim." They laugh.

"Well, little guy, you've got some pretty good hops there, and I love that crossover," says Al.

"I call me and Jordan TnT—for Tio 'n Taxman. I think the three of us can be TnT and da Tank!" says Tio with a huge smile. They all high-five and laugh. "I gotta go. See y'all Saturday morning." Tio jumps up and gets on his bike.

Jordan says, "Nice run, Tio. Be safe."

Al just waves as he is still stuffing the sausage in his mouth.

"So tell me about Gambo's deal," Jordan inquires of Al.

"Oh, man, it's sweet. That Carmen Policy [president of the San Francisco 49ers] is a true capologist, like his reputation. No wonder San Fran won the Super Bowl this year," says Al.

"Don't remind me. They beat the Chargers," Jordan recalls. He was a little torn during the Super Bowl in January. His HS teammate Sal Gambadoro was Al's first client as an NFL player's agent and was drafted by the SF 49ers in the 1992 NFL draft out of Rutgers University. He just finished an outstanding season capped off in the Super Bowl. However, Jordan has been a San Diego Charger fan ever since his youth. He was happy for Gambo when the Niners won, but the Chargers have still never won a Super Bowl, and in fact, this was their first appearance in the big game.

"Policy is big on signing bonuses which are player friendly but can be spread out over the length of the contract so as to not count too high against the salary cap," Al explains.

"Check it out—$1,000,000 signing bonus with three years at $400K a year and a team option for the fourth year," Al says proudly.

"That's awesome. How does the team option work?" Jordan asks.

"There are many ways to structure that. In this case, if the team picks up the fourth year, they pay him $400K. Or they can pick up the option and allow him to become a restricted free agent. In that case, we can negotiate with any team, and the Niners can either match the offer or let him go and get compensated a draft pick, to be determined. I came up with that restricted free-agent option. If they don't pick up the option, he becomes an unrestricted, free agent. Team and player friendly!" Al is obviously very excited.

"I'll bet Gambo is thrilled. I'm happy for him. Congratulations, Al."

"Oh, yeah, Gambo loves it. Thanks, man," Al confirms.

"Hey, you looked pretty good out there, but huffin' and puffin' a bit. You gonna be ready for the Final Four?" Jordan asks Al.

"I have to admit I need to drop some weight before then. What's the date this year?"

"April 1 to 3. Less than a month away. In Seattle this year."

"You have tickets yet?"

"No. You know I like to wait until the last minute and check the secondary market."

"Scalpers?"

"Yep. Cheaper," Jordan confirms.

"See ya Saturday morning to play ball here at eight," Jordan says, and Al confirms.

The friends shake hands and go their separate ways.

Last year, Jordan and Al ran a little con game at the NCAA Basketball Final Four weekend. They bought upper deck tickets for the two semifinal games on Saturday and finals on Monday. Annually, Epstein, Levin & Ohlman purchase luxury suites for the semifinals and finals. On Sunday, the CEO, Alexander Epstein, sponsors a company party and buffet that features a two-on-two basketball tournament for employees and guests (rules are that at least one participant on each entry must be an employee). The winner receives a nice cash bonus and tickets in the suite for the finals. Epstein is a big sports fan, super competitive in everything, and hates to lose at anything.

Jordan found out where the two-on-two tourney was being played. He and Al got there early, and though uninvited, they began shooting hoops on the court prior to the arrival of Epstein's entourage. As the group showed up, Epstein stated that they had the courts reserved. Al would say that there must be a mistake because they had also reserved the court. Of course, no one had time to try to straighten things out on a Sunday. Al suggested that he and Jordan would challenge the winner of the tourney. The stakes would be their respective tickets to the championship game on Monday. If Jordan and Al win, they swap tickets. If Epstein's team wins, they get the extra tickets to give away or sell.

Epstein sized them up. He noticed that even though Al was big, he looked out of shape, and he also didn't know who Jordan was at this point. Epstein, not wanting to delay his gig any longer, agreed to the terms. The outcome was exactly how the friends had planned. They beat the winners and scored the luxury suite tickets to the finals. Epstein glowered at them during the entire event. In fact, as they flew home after the game, one of the biggest pleasures they derived from the entire experience was how pissed off they made Epstein.

Jordan knows that, this year, Epstein will be looking for them. In fact, he had already investigated these two con artists and found out that Jordan works for David Jacobs. Epstein initially wanted him fired immediately. David defended him, explaining that he was his top producer and was a competitive former college athlete.

He actually laughed and said, "Come on, Alex, firing him would be like quitting. Find some ringers and beat him at the next Final Four shindig."

As Epstein thought it over, he decided that was exactly what he would do.

CHAPTER FOUR

March Madness

Based on previous experience, Jordan anticipates this reaction during the meeting with Alice Johnston. He places the box of tissues on his desk before she enters his office.

Alice enters the Jacobs & Goodman office suite ten minutes late for their three thirty scheduled meeting. That also is to be anticipated. Jordan knows that the first twenty minutes or so, he needs to allow her to vent over the frustrations and stress currently in her life. On cue, the flood gates open within the first few minutes as she attempts to articulate everything going wrong in her life. Jack Arbuckle contributes most profoundly to her level of stress.

Alice is a thirty-nine-year-old victim of a nasty divorce that was finalized almost two years ago. She is the mother of three children ages two, four, and seven. She's of medium height and is a little more than slightly overweight but not obese. Her hair is a musty brown and usually worn up in some type of bun on top of her head. She has a ruddy complexion that becomes more distinctly red in the face as she expresses frustration, anxiety or anger. Today she is wearing a beige pullover long-sleeved sweater and blue jeans that appear to be a size too small for her thick thighs and wide hips. Her fingernails are closely cut and nonpolished on her worn hands, which obviously participate in many motherly activities daily.

Her ex-husband, Donald Johnston, is the father of all three of her children. They were married for nine years. In the divorce from

Donald, she was awarded custody of the children and kept residency of the family home.

Currently, Donald is staying in a halfway house while attempting to overcome an alcohol addiction. He has no visitation rights with the children. He did maintain, through court order, 50 percent equity in the house they purchased jointly in 1991, just after the birth of their second child.

Alice responded to the newspaper ad in the *LA Times* from Jacobs & Goodman. She was very motivated by the "settle for pennies on the dollar" story of Ron Kessler. She was screened by the call center and had high hopes when she first came to the Sherman Oaks office and met with Jordan Duncan in October of 1994.

As Jordan listened to her story, he discovered that just prior to the divorce settlement in the fall of 1993, the Johnstons were audited for the tax years of 1989 through 1992. Donald and Alice owned a restaurant in Thousand Oaks, which is in San Fernando Valley about thirty minutes north of Sherman Oaks off the 101. The restaurant has been closed since just before the divorce. The equipment and furniture that wasn't leased was sold at a forced sale liquidation. The proceeds went to the divorce attorneys and court costs.

The IRS revenue agent who conducted the audit found evidence of unreported income as well as unsubstantiated expenses that were claimed on their original tax returns. The returns were filed married jointly, signed by both spouses. They received a tax bill from the IRS Service Center for $65,000, which has since grown to over $80,000 with penalties and interest.

By the time the case escalated through the Collection Division to the desk of Jack Arbuckle, the divorce was finalized, and Mr. Johnston was in rehab. Alice, having small children at home, with only one of the three is in school, decided that to try to stay financially afloat, she would open a day care center and run it out of her finished basement.

Unfortunately, having equity in the house that was encumbered with a tax lien, an OIC was not possible. Alice could not qualify for a refi on the mortgage. If she sold the house, her credit was now shot, and she couldn't even qualify to rent a place large enough to house her family. She would probably have to find a job waiting tables somewhere and wouldn't be able to afford day care for her children.

Jordan knew he was letting her down when he informed her that the best he could do at the time was negotiate an installment agreement. He worked the numbers to show that she could only afford an IA of $500/month. Jack hard-balled him and disallowed expenses in order to double the monthly payment to $1,000. Arbuckle had 53'd Donald Johnston (Form 53 is used for CNC status). Therefore, the entire liability was on Alice for the time being. All Jordan could do was convince her that it would be temporary until Donald came out of rehab and got a job.

Alice paid the IA in November, was late, but paid in December. During the Christmas / New Year's school holiday of two weeks, her income was essentially cut in half. She couldn't come up with the $1,000 in January, and Jack wanted to seize her property. He would have, if not for the fact that Alice had retained J&G and Jordan stepped up on her behalf. In February, she paid the $1,000 on time but couldn't pay any extra to make up for January's deficit. Jordan convinced Jack to tack on January plus the interest to the back end. When Alice came up with only $500 in March, Jack was ready to satisfy his seizure fever again.

During the past week, Jordan did some research to find an alternative, more effective solution for Alice. There was no doubt she was on a sinking ship and on the verge of losing everything. There was no telling when Donald might be able to take some financial responsibility, and Arbuckle seemed fixated on collecting solely from Alice with the intent to eventually seize her house and any other assets that she might have in order to close the case. Jordan knew that if he wasn't on the POA and negotiated an IA, Jack would have already hit her bank account and started the seizure process.

After listening to the excruciatingly sad and difficult update of Alice's current hardship, Jordan is ready to share his newfound strategy with her. Part of this strategy will be to convey the circumstances as dire as possible, and he needs to hear it firsthand from Alice.

"Alice, my heart truly feels for you and your children. I'm so sorry that you have endured such a difficult time. I've done some research, and I believe I've found a solution to get you out of this mess for good! However, it is going to take total transparency on your part. I need you to cooperate and sacrifice a little longer," explains Jordan.

"How can you possibly get me out of this without me losing my house, my car, and my children?" she asks with tears still streaming down her flushed cheeks.

"Through the offer in compromise, there is a provision called the innocent spouse relief. I think we can qualify you for that."

"How is that possible? I was married to the jerk during the years audited, and I signed a joint return."

"True, but here is the key..." Jordan pauses for a couple of moments to make sure the next question he poses is worded correctly and that Alice understands the significance of her answer and gives it truthfully. "This is very important, so think carefully before you answer. Did Donald include you in keeping the books for the restaurant? And were you at all involved in preparing the tax returns?" Jordan inquires while looking intensely into her eyes.

Alice doesn't need to think too deeply. "No, not at all. He did all the bookkeeping and hired an accountant to prepare the taxes. I never even met the man. Donald just brought me the returns after they were completed and showed me where to sign," she answers directly.

Jordan responds quickly and with renewed energy, "That's what I thought. He acted alone and was responsible for the errors on the return. You were an innocent victim of his negligence. There is the Form 656 for OIC and another Form 8857 for the innocent spouse relief. It will be necessary for me to review the original tax returns and the audited returns to substantiate this submission of forms. I need you to pay another $500 now for the balance of the March payment to avoid any further collection action. Then I will submit the forms before April 1, and all collection activities will be suspended. Arbuckle will have to review the case. He knows I will appeal it if he tries to dismiss the innocent spouse submission without due consideration of the facts. Can you do that?"

"I will have to! I can call a couple of the moms that I know well enough to ask if they will front me next month's fees. They are aware of the pressure I am under." Now Alice seems to have renewed energy. "Oh, Jordan, do you really think you can pull this off?" Alice asks hopefully.

"I think we've got a decent shot," replies Jordan without trying to make any promises.

"Okay. I am going to write you a check for $500. Please wait until tomorrow afternoon to deposit it in the bank," Alice pleads.

"No problem. I will arrange to make the payment to Jack on Wednesday."

"Great. One last request, Jordan…" Now it is Alice pausing for effect. Jordan observes that her bloodshot eyes are staring at the plaque on his desk. She continues, "When you have those forms filled out for the innocent spouse, would you please ram them up that son of bitch's ass and tell him that is from me!" Alice says with no sense of humor but with intense anger.

Jordan smiles, grabs her hand, and can't help himself in saying, "We are going to win this, Alice." He has every intention of fulfilling that promise. He knows it will be a hard sale to Jack Arbuckle, and it will be imperative that he presents her case convincingly.

She puts her other hand on top of his and says, "I believe in you, Jordan." She smiles for the first time in a while and takes out her checkbook.

After Alice leaves, Jordan calls Arbuckle to inform him that a courier will deliver a money order for $500 on behalf of Alice Johnston on Wednesday, March 15.

Jack smirks and says, "She's going down, Superstar. I know it, you know it, and hell, she even knows it. The sooner, the better. We need to put this woman out of her misery, so she can move on with her life in a downsized lifestyle that fits her pathetic existence."

Jordan thinks to himself, *If I were in a room with Jack Arbuckle alone right now, I would grab him by the throat and squeeze until his eyeballs were ready to pop out of their sockets! I would command Jack to beg for the right to continue his pathetic existence.* But on the phone, he simply responds, "I'll contact you again before April 1." Then he hangs up. He is not going to give Jack any advance warning about the forthcoming innocent spouse relief forms that will be submitted.

Since he stopped playing football after his senior year at UCLA, Jordan has changed his training methods and only lifts weights three times a week and then just to keep his muscle tone. More out of convenience and the abundance of equipment, he trains at Gold's Gym in Venice. It is on Hampton Drive and Sunset Avenue three blocks from the beach, where the basketball courts are located.

Joe Gold opened the first Gold's Gym in August 1965, in Venice Beach, long before the modern-day health club existed. Gold's at Venice became known as the mecca for bodybuilding, and in 1975, the film *Pumping Iron* was filmed there. The movie detailed the epic bodybuilding battle between Arnold Schwarzenegger and Lou Ferrigno for the 1975 Mr. Universe and Mr. Olympia titles.

Twenty years later, Gold's is brimming with celebrities and yet seems to be the only place in LA where the famous can go about their workouts without being overly bothered. Jordan likes that the members at Gold's are serious about their workouts, and it isn't a social gathering place.

After ballin' with Tio and Little Al on Wednesday evening, Jordan goes to Gold's on Thursday, March 16, after work. Since he rides his bike from Santa Monica, it serves as a warm-up. He starts lifting as soon as he arrives and spends about an hour and a half on the weights. He finishes his workout with twenty intense minutes on the Stairmaster, as it works his quads, calves, and glutes while giving him a good cardio workout.

During his Stairmaster time, Jordan can't help but notice an attractive young lady going lickety-split on the elliptical. With her arms and legs moving in unison at an extremely fast pace, she seems to accelerate to full capacity with 100 percent effort for a period of time. Then she decelerates to catch her breath before turning on the jets again! He is mesmerized watching her routine. He also notices that she is wearing a half T-shirt in Bruin blue with UCLA in gold letters across her chest.

It is not Jordan's style to fraternize at a gym, especially at Gold's, but he can't help himself from following her over to the drinking fountain after she finishes the workout. As she stops drinking, he is standing behind her.

He says, "That looked like quite a workout. I was on the Stairmaster and felt like I was in slow motion seeing you moving so fast." It's Jordan's attempt to start a conversation.

She laughs and says, "Yeah, I was doing high-intensity interval training. It is a great workout."

He responds, "I've never tried the elliptical. Looks like it has a lot of moving parts."

Again, she chuckles and says, "It's not really that difficult, just a matter of getting your arms and legs in sync. I like it for HIIT because it is such low impact on the joints. I'm Janne, by the way." She extends her hand.

Jordan takes her hand and feels a little foolish. "I'm sorry, I should have introduced myself. I'm not used to meeting people here. Jordan Duncan," he adds with a smile. "Do you go to UCLA?" He pointed toward her T-shirt.

"Did. Class of '94," Janne replies.

"Cool. I'm an alumnus also. Class of '92," Jordan states rather proudly.

"Wait. Jordan Duncan? Weren't you on the football team?" Janne asks as she slightly cocks her head and raises her eyebrows a bit.

"Yes. I was. Surprised you recognize the name. Are you a football fan?" Jordan asks as he thought it kind of cute the way she asked if he was on the football team. Sounds like a question you would ask while in high school.

"No, I'm not really a big fan, but I liked to go to the games sometimes with my friends. More of a social event. However, I remember someone saying the name Jordan Duncan as the player who made that amazing catch to beat USC at the Rose Bowl. That was the most exciting game I ever went to at UCLA!" Janne recalls with enthusiasm.

"Hahaha, thanks for remembering the one highlight of my football career at UCLA."

They both laugh.

"Hey, do you want to go get a cup of coffee or something?" Jordan blurts out without thinking that maybe drinking coffee right after an HIIT workout isn't the best idea.

"Actually, I'm meeting my personal trainer here. She should be arriving any minute."

"Well, maybe another time," Jordan replies.

"Okay. I go running along the boardwalk on Sundays. Rain check for the coffee then?" asks Janne.

Jordan doesn't hesitate as he says, "Sure! Do you want to just meet here at around 9:00 or 10:00 a.m.?"

"Ten would be great!" exclaims Janne.

"Great. Nice meeting you, Janne." Jordan initiates the handshake this time.

"Likewise, Jordan." She takes his hand with a smile.

As Jordan rides his bike home along the trail to Santa Monica, he wonders why when he is so confident while talking tax resolutions, playing b-ball, surfing, or even working out, he felt so awkward trying to ask Janne out. (Her name is pronounced Jayne, even though there are two *N*s.)

He can't really come up with an answer to that, but he can't stop thinking about her. She is about 5'6" and has long brown hair, which she had in a ponytail as she worked out. She must do this regularly based on her obvious athletic-looking build and toned abs. She has milk chocolate–colored eyes that are almond shaped. She looks to be of Asian descent and has gorgeous skin and a beautiful natural smile that seems to come easily and often. She is definitely very confident in carrying on a conversation. He likes that she didn't try to act as though she was a big football fan when she realized he played football at UCLA.

One silver lining to the dreadful state of affairs for the LA sports scene in 1995 is the resurgence of UCLA basketball. One of the greatest dynasties of NCAA sports and arguably of any team sports had been UCLA basketball teams of the sixties and seventies. Ten national championships in twelve years under the leadership of the great John Wooden.

However, it has been twenty years since the last championship. This year's team has just received the number one seed in the west region for the 1995 March Madness dash to the Final Four. Jordan is excited to follow their quest as he meets Al at their favorite local sports bar, Big Dean's Ocean Front Café, on the Santa Monica Boardwalk Friday, March 17. It is a short walk from Jordan's apartment complex, so Al parks there and walks over with him. They arrive early to get a seat at the bar, where the flat-screen TVs are larger than the ones outside on the patio. Mary-Lou, the bartender, has been there a long time as she seems to know all the locals on a first name basis, which includes Jordan.

"Hey, Mary-Lou, thanks for saving us prime seats for the Bruin game," Jordan says with a big smile as he and Little Al park themselves at the bar.

"Anything for you, honey," she responds with a grin.

It is understood that it's always first come, first serve at the bar of this most popular beach front location. The burgers are so good, as are the chicken wings. And there are a wide variety of drinks, so the locals continue to frequent Big Dean's even during the tourist season. They offer live music out on the patio during the warmer months of April–October.

March Madness has become one of the greatest sports spectacles in the country—three weeks of single elimination, win or go home, and exhilarating action across the country as schools battle for the honor and privilege to go to the Final Four during the first weekend in April.

UCLA is playing the first two rounds (provided they win the first) in Boise, Idaho. Their game tonight is against the number 16 seed in the West, Florida International.

Big Dean's is overflowing by the time of the Bruins' tip-off, and the noise level is deafening. Jordan and Al enjoy the camaraderie at the bar. Mary-Lou is working like a magician, keeping everyone full, hydrated and happy. They have already devoured their respective plates of wings and are on their second round of tall frosted mugs of beer by halftime.

UCLA cruises to a 92–56 win. The boys had called it quits on the drinking at two beers even though they won't be driving tonight as Little Al is spending the night at Jordan's. They are playing hoops at 8:00 a.m. Saturday. Jordan and Al realize they must prepare physically for the Final Four as it is only two weeks away before they go up against whatever Epstein brings to the party. They have agreed to play three times each week—Monday, Wednesday, and Saturday. Teaming up to play two on two together to work on their timing in the pick 'n' roll and defensive switches.

Sundays generally start early for Jordan as it is surfing day! He is especially excited about this Sunday as he will see Janne again.

Normally, Jordan likes to strap his board on top of the Bronco and head up the coast to Pacific Palisades or Malibu to surf on Sunday mornings. Other times, to mix it up, he will go south down to Manhattan, Hermosa, or Redondo Beach. The tides and surfing conditions will help dictate whether he surfs his longboard or shortboard. Today, because he doesn't want to chance running late in meeting Janne, he simply grabs his shortboard, slips into his wetsuit, and jogs just north of the pier at Santa Monica Beach to surf.

After some nice, refreshing wave rides in the sea breeze, Jordan returns home. He showers, shaves, and puts on some casual board shorts, a Hawaiian-style button-up short-sleeved shirt, and his Doc Marten sandals. He decides to drive and park on the street near Gold's.

After arriving at 9:50 a.m., in a couple minutes, he sees Janne walk across the street on Sunset to the corner of Hampton, where Gold's is located. She obviously just finished her run as she is in black compression pants to her calves with aqua-colored shorts and a matching short-sleeved dry-fit top. Her hair is down and goes about halfway to the small of her back.

"Hi," she says as she approaches. She extends her hand. "I wouldn't be so formal with the handshake, but I'm kind of sweaty."

Jordan laughs and says, "No problem. I was thinking maybe we could go over to the Blue Bottle Coffee shop on Abbot Kinney. It's less than a mile from here, and we could just walk."

"Sounds great! I love the iced coffee there," she responds happily.

It is quite a small shop, but after getting the New Orleans iced coffee and a couple of slices of banana bread, they go outside and sit on chairs with a small table between them along the sidewalk on Abbot Kinney.

"I didn't think to ask you the other day, but do you live around here?" Jordan asks.

"Actually, I live in Brentwood. As I mentioned on Thursday, I have a trainer who works at Gold's, and I love to run along the beach," Janne replies. "How about you?"

"I live just up the coast in the Mariner Village Apartments on Ocean Avenue in Santa Monica."

"Oh, wow, that's right on the beach. Must be nice!"

"Yeah, I enjoy it since most of my nonwork time is spent playing basketball at the Venice Beach courts, working out at Gold's, or surfing. It is very convenient," Jordan responds with a grin.

"Where do you work? What type of business?" Janne inquires.

"Right out of college, I took a position with a tax resolution firm in Sherman Oaks."

"Hmmm, interesting. Tax resolution—what exactly does that entail?" Janne asks inquisitively.

"We represent people to the IRS that have tax debts. I have become an enrolled agent so that I can negotiate settlements on their behalf."

"That sounds very interesting. What is your degree in?"

"Economics."

"That makes sense."

"What do you do?" Jordan asks.

"Well, I received my master's degree in political science. I am currently working on the presidential campaign staff for Steve Forbes. Have you heard of him?"

"Sure, *Forbes Magazine*. He actually is from a small town in New Jersey near where I went to high school."

"So you're from back east?"

Jordan chuckles. "No, I would never claim that. I was born in San Diego. My dad died when I was an infant, and my mom remarried when I was fourteen. Her new husband is an investment banker in New York. So he dragged us across the country to live. I went kicking and screaming." Jordan is now laughing out loud.

"Oh my, I'm sorry that you never knew your real dad. That must have been hard on you," Janne states empathetically.

"If I had a therapist, I'm sure he or she would say that. But I really can't complain about my upbringing. Living back east turned out to be a good experience. I had an outstanding high school football coach, and that helped me get a scholarship to UCLA. I've always been close to my mom, and I now have a little sister, who just turned ten years old. They still live in New Jersey, but they came to some football games and my graduation at UCLA. It's nice to be back living in SoCal. I feel most comfortable here," Jordan says as he realizes that he hasn't talked to anyone other than Al about his past. "How about you? Did you grow up around here?"

Janne takes a deep breath and starts talking. "For the most part, yes. But like you, my early years were a little complicated. My father was an American soldier drafted into the Vietnam war. He met my mom over there, and they married. I was born in Saigon in 1971. We were not allowed to come to the States with my dad when he was to be discharged, so he stayed until 1975. When Saigon was falling, we left and came to California. I've lived here ever since. However, my mom passed away when I was ten." She lets out a big exhale as she doesn't share her backstory with many people either.

Jordan is wide-eyed and silent for a moment. He feels a connection with her over the fact that both of their fathers were forced into the Vietnam War. He doesn't know what to say but would like to open up with Janne and get into a deeper conversation.

For the time being, all he can manage is "Wow, I'm so sorry about your mom. Vietnam is where my father died. He too was drafted into the Army in the sixties."

They just stare at each in silence for a moment. They each don't know exactly what they are feeling, but there is definitely some kind of bond.

Janne inhales and exhales again, smiles, and says, "One of Mr. Forbes's most important platforms is tax reform." Jordan is glad that she segued the conversation nicely back to work and politics.

He smiles. "But isn't that the way presidential elections always go? Republicans promise tax cuts, and Democrats promise tax increases only for the super rich and corporations?"

Janne laughs. "Pretty much. However, Mr. Forbes is presenting a complete overhaul of the tax system. No more complex tax codes!"

"Ouch! If he eliminates the IRS's bullying of US taxpayers, I will have to find a new line of work." They both laugh.

"Hey, have you by chance been following our alma mater in the NCAA basketball tourney?" Jordan asks.

"You mean March Madness? I filled out a bracket with some others on the campaign team. Of course, I have us winning it all!" Janne proclaims gleefully.

Jordan smiles. "That's good. And appropriate. They play this afternoon. I'm watching it with a buddy of mine over at our favorite sports bar on the Santa Monica Boardwalk. Would you like to join us?"

"Oh, that sounds like fun, but I have other plans." Janne sounds genuinely disappointed.

Jordan quickly replies, "Well, if they win, they play again Thursday night. Maybe after your personal training session, we can watch it together?"

"You know I might even see if I can reschedule for Wednesday. So far, you've only seen me all sweaty!" Again, they both laugh.

"I'm not complaining, but that sounds good. Should I call you to make sure Thursday works?" Jordan asks hopefully.

"Yeah, sure." She recites the number as Jordan stores it into his phone.

"Cool. I'll call you. Go, Bruins! Should we start heading back? Where are you parked?"

"I park in the lot by the pier in Santa Monica. Sometimes I run north to Pacific Palisades Park—I love the trail there—and sometimes south to Venice Beach or Marina Del Rey if I'm feeling ambitious."

"Since you are cooled off and full of coffee, I will drive you back to Santa Monica," Jordan offers as they start walking toward Gold's Gym.

"Thanks. Since you're going that way anyway, huh?" She nudges him with her shoulder while smiling. They both laugh again.

There is a comfort level and an obvious attraction between them. Each of them is curious to learn more about the other's past and present.

Big Dean's is jam-packed again Sunday afternoon. Jordan and Al made it in time to get front-row seats at the bar, and Mary-Lou doesn't skip a beat in keeping everyone well hydrated while stuffing their faces.

Watching the game isn't as carefree as the first-round game. The number 8 seed, Missouri Tigers, is leading the Bruins by eight at halftime. UCLA fights back to take the lead by one in the last minute of the game. Then shockingly Missouri scores with 4.8 seconds left to take a 74–73 lead. The bar is almost silent except for some mumbled cursing as UCLA calls timeout.

Discussing strategy for the last shot selection, the consensus at Big Dean's is that they must get the ball into the hands of their All-American and leading scorer, Ed O'Bannon. They inbound the ball under their own basket to point guard Tyus Edney, their second-best player. Edney streaks down the left side of the court and dribbles behind his back at the Missouri free-throw line while crossing the key. Just as the clock turns to a second left, he tosses up a one-handed shot over the outstretched hand of the Tiger center. The ball kisses high off the glass backboard. With almost perfect synchronicity, the red light around the backboard blazes, the game ending buzzer sounds, and the ball drops through the net. Bedlam ensues on the court as the Bruin players jump for joy. In the bar, complete strangers are hugging and high-fiving, and it's probably the same across the entire county of Los Angeles.

Even the cool and collected Mary-Lou is screaming "Oh my god!" with her hands on top of her head.

On to the Sweet Sixteen for the Bruins in a most spectacular fashion!

On Monday, March 20, while on his commute, Jordan calls the office to confirm that Arthur Gibson will be there today. He is already in, Vanessa confirms. Currently, he is in David's office in a meeting that includes Marlin and Karen Wallach.

Jordan is anxious to get Arthur's perspective on the innocent spouse relief. He wants to make sure he maximizes his potential for a successful outcome on behalf of Alice Johnston.

Upon arriving at the office, Jordan makes a few phone calls and confirms his 12:00 p.m. appointment. He asks Vanessa to let him know when Mr. Gibson is alone in the conference room.

After giving Arthur a few minutes to get situated but not enough time to get fully immersed in his next project, Jordan knocks on the door of the conference room and walks in.

"Hey, Jordan. How are you?" says Arthur with a big smile as he stands to shake his hand.

"I'm great, Arthur, how about you? When did you arrive in LA?"

Jordan and Arthur have met several times. Arthur admires Jordan's desire in learning as much as he can about the Internal Revenue Service and the functions and protocols of its various divisions. In fact, Arthur set Jordan up with study material and classes to prepare him for the enrolled agent exam back in 1993.

"I flew in yesterday. Will be here all day today and will visit the Service's Los Angeles District Office tomorrow. Will catch the redeye back to Virginia tomorrow night." Arthur quickly explains his itinerary.

"Got a couple of minutes? I was hoping to run something by you and get your expert opinion." He purposely did not preset an appointment with Arthur because, quite frankly, he didn't want David in on this more technical meeting. Sometimes David likes to get his hands into issues that might convolute what Jordan wants to accomplish. With David Jacobs, it always comes down to what is best for revenue generation in the business model for J&G, which can be different at times from what is best for the client.

"Sure. What's up?" Arthur responds as he takes off his jacket. Arthur Gibson always wears a suit when working. Today he is looking very sharp in a tan suit, a dark-brown long-sleeved dress shirt, and a striped brown, white, and gold tie. He is wearing a pair of brown Ferragamo wing-tipped shoes that look spit-shined.

Arthur is an African American in his early sixties and stands at 6'5". He played football at the University of Michigan back in his collegiate days. He was an offensive lineman, but since then, he has trimmed down considerably. Though he is naturally big-boned, he does not appear overweight whatsoever. He went to law school at Georgetown University and received his law degree with an emphasis in taxation. From there, he went to work for the Internal Revenue Service, where he had interned as a law student. He reached the level of regional director and had an integral participation in the revision and more fully implemented offer in compromise program in the early '90s. He retired from the service at the end of 1992 and became a tax consultant specialist for Epstein, Levin & Ohlman Tax Consultants and their affiliate, Jacobs & Goodman Tax Resolution. The move was rather seamless and natural. He is considered a valuable asset to each firm. He is highly respected by Alexander Epstein, David Jacobs, and all their associates.

"I have been working with a tax client since last fall. She was hoping that we could submit an OIC on her behalf. In filling out the financials, it became apparent that an OIC wouldn't be feasible. She is divorced but has a joint liability for the tax years assessed. The ex-husband is currently in rehab for alcohol addiction and unemployed. She was assigned a very tough RO. He 53'd the ex. I was negotiating an IA for her, and the RO rejected my proposed amount by disallowing expenses. We ended up with an IA of $1,000 per month. It is extremely difficult for her to manage. In the past five months, she has missed one month and was late on two other occasions. The RO wants to seize her real estate property. In doing some research, I feel that she is a good candidate for innocent spouse relief. I've never submitted one before, and I wanted to hear your thoughts and perspective on it." Jordan lays it out.

"Whew, innocent spouse relief is a tough road to go down. I'm sure you have read the qualifying criteria," Arthur says.

"I have and confirmed with her that she had no part of the bookkeeping of the business. It's a restaurant since closed, by the way."

She also never even met the accountant who prepared the tax returns for the years audited," Jordan explains.

"Have you seen the audit?"

"Not in its entirety, but I read the summary. It was concluded that the taxpayers underreported income and overstated deductions."

"Okay. There is one other caveat that I have seen come into play that is not spelled out in the manual per se. If the unaware spouse reaped financial benefits from the fraudulent tax returns, it could be a sticking point in getting them off as an innocent spouse," Arthur instructs.

"I will have to look into that," says Jordan.

"Get a copy of the audit, the original tax returns, and a sworn statement by your client as to level of unawareness. Might help contacting the accountant also. However, be aware that he could be an associate of the husband and not willing to divulge any pertinent information. Look for evidence of how they spent the excess revenue of not paying their fair share of taxes. Then I will be glad to review it before you submit."

"I would really appreciate that. This poor lady is a mess. Three little kids, and she is working very hard to try to keep her home."

"You genuinely care about your clients, don't you?" asks Arthur.

"Yes, I do. I give them my word that I will get them the best possible solution. You know I'm not one of those guys that tries to always portray the IRS as some kind of evil monster. Most ROs that I've dealt with seem reasonable. But with all due respect, the system is set up in a guilty-until-proven-innocent manner, and these people need help in minimizing the damage of not filing or being audited and overwhelmed with penalties and interest that can ruin them financially."

"I admire your efforts in advocating for your clients. I'm not sure having their best interests at heart is always the case with tax professionals."

Jordan doesn't quite know if that is a reference to E, L & O and J&G, but he gets the feeling that may be the case.

"I appreciate your support, Arthur. You've always proven to be a straight shooter with me," says Jordan with a smile as he stands. "I'll work on this innocent spouse and get back to you."

After two great sessions of b-ball on Monday and Wednesday, Jordan and Little Al are feeling pretty good about their respective games and teamwork. Al is getting in better shape and has even run full court a couple of times on the main court, holding his own against some stiff competition. After Monday's run, Jordan tells Al that he has invited Janne to watch the UCLA game Thursday night. He suggests Al get a date and join them or just show up alone and watch it with them.

Little Al laughs and responds, "I'll get a date, Mister One Girlfriend in Twenty-Five Years. I'm very curious to meet this woman who has captured so much of your attention. But I wouldn't want to steal her away from you in a threesome." They both laugh.

"I don't think Big Dean's will work. Too small. How about O'Brien's on Wilshire?" Jordan suggests.

"Sounds good. I'll just meet you there."

Jordan calls Janne and asks if she is okay with him inviting his buddy and a date to join them. She has no problem with that, so he arranges to pick her up. They all agree to arrive early and have dinner before tip-off.

Janne looks splendid in Jordan's opinion as he sees her for the first time in nonworkout clothes. She is dressed elegantly but casually in a light-blue short sleeveless slip dress. Over that is a white cardigan cotton-blend sweater. She wears two-inch open-toed white heels. She applies a little makeup with lipstick and earrings.

She looks marvelous, Jordan thinks.

Jordan dons a blue polo shirt with loose-fitting 501 jeans, a light-tan corduroy jacket, and brown loafers. Al no longer wears his hair long but rather neatly coiffed, parted in the middle to just touching his ears on the sides, and he is clean-shaven as well. He has on a white button-up long-sleeved cotton shirt with a navy blazer and dark-blue jeans with black Sketchers.

Al's date is named April. Jordan has met her before with Al as she is a paralegal that helps him with some contract work. They have been dating casually for the past six months. Tonight April has on a trendy pantsuit with chunky heels and a light sweater.

After introductions, they are seated and order dinner and drinks. As is common in social settings, Al is comfortable asking questions of Janne in a nonthreating manner to get to know her. He admires her confidence and wit as they all get along and have some good laughs. Janne is a little taken aback when Jordan and April refer to Alvin as Little Al during the conversation. Al explains that his dad, Big Al, is six feet seven inches tall, so he has been called Little Al by his mom and peers pretty much his whole life.

Of course, the boys can't help but tell a few stories of their high school football exploits. Janne inquires of Jordan if it was Big Al that he was referring to the other day when he mentioned the great coach that helped him get a football scholarship to UCLA.

Jordan confirms it, but Al clarifies that statement by saying, "Actually, Big Al landed him a scholarship to play at his alma mater, Penn State. Jordan crossed us all up when he bolted for UCLA in the eleventh hour!"

The girls don't know if there is some animosity built into that until Lil Al laughs and says, "It all worked out for the best, as pretty boy here never would have cut it at a blue-collar program like Penn State."

They all laugh as Jordan just shakes his head smiling and confirms, "True, no beaches in Happy Valley, PA."

The food is good, the drinks are tasty, and the company is delightful. UCLA plays an excellent game in winning 74–61 over Mississippi State.

Before they part ways, Al says, "One more win, and your Bruins are going to the Final Four!"

"That would be so awesome," says Janne. "I'm actually going to the Final Four this year in Seattle."

Jordan and Al look at each other in a surprised but excited way.

"We're going too!" blurts out Jordan.

"Really? How cool," Janne says.

"Yeah, how did you get tickets?" asks Jordan.

"We have a big rally and fundraiser in Seattle lined up on Friday. Mr. Forbes thought it would be excellent exposure to get a suite at the Final Four and go to the banquet on Sunday evening to rub shoulders with some big donors."

"That makes a lot of sense," replies Al.

"How did you guys get your tickets?" Janne asks.

"The CPA firm that owns our tax resolution business has a suite every year at the Final Four, and uhhh…we kind of finagled our way in." Jordan haphazardly tries to explain as Al just laughs.

"Sounds like everyone is going but me!" says April in a frustrated tone.

"Well, let's take one step at a time. The Bruins aren't there yet!" proclaims Al. "Should we do this again on Saturday afternoon to cheer them on?"

They all agree that it would be fun.

When Jordan drives Janne home, he parks in front of the duplex where she lives.

She says, "I would invite you in, but I have a roommate."

"No problem. I'll call you tomorrow about Saturday."

"I had a really good time tonight with you, Jordan. I like your friend Little Al too," she says, smiling.

Jordan leans over and kisses her lightly on the mouth. "I had a good time too. Let me walk you to the door." He goes around, opens her door, and walks with her along the sidewalk to the front door with his arm around her shoulder. They kiss again, a little longer this time.

Then he says, "Good night, Janne."

She smiles and says, "Good night, Jordan. Drive safe."

On Saturday, the group of four decide to have lunch and watch the game at Big Dean's Ocean Front Café as the ladies think a walk along the Santa Monica Pier and boardwalk after the game would be fun and just what they need after eating and sitting for so long. Even though it is jammed full of people, the openness and cool sea breeze are a welcome change from the confinement of a typical sports bar. They sit at a table out on the patio.

In a thrilling, high-scoring game, the Bruins pull out a 102–96 win over the number 2 seeded UConn. Everyone is excited, and it seems to carry over on their walk. People just appear to be in a better, friendlier mood in LA today. UCLA is going to the Final Four!

The following week is hectic for Jordan. He gathers the tax returns that were audited for the Johnston's, reviews them along with the official audit, and fills out the Form 656 (for the OIC) and Form 8857 (for the innocent spouse tax relief). He prepares the forms and supporting documentation and fax's a copy to the office of Arthur Gibson in Virginia. Arthur gives his blessing to the submission on a phone call to Jordan.

He sets up a courier to deliver the forms to Jack Arbuckle on Thursday, March 30. Prior to that day, he instructs Alice to open a new bank account without closing her old account. He tells her that as a precaution, she should put all her money, except for a token amount, into the new account. This scares her, but he explains that more than likely, nothing will happen. However, with Jack Arbuckle, you just never know how he might react when he receives the innocent spouse submission. Jordan includes a letter to Jack with the forms explaining that he will be out of town and unavailable to contact until Tuesday, April 4.

With it being only a couple of weeks before April 15, when federal and state income taxes are due to be filed, the office is quite busy. Karen Wallach hardly leaves her office until after the 15th. Jordan does not like preparing tax returns and limits his efforts to his own client base. Tonja stays extremely busy to make sure all cylinders are running smoothly and deadlines are met or extensions filed.

David calls Jordan into his office early in the week and tells him that Epstein has decided that it is an unfair advantage for Jordan and his teammate to only have to defeat the winner of the tournament to win the bet. Therefore, David extends a formal invitation to Jordan to participate in the company tournament. There will be eight two-man teams who will play a single-game elimination tournament on Sunday, April 2. The games will be played in a designated gym that has been reserved for the entire day. Games will be played to twenty-one points. The first team to get twenty-one or more wins. Two points will be awarded for each basket, and three points awarded for shots made from beyond the three-point line. There will be no free throws taken.

Jordan listens intently as David reads these rules, and when David asks him if he has any questions, he responds with a smile on his face, "Are we invited to participate in the company party with the buffet?"

David laughs and assures him, "I will personally make sure that you are."

Jordan asks, "Will you be there?"

"I wouldn't miss UCLA being in the Final Four. I am almost as excited to see you and your buddy go up against whomever Alex brings to challenge you!" replies David with a grin. He hands Jordan the invitation, which includes the times and addresses of the various activities.

CHAPTER FIVE

Final Four

The flight time from LAX to Seattle, Washington, is two hours and forty-five minutes. It is the first time in a while that Jordan and Alvin can sit and chat without interruption. Janne had invited Jordan to attend the fundraising dinner on Friday night in Seattle, but he needed to finish up some work and scheduled his flight with Al on Friday evening.

She has extended an invitation to Jordan as her guest to attend the Final Four banquet on Sunday night, which will be held in a banquet hall inside the Kingdome, where the Final Four games are being played. He accepted and is looking forward to the event. The tricky part will be getting Al in also. But they will work out those details later.

"So we are invited to participate in the company tournament this year, huh?" Al says with a chuckle.

"Yep. Something about us having an unfair advantage in simply playing his champion for all the marbles. We are fresher because they played a couple of games already," Jordan explains.

"Well, I guess there is some merit to that. I'm just a little surprised that your guy Epstein would invite the likes of us to play in his prestigious tourney!" says Al humorously.

"Surprised me too. This dude does not like me at all. I hear he is super competitive though, and the way we conned him last year infuriated him to no end."

"Then he will be more pissed this year when we win his entire tournament," Al states confidently.

"You can bet that he will stack a team to keep that from happening."

"Doesn't at least one player have to be an employee?"

"Yeah, I think I know who that will be. Todd Morrison is a junior accountant at the firm. I met him at the taxation course offered by the IRS to prepare for the enrolled agent exam. The dude played QB at UNLV. Claims he was an All-State basketball player in high school as well."

"How big?"

"Not that tall, maybe six two. I'm not that worried about him. But remember, he is the employee. No doubt, Epstein will pair him with a ringer."

"Nothing we can't handle. Playing at the Venice Beach courts has been great preparation. We competed against some badass ballers down there!" says Al.

Jordan nods in agreement. "We will just run our pick 'n' roll. When guys haven't played together like we have, it drives them crazy trying to figure out how to defend it. On defense, we just need to keep them off the offensive boards. They will miss shots. We need to rebound those misses." Jordan lays out the plan.

"Yep," Al agrees.

"Tell me more about Janne. She seems really bright, and of course, gorgeous!" Al asks his buddy.

"Haha, I didn't see this coming for sure. I like her, and I think we have things in common."

"You're not going to tell me anything more, are you?"

"Nothing more to tell. I want to keep seeing her and get to know her."

"Fair enough." Al nods his head.

"What's with you and April?" Jordan flips the questioning.

"She's great. We get along really well and have fun together. It is hard to be in a serious relationship with someone you work with. So for now, we keep it on the casual side. I am extremely busy preparing for the draft. Picked up some promising clients, and have been doing a lot of homework on them and potential teams."

Just as the month of April is the busiest season for tax professionals. With the NFL draft coming up in a few weeks, player agents are experiencing their busiest season as well. Al, being a relative newcomer in the field, likes to find what he calls diamonds in the rough. Players from smaller schools or perhaps a large school but have suffered injuries. They have talent but might fly under the radar of big agents and scouts. He has some connections and has signed some drafted players, but his bread and butter are undrafted free agents. He looks for high character guys with skills that have a lot of heart and desire to play professional football. The NFLPA rules limit fees paid to agents at 3 percent of their playing contract.

Therefore, he finds his clients an opportunity where there might be the best fit to make the team. If they stick, he can renegotiate after they prove themselves valuable for a bigger contract. He takes a chance on the player, and they take a chance on him. So far, it is working out well for both, as well as improving his relationships and reputation within the NFL organizations. It takes a lot of study time with film and phone calls.

Al is enjoying the process and is determined to be successful. He is getting a nice payday with the Gambadoro contract.

Saturday is a huge day at the Final Four. Fortunately, the weather cooperates in Seattle, and other than some interesting formations of fluffy white clouds, the sun is shining, and the skies are blue. TV cameras and crews congregate in abundance across the grounds at the Kingdome. Excitement is in the air as groups from all four schools are well represented. The semifinal round matchups will feature Arkansas, the defending national champions and winners of the Midwest Region playing against the 1993 national champions, North Carolina, who won the Southeast Region. UCLA, winners of the West Region, will take on Oklahoma State, a number 4 seed that prevailed in the East Region.

The pageantry of college athletics is on full display in the emerald city. Collages of color and mascot logos from each school, cardinal red Razorbacks from Arkansas, orange and black Cowboys from

Oklahoma State, Carolina blue Tarheels from UNC, and Bruin blue and gold from UCLA dominate the landscape. They roam from local restaurants through the tailgating parking lots and up the stairs to the entryway of the arena. Food, drinks, laughter, cheers, and bantering between the various groups, along with their respective pep squads, keep the energy level high and the noise level even higher!

Some say following college sports acts as a sort of fountain of youth. People in their fifties, sixties, seventies, and even older travel great distances, with many electing to pile into RVs to venture thousands of miles, each donning the colors and logos of the hometown schools. Some are alumnus that have relocated to various cities or rural towns across the nation, while most never even attended the school of their allegiance but reside near or simply within the state boundaries of their favorite teams.

Grown men and women, college students, professionals, laborers, contract workers, schoolteachers, and government employees follow recruiting efforts like it is a missionary endeavor to strengthen the fold of their devoted faith. Often wagers are placed legally and illegally, office pools including nonsports fans, filling out their "brackets" in a contest for some sort of prize, demonstrating an almost cult-like dedication.

There is no denying that the Final Four, the crowning jewel accomplishment of the fast and furious past three weeks of March Madness, has become a spectacular sporting event. It is viewed by tens of millions across the country and generates over a billion dollars in revenue. Sadly, only one of the four teams will leave fully satisfied and victorious, thus the remaining 75 percent of students, fans, players, and coaches will leave disappointed. However, you would be hard-pressed to find maybe a handful of people that would say they regretted attending the majesty of the Final Four!

This year, since UCLA is playing, Jordan purchased tickets from a scalper in the lower section of the arena rather than the upper section as he had done last year. The boys keep the drinking and eating to a minimum as they want to make sure they feel lean, quick, and sharp in their games tomorrow. Both of them are wearing UCLA colors as they enter the arena after conversing with many UCLA fans and find their seats.

UCLA–Oklahoma State is the first game played. The biggest concern for the Bruins and their coaching staff is controlling Bryant Reeves the Cowboy big man. He has a dogged desire to grab every rebound and, for a big guy, has a nice touch around the basket with either hand. At this juncture of the season, UCLA coach Harrick has done an outstanding job of balancing his attack by implementing younger players into the playing rotation. They complement the formidable seniors nicely. The game is tight the entire first half, and the halftime score is tied at 37. The second half sees the Bruins use their superior depth, experience, and youthful exuberance to pull away and win the game by a final score of 74–61.

The nightcap of the doubleheader is another extremely competitive first half, with North Carolina going to the locker room at intermission with a 38–34 lead. The team with the deeper roster prevails in this contest during the second half as well. The Razorbacks return to the championship game for the second year in a row by beating the Tarheels 75–68.

After the Arkansas–North Carolina game, by the time they file out of the arena and into the parking lot, where Jordan can call Janne, it is after 9:00 p.m. They exchange excited recounts of the UCLA victory and agree on how fun the championship game promises to be. With Jordan playing in Epstein's two-on-two tournament, Janne wishes him luck as they look forward to tomorrow night's banquet!

Sunday, April 2, is another beautiful day in the great northwest. With the temperature in the midsixties, the sun prevails through intermittent clouds. Jordan and Al drive their rented car to the designated gym, where they will participate in the tournament. Epstein has rented the use of a Catholic Parochial Junior High School gym, wherein the games will be played. Since it's a Sunday, there are no church services held on campus, and the school lot is empty except for vehicles of the participants and spectators.

There will be two games played simultaneously, one on each end of the full-court gym. Epstein has made sure that Jordan and Al will only meet his "select" team if both make it to the finals. Upon arriving, Jordan spots Todd Morrison quickly, and sure enough, his teammate stands out in the crowd of other participants. He is an African American young man in his twenties that stands at six feet seven inches with a very lean build. His legs are long but, other than some definition in his calves, quite thin. His fluid motion with the ball indicates that he has played a lot of ball in his youth.

As they are changing into their games shoes, Al leans over to Jordan and asks, "Do you recognize the ringer?"

"I'm pretty sure I've seen him, but I can't quite place where."

Little Al is wearing navy-blue shorts and a gray T-shirt with "Penn State Football" in navy-blue across the front. Jordan wears his "lucky" blue UCLA gym shorts with a light-gold tank top. He spots David, who is in jeans and a UCLA T-shirt. They exchange greetings and handshakes as Jordan introduces Al to David.

"My gosh, you boys here to play football or basketball?" David asks with a smile as he sizes up Little Al, knowing Jordan's football pedigree at UCLA.

"Whatever it takes to win," Al responds without a smile.

David gives an uncertain chuckle as he doesn't really know how to interpret that declaration. Al is in his no-nonsense, intimidation mode today.

"Well, Alex certainly didn't disappoint in finding a ringer to challenge you boys this year," David states.

"Hadn't noticed," Al says stoically.

"We're going to warm up, David. I'll catch you later," Jordan says.

"Good luck!" is David's last wish.

Alexander Epstein makes sure everyone knows who is in charge. He makes his way to the center of the court. He is wearing a black designer warm-up suit zippered halfway up to his chest over a white polo shirt and a whistle on a thin chain around his neck. He is flanked by a muscular mature man wearing cargo pants and a tight black T-shirt. He has short-cropped hair and a grim expression on his pronounced jaw cut visage.

Epstein blows the whistle loudly and distinctly calls all participants to the center court. There are eight teams of two players each for a total of sixteen players. Epstein reviews the rules quickly that were spelled out on the official invitations mailed to each employee participant of the tournament. The only criteria for a teammate in the tourney are that they cannot be a current college or professional athlete. He gives the assignments for the first round, which will take place in back-to-back games on each end of the court. There will be a fifteen-minute break to give the winners of the second games played time to rest. The second round will be played simultaneously as well on each end of the court. A fifteen-minute break will precede the championship game.

It is reiterated that the winning team will receive a $500 cash bonus to be split between the players and two tickets to the championship game in the E, L & O suite on Monday evening. He asks if there are any questions.

"Yeah, will the tickets allow us access to the Final Four banquet tonight?" asks Al sheepishly.

"No," Epstein's replies. "Okay, let's get started," Epstein barks to all.

There are bleachers on one side of the gym, where David, Marlin, and many prominent clients and employees of E, L & O, including Barry Levin, sit to watch the games. Epstein stands with his apparent "bodyguard" along the side of the court. He is positioned toward the end of the court, where Morrison and his ringer are getting ready to play. A coin flip determines who will get the ball first. It is losers outs, so when you score, the other team brings the ball back into play with their possession starting at the top of the key.

The competition is not bad as it is evident that everyone here has played ball at some level. But Al was correct when he said that they had stronger competition on the Venice Beach courts than what they will experience here, until the finals perhaps.

As they expect, Jordan and Al win their first two round games rather handily, as do Morrison and his running mate.

Just before they step onto the court for the final, Jordan stops and says to Al, "I recognize him now!"

"Yeah, who is he?"

"He is a kid from Compton that was highly recruited during my junior year at UCLA. Unfortunately for him, I remember reading, he got caught up in the AAU circuit. Played all over the country but never developed much toughness. I think he would have definitely toughened up if he just stayed playing on the outdoor courts and high school in his own Compton hood. Anyway, he went to USC with a lot of expectations put on him. As you can see, he never developed any upper-body strength and tried to rely on his finesse game and athleticism. He's too tall and not quick enough to play guard and not big and strong enough to bang inside. Ended up transferring out to some small school in the Midwest, I think. Never heard of him after that. His name is Isaac Robinson. Goes by Ike."

"So you're saying I should bang on him a little, huh?" suggests Al.

"Probably not a bad idea. He can shoot okay, handle the rock, and jump out of the gym."

As mentioned, Morrison and Robinson have had a fairly easy time advancing to the final. Jordan and Al played at the same time, so they haven't had a chance to watch them. They did hear oohs and ahhs from the spectators, assuming that was in response to dunks or other feats of athleticism from Robinson.

As they meet at center court, Epstein gives instructions. "Okay, for the final, I will flip the coin. The winner can choose to have the ball first or which end of the court they prefer to play on. Todd, you call it in the air."

"Heads," calls out Morrison.

"Heads, it is. What would you prefer?"

"We'll take the ball," Todd chooses.

Epstein looks at Jordan without saying a word. Jordan simply points to the north end of the court. As Todd is getting ready to inbound the ball to start the action, Epstein steps onto the court with his whistle in his mouth.

"Whoa, what are you doing there, chief?" inquires Al to Epstein.

"I'm going to call this game as the referee."

"No, no, you're not. We have played every game thus far, calling our own fouls without a problem," Al says, stepping forward with an absoluteness that Epstein can't believe and can't accept.

The bodyguard, whose name is Kurt Turlock, quickly steps between Al and Alexander. He is an alleged former Navy SEAL who is now officially the head of security detail for E, L & O. It is not evident why the CPA firm needs a security detail headed up by a former military man.

"This is the championship game of *my* tournament. It needs to be called correctly by a referee to ensure fairness," Epstein states with authority.

Jordan interjects, "Mr. Epstein, with all due respect, if you wanted the game to be called with refs, then you should have hired a high school or college referee to be here. Having an unqualified, obviously biased referee is not fair and will cause more problems than solutions."

Epstein is incensed and stares down Jordan with much disdain before turning to Morrison.

"We can play without a ref, Mr. Epstein. We're all used to it. If you think you are fouled, call it. You get the ball out of bounds, no questions asked." Todd looks at Jordan, who nods his head.

Epstein turns and starts walking toward the sideline. He looks up to the bleachers and announces, "We have mutually decided that the game will be played without a referee. The players will call their own fouls." He blows the whistle and, with some anger in his voice, yells, "Play ball!"

Todd tosses the ball to Jordan to check it and says, "Hey, Jordan, been a while." He has a smile on his face. "May the best team win."

"That's usually how it turns out," Jordan responds as he tosses the ball back to him.

No one has left the gym as even the other competitors have stayed and are seated in the bleachers, anxious to see how these two superior teams will fare against each other.

Al has dropped ten pounds in the last month and is playing today at 265. As he matches up with Isaac Robinson, who at 2 inches taller but not weighing even 200 lb. The contrast in their respective builds and body types is glaring, almost to comical proportions.

Little Al first started lifting weights under the tutelage of his dad at the age of thirteen. Having experienced the premature end of his professional football career due to knee injuries, Alvin Sr. was determined to train his son how to build his body correctly. He insisted that Al Jr. start constructing a strong foundation from which to build more weight, muscle, and strength. As most kids that begin weight training in their teenage years gravitate to the bench press and easy curl bar, Big Al insisted that his son focus on the squat rack, leg press, and dead lifts.

Even though he later developed a strong upper body, the foundation he began in his early years resulted in an enormously strong, thick lower body. His hips are wide, his butt is big. Each quadricep is so fully developed that one thigh is almost as big as a normal-sized person's combination of both thighs. His calves are massive, and his ankles are so thick that Al boasts often that he has never experienced a sprained ankle!

So with the ultralong and lean Robinson opposite the stout, broad Bockman, everyone in the gym is interested to see how it will play out. The other matchup is also quite interesting, featuring two former NCAA Division 1 college football players. Todd Morrison is 6'2" and is carrying 220 lb., which is 15 lb. over his playing weight at UNLV. Jordan Duncan is 6'0", 180 lb. Jordan figures that even though he is giving up a couple of inches in height and 40 lb. in weight, he can compensate with an advantage in quickness and athleticism. But he realizes that Morrison is no slouch when it comes to athletic skills.

Todd inbounds the ball to Ike on the right side, and immediately Al demonstrates that hand checking will be allowed. He makes sure that this thin, athletic opponent will understand that he won't be backing Al down into the post as he places his big left hand on the small of his back. Todd cuts to the baseline then circles back around to the left, a step ahead of Jordan and receives a pass. He faces up to the basket, dribbles one step left and puts up a sixteen-foot jumper. The ball caroms off the rim and is coming out of the basket cylinder when seemingly out of nowhere, Ike has both hands above the rim. And as soon as the ball clears the front rim, he grabs it and slams it through the basket!

Epstein yells, "Yes!"

Those in the bleachers enjoy the sequence and are conversing and laughing at how easily it appeared for Robinson to maneuver around Bockman.

As Jordan takes the ball to the top of the key to inbound, Al crosses in front of him and mumbles quietly, "Quicker than I thought, but he won't get within twelve feet of the basket again."

Jordan inbounds to Al, who is positioned on the right side of the free throw line. Jordan takes one step left then cuts right just above where Al is stationed. Al tosses the ball to Jordan, who is no more than a foot away. He immediately sets a granite wall of a screen on Todd, who runs right into him and practically falls down. Jordan is a step ahead of Ike as he drives to the basket. Ike realizes that he must switch onto Jordan. As Jordan elevates to go for the layup, Ike goes up with him and will no doubt swat the shot away.

However, as they have executed literally hundreds of times in the years that go all the way back to their high school days playing on the Taylor Park court, after setting the pick, Al rolls to the basket down the middle of the lane. With his considerable girth, he has sealed off Morrison. Jordan waits until Ike has committed to blocking his shot and softly lays the ball off to Al for an easy layup. Pick 'n' roll to perfection.

2–2.

As Ike receives the inbound pass from Todd, he backs away from Al and faces up to the basket about eighteen feet from the rim. He knows that he has quickness on his side and just needs to decide rather he wants to drive right or left past him. This is not Al's first rodeo up against tall, lean, athletically gifted ballers. He has a few tricks up his sleeve.

First, he gets in his defensive stance with his feet shoulder width apart, knees slightly bent. He stares right at the midsection and doesn't go for any head or ball fakes. Good players will use a series of jab steps before exploding into their drive to the bucket. Lil Al waits until Ike moves his pivot foot, which commits him to a direction, then Al lunges as Ike tries to go by him and sticks his thick knee into Robinson's quadricep muscle. Ike goes down in a heap of pain that will last for several more minutes.

Al raises his hand and says, "My bad, foul on me." He reaches down to help Ike to his feet and pats him on the butt.

Now he knows that Isaac Robinson will be settling for jump shots rather than trying to drive past this conglomeration of massive flesh, bone, and muscle that stands before him.

Todd Morrison was an outstanding athlete through high school and college. Though he has added weight and isn't as quick, his hand-eye coordination, footwork, and skill set in shooting a basketball remain superb. Jordan ascertains quickly that Todd wants to shoot jumpers and is in love with the three-point shot. Jordan has no fear of Todd driving past him, so he crowds him on defense. Todd does have a nice step-back move that he uses effectively with a little push-off with his forearm to create space for his jumper. He has the strength in his wrists to launch the three even as he is fading away.

The pick 'n' roll has many variations. It takes excellent timing and familiarity with your partner to execute all phases effectively. The combination of Jordan's quickness, scoring ability with either hand, and accurate outside shooting, along with Al's size, strength, smarts, and overall toughness—these two are hard to contain. They have such great chemistry on the court without any ego clashes as winning is what motivates each of them!

They trade some baskets as the stage is set on how this contest will play out. Ike can hit the outside jumper in the range of 16–18 feet. But as soon he shoots or if Morrison shoots, Little Al sticks his large derriere into him, and as he promised, Robinson comes nowhere near getting anymore put-back slams off offensive rebounds. Morrison hits a couple of threes, but Jordan stays in his face, and it is not easy for Todd to get a clean look.

Jordan and Al run a variation of the pick 'n' roll almost exclusively when they get the ball. Jordan can flair off that set and get an open jumper. He hits two three-pointers, and that keeps Todd honest in having to guard him all the way out to the three-point line. On the roll to the basket, Al does a great job of sealing off his opponent with his ample body, but Ike does create some issues with his length and outstanding vertical jump. He swats a couple of Al's shots away.

Leading 14–12 in a seesaw game, Jordan swipes the ball away from Todd as he is trying to go up for a three-point shot. He quickly grabs it and passes to Al. The ball comes back to Jordan as he appears ready to drive down the middle of the lane. Ike switches and clogs the lane about four feet in front of the rim. Jordan pulls up at the free throw line and drains a lean-in jumper before Ike can even contest the shot.

16–12.

"Time out!" yells Epstein.

"So the wannabe referee is now the coach?" asks a puzzled Al.

"Wasn't that a foul?" Epstein screams at Morrison.

"It felt clean to me" is Todd's response as he grabs for a towel.

"Each team gets one timeout," Epstein declares this newly instituted rule.

Jordan looks at Al, shakes his head, and says, "Whatever."

As Morrison and Robinson huddle with Epstein, he says to Ike, "Why are you settling for jump shots? You need to take the fat guy inside and just shoot over him from three feet. He will never block your shot." Ike doesn't respond as he simply looks into the rafters.

Then Epstein turns to Morrison. "You are bigger and stronger than Duncan. Back him in, and then do your fade-away."

Morrison is looking at him and nods his head in acknowledgment to the suggestion.

"Come on, you guys are way better than them. You are just letting them get into your heads. Let's win this and get out of here!" barks Epstein.

During the timeout, Jordan looks at Al, who is breathing rather laboriously. "You okay?" Jordan asks his buddy.

"Yeah, I'm good. I'm in this dude's head, but I have to concentrate to keep a body on him at all times."

"We're at sixteen. Next time we get the ball, let's see if we can drive the pick 'n' roll for a layup. Then when we're at eighteen, we run it again, but you fade back to the top of the key instead of rolling. That will give you a wide open three. Knock it down, and we're done!" Jordan lays out the plan.

Lil Al smiles and says, "I like it."

They grasp hands and collectively say, "Let's do it."

Morrison follows Epstein's plan and meticulously dribbles the ball while he backs Jordan toward the hoop. When he gets inside of eight feet from the basket, with Ike out front twenty feet from the rim, Todd turns toward the baseline and puts up a fall-away ten-footer. Nothing but net!

16–14.

"That's what I'm talking about!" screams Epstein as Todd has a satisfied look on his face.

Jordan and Al are unfazed. They inbound the ball and set up the pick 'n' roll. Ike jumps out to cut off Jordan as he is coming around Al's pick on Todd. Jordan splits the overplay by Ike, dribbling through his legs, and dashes for the rim. He has a step on Ike but knows how long his reach is. Maintaining his dribble, he takes a half crossover step with his left leg toward the right, giving the illusion that he will lay the ball up from the right side of the rim. Then he crosses to the left as he takes up his dribble and makes one long stride with his right leg. His reverse layup just clears Ike's outstretched hand. The ball kisses softly off the glass and goes through the net smoothly.

18–14.

Contrary to Epstein's instructions, Robinson receives the inbound pass from Morrison and takes two dribbles back, which surprises Al. With Epstein yelling "Nooo!" Ike's three-point shot swishes through the net.

18–17.

Epstein, in full coaching mode now, yells out, "Okay, let's get a stop. They are going to do the pick 'n' roll. No layups. Foul them if you have to!"

The pick 'n' roll is set up to perfection. As Jordan turns the corner to drive the lane, both Morrison and Robinson converge to stop him. Al does not roll as he has done all day. Rather he fades back to the top of the key just behind the three-point line. Jordan doesn't even look as he knows where Lil Al is standing. He whips the pass over his shoulder. Al catches it, takes a deep breath and shoots his two-handed set shot toward the hoop. The ball hits the back rim then front rim and rattles through the net.

Game 21–17!

Al stands at the spot where he launched the shot with both hands high in the air. Jordan jogs up to him with a huge smile and gives him a big bear hug. Thrilled, they compose themselves to go shake hands with Todd and Ike. All four players demonstrate good sportsmanship.

As Jordan and Al leave the court, they see Epstein with his hand rubbing his forehead as he shakes his head. The bleacher section is in a quiet hush as no one knows how to react.

David comes over and shakes hands with Jordan and, in a somewhat subdued manner, says, "Congratulations. Helluva game." It is as though no one wants to rouse Epstein any more than has already happened with the outcome of his tournament.

Little Al walks over to Epstein and says, "Thanks for the invite. That was fun. We'd like to get our cash and tickets now."

Epstein glares at him and then at Jordan. He is obviously furious. "You can pick up the tickets at will-call. I'll have David Jacobs pay you the cash when you return to Los Angeles."

"No way, José," Al responds. "Any tournament I've ever played in, the prize is awarded immediately. If we need to go to your hotel and pick up the tickets, we will. I know you can come up with $500 cash."

Jordan is proud to have Alvin Bockman Jr. as his best friend.

Epstein looks as though he is going to blow a gasket at the absurd gall of these brash punks standing before him. Kurt Turlock is braced for a fight.

"Relax, pal. We are simply asking for what is justly ours," Al says, defusing the situation.

"Janice, bring me the winner's prize," Epstein orders to a woman standing in front of the bleachers who is poised to deliver said prize when beckoned.

There are two envelopes, one with the suite tickets for the championship game that includes a VIP parking pass. There are two more tickets in that envelope that Epstein removes before handing the envelopes to David. He also gives him the envelope that contains five $100 bills. Upon handing the prize to David, Epstein walks away without saying a word or even glancing at Jordan or Al.

David now has a big grin as he hands the envelopes to Jordan and says, "You boys were outstanding!"

Jordan smiles and says, "Thanks, David."

Al just turns and says, "Let's get out of here and go celebrate. We've got 500 bucks to blow." They both laugh.

"Hey, do you want to stick around for the buffet?" David asks as they are walking away.

"No, I think we'll pass," hollers Jordan without turning around.

"Can I tell him to shove the buffet up his ass along with Epstein?" Al asks.

"No. I'd prefer you don't. He's still my boss."

They laugh as they walk to the car with great satisfaction.

That evening, Janne is able to procure two extra tickets for the Final Four banquet under the Steve Forbes campaign group. Janne explains that she mentioned him and his professional activities in negotiating with the IRS with Mr. Forbes, and he was intrigued. He would like to meet Jordan and perhaps set a time when they can further discuss the intricacies of the IRS Collection Division. She mentioned Al as his associate when obtaining the tickets from the campaign budgetary allocation person.

The banquet hall is decorated in a colorful display of arrangements focusing primarily on the NCAA Final Four logo and promotion of the great northwest as the host. Many dignitaries are in attendance, and it is a good strategic campaign move for Steve Forbes to be there.

Janne looks magnificent in a red sleeveless fitted dress with a halter neckline. It features a low cut and open back and is midlength. She is wearing three-inch pumps that are black with a red sole. She has red lipstick and modest-sized gold earrings.

She welcomes Jordan with a huge smile and big hug. She whispers in his ear, "Congratulations on your big win today! Wish I could have been there. By the way, you look very dapper tonight!"

Jordan is in a beige suit with an open-collared light-blue dress shirt. He smiles and whispers back, "You look amazing!"

Al is wearing a dark blue custom suit with a white dress shirt, blue striped tie, and black Gucci dress shoes. He smiles at Janne, leans down, and gives her a polite hug while saying, "You look beautiful, Janne."

"Thank you. I hear you were a star on the basketball court today!"

"As usual, Jordan scored most of our points, but I had fun knocking some people around," Al responds with a grin.

"Al was fantastic," Jordan confirms.

"Good enough to be called Big Al now?" Janne asks with a chuckle.

"As long as my old man is around, he is Big Al, and I am Little Al. I'm cool with that!"

"I understand. Hey, I would like you to meet Mr. Forbes before we sit down for dinner," says Janne.

"Sure," replies Jordan.

As he and Al turn to follow Janne toward Steve Forbes, they are confronted by Epstein, who has stepped away from his associates.

Alexander Epstein is five feet eleven inches tall with a thin physique. He looks well proportioned in his black tux, but Jordan noticed he is more skinny-fat looking in warm-ups. Not much muscle tone. He has a tanned face with a few wrinkles around his brown eyes. He is rather handsome with capped white teeth. His hair is well coifed, pepper gray, combed back, and held in perfect form by some kind of hair gel.

"What are you doing here? I specifically told you the tickets did not include an invite to this event," Epstein says, knowing full well that he removed the tickets to the banquet before handing over the envelope. He glares at Jordan with fury. "Leave now, or I will have you escorted out and cancel your tickets to the game."

"We are guests of someone else," Jordan says calmly.

"Who?" Epstein demands to know.

Jordan simply nods his head toward Steve Forbes, who is engaged in a conversation about thirty feet away.

"Steve Forbes?" questions Epstein.

"Yes, Steve Forbes and his campaign team."

"He is a Republican, promoting a tax reform platform. We do not endorse him!" Epstein is even more irritated now.

"I wasn't aware of a company policy as to with whom we can associate."

Just then Al steps forward and says, "Hey, look, we won your tournament fair and square and received the tickets to the game. This shindig is completely separate, and we are not here as your guests. So we bid you farewell this evening and will see you at the game tomorrow." He puts his hand gently on Jordan's back and nudges him to walk toward Forbes.

Epstein turns around abruptly and says, "Where is Jacobs?"

Janne was a few steps ahead of them before stopping when she realized they weren't proceeding behind her. "Who was that rude man?"

"That's the jerk I told you about who ran the tournament we played in. Has sour grapes, I guess."

"I want to hear more about him and his deal when we have time."

"Yeah sure, but not tonight. Let's go meet Forbes."

Janne waits for a break in the conversation. Then she says, "Hello, Mr. Forbes, this is Jordan Duncan, the man I told you about who negotiates with the IRS Collection Division. And this is his associate Al Bockman."

"Janne, you look stunning tonight!" says Forbes as he shakes her hand.

She smiles and says, "Thank you."

Steve Forbes then turns to Jordan and Al. He extends his hand first to Jordan. "I am very intrigued about speaking with someone who engages with the IRS in collections on a regular basis."

"Nice to meet you, Mr. Forbes. Yes, I help taxpayers negotiate tax debt settlements with representatives of the IRS Collection Division."

"Fascinating. You know one of the featured platforms in our campaign is tax reform. I've heard so many horrendous things about how the IRS treats American citizens, and of course, we all deal with an incredibly complex tax code. Perhaps we can set a time to chat about your experiences out there on the front lines. I think that would be very beneficial to my campaign," says Forbes as he reaches into the inside pocket of his jacket and pulls out a business card.

"I would be honored to meet with you," Jordan says as he takes the card.

Forbes then turns to Al. "Are you related to Alvin Bockman, the former Penn State and NFL player?" Forbes inquires.

"Yes, he is my father. Do you know him?" Al asks, rather surprised.

"He is an outstanding high school football coach and a pillar in the community near where I'm from in Far Hills, New Jersey," Forbes declares as he shakes Al's hand.

"No kidding. Small world. Jordan and I played on my dad's state championship team back in 1986," Al says proudly with a smile.

"I remember that. No one expected that a small school like Millburn could win the state championship. Quite a tribute to your dad and to you boys and your teammates."

"Thank you, sir. I will pass that along to my dad. I know he will appreciate congratulatory comments from someone as prestigious as you," Al says as Jordan nods his head in appreciation.

"Tell him to keep up the good work in helping raise stand-up young men and contributing so much time and effort to our local community. Enjoy the evening, gentlemen." He turns to Janne and says, "Thank you, Janne. Have a fabulous time tonight with your friends."

"Wow, what a cool dude," says Al to Jordan and Janne as they walk toward their table to be seated for the dinner and festivities.

"See why I latched on to his campaign?" Janne comments as she smiles.

"Wise choice. I look forward to hearing about his tax reform ideas."

The rest of the evening proceeds as a wonderful event. Jordan, Al, and Janne thoroughly enjoy themselves. Janne introduces the guys to other campaign workers, and they also get to shake hands with luminaries from the sports world, political arena, and corporate big shots.

They intentionally keep their distance from Alexander Epstein and his entourage, including David and Marlin.

Even though Janne is busy with campaign functions on Monday, the three friends have lunch in a trendy Japanese restaurant in downtown Seattle. They won't be sitting together at the game, and Jordan and Al will be going directly to the airport afterward.

"Go Bruins!" Jordan and Janne say to each other as they hug, smile, and kiss softly as they depart.

David is all smiles and high-fives with Jordan as they meet in the banquet hall adjacent to the entrance to the court where suite ticket holders congregate before tip-off. A variety of foods and drinks are readily available for all, laid out buffet style on long tables in the hall. Al has his hands full with a stacked plate of a hot dog, nachos, and soft pretzel in one hand and a beer in the other. He seems determined to gain back the ten pounds he dropped in the past month.

"Word of advice—try to stay away from Alex tonight if you can. He's still upset about you boys winning his tournament," says David.

"Is he going to hold this grudge forever?" Jordan asks. "It was just a basketball game."

"I think it is still in his craw how you guys played him last year. He waited a whole year to get revenge. So when it didn't turn out like he expected, well, he's not used to losing."

"Dude needs to learn how to chill out. He is going to die early if he doesn't," claims Al.

"Let's just enjoy the game tonight and stay away from him, okay?" asks David.

"No problem," says Al.

"Sure," says Jordan. "Go, Bruins!"

David slaps Jordan on the back and repeats "Go, Bruins!" with a smile.

The hearts of the Bruin faithful collectively sink when, in the first two minutes of play in the championship game, star point guard Tyus Edney goes to the bench after aggravating the wrist injury that he suffered in the Oklahoma State game. He would not be able to return.

Cameron Dollar the sophomore understudy to Edney at point guard for the Bruins steps up in his place. UCLA plays at a torrid pace, matching the speed and pressure of Arkansas's mantra, "Forty minutes of hell." The Bruins race out to an early eight-point lead but see the Razorbacks come back to close out the half trailing only by one: 40–39.

Jordan notices that Epstein is rooting for Arkansas. He doesn't know of any allegiance that he has for the Razorbacks but figures it is more of a case of rooting against UCLA. Jordan pretty much ignores everyone in the suite other than Al and an occasional high five from David. They have a great view of the court, a refrigerator filled with drinks, and their own server to bring whatever they desire to eat throughout the game.

The second half is truly blissful for Bruin fans. Dollar continues to spark the team as he dishes out eight assists and has four steals to ignite the Bruin Fastbreak. Freshman Toby Bailey plays out of his mind. He totals twenty-six points and nine rebounds, with several dunks that inspire the entire contingent of UCLA players, coaches, and fans. Senior Ed O'Bannon caps his All-American season and fabulous UCLA career with thirty points and seventeen rebounds. He is named the Final Four Most Outstanding Player as the Bruins blitz the Hogs, outscoring them 49–39 in the second half to win at 89–78.

It is UCLA's eleventh NCAA Basketball Championship, far and away most in the nation. The sweetness of this championship is that it is the first one in twenty years and the only one attained without legendary coach John Wooden at the helm on the sidelines.

Jordan and Al celebrate with many UCLA fans. Jordan makes a call to Janne, and they find a moment to rendezvous briefly in the depths of the Kingdome. Hugs, kisses, and laughter ensue. Jordan and Al eventually make it to the airport and fly home after a very fulfilling and satisfying weekend at the Final Four. They both agree that they couldn't have scripted things any better than the actual outcome. However, Jordan feels as though he has crossed a line and is a marked man in some way or another by the vengeful Alexander Epstein.

CHAPTER SIX

Gray May

Sitting across from one another in a booth at Fromin's Deli are David Jacobs and Marlin Goodman. It is not unusual for these partners to review the progress of their business and discuss various employees over lunch. Today, Monday, May 15, 1995, the dust has settled from the frantic tax season, and the numbers have been calculated as to revenues generated from tax return preparation in addition to the typical influx of tax resolution work that always surfaces during the first quarter of the year as taxpayers receive W-2s, 1099s, K-1s, and other documentation that apply to filing taxes.

Fear motivates action and the fear of owing taxes to the federal government, receiving threatening collection letters and in some cases, actual bank levies or property seizures seems to heighten during tax season. The volume of inbound phone calls increases significantly from January through April at the Jacobs & Goodman Tax Resolution call center.

David is finishing up his matza ball soup, and Marlin is working on his Caesar's salad with a side of a plain toasted bagel lightly covered with cream cheese. Both enjoy a cup of coffee with their lunch—David with cream and sugar, Marlin black.

David and Marlin's friendship goes way back to their school days in Brooklyn, New York, during the 1950s. After graduating in the same high school class, David left New York to attend the University of Miami. He received an accounting degree and subsequently became a CPA. Marlin also received a bachelor's degree in accounting from New York University (NYU). He, too, earned his certified public accountant credentials. In 1962 they both decided to spread their wings and move across the country together to Los Angeles to seek employment as CPAs.

Each of them is an avid Dodgers fan. In fact, they claim to be among the few remaining people alive who witnessed in person the 1955 World Series at Ebbets Field in Brooklyn and the 1965 World Series at Dodger Stadium in Los Angeles, both of which were won in a spectacular seven-game series by the Dodgers.

The Dodgers moving from Brooklyn to LA following the 1957 baseball season was heartbreaking for many Brooklynites. As David and Marlin recall, it had a major influence on their decision to move to Los Angeles as well. Jordan has commented to Tonja and Brookes that the only time he has witnessed Marlin laugh out loud is when he and David talk about going to those Dodger World Series victories.

The two lifelong friends couldn't be more different in appearance. David stands maybe 5'7" in his shoes and is about 30 lb. overweight. He has a full head of brown hair with a little gray at the temples and a tint of a reddish color on top that screams, "Just for men." He smiles a lot, is clean-shaven, and has a long Jewish-looking nose. Marlin, conversely, is tall at 6'1" and on the thin side. He wears a well-trimmed mustache that matches the color of his silver thinning hair, which he combs straight back to cover the balding at the crown of his head.

"We had our best tax season yet," remarks David. "Just under a 12 percent increase from last year on tax returns alone, 18 percent overall increase in revenue."

"Jordan remains the number one producing TDA," says David as he looks up from his sandwich to view the expression on Marlin's face.

Sure enough, Marlin's brow furrows a bit as he responds, "He worries me, and he should worry you too!"

"Why is that? Because he pissed off Epstein by winning his basketball tournament?" David says with some sarcasm.

"He is a maverick, marches to his own beat, and shows little respect to Alex, me, or you for that matter."

"I've never felt disrespected by him. As far as Alex goes, you saw how blatantly he tried to rig that tournament. He just hates to lose!"

"He makes off-the-cuff promises to his clients. He doesn't consult with you or me beforehand. That is disrespect in my book."

"He charges and collects appropriate fees. Besides, you used to say the same thing about Andy in Orange County, and that has worked out okay."

"Andy is controllable. Jordan does not seem to be intimidated by anything or anyone. I don't think when it comes right down to it, we can control him like Andy, Reed, Robert, or even Tricia. I'm just saying, be careful how much leash you allow him. He could be dangerous."

"That brings up a subject that I know you don't want to discuss." David stops eating and looks straight at Marlin. He continues, "Jordan has come to me again, wanting a 'big case.' Feels as though he has earned the right to handle a large case with big fees."

"See? That is exactly what I'm talking about! Just tell him Beverly Hills is my office and my territory," Marlin says with some irritation in his voice.

"His rebuttal is that big-dollar cases don't all have to travel to Beverly Hills. He could see them in Sherman Oaks. Can't you just throw him a bone, Marlin? The kid closes everything! Don't you have something that is not a trust fund recovery case but is a high-dollar amount you could send his way? It would help in your relationship with him."

Marlin is silent for a moment, thinking. "Okay, listen, I just met a new prospective client last week. I'm not sure I even want the case. Big liability. But honestly, I'm not clear on the nature of the debt nor what is currently going on with the IRS. If he wants it, he can have it."

"What do you mean you're not clear on it?"

"The guy was talking a hundred miles an hour in some kind of Spanglish—you know, half-English, half-Spanish rat-a-tat bullshit." He continues, "Something about border patrol problems that turned into IRS problems. Frankly, I don't want to deal with the wetback. Duncan can cut his teeth on a big liability case with that one. With one condition, he meets with him in Sherman Oaks and never in my Beverly Hills office."

"Okay, I will have him follow up on the case. Thanks, Marlin. A complex difficult case might cure him of wanting to deal with the big fish."

"I doubt it," says Marlin as they pay the bill and get up to leave.

As Jordan commutes into Sherman Oaks, his cell phone rings. Glancing at the screen, he notices an overseas number. Must be Leslie.

After she left for Europe, he received postcards regularly from Rome, Nice, Monaco, Barcelona, Lisbon, London and Paris. She travelled with a girlfriend. She finally settled in Paris and was hired as an assistant concierge at a resort hotel. She seemed happy, and Jordan was happy for her. Then last April 1994, he received a long-distance phone call from an overseas number. As he answered, at first all he could decipher was crying and his name.

"Oh, Jordan, I'm so sad."

After making sure that she wasn't hurt or in any danger, he listened to her pour her heart out. She had just heard the tragic news that Kurt Cobain, the iconic guitarist and front man for the rock band Nirvana had committed suicide at the age of twenty-seven. Leslie had always been infatuated with Nirvana's music and Kurt Cobain in particular. Jordan remembered one time he showed Leslie the only photo that he had of his late father, Edward Duncan, and she immediately said, "Oh my gosh, he looks like Kurt Cobain!"

Leslie felt as though Jordan was the only person who could truly feel her pain in receiving the tragic news. "I don't believe it… I feel so bad for Courtney [Courtney Love was Cobain's wife] and the baby! Francis Bean Cobain was only twenty-one months old when her father died.

"Jordan, I'm just devastated. I want to come home. I need you to hold me."

Jordan was able to calm her down as they spoke for over an hour and a half on the phone. He asked if she had spoken to her parents, and when she said that she had not, he suggested that she do that. She asked Jordan to come visit her, but he couldn't get away. Ultimately, she stayed and sent him a lengthy letter, where she explained in some detail why she felt so connected to the Nirvana music. The name Nirvana was taken from the Buddhist concept, which Cobain described as "freedom from pain, suffering, and the external world." Jordan didn't hear from Leslie again until receiving a Christmas card in December. She told him that her parents were visiting her over the holidays.

He answers the phone, "Hello."

"Hey, Jordan. It's me—Leslie. How are you?"

"Hey, Leslie. Good to hear from you. I'm good. How are you?"

"Great. Guess what. I have a boyfriend! His name is Nicola. His mom is French, and his dad is English, so he is fluent in both languages. He lives here in Paris but wants to come visit Cali! I told my parents, and they are excited to meet him and see me, of course. I've told him all about you. I would like you to meet him. I thought maybe you could teach him to surf! What do you think?" Leslie is bursting with excitement in the unique way that only she can be, as Jordan remembers.

"Wow, I'm really happy for you, Leslie. I would be glad to see you and meet him. Maybe you should let your dad take him surfing. You know I don't really teach surfing."

Leslie remembers how Jordan had told her that he could never teach someone to surf. The majestic ocean is the grand master of the surf. He explained that all you need is a board, a humble will to learn, respect of the ocean and other surfers, the guts to go out there, and the perseverance to not give up. A fearlessness about falling off the board and being gobbled up into a washing machine type of tumbling under water where you have little to no control until the wave spits you back out. Beyond that, it's just learning the feel and nuances of the board and the uniqueness of each wave. And oh yeah, it's probably a good idea to have a sense of balance and a surfboard leash so that you're not constantly trying to find your board after you wipe out.

She laughs. "Yeah, maybe I'll just take him out and let him try it on some small waves to start. But you'll meet him?" she asks excitedly.

"Sure. Just let me know when you're coming. I'm really happy for you Les. You sound great!" Jordan says sincerely.

"Thanks, Jordan. Good talking to you. I'll let you know the plans. Love ya. Bye."

Jordan has a feeling that he probably won't see Leslie again. He thinks she will have second thoughts about introducing her boyfriend or her parents will talk her out of it. Meeting the ex is generally not a great idea. But he genuinely is glad that she is happy—because he is too!

There were no messages from Jack Arbuckle when he arrives at the office. Jack has been fighting the innocent spouse relief for Alice Johnston and seems more determined than ever to seize her property and close the case. However, he has an obligation to go through the process of considering the submission of innocent spouse. That necessitates time because there is a lot of information to decipher.

Jordan has discovered that the Johnston's had put $100K down on the purchase of their home. He must show that those funds were either not derived from cheating on their tax returns or that Alice did not personally gain from that transaction. His biggest obstacle currently is keeping Arbuckle at bay as he wades through piles of data.

After obtaining all the financial information from the Williamsons and filing their missing returns, it appears as Jordan initially thought—an OIC is the best possible outcome. He has informed them and set them up on a payment plan to cover the costs of J&G fees. He also has an idea of how to get Tio a better-paying job to help his parents with the offer amount. He needs to visit a former client to see if that plan can be implemented.

He is wrapping up a couple of other OICs that he has been working on. As he is at his desk, working on these various cases and making phone calls, Tonja sticks her head in the door.

"Got a minute?" she asks.

"Sure, come on in."

"Marlin wants to see you in his office. But before you go in, I just want to give you a heads-up."

"Okay. I'm surprised that Marlin is here and that he wants to talk to me."

"Well, you know how I tend to get information from DJ about things, right?" Tonja begins.

"Yeah, go on."

"Last week, David and Marlin went to Fromin's for their monthly powwow to discuss, well, everything. Upon returning, David had a few things for me to do as usual, and he happened to say, 'I wish Marlin could just see what I see in Jordan.'"

Tonja continued, "I said, 'What do you mean, David?' He went on to explain that Marlin seems to think that you don't respect him, David, or Epstein."

Jordan shakes his head and lets out a noticeable sigh. "You know respect goes both ways. I feel like David treats me with respect, and I reciprocate it. Marlin hardly acknowledges me, so I don't go out of my way to talk to him. Epstein, now that is a different cat altogether. He just hates me because I won his basketball tourney."

"My advice is, when you go in there, be respectful and just hear him out. I have no idea why he wants to talk to you," Tonja suggests.

"Will do. Thanks, Tonja."

Jordan knocks on the door to Marlin's office in the Sherman Oaks suite, which always remains closed whether Marlin is present or not.

"Enter!" Marlin commands.

Jordan walks in and confidently says, "I heard that you wanted to see me."

"Yes, have a seat."

"David tells me that you are asking about working a big liability case," Marlin says, foregoing any small talk.

"Yes, I believe that I can handle that and generate additional revenue."

Marlin gets right to the point. "I've got a new potential client that I met with in Beverly Hills. I don't know the particulars about his case, but the liability is $160K and growing. I would like to hand that over to you. However, you will be required to meet him here in this office."

Required, Jordan thinks. *How typical of Marlin*. "Sounds great. I appreciate the opportunity. Do you know where he stands in the collection process?"

"No, there was a bit of a communication barrier. He speaks English, although with a heavy Spanish accent. I started a brief file, which I will hand over to you. Frankly, all that I know about it is right here. We didn't spend much time together," Marlin explains as he slides a manila folder across the desk toward Jordan.

Jordan opens the file and sees the name Jaime Delgado with a phone number and $160,000 circled next to the name. The next page is a copy of the form that was faxed to Marlin from the call center. It doesn't contain much info other than "Possible OIC, need more info."

"Not much to go on, but no problem. I'll call him and set an appointment to meet him here in Sherman Oaks. Anything else?"

"No, just keep David in the loop on everything you do with it. Don't be too eager to promise an OIC," Marlin advises.

"Okay, thanks, Marlin," Jordan says as he stands and leaves the room with the file in hand.

Jordan decides to waste no time in contacting Jaime Delgado. Just before he dials the number, Tonja bursts into his office. "Well?"

"He gave me a big liability case, $160K." Jordan hands her the file.

"Did he talk to this guy yet? There isn't much to go on. That is a terrible entry by the call center. I'm going to show this to JoJo," responds Tonja with a disgusted look on her face.

"No, please don't," Jordan is quick to respond.

"Marlin said he met with the guy and had some communication issues caused by the dude's accent. I'm a little curious as to why Marlin gave this up, but like you advised, I want to show respect and gratitude for the opportunity. If I start causing inner-office conflict right away, that won't look good," Jordan explains.

"Yeah, I see your point. Let me know what this guy has to say when you reach him. Good luck." She is out the door before he even says goodbye.

Jordan dials the number in the file. "Delgado Transport."

"Is this Jaime Delgado?"

"Who wants to know?"

"This is Jordan Duncan from Jacobs & Goodman Tax Resolution."

"Oh, okay, yeah, this is James Delgado. I am Mexican, but in the US, I go by James, not Jaime," he explains.

"Okay, James. I was given your contact information by Marlin Goodman. I'm following up on your visit with him last week."

"Are you his assistant or something?"

"More like a colleague. I am an enrolled agent with the authority to represent taxpayers to the IRS. I'm employed by Jacobs & Goodman."

"The other dude's name is part of the company name. Am I being sent to the second string now?"

Jordan fights back a chuckle. "No, we work as a team. What I'd like to do is meet with you in person and hear more details about your tax situation. I will tell you what I think we can do for you. Then you decide if you want me to represent you. Sound fair?"

"Okay, but I gotta tell you that Goodman *hombre* didn't say much at all. I left not impressed. If you didn't call, I wouldn't have called back." James Delgado is direct, and Jordan admires that.

"Can you meet me next Thursday or Friday in my Sherman Oaks office?"

"So I don't have to go to Beverly Hills? Finding parking there is a pain." Delgado sounds relieved.

"Nope, my office is on Ventura Boulevard in Sherman Oaks, across from the Galleria."

"Thursday is better for me. Afternoon is best. Say, 3:00 p.m.?"

"That works. Vanessa will call you to confirm and give you the address and directions. We have our own parking."

"Bueno. See ya then. Hey, Jordan."

"Yeah?"

"This is muy complicado, man. It ain't gonna be easy."

"The IRS is complicated. I'm prepared. See ya Thursday," Jordan says confidently.

Jordan feels a sense of excitement with the challenge before him. For some reason, he already likes James Delgado. He is direct, and there won't be any difficulty in gathering information. Strange, there is an accent, but he had no problem understanding everything Delgado said.

Jordan enters the Pacific Coast Bike Tours, located on the boardwalk at the Ocean Front Walk in Venice just across from the Muscle Beach workout platform. He asks for Thomas Paranucci, who is the owner.

The girl at the front desk asks, "May I tell him who you are?"

"Sure, tell him it's Jordan Duncan. He knows me."

From the backroom, where the bikes are located, out bounds the affable and very charismatic Thomas Paranucci.

"Mio buon amico, Taxman!" With a big grin, Tommy embraces Jordan with a big bro hug.

"How are you doing, man? I haven't seen you recently out on the courts!"

Thomas Paranucci has been a Venice resident for over twenty years and has accumulated a wealth of information about the area and its rich, colorful history. He opened Pacific Coast Bike Tours, catering to tourists from around the world as well as local Angelinos. Each tour is dedicated to sharing the hippest town in all of California.

They lead groups of people on beach-cruising bicycles along the fifteen-mile Santa Monica Beach bike path. They veer inland to check out the famous Graffiti Art Park. The tour features art galleries and unique local businesses and shops. The ride concludes through the stunning Venice Historical Canal District.

The charismatic tour guides (taught and mentored by Tommy himself) cover Venice's history in a quite-entertaining manner. They recite tales about the film stars, artists, authors, and poets who have contributed to making Venice the most eclectic seaside community.

Jordan met Tommy last year when he came to the Sherman Oaks office with a tax problem. In the early 1990s, the IRS went on a rampage, as they tend to do, targeting businesses suspected of wrongly classifying workers. Tommy had only worked as an entrepreneur prior to opening Pacific Coast Bike Tours. Therefore, when he started the company, he paid his employees as independent contractors on a 1099. The IRS did an internal audit, determined that his workers should have been classified as W-2 employees, and slapped him with payroll taxes, penalties, and interest of over $20,000. They just sent him the bill (tax assessment) without any interview or discussion of his business practices.

Jordan took POA, realized that Tommy was well capitalized in starting his business, had fantastic growth potential, and was not a candidate for an OIC. However, upon further review and negotiations, he was able to justifiably convince the IRS representative that when starting the business, the employees did qualify as independent contractors and it wasn't until a growth stage later in 1993 that they became full-time W-2 employees. The tax was dramatically reduced, the penalties were abated for the most part, and a significant decrease in interest charges were all reassessed. Jordan set up a modest IA for Tommy with the ACS and helped him find a competent CPA to handle his payroll and change the working classification of his employees. Tommy was grateful to Jordan, and now business is booming. Pacific Coast Bike Tours has received nothing but excellent and glowing reviews!

"Yeah, I went up to the Final Four to see my alma mater return the championship back where it belongs," Jordan says with a smile.

"Eccellente!" Tommy was born and raised in the US but comes from Italian heritage. When he learned that Jordan is half Italian and had helped him deal with the IRS, he felt that he had a *fratello d'armi* (brother-in-arms) type of relationship with him. He also loves to shoot hoops and often goes just a couple of hundred feet down the boardwalk to the Venice Beach basketball courts to engage in a game of three on three.

"What brings you in to see me today, *mio compagno?*"

"You remember meeting the dude I run with on the courts, named Tio?"

"The skinny black kid that talks a mile a minute and has incredible hops?"

"Yeah, that's him," Jordan says with smile and a chuckle. "He is a native of Venice and has been working part-time as a bike courier. He has a dynamic personality, has no fear of speaking to complete strangers, as you have witnessed, and knows this town. I'm helping his parents with a tax problem, and they could really use some extra money in the family. I was wondering if you might have an opening for a full-time tour guide?"

"Any problems with alcohol, drugs, or anything? We do background checks and drug testing. But if he's clean, I could put him on and see how he does," Tommy says with a smile.

"I'm pretty sure he's clean. I will have him come in and talk to you. Thanks, Tommy, this means a lot to me and even more to the Williamson family!" Jordan responds with a hand clasp and a bro hug.

"*Ciao, mi amico*, and don't be a stranger. Let's go hoop sometime soon."

"You got it. Take care, Tommy," Jordan says as he turns to leave.

Jordan goes straight to the Williamson apartment to share the news that their tax case has been assigned to a revenue officer. They drew Bobbi Sinclair, which is a huge upgrade from Jack Arbuckle! He informs them that he will be submitting an offer in compromise soon. He also speaks to Tio about Pacific Coast Bike Tours and shares that Thomas Paranucci might have an opening for a bike tour guide. Everyone down on the boardwalk, whether it be vendors, business owners, ballers, weightlifters, skaters, bikers, walkers, runners, surfers, or those that just hang out, know about Pacific Coast Bike Tours. Tio is beside himself with excitement. It would be his first full-time job with a legitimate paycheck. He can hardly believe it when Jordan tells him that they offer employee benefits like health insurance and paid time off.

Irma is in tears as she hears Jordan explain all this to Tio. She gives Jordan a big hug and says, "God sent you to this family, Jordan Duncan. We are grateful to the good Lord and to you, honey." Tyrone has a thankful expression as he grasps Jordan's right hand with each of his hands and nods with an appreciative grin.

Tio says, "Yo, Taxman. Thanks, bruh!" He goes through the handshake routine they do and a quick bro hug.

Jordan smiles and tells everyone that he will be in touch. As he leaves the dilapidated apartment complex, he feels a warmth from within and realizes that this is what he loves most about his profession.

It is Thursday, May 25, 1995. Along the southern California coastline, in the beach cities, they refer to this time of year as Gray May, followed by June Gloom. This is due to the lingering gray misty fog from some mysterious source within the conspicuous waters of the mighty Pacific that extends like tentacles over the shoreline until early afternoon almost daily during this time of year. It hovers as if in a protective mode, perhaps safeguarding the final days of the grand migration north of the magnificent, beautiful gray whales from the onslaught of tourist hordes migrating west to the awe-inspiring California beaches. The temperatures are in the midsixties, in the air, on the land, and in the water.

Jordan enjoys this time of year to surf because kids are still in school and tourists don't come to the California beaches to frolic in the fog. From July until mid-November, the brilliant sun will illuminate and bake the sand, sea, and anyone or anything absorbed therein. There will be plenty of beach worshipers that will congregate to swim, surf, boogie board, body surf, paddle board, or jump the waves near the shore. Beach volleyball is immensely popular in SoCal, along with beach cruisers, joggers, walkers, and skateboarders. Rollerblading has become the new exercise du jour. In Santa Monica and Venice, there are even gymnasts, weightlifters, and hoopsters demonstrating their skills. Of course, the majority of folks just come to hang out and lie down or shop and dine along the boardwalk and pier. Serious local surfers arrive early and leave early in the summer months.

Surfing during the early mornings in May and June offer no crowds of people, and the waves continue to roll in regardless of the visibility.

This day, Jordan decides to surf before going into the office to meet James Delgado. Surfing helps him relax and clear his mind, giving him a sense of humility derived from the enormous power and unpredictability generated in each wave. He also feels a sense of confident invincibility as he controls his ride, gliding, attacking, and pulling out of the wave on his own terms. The mixture of humility and invincibility is the state of mind and persona he desires to maintain while meeting Delgado.

The appointment is at 3:00 p.m., but Jordan has much to do prior to that, so he is on his commute by 9:00 a.m. As he drives up the 405, he turns on the radio. The OJ trial is slugging its way forward. Allegations are made of planted evidence and perjury of testimony. The general mudslinging between prosecutors, defense attorneys, and witnesses is prevalent.

Seems like this will last all summer, Jordan thinks to himself.

The aftermath of the horrendous Oklahoma City federal building bombing on April 19 is still being reported; 168 people have been found dead. A couple of white supremacists have been arrested and indicted for those murders. The tension continues to mount in the city and in the country.

At 2:55 p.m., the door to the Sherman Oaks office swings open, and in bounds a handsome forty-five-year-old Hispanic man wearing khakis, a blue Hawaiian shirt with the top two buttons undone, a gold chain around his neck, and white canvas boat shoes. He stands 5'10", is of medium build, and has thick black curly hair that is not neatly combed and hangs just over the tops of his ears. He sports a black mustache with a neatly trimmed goatee. His brown skin is augmented nicely with a flashy smile of straight white teeth, which he seems to enjoy displaying.

"Hola, senorita! Are you Vanessa?" James Delgado inquires as he quickly ascertains that Vanessa is of Latina heritage.

"Yes, I am," responds Vanessa with her own attractive smile.

"*Dios mio*, you are prettier in person than I even imagined talking to your sweet voice on the phone. Me llamo, James Delgado," he says as he takes her hand and bows his head slightly.

"Nice to meet you, Mr. Delgado. I will let Mr. Duncan know that you have arrived."

"Gracias." He lets go of her hand and steps back a couple of steps.

"Mr. Duncan, James Delgado is here in the lobby for his three o'clock appointment."

"Great, I will be right out."

"He will be right with you," Vanessa informs Delgado.

Jordan walks down the short hallway into the lobby with his accustomed polite, professional smile and hand extended as he approaches Delgado.

"Hello, Mr. Delgado, I'm Jordan Duncan."

"*Valgame*, you look like you could be a movie star," says Delgado as he shakes Jordan's hand with a smile.

Vanessa lets out a little giggle as Jordan says, "Not hardly. Please come with me to my office."

As Delgado sits down and they exchange a little small talk, Jordan learns that Jaime Delgado was born in Sinaloa, Mexico, in 1950. He came to the United States in 1970 to live with an uncle and work with him on the docks in Long Beach cleaning and repairing boats and yachts. He became a US citizen in 1977. In the early 1980s, he met some friends from Mexico who introduced him to an association that helped find employer sponsors for Mexican immigrants to get working visas and green cards in California. Delgado started working for them and did a few "side jobs" of actually driving to Mexico and physically moving his clients with their belongings to El Norte (US) in a van that he purchased. He was a regular at crossing the border and had the proper visa and paperwork.

By 1990, with the Immigration Act of 1990 signed into law by President George H. W. Bush, James Delgado went into business for himself. The law significantly increased the number of immigrants that were legally allowed into the country. He quickly learned about the five distinct employment-based visas categorized by occupation that were created by the new law. The category that fit his connections of both employers and workers was the EB-3. Essentially those are skilled workers (at least two years of job experience or training) or unskilled/other workers (no experience). The most common job placements that he works with are unskilled: caretakers, housekeepers, janitors, landscapers, nannies. Sometimes he is able to place skilled workers in these categories: journalists, computer scientists, graphic designers, supervisors. The forms and paperwork are rather extensive. However, he works diligently and sets himself apart from his competition by his willingness to physically move and deliver his clients to their employers.

"I appreciate you sharing that background with me. I learned something new. I never realized what a vital part of immigration finding jobs and people to match those jobs would be," Jordan says emphatically.

"*Si*, I kind of created a career out of bringing people across the border legally by finding them jobs first," Delgado says proudly.

"So explain to me now. How did you run into problems with the IRS?"

"*Ahi es donde las cosas se complican.* This is where it gets complicated."

"It actually started when some workers that I brought over as a skilled labor group, graphic designers, bailed on their employer after a couple of months and started dealing drugs—weed, coke, and even heroin." Delgado starts to explain. "Eventually, they got busted and, during their interrogation with the DEA, coughed up my name as how they got into the country. I think it was some kind of plea bargain, and they didn't want to reveal their true source. So basically, they threw me under the bus," He continues. "The DEA contacted me and brought me in for questioning. They discovered that I am originally from Sinaloa, which happens to be the drug cartel capital of Mexico. They assumed there must be some connection between me and the cartel, especially when they found out what I do for a living, bringing Mexican immigrants to El Norte. They opened an investigation, and believe me, it was not good for my business having the DEA interview my employer contacts. They found no connection, and luckily, I was able to convince most of my sponsors that it was all a misunderstanding. But don't get me wrong. I lost some business over it and mucho dinero!

"Next thing I know, the IRS is doing an audit on all my finances. They claimed that I underreported income on my tax returns and even stuck me with an excise tax on a boat that I purchased. In fact, they had a couple of *cabrones* from their Investigative Division interrogate me for tax evasion. They couldn't find evidence of that, so they just gave me a huge bill with all sorts of penalties and interest, which totaled $160K!" Delgado is now wiping his brow, and the smile is gone from his face.

"I know the interest continues to rise, so who knows what it is now? Some dude from collections contacted me, but I told him I had to talk to my attorney. He gave me until June 1 to pay in full, or he was going to start taking my assets. Can they do that without any court order?" Delgado is obviously very frustrated by the whole ordeal.

Jordan listens with a calm but concerned look on his face. "Wow, that is quite a story. Sounds like they are trying to pull a Capone on you."

"*Que quires decir?* What does that mean?" Delgado asks with a perplexed look on his face.

"Have you ever heard of Al Capone?"

"The gangster?"

"Yeah." Jordan sits back in his chair, clasping his hands behind his head.

"Al Capone was a bootlegger and mobster back in the 1930s in Chicago primarily. He became the number one enemy on the FBI's Most Wanted List. But they couldn't find enough evidence to convict him. So they turned to the IRS and investigated him on his tax returns and audited all of his financial dealings. Eventually, they found enough evidence to convict him of tax evasion and sent him to prison."

"Chueco!" Delgado is now on the edge of his seat. "That is exactly what they are doing with me, *vato*! You can stop them, right?" Delgado seems excited simply by the fact that Jordan recognized so quickly what was going on.

Jordan leans forward in his chair. "I believe there is a huge difference between your case and Al Capone's. I think he was guilty of criminal activity. I don't believe that you are. You might owe some back taxes. I won't know that until I look into it. I do know how the IRS can trump up tax assessments in order to intimidate and bully citizens into paying. That is what I intend to correct in your case!" Jordan continues, "You are right. It's complicated. But we need to focus on the tax assessment and not the criminal elements. The way the IRS works on tax liabilities, you are guilty until proven innocent. On federal criminal charges, you are innocent until proven guilty. So we start proving that you don't owe the tax and leave them with the burden of trying to prove you did anything criminal."

"I like it!" exclaims Delgado. "Now I got the right hombre on my side. You should be a partner here rather than that old fossil Goodman. He didn't even want to hear my story, man," Delgado remarks, quite animated.

"So what do we do next?"

"Let me ask you this… Do you remember the name of the reve-nue officer who contacted you, and do you have a copy of any forms they have sent you?"

"Dude's name is Jack Arbuckle. A real *tramposo*, if you ask me."

Jordan puts his face in his hands.

"Is that bad? Do you know him?"

Jordan looks at him without any discerning expression and sim-ply says, "This is going to be a war, James."

"Call me, Jimmy. That's what my friends call me. I need you to be my friend, Jordan. *De acuerdo?* Deal?" Jimmy extends his hand.

Jordan shakes his hand but says, "We haven't discussed fees."

"How much?"

"First thing I need to do is take power of attorney just for these tax matters. That will keep Arbuckle from contacting you directly. Did you receive what they call a CP–504 notice of intent to levy?"

"Si, I believe I did. About a month ago."

"That is why Jack is giving you until June 1. It is a thirty-day notice that is mandatory before they can levy your bank accounts and start the seizure process on your assets." Jordan continues, "We require a $1,500 fee to take POA. Then our fees are based on the hours of time required to resolve your problem. I'm going to be straight up with you, Jimmy. I don't know how much of this $160K I can get knocked off, but from what you explained to me, I'm certain that they have trumped up the charges excessively. This is going to take a long time to sort out and a lot of negotiating with Arbuckle. He is the toughest RO to deal with in the entire LA District office. I think a retainer of $10,000 will be reasonable. I will protect you from collection activity and start working right away on your financials, which will be critical to the outcome of your case. When we have your financials completed and I review the audit they performed, I can give you a fairly accurate idea if the $10K will be sufficient to handle the case. My goal is to allow you to continue running your business as usual as I work the case for you."

Jimmy Delgado stares at Jordan, studying him with his eyes slightly squinted for a period of a couple of minutes. Neither man speaks. Finally, Delgado says, "I follow my gut on most decisions I have to make about people." He pauses. "I'm usually right about who's *el bueno y* who's *el chueco*. I have a good feeling about you, Jordan. Let's go to war, *amigo!*"

Jimmy and Jordan both smile and shake hands again.

Delgado pulls out his money clip and counts out fifteen $100 bills. "You get your paperwork going, and I will go to my car for the balance." Delgado gets up and leaves the room with $1,500 lying on the table.

Jordan nods his head. He didn't really expect Delgado to pay the entire balance at once, much less today. He knows this is the big case he's been looking forward to working on. However, he also knows it is going to be an extremely complex and difficult case. It flashes through his mind that Marlin sensed the same thing when he so easily handed it to him.

Delgado returns, counts out the remaining $8,500 in cash, and signs the POA and client agreement form.

When they walk out to the lobby, Delgado turns to Vanessa and says, "Adios, bella dama."

She smiles and says, "Goodbye, Mr. Delgado."

Jimmy winks at Jordan then turns to walk out the door and says, "Adios, mi amigo."

"Adios," Jordan replies with a smile.

CHAPTER SEVEN

June Gloom

"You are mistaken when you think I have a quota to meet, Superstar. There are no quotas. Just feed the beast, close cases, and move on!"

Jack Arbuckle is in a philosophical mood today, thinks Jordan.

Jack continues, "I don't get you, Duncan. For some reason, you seem to gravitate to bottom feeders, like that loser Alice Johnston. You do this every now and again. Maybe you see yourself as some kind of hero—"

"I'm no hero, Jack," Jordan cuts him off.

"Well, for whatever reason, you tend to get personally attached in trying to help these people who are going down. You see, for me, it's not personal," Jack explains. "They're all the same. They make financial mistakes, sometimes unintentional, sometimes intentional. Doesn't matter to me. In their mind, they are never to blame. Somebody else is always to blame. The reason doesn't matter. They have stolen from the federal government, and my job is to collect what they took." Jack is on a roll, and Jordan decides to just let him go for the time being.

"Owing taxes is rarely the only problem these people have. They are bad money managers, and it is usually a symptom of deeper personal problems. Again, it doesn't matter to me. I don't have problems. They do. They don't have power. I do! Enforcement of power feeds the beast and closes cases." Jack pauses.

Jordan responds to Jack's diatribe, "We just see things differently, Jack. I won't disagree that my clients have usually made mistakes. I mean, really, who among us hasn't?" He finds it remarkable that Jack doesn't butt in at this point to deny that he makes mistakes.

"In its mandate to collect as much as possible or, as you put it 'to feed the beast,' the IRS takes on the persona of a 'supreme' agency. As you stated, you have been given enormous power, ironically without any need for due process. You inflict that power to enforce payment. However, you don't just try to collect what is justly the government's taxes. No, you charge enormous penalties on people that don't exactly follow the ridiculously complex tax code. Then tack on interest that retroactively starts to compound years before the tax is even assessed in the case of an audit." Now Jordan is on a roll.

"The dysfunction between the divisions in the IRS would be laughable if it weren't so inept and unfair toward the taxpayer. The revenue agents do the auditing and assess taxes that are owed, again without due process. Then you, as a revenue officer, enforce collection on those assessed taxes. Ironically, when we are negotiating necessary expenses in determining ability to pay, your mindset is to disallow expenses as it will lower the monthly amount they can pay toward the back taxes due. Therefore, creating a vicious perpetual cycle of tax debt. You are so focused on 'feeding the beast' and closing cases that you don't care one bit about eliminating the source of the problem."

Jack snickers. "Blah, blah, blah... You know what, Superstar? I am eliminating the source of the problem. These people just don't know when to quit. Their failing business or lame lifestyle is like having a terminally ill pet. They just can't let it go. They keep pouring money into it, trying to revive a dying dog. Going to a tax pro is like going to the empathetic veterinarian. They just keep pumping false hope into these poor souls. I, on the other hand, do them the real favor by putting this dying pet down. Put them out of their misery for everyone's best interest. Like the song says, 'You got to be cruel to be kind.'"

Jack concludes his speech with "I think that, unlike most tax consultants that don't think twice about taking money from these losers and filling them with false dreams of redemption, you actually believe that you can help them at least temporarily. I know you are young and somewhat naïve. After all, you went to UCLA to play football instead of SC…" At this, Jordan rolls his eyes. "So I'll tell you what I will do. I am going to place Alice Johnston into a 53 for the time being. We will revisit it down the road and see if her deadbeat ex-husband gets out of rehab and can contribute to this tax bill."

"I appreciate your attempt to placate the situation, Jack. But this is an innocent spouse case. The decision isn't how much will you collect from her and how much from Donald. The question is whether she is liable for any of it."

"I don't know if you are just ignorant or if you are trying to cut and run." Jack is quick on the comeback. "The question is, how much did miss Alice in Wonderland benefit from her idiot husband's cheating? I'm willing to let the dust settle a little and see what number we can come up with. If you don't want that, then I will enforce the IA we already have in place, and Alice can just go crawl right down her rabbit hole!"

Jordan pauses for a moment to think. "A 53 requires the sign-off from the branch chief. I am going to talk to Bobbi and make sure she knows that I am not pulling the innocent spouse relief off the table."

"Relax, it's just being postponed until we can figure out how much of the down-payment on that house came from the unpaid taxes. I'm giving you a break by not reinstating the installment agreement."

"Okay, 53 it, and I'll let Alice know."

At least there will be no collection pressure on her, Jordan resolves in his mind. He considers a 53 on the Johnston case a stalemate for now with the final outcome to be determined. However, he knows Jack will likely concede that the innocent spouse relief is viable, or he would never offer the 53 status. It's not as a "break" to him or Alice. Jack is doing it because he knows he won't win and he is going to try to get something out of Alice before he quits fighting. Jordan feels confident that he can ultimately show Alice did not benefit from Donald's error. He's got Jack in check, and checkmate is within reach!

"Next item of business. I don't know what you were thinking when you took on the case of that criminal Jaime Delgado. I'm telling you right now, Superstar, I will in no way be lenient on this case," Jack states, and Jordan is wondering when Jack has ever been lenient.

Jordan responds, "I heard his story, and it sounds as though there was no evidence to prosecute for criminal activity by the DEA nor the CID. It seems it is just another collection case. Isn't that why you are involved?"

"Oh, you have heard just one side of the story—and from the side of the crook. Believe me, the CID is not done yet. In the meantime, there is a tax assessment, and I will enforce collection action ASAP." Jack is back to having seizure fever!

"I filed a POA, so you need to go through me. I intend to comply with the necessary financial forms to determine ability to pay. In the meantime, we need to suspend collection activity," Jordan replies.

"Don't mess with me on this one, Superstar. I already know he has a sailboat that is worth over $100K, and I intend on seizing it… soon!"

"I have work to do, Jack. Please send the Johnston 53 over to Bobbi. I will contact her tomorrow. Have a nice day." Jordan hangs up the phone.

On Sunday, June 11, which is Janne's twenty-fourth birthday, Jordan and Janne drive up the coast thirteen miles from Santa Monica to Malibu to have brunch at Duke's, which is located right on the edge of the Ocean on Pacific Coast Highway 1. They are greeted by a hostess named Kathy Zuckerman. Back in the late 1950s, when her name was Kathy Kohner, she was the inspiration of the novel entitled *Gidget, the Little Girl with Big Ideas*, which was authored by her father, Frederick Kohner. She is a delightful petite woman who is now in her fifties and maintains the spirit and coolness of the Surfrider Beach, where she learned to surf and hang out with the other California teens of the times. The book rights were sold and converted into a 1959 movie and later a 1965 TV series starring Sally Field, both simply called *Gidget*.

The view is spectacular as they are sitting at a window booth that is literally splashed with seawater from waves that carom off the rocks just below. In the not-too-far distance, they see sea lions and dolphins frolicking about.

"So how is the campaign progressing?" Jordan asks.

"It is going well. I am learning a lot, as is Mr. Forbes. He wasn't planning on running for president. As you know, he is a very successful businessman and editor-in-chief of *Forbes Magazine*. He just really believes that a flat tax would be a 'renaissance' for the economy and change the cultural of Washington."

"I can't argue that a change would be good."

"His father, Malcolm Forbes, passed away in 1990, and then his mom died in '92. It's been tough on him."

"Yeah, I can imagine." Jordan sympathizes.

"Tell me more about you. I know you work in tax resolution, which I must say I find very intriguing. You played football in high school and college. You like to play basketball, work out, and surf. What are your dreams for the future? What would make Jordan Duncan most happy?" Janne asks with genuine interest.

Jordan lets out a little chuckle. "Honestly, as superficial as it sounds, I don't think too far ahead. Right now, I'm twenty-five years old and enjoy my good health, and I really get a charge out of helping people that are in trouble. As far as long term, like having a family or something, I figure maybe that will be my desire someday. I try not to get too wrapped up in politics, religion, or any civil or social issues. I like to stay as drama free as possible." Jordan smiles and reaches across the table to take Janne's hands in his. "What about you, Janne Sawyer?"

"Obviously, I do like to get involved in politics and in trying to make a difference on a more macro level." She is smiling too. "But all work and no play would make Janne a dull and sad girl."

"Here is a political question for you. It's kind of loaded since it has affected each of our lives rather dramatically," Janne says as she looks directly into Jordan's blue eyes. "How do you feel about the Vietnam War?"

"Hahaha, I can say unequivocally that I am not a big fan of that historically embarrassing tragedy of a war," Jordan responds immediately. "And you?"

"Mixed feelings. I am not a proponent whatsoever. However, I wouldn't have the parents that I have, nor would I even be who I am if the circumstances of that war didn't exist. But I certainly do agree that it was a terrible war. My dad is still affected to this day. I'm so sorry about how you lost your father and the effect it most certainly has had on you and your mother," Janne says with much empathy in her voice.

"I really would like to talk in more detail about our respective feelings on that subject sometime. But now let's go for a swim in the ocean, a walk along the beach and back down to the pier to watch the sunset, and then a nightcap at my apartment with a great view of the Pacific Ocean!" Jordan smiles, still holding Janne's hands.

"That sounds like a perfect birthday!"

On Monday morning, Jordan is in Brookes's office when Tonja goes swooping past the open door. She stops, backtracks, and sticks her head in. "If you're talking about the Delgado case, wait for me. I have to give something to DJ, and I'll be right back."

"Okay, I won't let him start until you're back," says Brookes with a smile.

"I don't think this place would function without that woman."

"No doubt," Jordan agrees. "I'm going to need her help with Delgado."

"Do you really think he is on the up and up?" Brookes inquires.

"Yeah, I think so. But the DEA and the CID have put this guy through the ringer, and I don't think he trusts many people at this point."

Tonja is back. "What did I miss?"

"Nothing." Jordan begins to explain the situation. "As I told you both, Delgado swears that he has done nothing criminal. And the DEA and CID have found nothing to prosecute. But Arbuckle informed me that the CID is still investigating."

"I don't know if you have heard this, Tonja. I know you haven't, Brookes, but Arthur explained it to me this way. The CID investigations work in reverse order of regular law enforcement investigations. With police detectives, step 1 is the crime, and step 2 is finding the criminal. When the special agents of the Criminal Investigation

Division of the IRS begin a case, it usually comes from allegations that someone may have been fraudulent in a tax crime. Step 1 is the suspect, and step 2 is the crime."

"Aha," says Brookes, "that does put a different light on things."

"So they don't really know if there has been a crime committed. They only have someone to investigate," Tonja adds.

"Exactly!" confirms Jordan.

"Therefore, I say we represent him at his word that he committed no crime and he simply has a tax debt, just like all our clients."

"I like it," says Tonja as Brookes nods his head.

"Do you think it's an OIC?" Tonja asks. "You got a nice fat fee from him."

"I'm thinking OIC doubt as to liability," Jordan responds.

"Jordan, I've heard those are next to impossible to get approved. We've never even tried one as far as I know. Maybe Marlin has. God only knows what he does—well, God and David."

"Here's my theory," Jordan begins as he sits on the edge of his seat with his hands on the desk in front of him, his eyes rotating from Tonja to Brookes. "I believe that the DEA thinks he has connections to the drug cartels in Mexico and his business is some kind of a shell to masquerade what he does. They couldn't find evidence of that, but I'm guessing those guys don't give up easily. So they bring in the IRS, knowing that if this dude is bringing Mexicans across the border regularly, there has to be cash involved. If cash is involved, we know that there is a good chance that not everything is declared on tax returns and the proper taxes aren't being paid. The CID does their ass-backward investigation, while at the same time, the Examination Division runs an audit. Of course, there is no due process, so they undoubtedly bloat the numbers on guesstimations of his cash receipts, trumped-up penalties, retroactive interest, and Mr. Delgado has a $160K tax liability. He has too many assets to do an OIC doubt as to collectability. The IRS has slapped a lien on his house and is looking for his bank accounts to levy. They will try to bleed money out of him and put him out of business until (a) he gives up the name of his connection in the cartel, for which they will probably plead him out to a lesser charge; (b) the DEA finds evidence on its own; or (c) the CID finds evidence of tax fraud, for which they throw him in the slammer until he gives up names."

"Unbelievable," says Brookes. "Are you sure you are only twenty-five years old? That is quite a theory!"

Jordan smiles and lets out a little laugh. "I'm not really that smart, Brookes. That is basically the Al Capone theory, modernized to fit the Delgado case. However, like I said to Delgado, the big difference is that Capone was a known gangster. The FBI just couldn't pin anything definitive on him, so they handed the case over to the IRS. With Delgado, I think the DEA is on a fishing expedition, hoping to land a bigger fish within the drug cartel. Like I said, I believe Delgado when he says he isn't linked to the cartels and that he runs a legitimate business."

Tonja adds, "You know, I think you could be right on target, Jordan. When are you going to tell David all of this?"

"Not until I can dig through the audit and see what I come up with. Don't say anything to David. He doesn't like it when TDAs go outside of the box." Jordan looks first at Brookes and then at Tonja.

Brookes just raises his hands as if in a surrender. "Not me. This is out of my realm of work. I just make the phones ring."

"That's right, and you are the best at that," Jordan reaffirms. He looks at Tonja. "Tonja?"

"He is going to ask me. He knows you got ten grand from the guy. You know I can't lie to David."

"I'm not asking you to lie. Just tell him the truth: 'Jordan, as far as I know, is trying to get an OIC,' which is the truth. Just don't spill out my theory about the DEA and CID nor the words 'doubt as to liability.'" Jordan smiles at Tonja as he gently punches her shoulder.

"Yeah, I can do that. That is the truth," Tonja says.

Brookes nods his head.

"I have another question," Tonja interjects. "You've given us your theory on what the DEA and IRS are doing, but what are we going to do in the meantime with Delgado?"

"Treat it like any other collection case. First, we review the audit and shoot it full of holes. Maybe we will find Delgado does owe some back taxes. Then I get a lot of penalties abated and set up an IA. But my gut tells me they fabricated the whole thing. Delgado says that his accountant is very meticulous with his records. That is why I'm thinking we might go for the OIC doubt as to liability."

"Sounds good to me. Let me know what I can do to help." With that, Tonja stands and heads out the door.

As Jordan is stepping into his office, JoJo comes out of the call center across the hall. "Jordan, I need to talk to you."

"Come on in, Jo. What's up?"

"What a day. The phones are going crazy. One of my tele-marketers got a weird call that I want to run by you before we set an appointment. This dude calls and says he has a tax debt of over $100K. Doesn't give specifics, but he insists that he meets with Jordan Duncan. The rep tells him that, on liabilities over $100K, we refer them to one of the firm's partners, Marlin Goodman. Normally, that makes people feel special, and they set the appointment. This guy says, 'No, that won't work. I need to meet with Mr. Duncan.' When asked for details about his tax debt, he says, 'I prefer to discuss that with Mr. Duncan.' The rep told him that she would have to get authorization to set the appointment with you and asked for the guy's phone number to call him back. He said, 'No, I will call you back tomorrow. Please have an answer by then.' I was going to ask Tonja, Marlin, or David what to do with that, but thought I'd ask you first."

"Did the guy give his name?"

"Robert Davis."

"Doesn't ring a bell," Jordan comments. "Well, you know I don't like to break protocol around here, Jo…"

JoJo cuts him off, "Yeah, and I don't like to drink a glass or two of wine every night after working here all day." They both laugh.

"I'd be glad to meet the guy. I don't think we want to scare him off. Maybe you could have his call transferred to you and find out how he got my name. Then set the appointment. I'll meet with him, feel out the situation, and then we can decide if I should work it or if we should turn it over to Marlin," Jordan proposes.

"Okay, mind if I run that by Tonja? You know how she gets pissed if I break protocol and something goes wrong," Jo says with raised eyebrows.

Jordan smiles. "Yeah, go ahead and run it by Tonja. I don't want anybody getting their feathers ruffled. But my opinion is, a referral is a referral, no matter how much they owe."

"I agree, amigo. I will talk to Tonja and follow your plan," Jo says.

JoJo Montanez is originally from Peru. She has spent most of her life in California, being raised by her divorced mother while her estranged father lives in Peru. She is tall, 5'8", which is extremely rare for those of Incan ancestry, which she is partially. She is quite striking in appearance and has long straight black hair, which extends all the way to her buttocks. Her eyes are large and very dark brown, almost black in color. Her nose is a little on the flat and broad side, evidence of her South American Inca heritage. Her skin is a rich brown toffee color with a nice complexion. She has a rather curvaceous figure. She was married once to a Mexican guy but doesn't like to discuss the nasty divorce.

Her personality can be abrasive at times, and she tends to be loud on occasion. Her and Tonja have had their share of run-ins; however, they coexist in a working relationship on the insistence of David. There are strong rumors in the office that David and JoJo have a relationship that extends beyond the confines of the office walls. David is married and has six kids, two of which still live at home. Anything in his life beyond his love of his business, family, the Dodgers, and UCLA sports remains very discreet. He puts his business success as a top priority and considers Tonja a key component to the success of J&G. Jo is quite aware of that hierarchy in David's life and does her best to work cordially with Tonja. The relationship between Tonja and David is close enough that she is aware of his extracurricular activities with JoJo. She stays professional and insists on workplace efficiency without letting personal feelings get involved. It seems to work, but sometimes Jordan thinks there could be a time bomb ticking and ready to explode if the business were to experience more trying circumstances and conflicts.

JoJo clears it with Tonja to set the appointment with Jordan. Mr. Davis remains vague on the phone and only reveals that he was referred by an anonymous source. The appointment is set for Thursday, June 22. Jo is clever enough to schedule it on a day when Marlin will be in Beverly Hills and at a time when David also will be out of the office.

Robert Davis is in the lobby at 9:45 a.m. on June 22, drinking a cup of coffee while waiting for Jordan to arrive. He is fifty years old and has short gray hair parted on the side. He is business casual today, wearing slacks, a white and gray pinstriped open-collared dress shirt, and a charcoal sports coat. He is of medium height and weight. He would not stand out in a crowd. He's not particularly handsome but not unattractive either.

Jordan arrives at 9:52 a.m. for their 10:00 a.m. appointment. "I hope you haven't been waiting long," he says as he extends his hand to Mr. Davis. "Jordan Duncan." He introduces himself as they shake hands.

"Not at all. Nice to meet you."

Davis follows Jordan to his office. "Please sit down and tell me about your tax issues. Who referred you to me and why?" Jordan has been trying to figure out, along with Tonja and JoJo, who referred this man to him and why he wouldn't divulge the name over the phone. He is a little suspicious that he may be getting "shopped" by the IRS.

Although the CID must declare who they are prior to asking any questions about a potential suspect or case, occasionally the Internal Revenue Service will send decoys to disguise themselves as potential clients to make sure tax professionals are not trying to entice taxpayers to be anything but honest and transparent with the IRS.

"First, I apologize for the discrepancy with your call center. These issues tend to be personal and the circumstances somewhat embarrassing."

"No problem. I understand, and I can assure you that what you tell me will be respected in as much of a confidential manner as you desire."

"I appreciate that. Do you mind if I ask you a few questions before I explain my situation and from whom I received your name?"

"Sure. Fire away." Jordan is bracing himself to make sure he measures his words carefully and will not to be misconstrued by the IRS if that is who is asking the questions. He has the Delgado case on his mind.

"Thank you. How long have you been working for Jacobs & Goodman Tax Resolutions?"

"Since August of 1992."

"I understand that you are an enrolled agent. How long have you had that designation?"

"Since February of 1993." So far, the questions are right in line with what Jordan would expect from the IRS.

"So obviously you are familiar with the tax audit protocols. In your opinion, what triggers an IRS audit?"

Okay, here is where they are going to try to catch me in implicating the IRS in some kind of audit conspiracy, Jordan thinks to himself.

"Many things can raise the red flag for an audit is my understanding. I'm not sure just what constitutes a red flag as my interaction with taxpayers is always post audit and I work with the Collection Division. However, I have been told that most audits are random in nature."

How's that for a vanilla answer? Jordan thinks proudly.

"How much do you know about Epstein, Levin & Ohlman Tax Consultants?"

Jordan didn't anticipate this question. "Not too much, other than they are the parent company to the company I work for. For clarity, you would have to ask one of the partners, David Jacobs or Marlin Goodman."

"Have you ever worked for Epstein, Levin & Ohlman? Do any of their partners sign your paychecks? Do you have a pension or any type retirement plan with them?"

"I'm not really sure where you are going with this, but the answer to all those questions is no. I am an employee of Jacobs & Goodman Tax Resolution, which is a limited liability company and separate from E, L & O to the best of my knowledge." Jordan is starting to get a little annoyed at the line of questioning. These are questions for David and/or Marlin, and he isn't interested in anything to do with E, L & O.

After a short awkward moment of silence, Davis says, "It is critical that I have your word of total confidentiality from here forward, Mr. Duncan. I was referred to you by Arthur Gibson. He spoke very highly of you and assured me that you are a man of integrity."

"I know Arthur and have tremendous respect for him. I am flattered that he vouched for my sense of integrity. You have my word that whatever you share with me will not be repeated to anyone in this firm other than whom you may designate as a need-to-know."

"First of all, my name is not Robert Davis. It is Royce Dawkins. It was necessary to use an alias to get through your screeners and meet with you as a client. Up until just over six months ago, I was the chief financial officer of a firm that was represented by Epstein, Levin & Ohlman Tax Consultants. The name of the company isn't relevant at this point. A rather auspicious audit was conducted by the IRS with little prior notice. That in itself raised a red flag for me as the CFO, as I was not asked for much input nor participation. When it was completed over a two-month period, I questioned some of the infrastructure changes they recommended based on results of the audit, and the next thing I knew, I was terminated. They offered a substantial severance package with the condition of a strict nondisclosure agreement. In essence, they would pay me in stock to keep my mouth shut about what happened as a result of the IRS audit. The management level changes that were proposed would be public knowledge soon enough. They seemed more concerned about the information that was exchanged during the audit."

Jordan is interested; however, he isn't seeing a path that would lead to sharing this information with him. So he interjects at this moment, "I'm sorry to interrupt you Mr. Dawkins. This is quite interesting, but what is the connection to me that prompted Mr. Gibson to set up this meeting?"

"That is a good question, and I will get to that if you will bear with me for a few more minutes."

"Sure. Go ahead." Jordan decides to patiently hear him out.

"After they gave me the offer, I asked for time to think it over. Fortunately, I have been frugal in my lifetime. I had a good income, and my wife also has a good income. Money wasn't the major consideration, but I suspected the legality or at least the ethical ramifications of their decision. I met with a legal representative of the firm, and he advised that I take the severance and move on. I then met with an outside attorney, and he advised that even though there might have been some ethical improprieties, no criminal or civil laws had probably been breached. He also advised that I take the severance and move on."

Dawkins takes a deep breath and continues, "I remembered one person with whom I felt most comfortable within E, L & O was their tax consultant, and I learned that he was a former high-ranking director at the IRS, Arthur Gibson. I decided to contact him to see if I could get input as to what happened in that audit. He was gracious with his time and agreed to meet with me at a neutral site. Mostly, he listened to my concerns."

Now Dawkins leans forward, looks around the room, and asks in a lower tone, "Are you absolutely sure that we can't be heard by anyone else?"

"No, we're good," Jordan reassures him.

"Mr. Gibson said to me, 'There may be merit to your concerns. I have been here in this capacity for almost two years and, prior to that, with the IRS for thirty years. There could be an unusual relationship between a CPA firm and a branch of the federal government in play here. As a former regional director for the IRS, I cannot get involved in making any allegations. I believe that if you genuinely want to pursue this—and I'm not saying it is the best decision for you to make—then you need to pry for more information. I suggest you start with the changes within your organization following the audit. Find out what you can in a discretionary manner. Then contact me and let me know what you come up with. If at that time, we mutually agree there could be some illegal actions taken, then we can look at it from the prospective of the CPA firm.'"

He continued, "I did as he asked and found out some things that caused us both to smell a rat, for lack of a better term." Dawkins pauses as he studies Jordan's face for a reaction.

Jordan does not visibly react.

Dawkins carries on, "The next step that Mr. Gibson suggested was to find out more information from the E, L & O perspective. That is where you come in. Arthur isn't sure as to how well connected the CPA firm is to the tax resolution firm. He stated that the only person that he felt comfortable trusting in the entire organization is you. He didn't know exactly how your protocols work regarding working cases. So he suggested that I call on you and set an appointment to meet with you. Then if you are willing to help us gather more information from within the firm, we will allow you to decide how that can be accomplished." Royce Dawkins now waits for Jordan to respond.

"Again, I am honored that Arthur has trust in me. That is quite a story. I'm not really sure what you are asking me to do. I guess, first of all, I need to know just what you found out from your company and what you suspect is going on with E, L & O and the IRS."

"Okay, that is a fair question. I would need to meet with you another time to explain everything that I found out from the company perspective. To be very blunt, I believe—and Arthur also suspects—that Epstein, Levin & Ohlman Tax Consultants is in cahoots with the IRS in targeting audits and then working deals in a win-win scenario."

"Wow! Those are strong allegations!" Jordan exclaims with his eyes wide open. "How do you think I can help you prove that?"

"We are not sure. Arthur says that you have a strong sense of fair play and an uncanny care and concern for your clients. If there is anyone on the inside who could possibly get additional information to help substantiate our case and blow this thing open, it would be you."

"Hahaha, Arthur said that, huh?" Jordan sounds amused.

"Do you disagree?"

"Not necessarily. I just think that he perhaps overestimates my ability to gather the information you are looking for. Honestly, I wouldn't know where to begin."

Dawkins appreciates Jordan's humility and frankness.

"Mr. Gibson will assist you. We are in a precarious situation wherein we can't infiltrate the CPA firm. Neither of us are attempting to gain anything financially. We simply feel a moral obligation to expose a huge transgression on the part of the IRS, which affects the economy and integrity of the entire nation, and bring to justice fraudulent activities on the part of the CPA firm."

Jordan believes Dawkins sounds sincere and not like he is grandstanding.

"Well, this is not at all what I expected out of this meeting Mr. Dawkins," Jordan says with a slight grin. "I will need to speak to Arthur to confirm all that you have told me."

"Of course. Absolutely!"

Jordan adds, "Then I will need to think about it."

"I completely understand," Dawkins agrees. "If it will help, we can meet again at a neutral location, and I will explain to you what I found out happened in the audit."

"That would probably help," Jordan says as he nods his head.

"When and where would you like to meet?"

"How long are you in town?"

"As long as this takes to give you the necessary information."

"Let's meet tomorrow for lunch across the street at the Galleria food court. Dress casual, and here is my cell phone number. Call me when you get there, anytime after 11:30 a.m.," Jordan instructs.

"Okay, sounds good. I appreciate your time and consideration, Mr. Duncan." Dawkins extends his hand.

Jordan shakes his hand and says, "Call me Jordan. I admire your courage in doing this."

Jordan walks him out to the lobby, and they say goodbye.

As Jordan sits at his desk, trying to contemplate everything he just heard, JoJo comes across the hall into his office, followed immediately by Tonja.

Tonja asks, "Well, tell us. Who is Robert Davis? Who referred him, and what's his deal?"

Jordan, trying to think quickly and keep his normal cool demeanor, replies, "Hate to disappoint everyone, but his liability isn't nearly as much as he thought. He doesn't qualify for an OIC. Like a lot of people, he freaked out over an audit and called a friend who he had remembered went through the same thing. His friend gave him my name."

JoJo is quick to ask, "Who referred him?"

Jordan knows that Jo has an uncommon ability to remember almost all the names of previous clients as they are screened and subsequently scheduled for appointments. He thinks quickly and pulls a name out of his past repertoire of successful OIC clients. "Remember the Parker couple from early last year?"

"Yes, of course," responds Jo as Tonja nods her head. "But why didn't he just tell me that on the phone?"

"Yeah. Why the big mystery?" adds Tonja.

"Look, I don't know what was going on in the guy's head. He just panicked over being contacted from the IRS with a tax debt. That is not unique." Jordan can't help himself from sounding defensive for the guy and rather dismissive to his coworkers. "But the mystery was totally overblown. I told him probably the best I could do is get him an IA and stretch his payments out over three years. He is going to think about it and let me know what he wants to do. End of story."

"Did he at least give you a phone number so we can follow up?" asks Jo.

"I will follow up. Don't worry about it, Jo. I appreciate everyone's interest, but it was a lot to do about nothing big. I've got some calls to make, so I will see you all later," Jordan says as he stands up and starts walking to the door, even though it is his office where they are sitting. The women take the hint and file past him out the door.

On her way back down the hall, Tonja steps into Brookes's office. "Got a minute?" she asks, closing the door behind her, and sits down. She knows that Brookes always makes time for her.

"Sure. Have a seat," he says, smiling.

"Jordan is acting awfully edgy about that Robert Davis appointment."

"What do you mean?"

"He was quite short and abrupt when questioned about the appointment. Not like him at all. Should I go talk to him, one on one?" Tonja asks with concern.

"I'd give him a little time. Whatever it is, he will figure out what to do, and I'm sure he will share it with you. He tells you pretty much everything, right?"

"Yeah, I guess so."

"TONJA!" comes a holler from David Jacobs's office.

"Gotta go." Tonja jumps up and scurries out the door.

"Is Jordan here?" David asks while studying papers on his desk.

"Yes. I think he is in his office, making some phone calls."

"Tell him I'd like to see him," David says without looking up.

Tonja decides to walk down to his office rather than use the intercom. She taps on his open door and says, "DJ would like to see you."

Jordan looks at her, stands up without saying a word, and shakes his head as he walks past her down the hall. "I didn't say a thing," she remarks from behind him as he heads toward David's office.

Jordan walks into David's office, hoping that this is not about Robert Davis. Before heading to the sitting area with the plush chairs and a couch, where they usually chat, he stops, "You wanted to see me?"

David looks up and, without standing, says, "Yes, have a seat." He points to one of the two chairs placed in front of his desk. As Jordan sits, David asks, "How are things going with the Delgado case?"

"Good. Filed the POA to stop collection activity while we can sift through the audit and gather his financial information."

"I got a call from Jeffrey Woodruff. Do you know who that is?" David asks.

"Yeah, he is the IRS LA District director."

"He informed me that Jaime Delgado is being investigated by the Criminal Investigation Division. Did you know that?"

"Yes, Delgado mentioned that they had investigated him but hadn't pressed for prosecution because there was no evidence of fraudulent activity. I assumed the investigation was completed."

"It's not. Why didn't you tell me about that?" David inquires with a concerned look on his face.

"Delgado came to us—actually, to Marlin originally—because he has a tax assessment and has been assigned to a revenue officer who was threatening levy and seizure action. I made it clear to him that we will be representing him on that front. He paid us $10,000, and I am trying to give him his money's worth." Jordan sounds defensive.

"When we take power of attorney, we are representing our clients in *all* tax matters with the IRS. If we have a potential client that is being investigated by the CID, I need to know before we can agree to represent them. This is a fundamental requirement of your position. You cannot arbitrarily decide who we will represent with a POA. Last time I checked, the names on our LLC documents are Jacobs and Goodman. Duncan is not on it, so he would not be held liable for anything. Understood?" David is very straightforward when he wants to make a point.

"Yes, sir." Jordan doesn't stop looking at David eye to eye.

"Keep me in the loop on everything that goes on with Delgado. If you are contacted by the CID, I want to know before you agree to meet with them. I will be in that meeting. Understood?"

"No problem."

"What about your other cases? Anything new worth discussing?" David is definitely not talking to Jordan like his prodigy golden boy today.

"Not really. Some OICs that are fairly routine and some IAs."

David nods his head and says, "Okay, that's all." As Jordan gets up to leave, David repeats, "Keep me in the loop *on everything!*" Jordan gives him a thumbs-up as he walks out the door.

Jordan sticks his head into Tonja's office and points down the hall and shows five fingers to suggest that she follow him to his office in five minutes. They use this signal as David's office is too close to speak out loud. Tonja enters and sits down in front of Jordan at his desk.

Jordan begins, "He knows about Delgado and the CID investigation. Woodruff called him directly. I explained that we are strictly working with the Collection Division on it. He just wants to be present if the CID wants to interview me. No problem. I would want him there. No mention of OIC doubt as to liability because I don't even know if that is feasible yet."

"Okay, good," Tonja responds. "I just didn't want you to think I told him anything. He never asked me anything about Delgado."

"Yeah, okay. Hey, about this Robert Davis, I know it sounds kind of weird right now, but everything is still very vague. I will try to get more details, but let's just keep it under wraps for now, all right? If I find out that it's anything more than I told you guys, I will share it with you."

"Yeah, sure," Tonja answers, even though in her mind it seems weird.

"I don't want David, Marlin, or Jo asking me any questions about it. Okay?"

"They won't get anything from me. I don't know anything to tell them," Tonja remarks. "But I won't initiate any conversation about it."

"Thank you, Tonja."

She smiles, puts her hand on top of his on the desk, and says, "I trust you, Jordan, and you can trust me. You know that, right?"

He smiles. "Yes, I do." She has never given him a reason to not trust her.

Tonja walks out, and Jordan lowers his face into his hands and thinks, *Office politics, I can do without it, but it's part of the game, I guess.*

For the first time since he can't even remember when, Jordan did not sleep well last night. He walks into the Galleria mall complex. The Galleria on Ventura Boulevard is a conglomeration of specialty shops, gallery events, and dining establishments. It's claim to fame, so to speak, is that it was used as the mall scene in the movie *Fast Times At Ridgemont High* in 1982, which has now amassed somewhat of a cult-like status among high school–era movies. Jordan spots Dawkins standing in front of Hana's Grill. He is wearing business slacks and a buttoned-up long-sleeved plaid shirt with no jacket.

That is about as casual as this guy gets, Jordan figures.

They shake hands and take a seat outside of the restaurant area. They are isolated from anyone else.

"Before you tell me what you discovered from within your company, let me tell you what I am going to do about Robert Davis. I am going to tell the office staff that you are a financial planner and embarrassed about this faux pas you have committed in owing back taxes. Therefore, you wanted this to be as discreet as possible and work directly with me only. I will explain that after we discussed your financial situation, I determined the best we could do for you is set up an installment agreement. After talking to your personal accountant, you discovered that he could do that for you at a much less expensive rate."

"That works for me. I'd like to pay you something for your time." Dawkins is obviously very anxious to get Jordan on-board to help him in his quest to discover the truth.

"No, that's not necessary. Just tell me what you discovered about this audit."

"Okay, thanks. Well, you may or may not know, but things have taken a turn in the corporate world in the past few years. Since coming out of the recession of the late eighties, many corporations have gone through what they have termed downsizing. We are experiencing a difference from past downturns in the economy where big manufacturing companies implement large layoffs of blue-collar workers. We are now in a more tech-driven society, and more than ever, white-collar jobs are being eliminated for budgetary reasons." Dawkins knows that he isn't here to give Jordan a lesson in economics, so he decides to get more directly to the point of interest.

"It is not uncommon for CPA firms to suggest a restructuring of leadership from the top down. But what is happening in some isolated cases, and I believe with Epstein, Levin & Ohlman Tax Consultants is that they are working with top executives to increase their compensation exponentially while the shareholders pay the price."

"Here is how it works. Compensation for corporate executives is generally in the form of salary and bonuses based on bottom line profits. What CPA firms like E, L & O have been trending toward over the past few years is having stock shares included in the executives' compensation. They take their yearly salary in appropriate pay periods. However, they defer receiving their bonus and stock dividends, keeping the funds within the company as the stock price increases. The money that is growing with interest is generally put into a separate account that is owned by the company and invested for the executive through a trust. Therefore, it can't be used to finance the company's operations. But here is the catch and shows why it behooves the IRS to get in on the game. Money that is deferred for the executives is not taxable to them. However, it cannot be deducted on the company's tax return."

Dawkins continues, "So in essence, executives receive interest-free, tax-deferred loans that are put into a trust for them and cannot be used to grow the company. Someone has to pay the price for such an arrangement. It is the shareholders of the company. Because this deferred compensation is not deductible for the company, it is taxed at the corporate rate of 35 percent. This means that each million dollars of deferred pay costs the company $1,350,000, the amount of the deferral plus the corporate income taxes that have to be paid."

Dawkins pauses and waits for a response from Jordan.

"Is all this legal?" Jordan asks.

"Amazingly, everything I described to you is legal. However, if there is an agreement in place between Epstein's firm and the IRS wherein they are jointly benefitting financially, that is illegal. This is how we, Arthur and I, believe the scam is occurring." Dawkins has his elbows on the table with his hands clasped as he continues to explain his theory. "E, L & O is basically recruiting executives to take part in this type of accounting, and when they bring their corporations into the fold, the IRS subsequently audits them. This method will generate hundreds of millions of tax revenue for the IRS, and post audit, the company goes through a downsizing of midmanagement white-collar employees to save costs. The company then experiences a bottom-line growth period on paper as they have cut costs before they have to ramp up their management team. The IRS taxes them at 35 percent on those bottom-line profits. We also believe that it works the other way around wherein the IRS leaks to E, L & O which corporations they will be auditing in the future so that they can target those executives. Again, the transactions are legal. What Arthur has explained to me that is illegal is what they call target auditing, wherein the audits are orchestrated as collaboration between the IRS and the accounting firm."

Jordan thinks he is following this line of reasoning but still is lost on what they want from him. "Sounds as though it could be feasible for sure. But where do I fit in?"

"We need two things from you. First, Arthur thinks the IRS cooperation with E, L & O could be trickling into the tax resolution business as well. He will have to explain that theory to you because I know nothing about it. We also need someone who can infiltrate the E, L & O database, which will help detect trends of corporate clients and targets for auditing. Again, you will get a better explanation and directions from Arthur. There just isn't anyone within Epstein, Levin & Ohlman Tax Consultants that Arthur feels we can trust. Again, he thinks highly of your level of integrity and says that you are bright, fearless, and resourceful."

Jordan responds, "Wow, this is a lot to digest. But I will say, everyone has their threshold of fear just like everyone has their threshold of pain." Dawkins nods his head in agreement. Jordan continues, "I will contact Arthur, but I'm sure he will only want to discuss this face-to-face. I know he is coming to town in a couple of weeks for a weekend of meetings that are scheduled. I will confer with him about getting together privately." Jordan exhales and runs his hands through his hair.

"Fair enough," Dawkins replies. "I appreciate you taking the time to hear me out and consider my proposition. Although I have a good feeling about Arthur Gibson and so far he has been a straight shooter with me, I needed to feel comfortable with you as well. I felt as though there was no better way than through your work environment. You seem very professional and competent, especially considering your youth." He smiles. "Maybe that is an advantage in your aggressiveness and fearlessness. I'm sorry if it caused you any difficulty."

"Yeah, too young to know better." Jordan returns his smile. "Don't worry about the work. I will smooth it over. I'm just glad that you didn't mention Arthur's name as a referral source."

"Thank you," Dawkins says as they get up and shake hands, and this time, Royce Dawkins gives Jordan Duncan his cell phone number.

That evening, Jordan, Janne, and Al are sitting in a booth against the wall at Chez Jay's in Santa Monica. It is an old nautical-themed landmark bar on Ocean Avenue within a block of the beach and walking distance from Jordan's apartment. Jordan asked his friends to meet him here because it is an out-of-the-mainstream bar where they can talk in private. There are pails of whole peanuts on the tables and bar with shells that end up on the floor. It has red-and-white-checkered tablecloths, appears to be kind of a dive, but is comfortable. The jukebox doesn't play anything newer than music from the eighties.

"So what's up, D-Can? You don't seem your usual chill, cool dude self?" Little Al asks as he sits across from Jordan and Janne.

"Yeah, what's bothering you, sweetie?" Janne asks as she puts her hand on Jordan's arm.

"I really appreciate you guys coming here on short notice tonight." After Jordan met earlier today with Royce Dawkins, he went for a run along the beach for almost two hours to help organize his thoughts. "There is something going on at work that I need to tell someone, and you two are my best friends, whom I can trust to keep it strictly confidential."

"Absolutely," says Al.

"Of course," Janne adds.

"The call center manager let me know that there was a potential client who specifically asked for an appointment with me. Problem was, he stated he owed over $100K in tax debt. Normally, those go to Marlin Goodman, David's partner. The dude said he was referred to me and didn't want to see anyone else. He wouldn't reveal who referred him. Jo, the call center manager, who works under Tonja, cleared it to schedule the appointment with me. Now everyone, except David and Marlin, to the best of my knowledge, is curious about this mysterious client and who referred him. I met the guy yesterday, and he began by interrogating me with some odd questions about my affiliation with Epstein's CPA firm. Honestly, I thought it was some undercover IRS agent feeling me out with regard to the Delgado case."

Jordan pauses to take a swig of the bottle of Corona beer in front of him. Likewise, Al tips up his Heineken, and Janne relaxes herself with a taste of her glass of wine.

Jordan continues as Al grabs another handful of peanuts. "I have no idea what this dude is getting to, but I tell him quite frankly that I don't know squat about E, L & O. Finally, he gets around to telling me why he really came to see me. He gives me this story about how E, L & O represents the company in which he was the CFO. Apparently, there was this unorthodox audit from the IRS wherein he was not included. Subsequently, he asked the wrong people the wrong questions, and they canned his butt." Again, Jordan wets his lips with the Corona.

"So who referred him to you?" inquires Al.

"That's where it gets really weird. This is very confidential." Jordan quickly turns to see if anyone is within earshot of them. With the coast clear, he leans forward as Janne nudges closer to him, and he half whispers, "Arthur Gibson, the former IRS regional director, sent him to me. Arthur is now a consultant for E, L & O as well as J&G. He has been like a mentor to me since I've been with the firm. Helped me pass the enrolled agent exam."

"What? How is there a connection with this guy and Arthur?" Janne asks.

"I know. Blew me away too. Then he says that he will give me details if I want to meet him away from the office in private. So I set up a rendezvous at the Galleria today. He proceeds to tell me this wild story about how Epstein and his partners are in cahoots with the IRS, targeting audits that include legal accounting schemes that financially benefit the executives, the CPA firm, and the IRS. I guess the 'targeting' part is what is illegal."

"How does this involve you?" asks Al.

"That was exactly my question. Turns out Arthur vouches for my integrity and how I am the only person in either company that he feels he can trust to gather more info." Janne squeezes Jordan's arm and smiles warmly. "It seems that Arthur suspects the tax resolution company might be in on the scam as well. This dude says he knows nothing about tax resolution, and I will have to talk to Arthur to hear that theory."

"Wow, what do they want you to do?" Janne asks.

"I'm still not sure. The guy was vague. I told him that I would obviously have to confirm his story with Arthur. He encouraged me to do so. Arthur is coming to town for a three-day meeting/retreat that David has scheduled the weekend after the Fourth of July."

"What are you going to do?" Al asks Jordan.

"First, I need to meet with Arthur face-to-face and get the entire scoop. My inclination is to not get wrapped up in this and wish them luck. I will, to the best of my ability, confirm or deny anything they find. I just can't see where getting involved in any kind of information gathering in a secretive manner could benefit me in anyway. Besides, this guy might just be looking to avenge getting fired!"

"Don't you want to know the truth?" asks Janne with a concerned look on her face.

"Sure. But I'm not going to act like some kind of corporate spy just to bring down Epstein, even if he is a total jerk. If he is guilty, I hope he gets what he deserves. I wouldn't even know where to begin to gather information that could implicate him of being in bed with the IRS," Jordan says while shaking his head.

"Yeah, I guess so. But you will listen to Arthur with an open mind, right?" Janne asks with her eyes wide open in anticipation.

"Of course, I will," Jordan confirms with a smile as he gathers her hand into his.

"Holy hell, I thought tax work was boring!" says Lil Al.

"You know we got your back, whatever you decide to do, right?" Al reaffirms Jordan.

"Yes, we do," Janne concurs.

"Thanks, guys. I know I can count on you. I feel better already." Jordan smiles at both while proceeding to drain the bottle of Corona.

CHAPTER EIGHT

Hotel California

On Friday, July 7, the office is abuzz as preparations are being made for the sales meeting/retreat that is scheduled at the Sportsmen's Lodge in Studio City. It launches this evening with a happy hour get-together. Saturday will begin with a breakfast buffet catered by the hotel staff in a large conference room. David Jacobs will address the entire group and speak about the state of business in general and announce that there are changes that are forthcoming within the IRS Collection Division in regard to the offer in compromise program.

Arthur Gibson will be given the podium to explain the changes in detail and the ramifications therein to tax resolution. After lunch, the group will be split into three groups, which will adjourn into smaller conference areas: (1) the TDAs (Reed Franklin, Andy Gilliam, Robert Lopez, and Jordan Duncan) will meet with David Jacobs and Brookes Peterson to discuss the new marketing presentation and techniques; (2) Marlin Goodman will host the tax managers (Karen Wallach, Sterling Frey, and Tricia Sherman), and they will discuss various techniques and strategies in negotiating with the ACS and revenue officers; and (3) the admin group (JoJo Montanez, Vanessa Garcia, Sally James, and Sunshine Kesler), led by Tonja Farley, will review the call center screening procedures, scheduling of appointments, filing the power of attorney, and overall office protocol.

Saturday evening will feature dinner in the hotel restaurant and then free time, wherein the entire group can comingle, enjoy the amenities (including the bar and lounge area, a large lap pool and deck area, spa, billiard and ping-pong tables, and even a poker room). There is also a paved walking trail around the lush green grass and tree-covered facilities that features a large pond with fish, ducks, and water turtles.

Sunday will be another breakfast buffet and closing remarks from David Jacobs. David has generously made accommodations for all to stay in private rooms on Friday and Saturday nights. The main purpose is to make sure that everyone is on the same page with the changes within the IRS Collection Division and also have a team-building experience, both professionally and socially.

Jordan is in Brookes Peterson's office just after lunch, helping him prepare his marketing presentation. Tonja enters and sits down.

She says, "Whew, I don't know about you guys, but I can feel a tension in this office thick enough that you could cut it with a knife!"

"Yeah, I've noticed that people seem to be on edge. Do you think it's the hangover effect from the Fourth of July celebration or just a nervousness of planning this weekend event?" Brookes questions his comrades.

"I think the changes to the OIC protocols are significant enough, as you know, to alter our marketing. David and Marlin are probably concerned about the effect on the bottom line," Jordan remarks.

"Arthur has been in the conference room with them all day, only breaking to go to Fromin's for lunch," Tonja adds. "Do you think the Delgado CID investigation has anything to do with the tension, Jordan?"

"Nah, I don't think so. I haven't heard a thing from the CID. I really think it is just bottom-line revenue concerns."

"Have either of you ever been to the Sportmen's Lodge?" Brookes inquires.

"Not me," says Jordan.

"Oh my gosh…" Tonja chimes in. "This place has quite an illustrious history. Full of drama and stories of mythical proportions. It has been around since the 1930s and used to be where a lot of celebrities would hang out. The goldfish pond was once a trout fishing farm. Supposedly, VIPs could catch their dinner and take it to the chef, who would prepare it gourmet-style. Clark Gable and John Wayne taught their kids to fish there, legend has it. It also was an illicit rendezvous place for celebrity affairs. But of course, no one names names on that front!" Tonja recounts with a laugh. "Do you know the last line of the song 'Hotel California' by the Eagles?" Tonja asks to either one of her audience.

"You can check out anytime you like, but you can never leave…" Jordan recites the lyrics.

"Hahaha, yep. And this is what they say about the Sportmen's Lodge: 'You can check out anytime you like, but the memories can never leave'!" Tonja laughs, and her two friends join in.

"I better not mention that to my wife," says Brookes. "She is already not too happy that David insists I stay overnight rather than commute."

"You'll be fine, Brookes. We will help protect your honor, right, Jordan?" Tonja says as she playfully punches Jordan in the shoulder.

"Absolutely," Jordan agrees as all three laugh some more.

"Tonja!"

"Gotta go." She stands and exits, stage left to that familiar beckoning.

Back in his office, as Jordan is doing some follow-up on his caseload, his cell phone rings. He recognizes Janne's number.

"Hi."

"Oh, good, I wanted to catch you before you head over to the Sportsmen's Lodge," says Janne with a relieved tone that he was able to pick up the call. "Are you alone?"

"Yes. Just doing some paperwork before I leave. What's up?"

"First, I am going to miss you this weekend. Do you realize that this will be the first weekend that we won't be together since we met four months ago?"

"Wow. Yeah, I will miss you too. Believe me, I would definitely rather spend the weekend with you!" Jordan reassures her.

"Aww, that's sweet. Please be sure and call me tonight after you talk to Arthur! I really want to hear about what he has to say to you."

Jordan contacted Arthur, and they agreed to meet early in the bar lounge area of the Sportsmen's Lodge before the others arrive.

"Okay, I will. But please don't get too excited about this, Janne. I really don't think this is something I want to get involved with."

"Hey, I was thinking, if you need help getting info on the IRS, Mr. Forbes is well connected in Congress. He is good friends with Jack Kemp, the former US congressman from New York and a huge tax reform guy. Maybe you could bring it to their attention that the IRS is scandalous. You could be a hero, Jordan!" Janne sounds excited about the prospects.

"I'm *not* the hero type, Janne. I like helping people deal with the IRS on an individual basis. I don't want to try to fight the IRS on a national macro scale. Leave that to the politicians. If that is your thing, great. But it's just not me. Heroes usually end up with the short end of the stick, ultimately. No thanks!" Jordan is adamant about this, and Janne recognizes that perhaps she pushed a sensitive button. "Janne, don't talk to Forbes about this!"

"Oh, Jordan, I wouldn't do that unless you asked me to. It was just a suggestion to perhaps help you gather information. I understand your feelings, and I won't push you to get involved. But please call me tonight," Janne asks in a much more subdued manner.

"I will. Thanks for calling, and I will talk to you later," Jordan says before hanging up. For an instant, the thought that Janne might have a political agenda with this information about the IRS crosses his mind. He trusts that she won't go to Forbes or anyone else unless he thought it would be the best thing to do. At this point, Jordan cannot envision that scenario.

After hanging up, Janne wonders if Jordan's antihero attitude has anything to do with his father dying while at war in Vietnam. Someday she hopes that he will feel comfortable enough and close enough to her to share his feelings in a more profound way.

Jordan packed a suitcase and tossed it in the back of the Bronco before work so that he could go straight to Studio City in the afternoon. He checks in at the Sportsmen's Lodge at 3:30 p.m. He puts on some jeans and a T-shirt to get comfortable while talking with Arthur. They've agreed to meet at 4:00 p.m. in the bar lounge, where Jordan is waiting with a bottle of mineral water at 3:45 p.m. No sense in starting with any alcohol this early and not while chatting with Arthur. He will be as clearheaded as possible.

Arthur walks in at 3:50 p.m. and sees Jordan immediately. They agree that he will check in and be down momentarily to start the conversation.

Arthur sits down across from Jordan in the lounge, where they share a coffee table between them. He maintains his sharp appearance with a dress shirt and slacks but has removed his jacket and tie. He orders a dry martini, and they engage in some quick, pleasant small talk.

"I must admit, Arthur, dealing daily with tax delinquents and the Collection Division of the IRS, I'm not generally blindsided or shocked by anything or any situation. But this guy totally surprised me with his story. I did not see that coming at all," Jordan says with a chuckle.

Arthur returns the chuckle and says, "I hear you. When he came to me, I thought there was probably some truth to what he was suggesting, but I had no idea that it would extend to the level as it now appears."

"I know you want confirmation from me on Royce's allegations, and I intend to provide that. However, let me start by giving you some background on how the IRS operates."

"That would help, I'm sure." Jordan listens with anticipation.

As he takes a sip from his drink, Arthur inhales a deep breath, exhales, and begins speaking in his slow, deliberate manner. "As you know, I was employed by the Internal Revenue Service for thirty years. I actually began my career there under the Kennedy Administration in 1962!"

Jordan raises his eyebrows.

"Hahaha, yeah, I'm that old," Arthur continues. "I will be forever grateful to men like Dr. Martin Luther King, JFK, and many, many others during the civil rights movement, which allowed me to rise within the ranks of the IRS. However, during my long career, I have witnessed many changes and, sadly, a virtual merry-go-round of policies in regard to the tax code and the enforcement thereof.

"In this country, we have the dubious honor of having the most complex tax laws in the world. We can thank or blame, however you want to frame it, the US Congress for that distinction. It is far easier and more powerful to pass a law than to administer it. Congress passes the tax laws, which become part of the Internal Revenue Code. Today, the code has over 2,200 pages! One of the biggest problems is that Congress passes many tax laws for purposes other than raising money to govern the country. There are some purely political reasons for tax laws. Special interest groups that contribute to political campaigns get tax laws passed that are designed to give them special benefits. There are thousands of different interpretations of the code that are not exactly clear as to how the tax law should be applied. Congress has given the IRS the authority to interpret the codes through a series of regulations."

Arthurs pauses and sips from his martini glass and bites off one of the green olives from the plastic toothpick. He continues, "We should always remember that the IRS is the Frankenstein monster created by the United States Congress. But playing Dr. Frankenstein and pumping new juices into the monster is not the solution. It only exacerbates the problem! Congress, in a more perfect scenario, would stop the habitual routine of inserting favors into tax bills."

Arthur stops to make sure Jordan follows the significance of his background lecture of the Internal Revenue Service. "I'm telling you this so that as we discuss what Mr. Dawkins has revealed, you can perhaps see the relevance on a broader scale."

Jordan nods his head. "I'm following you."

"Okay, good." Arthur has his elbows on his knees and leans slightly forward in his chair. "This all brings us to what is currently occurring within the realm of the relationship between Epstein, Levin & Ohlman Tax Consultants and the IRS."

Jordan is ready to hear Arthur's take.

Arthur continues, "I won't rehash what Dawkins told you about the audit that his former company experienced with the IRS and Epstein's group, only in saying that I was not a part of it. My function with E, L & O is strictly that of a consultant in tax codes and how the IRS interprets them. As long as I have been with the service, there have been issues with tax shelters. That is how CPA firms earn their keep in the corporate world. As long as it is legal, I have no problem with corporations nor individuals for that matter, trying to pay as little as possible in taxes."

He makes it clear to Jordan that it is not the manner in which E, L & O did the accounting to minimize personal taxes and increase compensation for the executives of their clientele that has his concern. He reiterates what Dawkins told Jordan, that it is legal and becoming more commonplace in the corporate accounting world.

"What is most concerning to me is whether the IRS and, subsequently, E, L & O are targeting who is audited and whether they are working in conjunction with one another to increase tax revenue and accounting fees. That is highly unethical and illegal."

Arthur continues, "It is also of great concern to me as a consultant to E, L & O as well as the firm that employs you, Jacobs & Goodman, whether these irregular, unethical, and illegal practices are carrying over to the tax resolution business. That would include and possibly involve individuals and small business owners."

Jordan interjects with a question. "How do you think they could be pulling that off?"

Arthur hesitates in answering the question by looking around the bar area and glancing over at the reservation desk. "It is starting to get a little busy here as people are arriving for the weekend. Let's take a walk around the grounds, okay?"

"Sure." Jordan quickly stands and is actually glad for the suggestion. The fresh air and the opportunity to move his limbs is a welcome variation to their current surroundings.

As they walk along the path, it is quite pleasant. There are shade trees on both sides of the concrete walkway, which is wide enough for them to walk side by side. The sun is still shining brightly without a cloud in sight. There is a slight breeze with the temperature in the low eighties on this July summer day. They stop midway across the wooden bridge that crosses the pond. Arthur places his forearms on the wood railing and leans over to let the barrier absorb the weight of his upper body. Jordan mimics his stance, and they gaze down at the fish below, admiring the beauty. Lily pads spread unevenly atop the slightly rippled water, and ducks are swimming peacefully along the pond. At the far end, there is a short three-foot waterfall that descends over rocks into the pond from a stream that extends beyond the boundaries of the hotel complex and serves as a tributary of the LA River, which runs along the River Walk in Studio City.

"It has been in the back of my mind that Alexander Epstein is a man who is difficult to read and not to be completely trusted at his word. He has the air of a person who is accustomed to giving orders and not following them, for probably a very long time."

Jordan nods his head in agreement. "You won't get an argument from me on that."

"When he offered me a position as an independent consultant with flexible hours and time commitment, after consulting with my wife, I decided that it could be quite interesting and fulfilling to work on the consumer and business side of taxation for a change. My wife agreed as long as it wasn't a long-term proposition," Arthur shares with a chuckle.

"The plan was to consult with Epstein's group on corporate tax laws and to help David and Marlin with the tax resolution business that had just begun. I believe you started with them shortly before I came onboard."

"Yes, I started in August of '92," Jordan confirms.

"Well, as you know, I was involved on the IRS side of the policy change in the OIC program. So with that in mind, I have been working on a regular basis with David and Marlin on OICs that result from payroll tax delinquencies, which the IRS takes very seriously. Now listen carefully, Jordan, because this is where I believe you can help me ascertain whether these guys are up to no good."

Jordan nods his head.

"Like I said, the IRS pays close attention to unpaid payroll taxes. It considers them the most serious of all tax debts. Are you familiar with collection activity on payroll taxes?"

"I studied it in preparing for the EA exam, but at J&G, Marlin handles all the payroll tax debt work."

"That's what I thought, as whenever we discuss those cases, your name never comes up, which only makes me more suspicious. Are you familiar with the trust fund recovery penalty?"

"Sure, in theory. But like I said, I have never worked a case involving the trust fund recovery."

"The theory of tax law is that the employer acts as a preliminary collector for the federal government, holding its employees' taxes in 'trust' until it is paid to the IRS. So if the business doesn't pay the amount taken out of the employee's paycheck on time, the IRS views this as illegally borrowing or potentially 'stealing' money from the US Treasury Department. IRS revenue officers take a hard line on payroll tax debt."

"Yeah, that's what I've heard. Also, that it is extremely difficult to get an OIC accepted for an ongoing business that owes payroll taxes."

"The cases that Marlin handles with the help of David, I might add, are the cases that involve defunct businesses. When a business goes under, the IRS transfers the business payroll tax obligation to individuals. They pierce right through an LLC or any corporate shields. This is called the trust fund recovery penalty. The penalty is equal to the amount of taxes owed, so the liability is doubled right away, with interest continuing to compound. The trust fund penalty is transferred in full to any employee of the defunct business that the IRS has deemed as a 'responsible' person. They use a lot of latitude on determining who is responsible."

"Wow, that's hard line!"

"As you can imagine, your company charges premium fees to do an OIC on a trust fund recovery penalty case," Arthur adds.

"I'm sure they do, and I'm sure that is why Marlin works all those cases," Jordan says while shaking his head.

"The thing that has always made me a little curious, but until now I didn't worry much about, is that David and Marlin would take an extraordinary interest in all the responsible persons and then discuss who is the ideal candidate to represent for an OIC submission. I never considered where they received the information on 'all' responsible parties. They would run several scenarios by me. They often execute more than one OIC submission for candidates on the same debt."

"Is that legal?"

"As long as they don't go over the aggregate amount owed on the debt, they can submit as many OICs as they want and can get multiple offers accepted," Arthur answers in a rather matter-of-fact tone.

"So what are you thinking?" Jordan inquires.

"What if they are getting 'hand-fed' these cases by the IRS with a list of all the persons that are deemed responsible parties by the service? That way, J&G 'solicits' the most likely party for an OIC. They get fees and start the collection process for the IRS. David and Marlin are allowed to do as many OICs as they can convince to pay their fees, and eventually, the IRS collects the entire amount by process of elimination. Both the tax resolution firm and the IRS come out winners. Of course, it would be unethical and illegal."

"Do you think this 'feeding' of clients extends to the taxpayers that I deal with?" Jordan asks, somewhat afraid to hear the answer.

"Highly unlikely," Arthur answers immediately. "It wouldn't be worth the effort on the IRS's side to worry about individual taxpayers, and although the penalties and interest are certainly extreme, they don't warrant an effort to hand-feed clients for OIC opportunities."

Jordan is relieved to hear that. Then he asks, "What would you have me do to try to prove your theory?"

Arthur turns to look at Jordan in the face. "First of all, Jordan, I wouldn't ask you to get involved if I didn't think it was in your best interest. However, if my theory is correct, you need to get the hell out of there before they get busted. Even though you aren't directly involved, you are by association, and you do not want to be affiliated with them if they are in bed with the IRS.

"Secondly, I'm sure you want to know from a personal standpoint if the company you work for is ethical and, in the worst case, acting illegally. I had Dawkins come meet you because I wanted you to know whom we are working with and to hear the story of improprieties firsthand. It was his idea to pose as a fictitious client. There might be a point where I would ask you to try to procure information from the CPA firm's database. I can advise you on how, when, and if that is necessary. For now, I will work very discreetly with Mr. Dawkins to try to discover the validity of his theory of E, L & O working in cahoots with the IRS in targeting audits. What I would suggest for you now is to help gather information that would validate my theory of involvement by Jacobs & Goodman. What you discover, if nothing else, can be a 'canary in the coalmine' so that you can exit before the shit hits the fan." Arthur reveals his plan and Jordan's possible motives for involvement.

"You know this is all very surprising and sudden to me, right?" Jordan says as he is still gazing out over the pond.

"It shocked me too. But my plan is to find out what I can over the next few months, then retire by the end of the year. The decision I have to make if I discover this to be true is how I will reveal it to the authorities and to which authorities! But I won't sit on it—that I can assure you. I am not wired that way." Arthur is somewhat amused by his own statement.

After all, to whom do you go to call out the IRS? Congress? They are the creator and protector of the IRS! However, there are two political parties constantly at odds within Congress on the dealings with the IRS. If played right and presented to the correct party at the correct time, it might make a huge impact on the future operations of the IRS. Heads would roll, for sure.

Jordan, on the other hand, is thinking that he is capable of sitting on it if the IRS is in cahoots with Epstein. All it would do to find out is confirm his dislike and distrust of Alexander Epstein. Let others push for indictments and convictions. If David and Marlin are involved in illegal or unethical shenanigans with the IRS, that is a different story. He would certainly "get out of Dodge" as far as his employment. It wouldn't be difficult to find work with another tax resolution firm. They are sprouting up all over LA County these days. He must decide if he wants to be part of this inside investigation of J&G. How would this information affect Tonja, Brookes, and the rest of the staff? Does he want to risk getting fired by snooping around, searching for evidence of wrongdoing? It doesn't seem like the smart thing to do. However, that decision, he feels, would in some way be letting Arthur down.

Jordan turns to face Arthur and looks up to the larger man as he straightens up. "I truly appreciate your confidence and trust in sharing all this with me, Arthur."

"You're a good man with a very bright future in this business, Jordan. You have a genuine interest in helping your clients that I have witnessed. There is no doubt in my mind that you will land on your feet regardless of the outcome. I just thought you should know of my suspicions before I do anything. Whatever you decide to do, you have my support."

"Okay, I will think it over and get back to you soon," Jordan responds.

Arthur, while patting him on the back, says, "Let's go mingle with our group and have an enjoyable time. I have a presentation to give tomorrow morning, and then we will be leaving tomorrow afternoon."

"Sounds good," Jordan says with a smile.

Instead of walking directly back to the bar lounge, Jordan excuses himself to Arthur and continues to walk along the path that winds through the hotel property. As he contemplates about all that he has heard from Arthur and Royce Dawkins, he comes to the realization that Arthur Gibson is risking more than he would be by trying to discover whether or not Alexander Epstein and his CPA firm are in cahoots with the IRS. Like Dawkins, it's not a financial decision for Arthur. He could very easily walk away right now and simply retire with his federal pension and undoubtedly a healthy retirement account.

However, if he does uncover some unethical or illegal behavior on the part of the IRS, then he is willing to try to expose those improprieties to Congress and, in turn, the general public. Which would create a huge scandal on Capitol Hill! Why would he put his entire working career on the line like that? Obviously, he wouldn't, unless he had concrete evidence against them. But still, is it worth it? The only answer Jordan can surmise in his mind is that Arthur Gibson is a man of principle. His honor in serving the country is a matter of justice, not only in his own efforts and actions, but those of the organization that he represented his entire working career. That seems more important to him than his own ease of life in retirement. Jordan has a lot of respect for Arthur Gibson.

He returns to the lounge area. As the happy hour crowd has emerged, Jordan spots some of his work colleagues sitting at a table. He approaches to join them.

"Hey, JD. How are ya?" Andy Gilliam, the TDA from Orange County, jumps up to greet Jordan with a hearty handshake.

"I'm great, Andy. How are you?"

"No complaints. You remember Robert Lopez from the Inland Empire, right?" Andy points to the gentleman sitting next to him. Tonja and Brookes are also seated at the table.

"Of course, we've been in sales meetings together. How are you, Robert?" Jordan says as he shakes his hand.

Andy Gilliam is thirty-eight years old and is a former life insurance and annuity salesman. He is quite outgoing and personable. He has sandy-blond hair and is of average height and build. He loves sports but more as a fan than a participant, although he likes to brag to Jordan that he, too, played football in high school. Robert Lopez is the newest TDA as he was hired last December. He is forty-six and of Latino heritage. Though he has lived his entire adult life in the Riverside area, he is bilingual, which comes in handy in the inland empire (Riverside and San Bernardino Counties).

"Hey, Jordan, where have you been? You left early, and we thought you'd be here, saving a table and wetting your whistle!" Tonja says with a laugh.

"I checked in, changed clothes, and have just been wandering around outside. Beautiful facility and grounds. I walked the entire trail around this place," Jordan explains. "Any sign of the NorCal contingent yet?"

"No. Knowing Sterling, they probably worked a full day before catching a flight. I don't expect them until eight or nine tonight," Tonja states.

"Hey, man, I heard you smoked Epstein's ringers at his basketball tourney at the Final Four," Andy says to Jordan with a huge grin.

"Yeah, it was pretty cool. You should have seen Epstein. He showed up in designer warm-ups and a whistle. He wanted to ref the championship game," Jordan recounts to everyone present with a laugh.

"No way!" says Andy. "Oh, man, I would have loved to see the look on his face when you guys won!"

"Yeah, it was pretty epic."

"Wasn't David there too? Did he rub it into Epstein afterward? I heard those two are pretty competitive," asks Andy.

"No, you know, everyone was very subdued when we won. I think David knew how much Epstein wanted to get his revenge from last year and didn't want to trash-talk his former partner."

"That is awesome. Wish I was there. Congratulations, man." Andy tips his bottle of Budweiser to Jordan.

"Thanks. It did feel good, and we scored corporate suite tickets to UCLA's championship game!"

"Outstanding!" Andy concludes.

The small group discusses the upcoming day of meetings and share some "war stories" about their encounters with tax debt clients. They enjoy laughs, appetizers, and drinks. There's no sign of the NorCal group of employees. They do see David, Marlin, JoJo, Karen, and Vanessa all arrive and check into their rooms. Andy nudges Jordan, winks, and nods toward David and JoJo walking together toward the penthouse suite. Jordan just shakes his head and smiles. Knowing they are required to start the meeting at 8:00 a.m., meaning the breakfast buffet will be available between 7:00 and 7:45, they collectively decide to retire to their respective rooms at 10:00 p.m.

As Jordan enters his room, he suddenly remembers that he hasn't yet called Janne. He speed-dials her number.

"Jordan?"

"Yeah, hi."

"Is everything okay? I've been worried about you!" Janne says with a concerned tone.

"Everything is fine. I'm sorry. After speaking with Arthur, I ran into some employees from OC and the Inland Empire that I hadn't seen in a while. A group of us were just getting caught up down in the lounge area."

"No problem. How did it go with Arthur?" Janne inquires anxiously.

"Fine. He pretty much confirmed what the other guy said. For now, they are just suspicious. There is no concrete evidence of anything illegal."

"What does Arthur want you to do?"

"Nothing on the CPA side of things, which I was glad to hear because, like I said, I wouldn't know where to begin with that."

"And with your company?" Janne feels like she is having to pry things out of him.

"Arthur just has a hunch that David and Marlin could be involved in something irregular. He asked if I would like to try to get some answers." Jordan is trying to downplay the situation. "Honestly, I think it is a long shot that they are mixed up in any foul play with the IRS."

"What did you tell Arthur?"

"I told him that I would think about it and get back to him next week."

"Okay, well, thanks for the update. Have a good meeting. Can I see you sometime on Sunday?"

"Yeah, I would like that. I'll call you when I'm done on Sunday afternoon."

"Sounds good. Take care." As Janne hangs up, she can't help but think that Arthur must have more than a "hunch" to have this guy come meet him and then tell him that the tax resolution firm could be involved.

Why is Jordan downplaying this? she wonders.

Saturday morning is another gorgeous SoCal summer day with brilliant sunshine and temperatures in the seventies and climbing to a forecasted eighty-six by midday. As the employees congregate around the breakfast buffet, Jordan is surprised by a familiar voice from behind.

"Hi, Jordan. Can I bring you some orange juice or coffee?"

He turns around to see Sunshine's bright smiling face. She is wearing a cute off-white sundress with yellow polka dots that has spaghetti straps over the shoulders. She is carrying a tray of the afore-mentioned glasses of orange juice and ceramic cups of coffee.

"Sunshine, what are you doing here?" Jordan asks with a surprised smile.

"David said I could come and help out today. I am part of the front-office staff, you know."

"Cool. But they are asking you to serve?" Jordan inquires with an inquisitive look on his face.

"I don't mind. Where are you going to sit? I'll take your drink there."

"Anywhere is fine. I'll take a glass of orange juice. Thanks," he says with appreciation.

He follows her to an empty table and sits down. Almost immediately, Tricia Sherman leans over his left shoulder and says, "Hey, stud. You're looking good! Guess where I'm staying tonight. Just by chance, I'm in the room right next to you, and I discovered they have an adjoining door between our rooms." She has a seductive-looking smile on her face as she sits down next to him.

"Hey, Tricia. You look nice too," responds Jordan, ignoring the comment about the rooms, although he is positive that it wasn't "by chance." "What time did you guys arrive last night?"

"Oh my god, what a nightmare! Not until almost 11:00 p.m. I don't know why on the weekend *after* the Fourth, there would be so much air traffic. We ended up going into LAX rather than Burbank. Ridiculous, if you ask me!"

Tricia Sherman, born Patricia but long since has legally shortened it because she hated to be called by her childhood nickname, Patty, is a tax attorney who lives in San Francisco. She has a brilliant mind and attended UC Berkeley law school. She worked in corporate tax in Silicon Valley for several years until suffering from an extreme case of burnout. She quit her job and bought a condo in the Marina District of San Francisco.

After about six months of just "playing around" in San Fran and Marin County, she answered an ad from Jacobs & Goodman Tax

Resolutions for a tax manager in their Burlingame office. She interviewed with Sterling Frey. Not overly impressed with the setup and type of work, she declined their offer. David Jacobs then called her personally. She agreed to meet him at the Embarcadero at Pier 39 for lunch. David displayed his typical charm and offered her a position of working in the field, meeting with delinquent taxpayers, articulating the services offered, and then working the cases as a tax manager.

By functioning as both a TDA and a tax manager, he could meet her salary expectations. She has the highest base salary (much to the dismay of Sterling) and the highest overall compensation in the company behind David and Marlin, even though Jordan produces more revenue by at least 30 percent while also working his own cases as a tax manager.

She meets clients three days a week on the seventeenth floor of a business office building just on the other side of the bay bridge in Emeryville, which services the entire east bay area. The executive office suite offers a spectacular view of the San Francisco Bay, downtown San Francisco, and on clear days, you can see Alcatraz Island and the Golden Gate Bridge. The other two days, she has an executive suite in the financial district of San Francisco on Montgomery Street.

She is sharp minded, very professional in her appearance and mannerisms, and quite attractive, which in no doubt enticed David to do whatever he had to in meeting her employment demands. She is thirty-eight years old with shoulder-length dark-brown hair, which she keeps that way with coloring and is combed across her forehead. She has big blue eyes and a strikingly pretty smile. She stays fit and has obviously been artificially endowed in the breasts. She is pleasant and articulate and doesn't come across as pretentious or condescending.

After breakfast, David officially welcomes everyone and goes over the agenda. He then proceeds to give a presentation using a computer generated projection onto a screen in the front of the room. The figures and graphs demonstrate the increase in revenues from month to month and quarter to quarter. He breaks down the revenue into segments: (1) income tax returns, (2) power of attorney retainer fees, (3) installment agreement fees, (4) offer in compromise fees, by far the largest and most lucrative segment of revenue. Before relinquishing the floor to Arthur, David gives a brief explanation of how the OIC program is going to change within a short period of time. He encourages everyone by stating, "This will only change *how* we submit offers but should not impact the *quantity* of offers submitted."

Jordan can't help but wonder why there is no category for trust fund recovery fees that Marlin generates. He has always thought it strange as to how secretive Marlin's work is, and now it seems to be an elephant in the room obvious omission that no one ever questions.

Arthur Gibson is once again the best-dressed person in the room, in full suit and tie. David had expressed in a company-wide memo that these meetings were going to be "business casual" affairs. Arthur only knows one way to dress for a business meeting, particularly one in which he will be a featured speaker. Starting in college, he has always felt he was considered a football player first and a student second. Because of his race, he feels a need to prove himself worthy of the status that he has achieved. He was never going to be the fat, pampered ex-football player and never be considered unprepared nor underdressed for any occasion.

He is an outstanding public speaker. His elocution is perfect. He starts with a light-hearted comment about the irony of holding a tax resolution meeting in a venue that once accommodated Al Capone. That brings the anticipated laughter. Then he goes into his subject matter.

He starts with a brief history. "More than forty years ago, the offer in compromise program was authorized by Congress to give taxpayers a 'fresh start' based on their ability to pay their tax debt. However, for most of this time, relatively few taxpayers were deemed eligible to receive this relief. As you know, all that changed in 1992 when the IRS instituted the friendlier version of the offer in compromise. I was involved as a regional director for the IRS at the time and in working with Mr. David Jacobs." He points over to a smiling David, who nods his head in recognition. "A formula was designed that would be more reasonable in determining a taxpayer's ability to pay, and the IRS Collection Division was encouraged to look at offers more favorably as a method to collect revenue and close cases. Now everyone in this room understands this formula and process as you work with it literally every working day, and I must say you have done an outstanding job of submitting qualified offers. Jacobs & Goodman Tax Resolutions is the number one firm in the nation in OICs accepted. Give yourselves a round of applause." Arthur smiles as everyone claps their hands with smiling self-congratulatory praise.

Andy whistles and shouts, "Yes!"

"However, as with most tax-related programs, there is a sensitive balance mechanism always in play. Congress uses taxation and the IRS as its enforcement arm to generate revenue for the multitude of government programs. So as we have experienced what we call the golden age of the OIC program, there are those that believe the IRS has become too lenient on accepting offers. This translates into the belief that too many delinquent taxpayers are getting offers accepted that should be paying in full over time with more aggressive installment agreements."

Arthur continues, "To help create this balance of OICs, IAs, and paid in full by liquidating assets for delinquent taxpayers, starting in August of this year, the IRS has issued new 'guidelines' in setting standards for various types of expenses allowed. The service has defined three types of necessary expenses: (1) national standards, (2) local standards, and (3) other."

Arthur explains what constitutes national standard expenses, such as food, housekeeping supplies, apparel, and personal hygiene products. A list of the national standards is illuminated on the screen beside him. He pauses to allow people to view the various expense allowances.

"Local standards cover expenses that the IRS concedes are not amenable to determination on a national level. These are housing and transportation." Arthur now shows the local standards rates for Los Angeles County on the screen. He again pauses to allow the audience to view the numbers on the screen. "As you can tell right away, this is going to alter considerably the formula in determining offer amounts and installment payments."

There is collective murmuring in the room.

David stands abruptly and says to the group, "We will demonstrate in our afternoon sessions how this will *not* affect how we do business and how we fully anticipate continuing to submit offers in compromise at the same rate."

Arthur is somewhat taken aback by that statement but does not show it in his demeanor. He continues his presentation. "In wrapping this up, there are expense categories not included under the national or local standards that may be allowable if they are deemed necessary. This 'other' category would include; health care, child care, court ordered payments, any other secured debt or legal fees and possibly miscellaneous expenses that can be open for negotiation. Clearly the secret to effective negotiation will be convincing the IRS that particular expenses are necessary. That is where David and Marlin will be able to help you."

Arthur entertains questions from the group and then they break for fifteen minutes. For the remaining time in the morning session, Brookes Peterson does a fine job of presenting the slight changes that will be occurring in his advertising campaign. After he entertains some questions, the lunch caterers arrive, and the group breaks for an hour-long lunch period. After lunch, Arthur bids all a farewell as he heads for the airport. The afternoon sessions are very informative. In the group that consists of David, Brookes, and the TDAs, it is apparent that David will be insistent on keeping the quota of OICs submitted at the current quantity levels. Brookes has told Jordan previously that David Jacobs doesn't believe in the theory that you 'can't fit a square peg into a round hole.' His methods are to simply file down the edges of the square peg or dig a wider circumference of the round hole. He seems determined to practice that technique with the revised national and local standards set forth by the IRS of allowable expenses.

Jordan has found throughout the day that his mind is wandering in reflection of his conversation with Arthur yesterday afternoon. It does dawn on him that he needs to put pressure on revenue officers with whom he is currently negotiating an OIC. It certainly behooves his clients to get offers accepted before the changes in allowable expenses takes effect.

Dinner and free time follow the meeting schedules. Jordan sits at a table with the other TDAs, including Reed Franklin. Reed is an interesting individual. He is a retired college professor of philosophy at San Jose State University. He met Sterling Frey as a client before Sterling worked for J&G. Franklin had underreported some income from consulting gigs between semesters, which was discovered in an IRS audit. Sterling, who was working independently as a tax consultant, helped him resolve his debt through an installment agreement wherein they were able to get most of the penalties abated. Sterling was impressed with how Reed spoke in such a calming and articulate manner. When Sterling was hired by David Jacobs, who loved Frey's previous connection with the IRS as a revenue agent, he was allowed to interview and hire a staff.

Sterling contacted Reed Franklin to inquire if he would be interested in the tax delinquent advisor position. When Reed heard about the revised OIC program in '92, he was thrilled with the opportunity to present it to delinquent taxpayers, feeling as though he could empathize with the fear they were experiencing. The income potential excited him as well. He has done very well as a TDA in the Burlingame and San Jose offices. He has an excellent relationship with Sterling, a rather frosty relationship with Tricia, but he is well liked and respected by the other TDAs, as well as David and Marlin, each of whom are approximately his age. He also happens to be a big Stanford football fan and loves to engage in college football talk and debates with Jordan. He speaks with so much knowledge about the history and current affairs of Stanford football that Andy assumes that he is a former professor at Stanford. Reed never bothers to correct him.

David has generously allowed a per diem for each employee to cover their dinner, drinks, after-meal goodies, and entertainment.

After dinner, Jordan is walking into the game room. Sunshine runs up from behind, slides her arm through his, and says, "Guess what. I'm spending the night here!" She has a grin on her face.

"Are your parents okay with that?" Jordan asks with a doubtful look.

"Oh, they think I'm spending the night at a friend's house," she responds, still smiling. At least she is being honest.

"Did David agree to get you a room?" Jordan has doubts about that.

"Not exactly." She stops walking and grabs onto his hand. She looks at him rather sheepishly. "I was hoping maybe I could stay in your room."

"Hahaha, I don't think that is a good idea."

"Come on, I won't bug you. We could maybe bring a bottle of wine to your room and watch a movie together until we fall asleep. I brought some really cute PJs!" she suggests hopefully.

"Sunshine, I really like you and think you are a smart, attractive girl. You have a great future. But you are not quite seventeen years old! I could get in a lot of trouble letting you spend the night in my room."

"Ohhhh, okay. But hey, let's play a game of ping-pong. Bet I can beat you! Then let's take a swim in the pool and go in the spa!" She is persistent.

"Hahaha, that I can do, only if you promise to go home by no later than 10:00 p.m."

Jordan sounds like her father, Sunshine thinks.

"Okay, okay. Grab a paddle!"

Jordan would much rather play ping-pong and swim some laps with Sunshine than sit down and participate in the poker game that is being organized by Andy and talk more about the tax business. Robert, Reed, and Sterling join Andy for poker, nachos, and drinks. Jordan figures they will be so engaged for hours.

David, JoJo, Marlin, and Tricia are at the billiards table. Tonja, Karen, Vanessa, Sally, and Brookes are in the lounge next to the live band, which is providing the musical entertainment. They sit together on a couch, enjoy the music and drinks, and Tonja entices Brookes to dance with her. No doubt Karen will retire to her room early. Eventually, Brookes will challenge Tonja to a game of ping-pong and he, too, will retire earlier than the others. Vanessa and Sally engage with the men at the poker table.

Jordan and Sunshine finish swimming laps. She wants to race 200 meters in the 25-meter pool. Jordan wants to only go 100 meters, there and back two times. Sunshine gets her way, and Jordan has to really swim hard in the last 25 meters to overtake her and win by half of his body length. The spa is off in a corner under a couple of palm trees and has a hedge on two sides to ensure privacy. It is relaxing, and the water temperature is 102. It's hot enough to soothe sore muscles but not so hot as to force you to get out after only a short time. Jordan and Sunshine are the only people in the water.

She snuggles up next to him. "There is a lot I want to do and learn before I go away to college, Jordan."

She rests her head on his shoulder. Jordan decides to let her keep it there for now as he senses she is going to open up to him and it will allow him to give her some much-needed advice.

"Don't get me wrong. I'm not stupid, and I know how important getting good grades is. I want to go to a UC school, and they are hard to get into. So far, I have a 4.0 GPA. I'm on the swim team, belong to the drama club, and get along well with my teachers. I'm excited for my senior year."

"That's great!" Jordan remarks as he thinks how she sounds like a much better and more mature student than he was in high school.

"I'd like to get a scholarship to help my parents out and not have to borrow too much in student loans. I'll never be a good enough swimmer for that, so it will have to be in academics."

Jordan is impressed with Sunshine's mature approach until she follows up with…

"But I will only be in high school once. Part of my college preparation needs to include learning how to surf, drink, and have sex." She says this with a smile, grabbing tighter to his arm. "I can't think of anyone I'd rather have teach me these things than you, Jordan Duncan!"

Jordan can't help but laugh. He pauses for a moment, and knowing she is expecting a response, he says, "Sunshine, let me share a few thoughts with you. First, drinking is way overrated. You definitely should wait until college to try it. I can almost guarantee that you will be disappointed. You will experience way more regrets than pleasure from drinking. When you do drink, I suggest you remember one word: *moderation*. I wouldn't say that sex is overrated, but I can say that, sadly, you will also experience more regrets than pleasure in having a sexual relationship too early—more in the form of heartbreak. No matter what anyone tells you otherwise, trust me when I say a sexual relationship changes things between a man and a woman. Unless both are committed to building the relationship, someone will get hurt. More often than not, it's the girl. And it could have lasting emotional consequences."

Jordan takes a deep breath as Sunshine remains silent. "Someday, maybe in college, maybe later, you will meet some lucky guy that will match your enthusiasm for life, your sharp intellect, and your mature outlook. You will be attracted to each other on many levels. More than likely, he will be closer to your age than a nine-year gap."

He nudges her with his shoulder, and she lets out a little laugh. "I think you will know it when it happens. Then you can explore more of yourselves together physically, intellectually, and emotionally and see where it takes you. Until that happens—and it will only happen when you least expect it—enjoy your journey through high school and college. But make wise decisions. You're right. You can only live these times once, but the memories will last forever."

There is a moment of silence between them.

Then Jordan adds, "But I'll tell you what... I will take you surfing."

"You will?" Sunshine perks up. "Cool! I have the most awesome new bikini I want to wear when you take me surfing!"

Jordan laughs out loud. "Sweetie, you have no idea what those waves will do to that bikini. Mother Pacific gobbles up girls' bikinis in her powerful breaks and spits them out. She will totally embarrass you!"

"Oh my gosh..." Sunshine says with a certain amount of anxiety and fear in her tone of voice.

"Don't worry. I have a wetsuit that will fit you." Jordan almost relishes the idea of helping her experience surfing for the first time. "Let's get going. It's after nine thirty. You can shower in my room before going home."

As Jordan helps her climb the steps out of the spa and hands her a towel, she raises herself onto her toes and kisses him on the cheek. "Thank you, Jordan Duncan, for spending this time with me. I can tell you really care about me." She smiles. "You gave me good advice, and it means more coming from you than it would have from anyone else. I truly mean that!"

"No problem. I do really care about you. It would bother me a lot to ever think of you getting hurt. I will let you know a little secret."

Sunshine beams a huge grin. "Okay!" And she turns her ear to his face, thinking that he is going to literally whisper a secret to her.

Jordan obliges her by leaning over and putting his lips right up to her ear. "In a lot of ways, you remind me of my first girlfriend. And that wasn't until I was in college at UCLA."

"Really? See? I knew we had a connection!" she says joyfully and gave him a playful shove. "Someday you will have to tell me about her."

Jordan feels confident that Sunshine has received his message in the proper manner. She won't solicit any drinking or sexual experiences with him and, hopefully, with anyone else for a long time…as long as he takes her surfing. He intends to keep that promise.

Jordan is relaxing while lying on the bed in his room at 11:15 p.m., watching TV in just gym shorts and no shirt, when his cellphone rings. He thinks it is going to be Janne, but to his surprise, Tonja's number shows up.

"Hello."

"Hey, what are you doing?" Tonja asks, sounding wide awake.

"Just lyin' here, watching some boring movie on TV."

"Same here. Can't sleep. Wanna meet me down at the bar?"

"Sure, see ya in a few." As soon as he hangs up, there is a distinct knock on the door between his room and the adjoining room.

Oh no, he thinks as he suddenly remembers who informed him this morning that they were in adjoining rooms.

He walks over to the door and says, "Hello?"

"Open the door, silly," Tricia responds.

Jordan unlocks and opens the door, but no one is standing there. He takes a step into the room and repeats, more as a question. "Hello?"

There she stood in the doorway
I heard the mission bell

Standing a few feet back is Tricia. She looks completely different than Jordan has ever seen her. She has on black lingerie. It is very low-cut in the front, exposing at least three quarters of her breasts. It's strapless and high-cut on the sides, revealing her legs all the way up above her thin hips. The outfit exposes her back and is completed with black fishnet stockings and red stiletto heels. As soon as Jordan takes a step into the room, she advances two steps forward to be right up against him.

And I was thinkin' to myself
'This could be Heaven or this could be Hell'

"Hello, Mr. Duncan. Would you like to join me for some fun this evening?" she says in her most seductive tone of voice.

Jordan attempts to back away, but she has already put her arms around his neck. With five-inch stilettos, she is only an inch shorter than him, and she immediately kisses his cheek and starts nuzzling his neck.

Jordan gently but firmly pushes her back. "Wow, this is quite the seductive scene you've created," he says with a small manufactured chuckle.

"Of course, just for you!" she says as she advances forward again, placing her hands on his bare chest. "You have no idea how much I desire you right now."

As she leans in to kiss him on the mouth, Jordan turns his head and lifts his arms up between them and pushes her back, though not in a rough manner. This time, he grasps onto her arms to hold her in place.

Welcome to the Hotel California
Such a lovely place such a lovely place
Such a lovely face

"This can't happen, Tricia. I'm flattered that you would want to be with me, but I can't do it."

"Why not? Do you think I'm too old for you?" she asks with a pouty look on her face.

Jordan can smell the alcohol on her breath and knows that she is going to regret this scene in the morning.

"No. You are an extremely attractive woman. But I have a girl-friend, and I don't cheat on her," Jordan says without hesitation.

"What? When did this happen? No one has said anything about you being taken. I would have heard. Everyone would be talking about it."

"It's fairly recent, and I haven't told anyone in the office."

"Well then, no one has to know about tonight either. I won't tell anyone," she says again in her seductive tone, although she is getting obviously irritated by not being able to raise her arms. "Let me go."

"I will. Then I will step back into my room, and we will say good night to each other. Okay?"

She has obviously been drinking quite a bit. "I went to all this trouble to get all sexy… You're just going to walk away? It is rare that I would do this for a man. But if I do, I *never* get turned down!" She's still being quite defiant.

"Why don't you call Marlin? I saw you shooting pool with him earlier. Or Andy. I'm sure he would love to spend some time with you."

"Ewwww, Marlin is old enough to be my father. Andy is like thirty-eight going on eighteen intellectually!"

"Hey, like I said, Tricia, you are a gorgeous woman. If circum-stances were different, I'd consider myself very fortunate."

"Really?" she says with a smile forming on her face, but her eyes seem to be drooping.

"Yes. But now I am going to help you get into your bed so that you don't hurt yourself." Jordan can tell that she seems more intoxicated than he originally thought.

He holds her left arm with his left hand and puts his right arm around her back, slowly walking her over to the bed. He sits her on the edge of the bed and takes off her heels. He gently pulls the covers down and lays her back onto the bed, placing the pillow behind her head.

She seems almost asleep now but whispers, "Will you take off these stockings? They are very uncomfortable."

"I think you should keep them on. Good night." Jordan quietly but swiftly leaves the room. He makes sure to lock the door between their rooms.

Welcome to the Hotel California

He throws on a T-shirt, board shorts, and tennis shoes and goes out the front door of his room, heading toward the bar.

"Oh my gosh, I thought you got lost!" Tonja says with eyes wide open as Jordan enters the bar area and sits next to her at the bar.

"Sorry, right after we hung up, I got interrupted."

"Everything okay?"

"Yep. What are you drinking?" Jordan does not want to share the experience he just encountered with Tricia.

"Appletini," Tonja responds, lifting the glass in front of her, which is still about a quarter full.

"Another appletini and a captain and Coke," Jordan calls out to the bartender.

"Glad you showed when you did. I've already had to fend off two lushes," says Tonja, nodding toward two guys at the end of the bar.

"This place certainly lives up to its reputation," Jordan says with a smile.

"It certainly does. Welcome to the Hotel California..." Tonja smiles.

Tonja and Jordan spend the next forty-five minutes talking shop, reviewing the meetings and surmising how these changes within the OIC program might affect their business. Neither is sure how David can expect it to be business as usual in terms of OICs submitted.

They continue nursing their drinks and chatting until suddenly a very distraught JoJo Montanez comes storming into the bar a little after 1:00 a.m. She spots them and plops down in the seat next to Tonja.

She orders a margarita on the rocks with salt and says to Tonja and Jordan, "Dios mio, ese hombre es dificil!"

"Who is that? David?" Tonja inquires.

"Si. David," Jo confirms.

"What did he do?" Jordan asks.

"Well, you know he invited me to stay with him this weekend. I told him I don't think it is such a good idea, with the entire staff here. He says, 'Don't worry. We will be discreet.' He makes me hang out with him all night, shooting pool and playing cards with Marlin and that bitch Tricia. *So* boring!" Jo is visibly upset, but Tonja and Jordan just let her continue, trying not to laugh.

"So tonight he asks me to get ready for bed and that he will be right in. We are in the penthouse suite, so there is a separate living room from the bedroom. The doors are closed, but as I finish getting ready in the bathroom, I hear another voice in the outer room." Jo is being very animated with her hands as she talks. She stops to work on her margarita.

"He *calls* me on my cell phone. I'm right in the next room, but he calls me on the phone! Dios mio! He says that he needs to talk to Marlin for a while, tells me there is some cash in his money clip on the nightstand and that I should take enough to have some drinks at the bar and then bring up a bottle of Chardonnay when he calls me. There is a separate exit from the room through a door in the bedroom to an adjoining room." Jordan knows about those doors. "He asks me to leave that way. Apparently, the next room is Marlin's room. I'm not sure why. As if Marlin doesn't know I'm in there."

"Did he say what was so urgent?" Tonja asks.

"No. But this is what is really weird. I'm *not* going to go down to the bar in my lingerie, right?" They both nod their heads simultaneously. "So I'm changing into something casual." She points to herself. She's wearing fashionable sweatpants, a pullover top, and flip-flops. "As I'm about to leave, I hear a third voice through the door. Who could that be? I put my ear up against the door and realize they have Alexander Epstein on speakerphone. My gosh, it's like 4:00 a.m. back east!"

Jo takes another hard swallow of her margarita, which empties the glass, and she asks the bartender to hit her up with another. Jordan and Tonja refill as well.

She continues, "So now I'm curious. I keep my ear pressed to the crack in the double doors."

As she drinks again, Tonja says, "What did they say?" She wants Jo to finish the story before she gets too drunk.

"Epstein says, 'So are we clear on the need to close the Dawkins case?'"

Jordan almost spits up his drink when he hears the name Dawkins!

"Who is Dawkins?" asks Tonja.

Jo screens all calls and has a phenomenal memory for names. "I don't know any Dawkins. But occasionally, Marlin schedules his own appointments. However, he almost always gives me his calendar. I have never seen the name Dawkins."

Jordan tries to remain calm but needs to hear more. He asks, "Did they say anything more about the case?"

Jo turns to face Jordan and says, "Yeah, David asked Epstein, 'How do you propose we handle that?' I thought it was kind of strange. David usually is the one telling Marlin or anyone else, including Epstein, how they will handle cases."

"What did Epstein say?" asks Tonja.

Jordan is glad that Tonja is taking an interest in this scenario as well. He doesn't want to sound overly interested on his own.

"Epstein just said, 'Do whatever it takes, but we need to terminate it as soon as possible before it goes any further.' That was it. I left before David found out I was still around."

"What are you going to do?" Tonja asks Jo.

"Nothing. David would be very upset if he found out I was eavesdropping on his business conversation. I will just wait for his call, take him the bottle of wine, then screw his brains out. That's what he wants," Jo says as she shakes her head and takes another drink. All of a sudden, she becomes very animated and grabs each of them by the arm. "Promise me, both of you, that you won't say anything to David or anyone else in the office about this!"

Tonja puts her hand over Jo's and says, "Never. I won't even mention the name Dawkins."

Jordan also promises that he won't mention it to David or anyone in the office.

"Okay. Thanks, you guys. I'm so glad that you were down here. I feel better being able to tell someone. I think I am going to get out of this relationship. He will never leave his wife, like he says he will."

JoJo's phone rings. She gets the bottle of wine and heads back to the penthouse.

"Wow," says Tonja to Jordan. "I can't believe David told her he was going to leave his wife. I wonder if that is true."

"Nah. I think a cheating man will say what he needs to in order to keep his fling going. But there will be a price to pay somewhere sometime by someone."

"What do you think this Dawkins case is all about? And why are they talking about it on a Saturday night, uh, Sunday morning at 4:00 a.m. Eastern with Alexander Epstein? Must be something pretty big," Tonja says with a concerned look as she eyes Jordan.

"Yeah. I think we better keep a lid on it like we told Jo we would."

"You're right," Tonja agrees. "But we can talk to each other about it." She smiles.

Jordan smiles and nods his head in agreement.

"Gosh, I'm exhausted now. What an insane place, huh? Didn't I tell you this place is full of drama? A real-life Hotel California…" Tonja exhales.

"You can check out anytime you like, but the memories can never leave." They both say it together as they shake their heads in unison.

"Good night, my dear," Tonja says to Jordan as they give each other a hug, and she kisses him on the cheek.

Jordan says good night and realizes that this is the third woman who has kissed him tonight and not one of them is his girlfriend. There is something strange and mythical about this place.

Everything has changed now, Jordan thinks as he lies in bed wide awake. How do they know about Dawkins? And what does Epstein mean by "terminate" the case? He wonders.

CHAPTER NINE

Summer Heat

The full splendor of southern California summer has arrived in July, especially in the beach towns. Tourists are everywhere. Sunburned shoulders, backs, noses, legs, and arms are ever present as so many people from virtually all over the world descend upon on the beaches and surrounding business establishments. The retail and food venues are in their glory as sales through the summer months carry the bottom line through the remaining year. The local residents more or less put up with the inconvenience of the additional crowds because they, too, look forward to the warmer weather, ideal cool but tolerable water temperature, the money consumed in their community, and the overall energy that the summer brings to SoCal.

Santa Monica and Venice Beach residents are generally health conscious and fitness oriented, which is manifested by the various sporting and athletic equipment, trails, and apparatuses available up and down the coastline that separates them. Amazingly, the skaters, surfers, ballers, and bodybuilders, though very distinctly of different backgrounds, personalities, and ethnic origin, coexist with little conflict. This phenomenon can perhaps be attributed to the simple fact that they are all in love with the common features of the sun, surf, and SoCal vibes that transcend any animosity that might otherwise be present.

The predominant lifestyle attracts many fitness and health enthusiasts to their beaches and boardwalks year around, but the additional throngs of people in the summer months include many that come simply to gawk at others. The energy and upbeat lifestyle, including the music generated, can be quite contagious. Many utilize this exciting modification of the normal doldrums in their life as a welcome deterrent and stress relief. Hopefully, at least for a short period of time, it motivates them to a more active, positive lifestyle and mindset!

The SoCal energy on Sunday night at Chez Jay's is evident as Jordan, Janne, and Al rendezvous once more to discuss the dilemma Jordan faces. It is a little past 10:00 p.m., but it's still rather crowded in the small bar as a nice sea breeze passes through.

"Arthur was very straightforward with me. He believes there are some irregularities and possible illegal activities going on between Epstein's firm and the IRS."

"Does he think that it extends into your local office?" Janne inquires.

"He has a theory about that. I was a little skeptical at first mainly because I didn't think David needs to do anything like that to be successful. We have a thriving, legitimate business model that generates a lot of revenue. However, late last night, something was revealed that has my head spinning!" Jordan declares with much consternation in his voice.

"What's that?" asks Al. Janne also looking on with concern.

"You better take a drink before you hear this," Jordan warns.

Al throws back a long swig of beer, and Janne takes a healthy taste of her glass of wine. Jordan also takes a pull of his bottle of Guinness.

"I told you about the dude who came in the office disguised as a client, right?" Jordan says.

"Yeah. What about him?" inquires Al.

"The name he came in under as he set the appointment was Robert Davis. When he met with me the first time, he informed me that his real name is Royce Dawkins, which Arthur confirmed. I didn't mention that name to anyone, including you guys," Jordan reveals.

"I noticed you referred to him as dude or the guy," Janne confirms.

"Right. That was part of the confidentiality thing. So late last night—actually, it was past midnight—I was sitting at the hotel bar with Tonja, talking about the meetings and the possible implications to the business. In walks JoJo Montanez, the call center manager. I don't know if I ever mentioned it, but she sides as David's mistress."

"My gosh, the office drama you deal with," Janne says while shaking her head.

Al nods and chuckles. "Why does that not surprise me at all, having met the little con man one time at the Final Four?"

"Yeah, but what's shocking is what she revealed to Tonja and I. Now she had obviously been drinking pretty much all night."

"Probably the only way she could stomach being with the creep."

Jordan ignores Little Al's comment and continues, "Visibly distressed that David sent her down to the bar at 1:00 a.m. so that he could have a meeting with Marlin, she sat down at the bar. She proceeded to tell us that as she was getting dressed, she heard another voice in the outer room, where David and Marlin were talking. She pressed her ear to the door and distinctly heard the voice of Epstein on speakerphone."

"Didn't you tell me that he lives back east somewhere?" Janne asks.

"Yes. In Maryland," Jordan continues. "So yeah, at 4:00 a.m. back east, Epstein is on the phone, telling David to close the Dawkins case ASAP. I had never mentioned Dawkins's name to David."

"Wait a second," says Janne as both she and Al raise their eyebrows in unplanned unison. "What did they know about Dawkins?"

"As I told you before, he was the CFO of the firm Epstein represented through an IRS audit. He is no longer with the company, so I don't know what he means by having a 'Dawkins case.' But here is what really got me concerned. Jo kept listening and heard David question Epstein on how he proposed they 'close' the case. Epstein responded that they 'needed to do whatever it takes to terminate it.'" Jordan pauses and takes another swallow of his drink. "That's all that JoJo heard."

"Wow!" Al has littered the floor with peanut shells and stands to make his way to the bar for another round of drinks.

Janne says to him, "Better make mine a beer too." She looks at Jordan for a moment in silence. Then she says, "What do you make of all this?" She has a very perplexed expression on her face.

"I don't know. I didn't sleep much and was a basket case at the final session of meetings this morning."

Little Al returns and passes out the beers. "I gotta say, D-Can, this is getting pretty weird."

"Yeah. The thing that makes me most concerned is his use of the phrase 'Do whatever it takes to terminate.' Does that mean terminate the case or, if necessary, terminate Dawkins?"

"With that bastard, nothing would shock me. Hatred just spews from his eyes and demeanor," remarks Al.

"I only saw him once very briefly, but he seemed evil," adds Janne.

"I tried to call Arthur this afternoon, but he didn't pick up. I left him a message. I wanted to get his opinion. If I don't hear from Arthur, I am going to call Dawkins directly and warn him."

When Al went to the bar, he noticed and acknowledged a couple sitting together. They appeared to be in their early fifties. They nodded to him and smiled. Al saw that the man, who was wearing a denim button-up shirt with the sleeves cut out and a navy-blue bandana, had a tattoo on his shoulder of the Marine Corps logo and motto: "Semper fi," meaning "forever loyal." As the three friends are nursing their drinks for a moment, reflecting on what Jordan just revealed, they see the former Marine walking back from the jukebox... Then the music starts.

I, I wish you could swim
Like the dolphins
Like dolphins can swim

"Oh, David Bowie. I love this song," says Janne with a smile.

I, I will be king

And you, you will be queen
Though nothing will drive them away
We can be heroes just for one day
We can be us just for one day

"So this new info puts things into a whole different perspective for you, doesn't it?" Al asks as he looks at Jordan, beer bottle still in his hand.

And the shame, was on the other side
Oh, we can beat them, forever and ever
Then we could be heroes just for one day

"Yes, it certainly does," Jordan responds with his bottle in hand.

We can be heroes
We can be heroes
We can be heroes just for one day

"What are you going to do?" Janne asks with her beer bottle in hand.

Jordan pauses for a moment, then looks at Al and then at Janne. "I think it's time for me to 'man up' and find out what the hell is going on. I need to help these guys!"

"That a boy! You know we are with you all the way. Whatever you need!" Al raises his bottle to the middle of the table.

"I'm in. Let's do it! We can be heroes," says Janne with a smile and raises her bottle to Al's.

"To us! We can be heroes…just for one day!" Jordan touches his bottle with the other two.

As the three friends walk past the bar on their way out, Al stops and extends his hand to the tattoo guy. "Thanks, man. That was the perfect song at the perfect time."

The man shakes Al's hand and says, "No problem."

His wife says, "You kids looked a little stressed. You look better now."

Janne speaks to the gentleman. "And thank you for your service." She points to his Marine Corps tattoo. "The Marines helped bring me and my family to this country from Saigon in 1975."

"I know. I was there." He returns her smile. "It was time to help put an end to all the suffering. Semper Fi!"

All five of them nod their heads respectfully, say goodbye, and wish one another well.

On Monday morning, July 10, Jordan is driving into the office when his cell phone rings.

"Hello, this is Jordan."

"Hello, Mr. Duncan. This is Arthur Gibson returning your call." Arthur is not sure if Jordan is alone or whether he might be on speakerphone.

Jordan proceeds to tell Arthur about the episode at the Sportsmen's Lodge involving the name drop of Dawkins. Arthur is also surprised and perplexed as to how those three would be intertwined with Royce Dawkins. He remains calm and tells Jordan that he will contact Dawkins. He advises Jordan to not say anything at the office to anyone. Jordan agrees and tells Arthur that he has thought more about what he shared and is willing to help in any way necessary. Arthur is pleased to have his commitment and says that he will call him after speaking to Dawkins.

Jordan knows that he needs to expedite the Williamson OIC. He calls Bobbi Sinclair, saying, "Hey, Bobbi, Jordan Duncan here."

He has a good working relationship with her as they extend mutual respect. He has an inclination to go to her more often; as the branch chief, she is technically over Jack Arbuckle. However, he is not clear as to how the hierarchy works within the Los Angeles District. So he chooses his battles on when to include Bobbi as it pertains to Jack's brazen authoritative methods on taxpayers. Generally, Jordan deals with Jack one on one. He figures that he would lose any leverage he might have in negotiating if he tried to constantly go over his head. Besides, the IRS gives an overabundant amount of power to revenue officers in making collection decisions.

"Hey, Jordan, how are you?" Bobbi always sounds upbeat and genuinely happy to hear from him. That is rare when calling an RO of the IRS.

"I'm good. Just wanted to touch base with you on a couple of cases. Where are we on the Williamson OIC? And what is the latest progress on the Alice Johnston innocent spouse relief?"

"Well, on the Williamson case, I am having a hard time justifying a $3,000 offer. It is our policy here to never accept an offer for less than $5,000."

Jordan has done some homework on this and says, "Is it your office protocol, or is it an official IRS policy to not accept offers less than $5,000? Because protocols can have exceptions, and I think you will agree that the numbers indicate that a $3,000 offer is warranted."

"My gosh, listen to you… For a young guy, you certainly have progressed rapidly in this position!" Bobbi says with a chuckle. "Technically, there is no official IRS policy on the amount of an offer. As you know, we follow a formula to determine the collectability potential. There are times, however, wherein the formula spits out a zero or even a negative number. So to make it worthwhile, we have set the $5,000 benchmark as the number that makes it worth our time in working the case. I guess there can be exceptions if justified. Let me look it over again and consider your offer more closely."

"I appreciate that, Bobbi. Maybe if you came to their residence and viewed firsthand how they live, it might help you justify accepting their $3,000 offer. I'm telling you—it is a hardship case."

"I will take your word on that, Jordan. It would only drive my cost on this case higher if I was to make a field visit. I will take a close look and get back to you before the end of the month. Now as far as the innocent spouse for Alice Johnston, that is more complicated," Bobbi continues. "As previously noted, we have to examine to what degree she benefitted from the underpaid taxes. I understand there was a substantial down-payment made on their place of residence, which was purchased during the time period in question."

"Yes, but I have submitted all her expenses associated with starting her day care business. Those costs offset her half of the down-payment."

"That will have to be determined. Unfortunately, when we place a case in a status 53, it goes to the bottom of the pile of priority cases. Technically, it is buried in a 53 for a year," Bobbi says apologetically.

"One of Jack's little tricks, huh? Unbelievable. That guy is like a pit bull. Just doesn't know when to let go of a case. I thought it was IRS policy to close cases with expediency," Jordan counters.

"Using your terminology, Mr. Duncan, that is more of a protocol than an official IRS policy, and there are exceptions. Innocent spouse relief cases are an exception to the rule of quick case closure."

"Okay, Bobbi. I will tell Alice to continue running her day care and not worry about collections for the time being. You don't have to wait a year, right?"

"That's right. I will revisit the Williamson case and get back to you and see what I can do in prodding Mr. Arbuckle along on the Johnston case. Nice chatting with you, Jordan."

"Likewise, Bobbi. Take care."

The office phone line rings.

"Hey, Vanessa, what's up?" Jordan answers.

"Call for you on line 2. Sorry, she wouldn't give a name."

"No problem. Thanks." Jordan pushes the line 2 button. "Jordan Duncan."

"Hello, Jordan, this is Tricia Sherman."

"Hi. How are you? Get back home okay?" Jordan asks in a pleasant tone.

"Other than feeling like a complete fool and probably still a little hungover, I'm fine. Just wanted to call and apologize for my behavior Saturday night. That was quite inappropriate and out of character for me."

"Don't worry about it. No harm, no foul," Jordan says, trying to keep the mood light.

"I appreciate you saying that. Obviously, I drank way too much that night and came on very strong. Thank you for handling the situation with class and tact. I'm hoping that you haven't shared what happened with anyone else in the company," Tricia says with a hint of hope in her voice.

"No, not at all," Jordan conveys with a blithesome tone.

"Thank you. You are a real sweetheart of a guy, you know? If you weren't so dang *hot*, I would just treat you like a younger brother!" Tricia says while starting to laugh. Jordan joins in her laughter.

"I have a lot of respect for you, Tricia, and I appreciate all that you have taught me about tax law. Jacobs & Goodman Tax Resolution is fortunate to have you onboard," he says with sincerity.

"Thank you, Jordan. Take care, and let me know if you have any tax questions that I can help you with." She sounds relieved as she hangs up.

On Monday, July 24, Jordan has not heard anything from Arthur other than to let things simmer down while he and Dawkins try and figure out how Epstein, David, and Marlin caught wind that Dawkins might be a threat to them. Royce Dawkins is keeping a low profile and decided to take a two-week vacation to Europe with his wife. Arthur is keeping a low profile with E, L & O. He currently is consulting on the affairs of the IRS as to how the national and local standards are going to be rolled out and the effects it will have on the Collection Division's activities.

Jimmy Delgado comes to the Sherman Oaks office to meet with Jordan to discuss his financials. As he enters Jordan's office, JoJo comes out of the call center.

"Ooh la la, what have we here? *Como te llamas bella dama?*" Delgado inquires.

"JoJo Montanez, *y tu?*"

"Jimmy Delgado. *Noto un ligero acento. Peruano?*"

"Si. Naci en Peru. Ahora soy ciudadana de Estados Unidos."

"Muy bien. Una princesa Inca. Yo soy de los Guerreros Aztecas de Mexico."

JoJo laughs. "Un placer conocerte, Senor Delgado."

"El placer es mio. Por favor llamame Jimmy." Delgado takes Jo's extended hand in his, raises it to his mouth, and kisses it softly while bowing at the waist.

Jo smiles as he releases her hand and says, "Me puedes llamar Jo." Jo is taken by Jimmy's charm and handsome features and is actually impressed by his self-reference as an Aztec.

Jordan is sitting at his desk while this impromptu conversation takes place just outside his office door. "Jimmy, come on in, let's get started."

As Delgado enters the office, Jordan says, "Shut the door behind you."

Delgado shuts the door and sits down. "My goodness vato, why didn't you tell me about JoJo when we first met? Were you saving her as a bonus after you resolve my tax case?" Jimmy Delgado is beaming with his ear-to-ear smile.

"Jimmy, she is off-limits to you. Already taken!" Jordan replies sternly.

"Oh, you mean you and her are already..." Jimmy makes some gesture with his hands that Jordan has never seen but whose interpretation he has no interest in hearing.

"No. She is the mistress of the president of this firm. And that needs to remain confidential. Understand?" Jordan's expression remains serious. "I'm not joking about this."

"Hahaha, you telling me that old sourpuss dude I met, Marlin what's-his-name, is banging that?" Delgado is laughing out loud.

"No. His partner, David Jacobs, the true head honcho around here, is in a relationship with her...discreetly!"

"Can't be that discreet if you know about it. I don't see no ring on her finger. Seems to me she's free game!"

Jordan can tell, Delgado is going to be a real handful in certain circumstances.

"I'm telling you, Jimmy, if you want me to represent you and give you the best chance of escaping this huge tax liability, you need to adhere to my advice. And as it pertains to JoJo Montanez, don't try to get involved. Clear?"

Delgado can tell that Jordan is not messing around. "Si, si, okay, vato. I was just messing with you. But I must say, if I had a girlfriend like that, whether it was discreet or not, I would slap a big diamond ring on her finger to claim my territory, *lo comprende?*"

"That's between them. None of my business. Nor yours. Let's talk about your tax case." Jordan changes the subject. "Like I told you, this is all going to come down to numbers. I've received a copy of your audit. A colleague of mine, Karen Wallach, is going to review it very closely. In the meantime, you and I need to discuss your current financial situation. It is critical that you be completely honest with me. I don't like surprises later in the case that the IRS might spring on me that you withheld in conjunction to your personal assets or income statement. All right? Are we clear on that?" Jordan feels the need to be extremely straightforward with Jimmy. He senses that Delgado will respect that approach and it will entice him to also be forthcoming with his financial information.

"Fire away. I am an open book to you, amigo, as long as I know that you are acting in my best interest. Like I told you before, I am a good judge of character, and I trust you, Jordan. Just don't betray that trust, and we will work well together." The smiling face and joking attitude have left Delgado's demeanor, for which Jordan is grateful.

"I have an appraisal of your home and your mortgage payments. You also have a rental in San Diego County that appears to have a slightly negative cash flow when you take into account the property taxes you pay. Is this the latest balance sheet and income statement from your accountant?"

"Yes. That was through the second quarter of this year," Delgado responds.

"Let's talk about this mysterious boat of yours that Jack Arbuckle seems so intent on seizing. There appears to be a huge discrepancy on the purchase price and actual current value. Tell me about it." Jordan raises his eyes from the documents on his desk and looks directly at Delgado.

"That revenue officer is crazy. First of all, I bought the boat on a distressed value sale. An auction. You know what a distress sale is?"

"Sure, like a foreclosure sale on a real estate property," Jordan replies.

"Right. You see, like I told you before, my uncle works at the Long Beach Harbor, and I used to help him out, cleaning and doing minor repairs on the boats docked there. I developed a love for boats and particularly sailboats. After I left the docks and I started making *mucho dinero*, I told my uncle to keep his eyes open for some good deals. A few years ago, 1992, he calls me and says there is a dude at the harbor that is falling behind on his payments for a sweet 1990 Catalina 42. One of the most 'cherry' sailboats around! So I check it out and go to the auction. I got a number in my head, but I don't think it will be enough. Next thing you know, I've got me a forty-two-foot sailboat!"

Delgado's smile is back as he relates this story. Jordan senses that Delgado never goes too long before flashing his ever present joie de vivre.

Delgado continues, "Later, in 1994, I get audited, and they include an excise tax on my boat. They listed the value at over $100,000, which might have been correct when it was new or if I bought it at full value. I only paid $74K." He is shaking his head in disbelief.

Jordan is familiar with the short-term, ill-advised attempt at a "luxury excise tax" the IRS instituted in 1991. It was such a disaster, having an adverse effect on the boating and aircraft industries, that it was discontinued after 1992. In an effort to "soak the rich," Congress passed a bill to exercise a 10 percent tariff on what were considered luxury items, such as airplanes that cost over $250,000 or boats priced over $100,000.

However, the largest effect wasn't on the rich, as they just spent their money elsewhere, but on the boat and aircraft manufacturing industries. Even though the luxury tax was in existence for only two years, it had devastating consequences to the boating industry in particular. Many people lost jobs, and they certainly weren't among the rich. Consequently, the tax only brought in a mere fraction of the losses occurred in the $12 billion boat industry.

"Where is the boat now?" Jordan asks.

"My uncle has a client at the Long Beach Harbor, who owns an additional boat slip out on Catalina Island. We got it covered in his slot there. I don't think the IRS will find it."

"Good. Leave it there until we get this mess settled," Jordan advises.

"Karen will crunch the numbers on the audit. I will make sure to point out to her what you just told me. Are there any other assets that you have not listed here? Transparency is of utmost importance."

Jimmy Delgado is silent for what seems to be nearly thirty seconds—a rarity on its own but also a reflection that he is once again weighing his trust meter on Jordan. "There was an incident. A little over ten years ago, I was asked to do a job in Mexico. The detailed circumstances were not made clear to me at the time, but the job paid very well. I performed the task and was paid in gold bars. I didn't know what to do with that, as I had no idea how to convert them into cash in this country or even in Mexico. So I gave them to a *compadre* in Mexico and asked him to stash them for me until I could figure out a way to convert it to cash and bring it to El Norte. They remain in Mexico, and I have not touched them in over ten years." Delgado relates that story unblinkingly, staring directly into Jordan's eyes. He is trying to gauge what kind of reaction his newfound compadre will have upon learning of this most unusual declaration.

Jordan tries to ascertain whether he heard the correct version and how much was omitted of this unexpected, extraordinary tale.

"Did this task have anything to do with drug dealing or anything with illegal drugs?" Jordan is thinking of the DEA investigation.

"No, not at all."

"Have you ever brought any of the gold into the United States?"

"No. Never." Delgado remains steadfast in his story.

"Have you ever declared ownership or listed the gold as assets or collateral on any type of paperwork or loan application?"

"No. Never."

"So in your opinion, is there any paper trail that can link you to these gold bars? Perhaps a written agreement with your colleague in Mexico?"

"Just a handshake. He is a very good, trustworthy compadre. My cousin."

Jordan pauses again, slowly shaking his head, and runs his fingers through his hair before speaking. "I have never asked a client to lie to the IRS. It can have severe ramifications for the taxpayer but also for my career. I am not going to ask you to lie now. If the IRS ever inquires about this, I advise you to tell them the truth. However, for the sake of our case involving your current tax situation, I don't see the relevance of bringing this information forth. The bars never came into the US. I advise you to never mention it again. I appreciate your honesty in sharing the information with me as it helps build my trust in you. But moving forward, let's not discuss this issue again. Agreed?" Jordan purposely does not inquire as to the perceived value of the gold bars.

"One hundred percent agree, vato!" The smile is back as Jimmy extends his hand. The Taxman and the Aztec shake hands. A unique and perhaps long-lasting relationship has been formed.

At a little after 5:00 p.m., Tonja comes into Jordan's office as he is winding down his workday, and she sits down. "DJ wants to see you. He knows you met with Delgado today, but he hasn't asked me anything about that case. However, he did ask about Robert Davis. You remember that weirdo that came in without letting anyone know who referred him?"

"Yeah, I remember. What did you tell him?"

"Nothing… There was nothing to tell. I just said that you met with him, and as far as I know, the guy never came back."

"Good. I will find out what he wants," Jordan says.

"Have you heard anything more about a Dawkins case?" Tonja inquires before he leaves the room. Jordan stops and turns toward her.

"No. Nothing. Have you?"

"Nothing at all. Are you going to ask David about it?"

"Not unless he brings it up. We told Jo that we wouldn't." Jordan can't imagine David bringing up the name Dawkins, although he is curious as to why, a month later, he asks about Robert Davis.

Does he know that they are one and the same? he wonders.

"The whole thing is just so weird. Jo was pretty drunk that night. Maybe she just misheard some things," Tonja says in a confused manner.

"My experience with people who drink too much is that it acts more like a truth serum than anything else," Jordan comments.

"That's true. Well, good luck, and let me know how it goes."

"Thanks. Will do," Jordan says as he steps out the door of his office and begins the trek down to the end of the hall, where David is waiting in his sitting area with a glass of brandy next to him on the end table.

"Hi. You wanted to see me?" says Jordan as he sticks his head in the door.

"Yes, come in, Jordan, and have a seat," David greets him while pointing to the couch, which has a coffee table in front of it. David is sitting on a cushioned chair across the couch. "Would you care for a drink?"

"A bottle of water would be nice," Jordan replies.

David stands and walks to the small refrigerator, pulls out a bottle of water, and hands it to him.

"Thank you. What's up?"

"I understand Mr. Delgado came in today. How is that case progressing?"

"Yes. We went over his financial documents, and I let him know that Karen is reviewing his audit. All is well. I haven't heard anything from the CID. Have you?" Jordan turns the question back to David. He has a feeling that this is just an icebreaker for what David really wants to discuss.

"No. But I don't expect to. Your name is listed on the POA as the contact person representing our firm. So that would come through you, and then you can notify me."

"I will as soon as I hear anything."

"Any chance of an OIC with Delgado?" David asks, sipping his brandy.

"Not sure. It is a large liability amount, but there seems to be some discrepancy on the value of his assets." Jordan recaps the case to David.

"Okay. Just keep me in the loop. Big dollar case."

David changes the subject. "What do you know about a Robert Davis?"

Okay, here we go, thinks Jordan. This conversation will be critical in the Dawkins case for sure.

"Not much. He came in about a month ago, specifically requesting to meet with me. Didn't give any info on his tax debt, so I was going in blind. Before he would answer any questions from me, he asked if I would answer some questions. It had all the markings of an IRS setup. Since it was just after I had met Delgado, I was pretty sure that was the case."

David interrupts, "You know that the CID has to announce themselves. Why didn't you come and get me?"

"I didn't think it was the CID. I just thought it was the Collection Division shopping me. The guy asked questions about how long I have been with the firm and about my credentials. I answered his questions, but he remained vague about his liability, so I told him that the best I could do would be negotiate an IA and that our fee would be around two grand."

"That's it? Did you meet with him again?" David asks suspiciously.

David just showed his hand in Jordan's mind. If he had asked if he talked to him again, then perhaps he didn't know any more. However, if there was another meeting in the office, Tonja would know about it. He obviously asked Tonja. Jordan is pretty sure David knows they met the next day at the Galleria. He decides to play it straight.

"Actually, he was acting strange, looking around like he thought my office was bugged. He asked if we could meet somewhere outside of the office. I didn't want to waste a lot of time with this guy, but I wanted to be cooperative with the IRS. So I told him that I would meet him at the Galleria the next day at lunchtime."

"That is highly irregular, Jordan. Why didn't you tell me about this?" David is starting to sound a little irritated.

"You were not in the office that day. Besides, since when do I need to come to you on everything? I feel like you are wanting to micromanage me lately. What's up with that?" Jordan decides to turn the tables and show some assertiveness that few do when interacting with David. But he refuses to be bullied.

David takes a longer drink from his glass of brandy and, in fact, finishes it. He reaches for the bottle and pours himself another round. The silence in the room is deafening to Jordan; however, he is determined not to be the one to break it. He takes a drink of water.

David looks at Jordan and continues to pause before speaking. "You know, Jordan, I really like you. I always have. And not just because you played football at UCLA or because you have become quite adept at your job. You are my number one revenue producer. But mostly, it's because I believe you are a good person. You have integrity, and you have been a loyal, hard-working employee. I have rewarded you well, as I do all my employees that produce excellent results. We have a successful business that benefits many delinquent taxpayers with a fresh start. It is a very fulfilling industry with a win-win scenario. Wouldn't you agree?" David is going with the soft approach as he realizes that Jordan isn't easily intimidated.

"Yes, I would agree with that assessment," Jordan replies calmly.

"Okay. I want you to listen very closely as this is extremely serious." David leans forward, and with his elbows on his knees, he looks directly into Jordan's eyes and says, "I know that Robert Davis came in here under false pretenses. His real name is Royce Dawkins. I don't know exactly why he came to see you, and I don't know exactly what he told you. But I am going to tell you what I do know about him..." David pauses for effect and to see if Jordan will deny or confirm anything. Jordan remains silent and waits for David to continue.

"Royce Dawkins is a disgruntled ex-employee of a firm that Epstein, Levin & Ohlman Tax Consultants represented at an IRS audit. Dawkins was their CFO at the time of the audit. When it was discovered during the audit that he wasn't doing a very good job, the company subsequently let him go. Although they offered him a generous severance package, he decided to try to fight them. He went to the company's legal team and was advised to take the severance because there was no case of unlawful termination. He just can't seem to let it go. He contacted Arthur Gibson and then came all the way out here to meet with you. None of us can figure out what he is up to at this point, but believe me, Alexander will find out, and Dawkins could very well end up behind bars." David again pauses to allow Jordan to respond.

This time, Jordan does respond. "I don't understand how all this involves me." Now Jordan is baiting David for more information.

"Well, either you are playing dumb as to what Dawkins shared with you or Dawkins is simply trying to find a weak link wherein he can try to inflict some kind of revenge on Epstein. Honestly, I don't know at this point. However, I am going to be straight with you, son."

Seriously, he is calling me son? Jordan ponders.

"Both Alex and Marlin think we should terminate you immediately for disloyalty. However, I feel like I need you now more than ever. We are entering a period of much more difficulty in our business model. For the past three years, offers in compromise have been gravy. I found the right advertising guy that makes the phone ring constantly with eager tax delinquents. These are basically lay-down cases for the TDAs. Everyone has made good money. Quite honestly, you, Tricia, and Marlin are the only employees that I trust moving forward, as it will take much more skill in salesmanship and negotiating to bring in the same revenue. Up until now, Marlin has handled all our payroll tax clients and large liabilities of over $100K. I am willing to let you handle many of the large liability cases and just keep Marlin on the payroll tax cases. Those are a specialty group with which Marlin has substantial experience. Your commission income will increase considerably with these high-liability cases, such as Delgado." Jordan can't help but think about Arthur's theory of how Marlin and David handle payroll tax cases. This only confirms to Jordan that he could be right on track. David is obviously waiting for a response.

"Disloyalty? Why? Because I beat Epstein's ringers in his personal basketball tournament? Because I got a $10,000 fee from a client that Marlin had kicked to the curb? Sounds to me like you have a couple of disgruntled partners."

"Man, Marlin was right. You just will not be intimidated or controlled." David takes another sip of brandy. "I'm not trying to intimidate you. Just work with me, son."

A thought immediately comes to Jordan: *If he calls me son one more time, I might get up, punch him in his big nose, and walk out of here for good.*

However, his cool demeanor takes control of his thoughts. He realizes David is setting him up nicely to get in closer and find out the real scoop as to what is going on. He remains silent to let David finish his proposal.

"Just stay out of Epstein's business. Don't talk anymore to this Dawkins character, as he has nothing to do with our resolution business. You have a good life, Jordan. Let's keep it that way. What do you say?"

"I have a couple of questions."

"Go ahead," David responds.

"How did Epstein figure out that Robert Davis came to see me and that he was, in truth, Royce Dawkins?" Jordan is perplexed by this question.

"Because I trust that you are going to continue to work with me and be very productive, I am going to level with you."

David doesn't level with many people, Jordan surmises.

"When Dawkins didn't take the severance, even after he was told that he had no unlawful termination case, Alex concluded that this guy could be trouble—if nothing else, in racking up attorney fees for E, L & O. So Epstein had him tailed by a private investigator." David continues, "He followed Dawkins to Arthur then out here. Alexander is about ready to put an end to it by pressing charges of harassment if Dawkins doesn't cease and desist immediately."

"Was the PI his personal lapdog Turlock?"

"Be careful, Jordan. These guys can be dangerous," David warns.

"Second question: what does Arthur have to do with all this?"

"Nothing to my knowledge. Epstein is talking to him as I talk to you. I'm sure Arthur will also agree to not speak anymore with Dawkins."

"You are a smart kid, Jordan. Just don't try to get too smart for your own good. Stick with me. Stay away from Epstein's business. Don't worry about Marlin. He knows how I feel about you, and he has seen you in action. He doesn't want to admit it, but he knows you are a key component to the success of our tax resolution business. Do we have a deal?" David stands and, with his hand extended, walks over to Jordan.

Jordan stands and says, "Sure." He shakes David's hand. David smiles as he grasps Jordan's hand with his left hand as well.

"One last question for you. What's going on with you and Sunshine? I saw you in the pool with her at the hotel."

"Hahaha, nothing. We are just friends and work associates. I didn't want to sit and play poker all night, and she asked me to go for a swim. Seemed like a good idea."

"Okay. I am good friends with her parents. So naturally I kind of keep an eye on her when I can."

Yeah, sure, Jordan thinks, *when you aren't too wrapped up with your mistress.*

Jordan leaves the room.

CHAPTER TEN

Game Plan

During a tension- and turmoil-filled year, any good news is greatly appreciated. Such was the case at 4:30 p.m. on Friday, July 28, when Jordan received a phone call from Bobbi Sinclair. In her typical enthusiastic manner, she informed him that the Williamson offer in compromise of $3,000 was accepted and that when it is paid, the case will be closed! She reviewed the conditions with him and faxed the acceptance letter to the J&G office. Jordan thanked Bobbi, waited for the fax to be transmitted, and then took off immediately to hand-deliver the letter to the Williamsons.

The reception at the Williamson apartment was one of great joy, relief, and satisfaction. Jordan explained that with the offer amount needed to be paid within thirty days, they would not be entitled to a refund for the current year (for which they would not qualify anyway), and they must stay current with their filing and tax payments for the next five years. They agreed that they could and would do that. Jordan had instructed Tio to cash and save his paychecks from the Pacific Coast Bike Tours in order to pay the offer amount. He had done so and was enthusiastically ready to hand over the cash to his parents to be finished with this tax albatross, which had been weighing down the entire family.

There were hugs and tears as Irma, Tyrone, and Tio all thanked Jordan and the good Lord for their delivery from this huge source of anxiety and stress. Jordan made assurances that he would guide them through the payment process and bring them the final release of liability statement.

Outside the apartment door as he was leaving, Tio said to him, "Taxman, you did it. I will never forget this, man."

Jordan smiled and said, "You've been blessed with extraordinary parents. Take care of them as they have done to you."

Jordan was able to talk with Arthur briefly after they had met with David and Alexander respectively. They agreed that it would not be wise to speak on the phone about anything relevant to Dawkins. Arthur would purchase a new phone, and Jordan gave him Janne's number.

Janne had arranged for Jordan to speak to her father, John Sawyer, on her phone. After a lengthy conversation, in which Jordan was able to ascertain that John might be an asset to them, he arranged to meet with him in person at his ranch in Yosemite Valley. They decided that it might also serve a good purpose to invite Arthur, Al, and Janne to meet as well. It was imperative that they have an out-of-the-way, discreet location wherein they could all meet and discuss the current status of what each knew and what they could accomplish moving forward.

August 15 is the deadline for tax filing extensions. Jordan had all of his clients already filed, so with the rest of the office helping Karen accumulate financial information for filings, it was a good time for Jordan to schedule a vacation. Typically, much like after April 15, the tax resolution business picks up after August 15. The 15th also happens to be Jordan's twenty-sixth birthday. So he cleared it with Tonja and David that he would take two weeks off, from August 7 to 20. He and Janne are going to take a road trip up to Yosemite Valley to meet John Sawyer and then back down the coast. They arranged the meeting with John, Arthur, and Al for Wednesday, August 9.

John runs a hiking/backpacking/camping tour guide business on the backside of Yosemite National Park. His participating partner is Peter Marshall, whom he met and served with in Vietnam. Pete owns a helicopter, which is also used in the business to transport serious outdoors enthusiasts to remote areas wherein they must utilize expert trekking, hiking, and climbing skills to traverse back to the home base.

The partners, along with a third nonparticipating partner, own a 6-bedroom, 4 ½ bath, 4,500 sq. ft. cabin, where they offer lodging and meals during the busy spring, summer, and early fall months. They are also opened during the winter for weekends only. At the ranch, they have a barn where they house 6 horses and a couple of pack mules to assist in their guided tours. During the summer months, they open an area for tent camping, and Pete will often stay in a trailer parked permanently on the property to allow for more guests.

Pete flies to Lake Tahoe periodically, where he picks up some fares flying high rollers in from the surrounding areas to casinos on the Nevada side of Tahoe or skiers at Squaw Valley on the California side. Much of their wilderness trek clientele comes from the source of these high rollers. Even though it is one of the busiest times of the year, John was able to secure rooms for Jordan, Al, Arthur, and Janne. They will stay Tuesday and Wednesday nights, with Wednesday reserved for them to discuss the game plan to expose the CPA firm working with the IRS. Al and Arthur are flying into Sacramento airport on Tuesday, and Pete will pick them up in his chopper. They will leave Thursday morning.

Jordan and Janne leave on Monday after the commute traffic taking the 405 and then merging onto the 5 northbound just south of Santa Clarita. After crossing over the grapevine, they take Highway 99 toward Bakersfield and Fresno. Monday night is spent in a hotel in Fresno. That leaves them just about two hours to finish the trip Tuesday morning. There will be plenty of time to visit with John before Al and Arthur arrive for dinner.

The conversation between Jordan and Janne on the first day of their journey is primarily focused on Jordan's work, the Dawkins situation, and the Forbes presidential campaign, which has absorbed most of Janne's time and energy.

As they finish the continental breakfast at the hotel and begin their drive to Yosemite Valley, Jordan asks Janne, "So how did your dad end up running an outdoor wilderness camp?"

"He has really been 'off the grid,' so to speak ever since he brought my mom and me to the United States at the end of the Vietnam War." Janne begins the backstory of her father's journey to the Yosemite Valley. "Because of the circumstances, which I'm sure he will explain to you better than I can, by the time we arrived in the US, he had to face military court. Luckily, with the help of two decorated servicemen who testified on his behalf, he was able to avoid any prison time. However, he was dishonorably discharged from the military and found work difficult to find. So he took us to his hometown of Sonoma. He got a job working on a ranch while he enrolled at Sonoma State University. My mom got quite sick, and soon after he graduated college, she passed away. My dad was very angry after my mom died. He and I moved to the Yosemite Valley when I was ten. We lived in a mobile home, and he homeschooled me while he took a job as a park maintenance worker inside Yosemite National Park."

Janne stopped talking, and there was silence for a couple of minutes as Jordan sensed that she had more of the story to tell. "I did attend public high school, and after I graduated, I received an academic scholarship to UCLA. My dad started taking night courses toward a law degree. It took him several years, but he got his law degree from San Joaquin College so that he could defend people in tax court."

Janne turns to Jordan, smiles, and takes his free hand into hers. She continues, "His first client and only client so far, I believe, was one of the guys who testified on his behalf in the military court, Peter Marshall. He is also his business partner, whom you will meet. He will tell you how they started the business with a third partner, who only shows up occasionally."

Jordan is interested in hearing about her father's history but wants to know more about what happened to her mother. "So you said your mom got really sick and passed away. What happened, if you don't mind me asking?"

"My mom lived in a small village in South Vietnam near the northern border not far from an area that was sprayed by the US military with Agent Orange. Though it was documented that the chemicals would only kill plant life, well, you probably know by now that it didn't turn out to be the case. It wasn't until we moved to the United States that she began to have problems with her blood cells that ultimately was diagnosed as lymphoma, from which she never recovered."

Janne takes a deep breath and then continues, "My dad has deep-rooted resentment over that war and the ramifications thereof. However, like I told you before, he always says that he has no regrets of going there, because he found my mom and they had me." She smiles again and squeezes Jordan's hand.

"Yeah, that is certainly understandable." Jordan empathizes with Janne for the loss of her mother.

The layout at the ranch is stunning. The turnoff from Highway 140 is a dirt road, and the location is on the backside of El Capitan, which is within the Yosemite National Park boundaries. There are pine trees on both sides of the dirt road leading up to the main cabin. It is a log cabin with a large porch in the front with a wood railing and two rocking chairs nestled against the wall. The cabin has two stories and a basement. There is an open entryway with a high ceiling all the way to the second floor.

The huge kitchen is to the right of the entryway, accessible by way of a short open walkway. There is a big sink with ample cupboards, a large side-by-side refrigerator/freezer, a walk-in pantry, and an island with five barstools that make up the kitchen area, which has hardwood flooring. Off the kitchen is a dining room, where rests a long oak table that has chairs to seat twelve and serves as a conference table when needed. A large area rug is below the table. A sliding glass door goes out onto a back patio from the dining area.

Straight in front of the entryway, there is a step down into an extremely large living room area with high-angled wooden beams. There is a fifty-two-inch flat-screen TV against the wall and next to a stone fireplace with evenly cut logs neatly stacked on the side. There are two reclining leather chairs, each with an end table and a large sectional couch with a coffee table in front. It has hardwood floors with a large brown and red-fringed area rug. There is also a sliding glass door that goes out onto the same back patio that is accessible through the dining area. To the immediate left of the entry way is a half bath and a door across from it leading to the master bedroom. This is where John Sawyer sleeps. It has an attached bathroom with a large sink and mirror and a walk-in shower enclosed by glass walls. Next to the bathroom area is an ample walk-in closet. There is an attached sitting room with a desk and computer, a leather-backed chair, and a bookcase in his suite.

There is a wall between the living room area and the dining area. Between those rooms is a door that opens to a stairwell leading down into the basement. The stairs open to a family room, which has a pool table and a couple of chairs facing a large-screen TV. Against the far wall, there is a bar area that can seat four with a keg of beer and wine bottles from John's Sonoma and Napa Valley collection built into the wall. There are two bedrooms and a Jack 'n' Jill bathroom between them that has two sinks. Attached is a toilet room with a shower. The laundry room is also in the basement.

A wide staircase just off the entryway before the walkway to the kitchen winds up to the second floor. There is a bonus room overlooking the living room with a wood railing balcony. A small couch, reclining chair, and beanbag all face a thirty-two-inch TV. There are three bedrooms upstairs. Two of them share a Jack 'n' Jill bathroom similar to the one in the basement. On the other end of the upstairs, past the bonus room and above the master bedroom, is another large bedroom. It has a walk-in closet and its own attached bathroom, sink, and shower. Pete sleeps here when the place is not fully occupied.

On the covered back patio is a ping-pong table and steps that lead down to a built-in spa that can seat ten. There is a wooden bench and railings that encircle the spa in a horseshoe configuration from the steps. Below the spa is a large grass area with trees and shrubs. Most mornings, just after dawn, there are several deer nibbling from the shrubs.

Just past the main cabin up the dirt road another one hundred feet is where a trailer is parked on the other side of the road from the cabin. It is backed against the forest with a big concrete circular area carved out of the trees behind it to create a landing pad for the helicopter. Beyond the trailer, another couple hundred feet, the dirt road ends in a turnabout fifteen yards in the front of the barn, where the horses and mules are housed. To the left of the barn is a chicken coup. Next to the coup is a large meadow where, at the far end, the trail begins toward the backside of the majestic Yosemite National Park. In the meadow, they accommodate tent campers. It is sectioned off to allow up to six tent campers at a given time without crowding them. There is a restroom facility in the meadow.

John Sawyer is average height, 5'11" with a lean, wiry physique at 170 lb. He has muscular arms from working around the ranch for many years. His hair is prematurely gray, but he still maintains a full head of hair that is medium length. He wears a goatee and only shaves about every third day. He lives in the cabin to be able to cook the meals and help plan the excursions. Pete also helps in the kitchen as both men enjoy cooking. Peter Marshall retired from the military after twenty years of service in 1985. He has not cut his sandy-blond hair since other than a trim around the edges. Most of the time, while working or flying, he combs his long hair straight back into a ponytail. He stays clean-shaven, stands 6'1", and weighs 210 lb. He doesn't appear to be outwardly muscular; however, he maintains what he calls his "army strength."

Typically, the guests stay one night and then go out on their adventure the next day. If it is a one-day trek, they can leave later that evening or stay another night, whatever they have booked. If the guests are going on a multiple-day adventure, John leaves Pete in charge of the cabin and leads the group on horseback. Unless it is a highly advanced group that needs helicopter access to the high rugged terrain. Pete is the pilot that puts them down in the middle of the mountains. For an extra fee, John will accompany them and lead them back. However, most of these groups are experienced enough to navigate themselves back to the cabin. After all, that is part of the challenge, along with rock climbing and trailblazing. There are no formed trails per se for them to follow. After a few years, there are some well-used pathways in which they can follow for much of their adventure; however, a compass is an essential piece of equipment.

When Jordan and Janne arrive in the Bronco at the ranch, John Sawyer and Pete Marshall are alone to greet them. They had a group of four people spend the night on Monday, but Pete took them out in the chopper to a destination high in the mountains early this morning. They will be on their trek for a week. John changed the bedding down in the basement bedrooms to get them ready for Al and Arthur. Pete will stay in his room tonight. Jordan and Janne take the other two bedrooms upstairs, while John stays in his usual habitat on the main floor.

No guests are scheduled to arrive until Friday. The weekend is totally booked with five people in the cabin Friday night and six campers in tents reserved. On Saturday morning, John will take the five cabin occupants out on horseback for an overnight excursion and return on Sunday. The campers are all going out, hiking the trails on their own, and don't have a schedule they need to follow.

After introductions, the four of them sit in the living room to chat. Janne brings her dad up to date on her activities with the presidential campaign. John is pleased that Steve Forbes is promoting a platform of tax reform and introducing a flat tax system. Jordan describes the type of work he does and the allegations brought forth by Royce Dawkins and Arthur Gibson. John is impressed with the maturity and level of aptitude that Jordan displays as he discusses the negotiations that he encounters on a daily basis with revenue officers of the IRS Collection Division.

"I studied tax law and have a good idea of how the tax system works and doesn't work, but I have little knowledge of the collection process other than knowing that the IRS wields too much power," John comments.

"It can be frustrating trying to negotiate settlements or payment plans when they can levy bank accounts or seize property at a whim with no due process," Jordan confirms.

John has taken an immediate liking to Jordan. That is rare because from his experience in life, people can be deceiving. He is usually cautious as to whom he trusts and respects.

There is something sincere and authentic about this young man, he thinks to himself. *He is confident but not cocky. He is articulate but does not waste words*. The obvious mutual attraction and respect that Jordan and Janne share helps win her father over as well.

"I want to hear more about the situation that brings you here and share some of my thoughts, but I think it best to save that for when your friends arrive and we can all enjoy a good night's sleep," John suggests.

Jordan, Janne, and Pete all agree.

"On a more personal level, Janne tells me that your father served in the Army in Vietnam." John just throws it out there, and even though Jordan is a little surprised, he is not offended in the least.

"Yes, my father, Edward Duncan, was drafted in 1967. He trained and became part of the 101st Airborne Division. He was then deployed to Vietnam. He fought in many battles, most notably the Battle of Hamburger Hill, which he survived." John sneaks a quick look at Pete, who is listening intently.

Jordan continues, "He had been given time off just prior to the holidays in 1968 and came home to see my mom, whom he had married before reporting to the Army when drafted. When he returned to Vietnam, my mother discovered that she was pregnant. My dad was scheduled to be released right about the time of my mom's due date. I came a couple of weeks early, but my dad was able to fly back and be there."

Jordan pauses and takes a drink of water that Janne had brought him as they were first seated. "Apparently, the army was offering specific drafted soldiers an opportunity to extend their service time for six months in exchange for benefits that were normally available only to enlisted men. As my mom has told me, they agreed that my dad would take the offer so that he could get his education paid for and receive GI benefits in purchasing a home someday. Unfortunately, they never got the chance as he was killed in December of 1969 in some kind of ambush."

Silence hovers in the room as Jordan finishes his rendition of his father's military service. Janne feels tears forming in her eyes.

Finally, after what seems to be several minutes, John speaks, "I'm very sorry for your loss, Jordan. I, too, was drafted into the Army in 1968. I saw many horrible things and much death. I'm sure it must be particularly hard for you to have never known your father and hear everything that transpired secondhand."

"Yeah. Fortunately for me, I have an incredible mother, who has never spoken one negative word to me about the war or my father's decision to go back when he could have stayed home. I know she loved him very much, and I have been the recipient of her love all my life. I owe any success that I have achieved and any positive character traits I might possess to her," Jordan states in a noble manner.

"She sounds like an amazing woman who had to endure an extreme heartbreak but had the wherewithal to raise an outstanding young man," says John.

Jordan nods his head in appreciation, and Janne smiles as she takes hold of Jordan's hand on the couch.

John continues, "If I may, with the help of Pete, I'd like to share some thoughts with you about your father from a perspective that perhaps you have not heard before."

"Sure," Jordan responds as he takes another drink of water. This is way more intense than he expected. He has never shared the story of his father's death with anyone other than Big Al and Little Al. He only heard the story once from his mother, and they never spoke about it again.

"First, let me start by saying that your father must have been exceptional in basic training. It is rare that a draftee would be invited to train with the 101st Airborne Division, right, Pete?" John turns to Pete, who is seated across from John in a chair turned backward that he brought in from the dining room so that he could face Jordan and Janne on the couch.

"Very rare," Pete replies.

Jordan senses that Pete is not an overly talkative type, which he appreciates, as it gives more clout to what he might say.

"Yes, my dad was an excellent athlete who starred as a quarterback on his high school football team. He was hoping to play at UCLA."

John and Janne both smile at that declaration.

"As I mentioned, I was drafted, but Pete came into the Army through the West Point Academy. He learned to fly and became a combat helicopter pilot. He was also involved in the Battle of Hamburger Hill. Tell Jordan what you remember about that battle, Pete."

Jordan's eyes widen as he looks toward Pete. He has never met someone who went to West Point, and he has never spoken to anyone who fought at Hamburger Hill.

Pete looks Jordan straight in the eyes and starts speaking. "In May of 1969, part of an operation called Apache Snow took place on a rugged jungle-shrouded mountain range in South Vietnam about a mile from the Laotian border. Rising from the A Sau Valley was a mountain called Ap Bia. From the valley floor, it was 937 meters high or just over 3,000 feet. On the US Army maps, it was referred to as Hill 937. It was the highest and steepest of the three ridges that extended from the valley. Later, after the ten-day battle, it was referred to by soldiers who fought there as Hamburger Hill because it resembled, according to a soldier, the results of a meat grinder, with human bodies from both sides having been shred about." Pete pauses, reaches to the floor, and takes his water bottle to wet his lips.

He continues, "I know all this firsthand because I was there. I made multiple insertions of combat soldiers, flew out dozens of wounded from hot LZs, personally engaged in vicious firepower encounters, and witnessed several comrades in choppers get shot down. The battle was primarily an infantry engagement, with the US troops from the 101st Airborne Division moving up the steeply sloped hill against well-entrenched troops of the People's Army of Vietnam [PAVN]. Attacks were repeatedly repelled by the PAVN defenses. Bad weather also hindered operations." Pete pauses again and turns to look at John. Jordan and Janne remain riveted to this story.

"As John mentioned previously, it was rare that drafted soldiers were in the 101st Airborne Division, also known as the Screaming Eagles. But the ones that made it were generally assigned to the 3rd Battalion, 187th infantry. That is where your father undoubtedly was in this battle. Me and many other pilots dropped those boys in makeshift landing zones during several runs." Once again, Pete needs to pause and drink some water. Jordan and Janne also sip from their water.

"What I witnessed and participated in over the next ten days was the bravest, most courageous display of grit and determination that I saw throughout my military career. Those soldiers were trekking uphill against an enemy entrenched on the high ground in bunkers, scurrying around through an advanced tunnel system that was nearly impossible to find and destroy. Our boys were often slipping and sliding due to the mud from the rains and blood from fallen soldiers on both sides. They continued for days, no one sleeping for more than a couple of hours in shifts, curled up in the wet jungle-like conditions on the side of that rugged steep terrain. They fought to within a hundred meters of the summit and nearly carried the hill but experienced severe casualties, including most of their officers. The battle was one of close combat, with the two sides exchanging small arms and grenade fire within twenty meters of one another. However, an exceptionally intense thunderstorm reduced visibility to zero and ended the fighting on May 17. Unable to advance, the 3/187th withdrew down the mountain.

"Two fresh battalions were airlifted into landing zones northeast and southeast of the base of the mountain on May 19. Both battalions immediately moved onto the mountain to positions from which they would attack the following morning. Lieutenant Colonel Honeycutt argued to General Zais that his battalion, the 3/187 was still combat effective. The general agreed to let the 3/187 continue in the fight. The 3rd Brigade launched its 4-battalion attack at 10:00 on May 20, including 2 companies of the 3/187 reinforced by Company A 1/506. The battalions attacked simultaneously, and by 12:00, the 3/187 reached the crest. The PAVN units that were still alive withdrew into Laos, and Hill 937 was secured by 17:00." Pete stopped talking, and there was silence in the room for a few minutes while everyone present tried to put into perspective what they had just heard.

"All told, US losses during the 10-day battle totaled 72 killed and 372 wounded. US estimates of the losses incurred by the PAVN included 630 counted dead, numerous others in makeshift mortuaries in the tunnel complexes they discovered dug into the mountain, and hundreds who ran down the backside into Laos, some being killed by air strikes on the way down. Your father, in my opinion, was part of the greatest battle victory of infantry combat that I have ever seen in my army career. They ascended that hill as young brave boys and came back as hardened, proven men of valor," Pete concluded.

Jordan had a lump in his throat that prevented him from speaking, but with moisture in his eyes and a swelling in his heart, he nodded a sincere appreciation to Pete for sharing his firsthand version of the Battle of Hamburger Hill. Pete nodded back to him with much respect for Jordan's father.

John picked up the conversation from there. "I was not an exceptional soldier. I believe that I was a good soldier who did my duty and tried to make good decisions. Pete was an exceptional soldier, as was our third partner, David Lackey, whom Pete met at West Point and who later became a captain in the US Army Rangers. Not many drafted soldiers became exceptional; however, your father, Edward Duncan, was one who certainly did. As you mentioned earlier, Jordan, your dad was offered an extension to stay in Vietnam. The Army started that program because with so many drafted soldiers, by the time they became useful and effective, they were sent home. Only the elite few were offered extensions to help train and protect the 'newbies.'"

John turns to look at Pete. "Pete will attest to the fact that this was one messed-up war! By the time your father and I arrived, the troop morale was low as it had become evident that the US was not there to win the war. So the soldiers banded together to fight for one another and save the lives of their brothers-in-arms. I experienced it along with my two lifelong friends. Why are we friends even though we come from such different backgrounds and have followed different paths?"

Again, John turns to Pete and then looks back at Jordan. "Because we experienced hell together. I can tell you without a shadow of a doubt that soldiers like your father saved hundreds of lives. There were so many kids over there that had no business being there. They were scared and totally out of their element, thrown into a situation of life and death, certainly not of their own choosing. Their only hope was the bravery, valor, and wisdom of the strong soldiers to their left and to their right. I can guarantee you that your dad did not go back to Nam to be a hero for his country. He went back for those underdogs that needed his help to survive and for what he thought was best in the long term for his family. I can also tell you without a shadow of a doubt that if it weren't for exceptional soldiers like Pete, Dave, and Edward Duncan, I never would have found my wife, Kim Le."

John pauses and looks at Janne, who nods her head to her father with a slight smile. "Yes, the elite soldiers of the US Army literally saved thousands of lives of South Vietnamese civilians. That beautiful young lady sitting next to you would not be here if it weren't for dedicated, courageous soldiers like Edward Duncan. For that, I will be forever grateful."

John stops as he is beginning to get emotional, with tears welling up in his eyes. Tears are now rolling down Jordan's cheeks, and Janne is crying quietly. Jordan puts his arm around Janne, and she buries her face into his shoulder. Pete walks over and puts his hand on John's shoulder, who is still seated.

"It was a crazy, ill-advised war. There were so many casualties and lives affected, even to this day. But I believe in my heart that honoring those that served and died and holding close those that served and survived is the best way to show respect and support for all that experienced it in one way or another," Pete says in a fitting conclusion to the conversation.

After hugging Janne and kissing her forehead, Jordan stands, as does John Sawyer. They embrace as Jordan whispers, "Thank you so much." He turns to Pete, gives him a bro hug, and says, "Your rendition of that battle and knowing that my father participated alongside of you gives me more comfort than you will ever know. Thank you!" Jordan wipes his eyes and smiles.

"My honor and pleasure to pay tribute to a courageous fallen comrade to his fine son," Pete replies.

John adds, "Whatever good you received inherently from your mother, I think you received the same amount of good genes and strong character traits from your father."

Jordan nods, and for the first time in his life, he sincerely believes that to be true.

"You better leave to go get his buddies," John says to Pete, who turns and heads to the door.

Janne walks over and does a three-way hug with her dad and her boyfriend.

When Al, Arthur, and Pete arrive, John has already prepared dinner. There is a stream full of trout not far from the ranch, and the men keep an ample supply of fresh trout on hand to serve their patrons. Tonight, John thinks that his daughter and her friends will enjoy this meal. He includes baked potatoes, a fresh cut salad, and zucchini along with one of his favorite Napa Valley white wines, the Sauvignon Blanc, which is a perfect selection to go with the fresh-water fish.

During dinner, Al comments, "This place is awesome. I would love to book some time here with my clients and potential clients. If I had known the setup, I would have brought my girlfriend to share the basement with me instead of Arthur!" They all laugh.

Arthur responds, "Ninety-nine times out of one hundred, I would prefer my wife to be here with me over you, Alvin. However, based on what we need to discuss while here, I will settle for you this one time."

Once again, laughter ensues.

Actually, the two physically imposing men hit it off right away. They spoke about college football, the NFL, the IRS, and their respective relationship with Jordan Duncan while at the airport and on the helicopter ride to the ranch.

After dinner, John insists on cleaning up, although Janne is just as insistent about helping. The others engage in a competitive game of billiards, wherein Jordan and Pete challenge Al and Arthur. They all decide to get a good night's rest so they can get started early in the morning to begin their deliberations on the upcoming game plan to take on the IRS!

Upon retiring to their respective rooms, Jordan and Janne meet in the Jack 'n' Jill bathroom that separates their rooms. Jordan puts his arms around Janne, and she rests her head against his chest.

He whispers, "Thank you, Janne, for bringing me here to meet your dad and Pete. I had no idea that we would talk about Vietnam and my dad like that. It was exactly what I've needed and was longing to hear my entire life. I cannot remember the last time I actually cried." He kisses the top of her head.

Janne looks up and says, "I had no idea that my dad had those kinds of feelings about the war, and that story Pete told was so intense and moving. The whole experience made me feel closer to my dad and also made me appreciate you even more for the man that you are in spite of losing such a great father before you ever got to know him."

They continue to embrace as they begin kissing each other passionately.

On Wednesday morning, August 9, after breakfast, the small group decide to congregate in the living room rather than sit in the more formal setting at the dining room table. John and Pete bring in two chairs from the dining room, with Al and Arthur sitting in the leather reclining chairs. Jordan and Janne sit together on the couch. Even though it his home, John has asked Arthur to lead the conversation and has agreed to contribute when asked.

Arthur begins by recapping his position within the IRS as a regional director for thirty years, his subsequent retirement, and his current role as a consultant to the CPA firm of Epstein, Levin & Ohlman Tax Consultants and Jacobs & Goodman Tax Resolution, which he explains to John and Pete is an affiliate company to E, L, & O. He then proceeds to lay out the manner in which the audit precipitated his meeting with Royce Dawkins. Arthur explains in great detail the allegations that were brought forth by Mr. Dawkins regarding E, L, & O being in cahoots with the IRS in the format of targeting specific firms for audit. He outlines how that arrangement, in theory, benefits both E, L, & O as well as the IRS. Before taking questions, he alludes to his meeting with Alexander Epstein just prior to making the trip to California for this meeting. He mentions that

David Jacobs was meeting with Jordan simultaneously, which he is sure was intentional so that they would not communicate in order to collaborate their stories as it pertains to their respective encounters with Royce Dawkins. Arthur asks the group if there are any questions.

John Sawyer is the first to speak up. "So to sum up your meetings with Epstein and Jacobs, respectively, where do things stand as far as your status as a consultant and then, Jordan, your employment status?"

Arthur answers first. "Epstein seemed to buy my explanation that I was approached by Dawkins pertaining to the audit. I explained to him that Dawkins thought perhaps E, L, & O had a hand in his termination. My story to Epstein was that I informed Dawkins that I had no such knowledge. Epstein wanted to know why Dawkins went to California to meet with Jordan. I relayed the story that Dawkins inquired about who would be the best person to contact in the Tax Resolution Division if he had an unresolved tax debt. I gave him Jordan's name." Arthur looks at Jordan, who nods his head in affirmation of the rendition.

He continues, "Epstein is not a man to be trifled with. He made it clear that he believes Royce Dawkins is nothing more than a disgruntled ex-employee looking for a way to place blame for his employment termination. His main concern is to not give him any ammunition that would involve E, L & O in a lawsuit. He was also quite explicit that if I wanted to continue as a consultant with his firm, I was not to interact with Royce Dawkins in any manner moving forward. I agreed to those terms."

Jordan confirmed that he had a similar conversation with David Jacobs and that he, too, agreed to cut off communication with Dawkins.

"So where does that leave Dawkins now?" asks John.

"As far as I'm concerned, Royce Dawkins was the trigger man that put this investigation, if you will, in process. I think that for his own good, we should thank him but suggest that he not communicate with either of us any longer," Arthur responds, and Jordan agrees.

John thinks for a moment and then says, "That sounds reasonable. If there is anything that he might discover within his former organization that he believes is pertinent to what we are trying to prove against E, L & O or the IRS, we can set up a mechanism for him to communicate with Pete or me in a covert manner." John looks at Pete, who nods his head in the affirmative.

Arthur agrees with that idea. He asks John how, in his opinion, he and Pete can contribute to implicate the IRS and E, L & O of illegal practices.

John responds, "Let me begin by giving you some background on how Pete and I first met and then the circumstances in which we became reacquainted. I think that will clarify as to what we bring to the table for this endeavor."

Arthur, Jordan, Al, and Janne are each interested in hearing the story.

"I was drafted into the army in 1968 at eighteen years old and deployed to fight in Vietnam. Early 1970, my platoon was ordered to assist in the evacuation of a village in South Vietnam to get the civilians out before an impending attack from the North Vietnamese or, as we referred to them, the PAVN. Before we accomplished our mission, we were hit by an ambush. I took a round in my gut and was unable to continue in the evacuation. Luckily, no vital organs were damaged, but I was bleeding heavily. I crawled into a ditch and tried to camouflage myself with brush and broken tree limbs. After the shooting stopped, I tried to climb out and proceed toward our escape route.

"I wasn't doing too well, and fortunately, I was discovered by a young woman from the village who had survived. She bandaged me as well as possible to stop the bleeding. I stayed with her in hiding for two days until I felt like I could at least hike out of there. The young lady, named Kim Le, insisted on helping me with my journey. I never would have made it without her. As we were evading and hiding when necessary, we heard choppers coming. The Americans had come back to gather their dead and see if there were any survivors. We were spotted by a chopper pilot, who dropped in abruptly so a crew member could jump out to help me aboard. There were other wounded soldiers already in the chopper. Army regulations stipulated that no civilians were allowed in official Army vehicles.

"I insisted that Kim Le board also or else they would have to leave me. I told the pilot that this young lady had saved my life and that she had no family to return to. Enemy fire began to spray around us. He yelled, 'Get them both onboard, and let's get out of here.'"

John turns toward Pete and points at him. "That pilot was Lieutenant Peter Marshall. He flew us to a hospital in Saigon. There, I thanked him and he said, 'I'm glad you survived, soldier, and had the decency to stay with the one who saved you.' There is no doubt that if we had left Kim Le behind, she would have been killed but probably not before she was raped and/or tortured. Pete saved her life as she had saved mine. I stayed in the hospital for the next few months. Kim Le never left me. Lieutenant Marshall also came to visit before I left, and we exchanged names and companies. Upon my release from the hospital, I was scheduled to be discharged from the Army in another month, as my two years were up. However, I had fallen in love with Kim Le. We were trying to teach each other our respective languages and communicating the best we could. Sometimes, I believe communication can be more profound without the spoken word."

Janne smiles at her father, and Pete just says, "That's for sure."

John continues, "I couldn't leave Kim Le behind, so I married her in Saigon. The next month, when I received my orders to return Stateside to be discharged, I was told that Kim Le could not accompany me even though we were married. We would have to make other arrangements for her to get to the US. There were no guarantees on how that would be accomplished. As we were weighing our options, we discovered that Kim Le was pregnant. As far as I was concerned, that made the decision easy. I was staying with my wife and child-to-be."

By this time, Janne is beaming with tears welling up in her eyes. Jordan holds her hand, squeezing it lovingly.

"We ended up staying until 1975, which was when the United States signed the treaty to evacuate Saigon, which would subsequently become known as Ho Chi Minh City. From there, we came back to the US, where I was considered AWOL and arrested. I faced military court. I had two material witnesses—by then Captain Peter Marshall and Captain David Lackey, an Army ranger who had led a village rescue mission in which I had previously participated.

"I did not know until my court date that Captains Marshall and Lackey were in the same West Point Academy graduating class and had remained in touch throughout the war. When Pete told Dave about my story with Kim Le, Dave put two and two together and realized that he had been attached to my platoon as a special operations advisor on that other rescue mission. He offered to help on my behalf. Having two decorated soldiers testify on my good character and worthiness as a dedicated soldier no doubt influenced the judge to not order any prison time. I was dishonorably discharged and placed on probation, but I could return to my wife and daughter."

John looks at Pete, and they exchange a respectful smile and nod of the head. "Now comes the tax part. Because I stayed in Saigon in 1970, I never filed a tax return. When I returned to the US five years later, it took about two years for Uncle Sam to come calling for back taxes plus penalties and interest." John looks at Jordan. "Sound about right?"

"Yep, they are usually about two years behind in contacting you, but penalties and interest don't wait," Jordan confirms.

"I didn't know anything about tax resolution firms, so I just got on a payment plan and paid it all back. As I was going to school and working, my wife developed symptoms of lymphoma, which were caused by her exposure to Agent Orange, which had been dumped repeatedly on the jungle surrounding her village. It was meant to reduce the foliage to better spot enemy movement. The ramifications were much wider spread than intended." John pauses, takes a deep breath, and continues, "Kim Le passed away in 1981. Janne and I moved to the Yosemite Valley. I started studying tax law as I thought there were probably other veterans as well as citizens that ran into problems with an archaic national tax system, like I had. After Janne earned a scholarship to UCLA, I received my law degree in taxation.

"About that time, I received a letter from Pete Marshall, who was working in the Silicon Valley as a corporate helicopter pilot. We got together for dinner and drinks, and I discovered that Pete had just recently been audited by the IRS and that they disallowed many of his write-offs. I studied the audit and discovered several mistakes made by the auditor. We decided to fight them in tax court. We ended up winning the case."

"Nice!" responds Little Al.

"Thanks. As we were going to celebrate our victory over the IRS, Pete invited Dave Lackey to join us. After a few drinks and laughs, when they discovered where I lived, Pete came up with the idea of this ranch. All three of us are avid outdoorsmen. Pete had made a lot of money piloting big shots around, and Dave had gone into the CIA after retiring from the Army Rangers when he had put in twenty years of service. I didn't have any money, so it was decided that I would put in sweat equity in designing, helping build, and running the ranch. Pete helps out around here flying customers to remote hiking and rock-climbing destinations. Dave has now left the CIA and works as a private contractor, doing security surveillance for private firms and individuals. His intent is to eventually build a cabin over on the meadow where we currently have campsites to live with his wife and help on the ranch once his three kids are out of school. Right now, he lives in Santa Cruz with his wife, daughter, and two sons. He and his two college-aged sons are over in Hawaii, surfing, as we speak.

"So after all that, to answer your question, Arthur, I believe that we can help formulate a plan and use our various skill sets to take on the IRS. Yes, I have some animosity built up. However, with the help of my two West Point graduate business partners, I have learned to take a nonemotional, military-style approach in planning operations. I believe that with my tax law knowledge and a desire to help my daughter, who has decided that this is a most worthy cause, I can be of some assistance. I volunteer my services!"

"Whew, that is quite a story, John, Pete," says Arthur. "I agree that you can definitely be of assistance to our cause. Let's define our cause and discuss how we might be able to expose the illegal activities that we believe are occurring."

Arthur continues, "We believe that E, L & O is working in conjunction with the IRS in targeting firms for tax audits. That is illegal. Also, we believe that the IRS is feeding J&G delinquent payroll tax offenders in order to help in their collections. Also, illegal. The question is, how do we accumulate evidence to prove these allegations, and to whom do we present this evidence?"

"If I may?" John inquires.

"By all means," Arthur replies, bowing his head.

John stands up and begins to pace slowly. "There is a term used in survival that the Navy SEALs take credit for, although Dave tells me the Army Rangers used it well before the SEALs commercialized it. Doesn't really matter who concocted it. The term is 'Two is one, one is none.'"

John explains, "The basic idea behind 'Two is one, one is none' is to have multiple methods to accomplish certain goals and tasks. For example, a sharp blade is one of the most important survival tools. That being the case, if your knife breaks or is lost, you are in big trouble without it. So you always bring two. I typically have three of them with me at all times.

"Carry redundant capability, not redundant gear. What I mean by that is, by having different solutions to the same problems, you have not only helped protect yourself against the risk of losing or breaking something deemed necessary but you have also increased your capability to solve the problem by more varied circumstances. Take, for instance, the example of the knife. I personally like to always carry a sheath knife. It allows me to cut almost anything, any size. But it is bulky. I also carry a folding knife, like a Buck knife. It is more compact but also very functional. Then for good measure, I bring along a multitool knife, like a Swiss Army knife. It can accomplish many functions, and although it won't cut quite as effectively as a sheath or Buck knife, it will nonetheless work as a cutting knife if the other two become nonfunctional."

John has everyone's undivided attention. "How does this theory apply to our situation? It can be especially important as the theory applies to mission planning. One plan means no plan. Two plans can be good for one. I like to take it one more step with three plans, which I call 'Two is one, one is none, and three is one plus one.' The third plan is your exit strategy—what to do if everything goes south."

"What I'm thinking is…" John begins to lay out his thoughts on a game plan. "Plan A is to expose E, L & O and the IRS in an illegal collaboration in targeting selected businesses for IRS audits."

He looks directly at Arthur, who nods his head in agreement.

John continues, "This would require that Arthur, if you still have connections within the IRS, see what data you might be able to collect. Perhaps a list of corporate audits from the past few years. Also, try to get access to data from E, L & O as to which of their clients have been audited and the dates. Pete and I will put this data into an algorithm to connect any consistencies or tendencies that can link the two lists."

John turns to Jordan. "Part 2 of plan A is to determine if the IRS is feeding J&G leads to payroll tax debtors and letting them assist in their collection efforts for substantial fees." He turns back to Arthur. "Is that right?"

Arthur confirms that is what he suspects.

"Jordan, perhaps you can find access to the payroll client files and look for sources," John says.

Jordan agrees that he can look into those opportunities.

Next, John looks at Janne. "I was thinking that you could act as a liaison between our efforts and the US Congress through your association with Steve Forbes. I'm not sure, but it seems logical that if we are going to expose illegal activities of the IRS, Congress would be the only route to go, right?" John asks as he turns back to Arthur.

"Yes, I believe so. But I think we need substantial evidence before Congress would even look into such allegations," Arthur responds. "That sounds like a solid plan, John. However, you mentioned having a plan B and even a plan C."

"Yes. Thank you, Arthur." John begins to lay out plan B. "There is something that I've studied as it pertains to IRS collection methods, and Jordan has confirmed it with me. I'm interested to see if you agree with this theory, Arthur. The IRS Collection Division abuses the power that it has been given by the US Congress, totally ignoring constitutional rights of taxpayers in terms of due process. They levy bank accounts, garnish wages, and even seize property without so much as a court order. I'm thinking that plan B could be to gather evidence of taxpayer abuse by the Collection Division to be able to persuade Congress to examine the IRS collection activities, which in turn could open the door to add on the target auditing allegations. Both of you could play critical roles in substantiating actual cases of this abuse. With an election year coming up, it might be something that Forbes and the Republican Party might adhere to in their tax reform platform."

As John concludes his thoughts on plan B, Arthur speaks up. "I think that is an excellent idea. Kind of an end-around play if you can excuse the football metaphor."

"I love it," Al chimes in. "Misdirection so that if the IRS or E, L & O suspect that we are on to their target auditing scheme, they won't have a clue that we are attacking them from the collections angle."

"Exactly," John adds. "Since the tax resolution firm that is firmly entrenched in collection issues is part of the entire E, L & O business structure, they will be subject to an investigation of their books and audits. This will open the back door to their target auditing collaboration."

Jordan asks, "What type of substantiation are you referring to?"

Arthur answers the question. "Some of your existing or past caseload—for instance, the way that woman for whom you submitted the innocent spouse relief was treated by the revenue officer. That is just one example of abuse of power. There must be hundreds of cases similar to that. I can put out feelers across the country to tax professionals, and I'm sure we can find ample evidence of abuse of power."

"I know I can personally give you several instances. I like this angle," Jordan replies.

"Okay, great. Now for plan C or the exit strategy." John is ready to wrap up his "Two is one, one is none, and three is one plus one" game plan approach. "Trying to expose or ultimately bring down a federal government agency is not only a monumental endeavor with long odds against success but it can also be full of risks." John pauses to make sure everyone gets the gist of this impactful declaration. "The obvious inherent risk of attacking the IRS is having your personal life turned upside down by way of financial audits and possibly more scrutiny. We have already seen what Epstein is willing to do to nip the Dawkins questioning in the bud. He hired a PI to follow him, and we don't know to what extent he will try to track Arthur's and Jordan's activities.

"If the IRS, E, L & O, and maybe even Jacobs & Goodman decide to turn the tables and take aggressive retaliatory measures, we have to be willing to abort the mission and have an exit plan. My suggestion is that plan C consist of going off the grid and being able to hide assets and maybe ourselves. Our third partner, Dave Lackey, could help in that regard. He has substantial resources with offshore accounts, alias identities, and ulterior locations to habitation. Each of you need to think of your personal circumstances and what you might be willing to do if plans A and B both blow up."

Silence perpetrates the room as everyone collectively ponders what John Sawyer has just laid out to them.

Before anyone comments on plan C, Al raises his hand and says, "I have two questions." He is looking directly at John.

"Fire," John responds.

"First, you mentioned everyone's role but mine. What can I do?"

Jordan is quick to reply. "You are my wingman, Lil Al. Do you still know how to pick locks?"

"Sure. That is something you never forget, as long as it's not too complicated."

"Good. That is where we will start. I need you to pick the lock to Marlin's office in Sherman Oaks," Jordan says, smiling.

"No problemo," Al says, returning the smile. "Second question—can any of us use this place as our off-the-grid habitation if all goes south?"

"Hahaha! Absolutely. We haven't even shown you the more covert features of our little nest egg here." John returns Al's Smile.

"Awesome. Count me in!" says Alvin Bockman Jr., who never backs down from an opportunity to help his best friend.

Arthur says, "I think we have a solid plan from which to move forward. Thank you, John. You were correct when you stated that you and Pete, along with your third partner, can be of assistance in our quest for justice."

John looks at Pete, who just nods his head. "Great. I appreciate everyone coming and we can start putting the plan into action. Of course, we need to follow certain protocols to make sure our internal communication is secure. Pete will go over that with you. Then if anyone is interested, I'd be glad to saddle up the horses and take you on an extended tour of our vast wilderness resort!" John stands, and everyone elects to take him up on the horseback excursion offer.

On Thursday morning, after a hearty breakfast of bacon, eggs, and hash browns with orange juice or coffee, everyone says their goodbyes. Pete loads Al and Arthur into his chopper for the trip back to Sacramento Airport. John offers to take Jordan, Janne, and his Bronco out for some four-wheelin'. They accept and decide to spend an extra night at the cabin, leaving on Friday morning. It was three days well spent for each of them that they will never forget.

John and Pete bid them farewell, and as they drive away, John turns to Pete. "Tell Dave I've got a job for him if he's interested."

"For you, he will be interested," Pete responds.

Jordan and Janne head west, spending Friday and Saturday nights in San Francisco. They have reservations at the Normandy Inn in Carmel by the Sea for Sunday to Tuesday. It is near Pebble Beach, and the two of them have a delightful time at the spectacular beach. They start driving south on the historic Pacific Coast Highway 1 after breakfast on Tuesday, August 15, Jordan's twenty-sixth birthday. They spend Tuesday night in San Simeon near Hearst's Castle and return home on Wednesday, August 16. It was a fabulous ten days together. Jordan and Janne have become extremely close in their relationship, and each feel good about their plan moving forward to take on the IRS.

On Thursday, August 17, Jordan had promised to take Sunshine surfing for the first time on her seventeenth birthday. It is a beautiful sunny day, and Jordan picks Pacific Palisades, where Perfect Day Surf Camp is located. It is an ideal surfing venue for beginners. He presents her a new wetsuit as a birthday gift. Jordan is pleasantly surprised at Sunshine's level of athleticism and willingness to keep trying after several failed attempts to get up. After the first couple of hours, she gets the hang of it and actually catches some waves. She tells him afterward as they change clothes that it's been the best day of her life so far.

They drive up the coast to Malibu, where Jordan treats her to a late lunch at Duke's with salmon and a virgin margarita. He tells her about his former girlfriend from UCLA. Sunshine loves romantic stories and thanks him for comparing her to Leslie. He delivers her home by 7:00 p.m. so that she can spend her birthday evening with her family.

CHAPTER ELEVEN

Working the Plan

Beginning with the announcement of the national and local standards being implemented into the IRS Collection Division computations, it has been evident that revenue officers have been stalling in accepting offers. Subsequently, Jordan has a backlog of almost a dozen OICs and at least as many IAs. It also indicates to him how fortunate it was to get the Williamson offer of $3,000 accepted during this apparent "dead time." He knows that this fortuitous event was a combination of his aggressive, proactive efforts and, probably more so, the fact that the revenue officer in charge of the case was Bobbi Sinclair. Not only is she the branch chief, meaning that she needs no one else's approval, but she also happens to be a rare revenue officer that shows some empathy toward legitimate hardship cases.

Since returning from Yosemite Valley, Jordan has been thinking about cases wherein he can expose the IRS Collection Division in their abuse of taxpayers. Alice Johnston is a good start, and he can think of some other scenarios. This thought process eventually comes around to Jimmy Delgado. He believes the manner in which the IRS is trying to either pin illegal activity or, if they can't prove that, then nail him for an exorbitant amount of back taxes due is certainly a good example of taxpayer abuse. He needs to figure out how to best frame the case to prove this point. He is going to need cooperation from Delgado, and he will have to set up Jack Arbuckle into demonstrating definitive abusive actions, the latter of which shouldn't be overly difficult, perhaps using the boat as bait.

Arthur Gibson is busy thinking about how he can pull resource data from within the IRS audit files without appearing to be suspicious of illegal activity. He remembers interacting with Shelley Davis, who is the acting IRS historian. In 1988, Ms. Davis was appointed as the first ever internal revenue service historian. She discovered that her position was not well accepted among her peers and, in fact, was stonewalled from any records that might be remotely embarrassing to the agency. She found Arthur Gibson to be one of the few senior officials of which she could receive transparent feedback. Arthur decides to contact Ms. Davis.

On the other front, he is contemplating how he can infiltrate the Epstein, Levin & Ohlman files of audited clients. He comes to the conclusion, based on the Dawkins debacle, that he will let things cool down within E, L & O and not expose himself to being followed by the personal sentry of Alexander Epstein, a.k.a. Kurt Turlock. Besides, if he can get ahold of the IRS corporate audit files, then there is a good chance the representing CPA firm will be listed somewhere in the file.

The Steve Forbes presidential campaign moves into full force with a nationwide tour where scheduling is organized for formal speeches, meet-and-greet functions, town hall gatherings, and Republican Party debates. Janne is invited to accompany the team. She will be on the road for the most part of the Republican primaries.

Jordan has completed just about everything he needs on Delgado's financial forms. He has documentation to substantiate his income and expenses. As Delgado enters the office suite and follows Jordan down the corridor, he noticeably looks across the hall from Jordan's open door and pauses as if contemplating opening the door to the call center.

"Don't even think about it," Jordan says as if he is reading Jimmy's mind.

"What? I can't even say *hola* to my new *amiga*?" Delgado displays a mischievous grin.

"The walls in this office have eyes and ears, Jimmy. So don't push your luck on the 'new amiga' idea. Like I told you, stay away from that, and let's concentrate on your case while we are here!" Jordan lectures.

"You know, amigo, for a good-looking young hombre, you seem to be missing the spirit of adventure and excitement in chasing the ladies that I would expect from you." Jimmy says this with his usual grin and sparkling cavalier-looking eyes as he pats Jordan on the back before entering his office.

Jordan lets out a noticeable sigh and says, "There is a time and a place for everything, Jimmy. This is neither the time nor the place for you to be tom cattin' around with my boss's lady! Shut the door, please."

"That's what I like about you, vato. You are way smarter than normal for your age and give me the voice of reason!" Delgado keeps his toothy grin intact as he shuts the door behind him and takes a seat.

"Thanks, Jimmy. I think you are way smarter than you want people to think, and you like to push the envelope to see what you may get away with from people." Jordan is matching wits with Delgado.

"Hahaha, *muy bien*, amigo. I like how perceptive you are. You know, I think we are a lot more alike than you would want me or anyone else to believe!" Jimmy is laughing at his own declaration of perception.

"Maybe, but let's get to work here."

Jordan senses that Delgado may be right. There is something about this dude that Jordan likes and admires. Perhaps, he thinks, it is his combination of being extremely transparent, somewhat cavalier, but under complete control just below the surface. He has a feeling that Jimmy has a genuine happy-go-lucky, engaging personality but knows what he wants and has a pretty good idea about how he is going to get it.

"Let's start with this boat. You told me how you bought it and how the IRS has inflated its value in order to stick you with an excise tax. I want to expose Jack's obsession with trying to prematurely seize property. So I am thinking of using the boat as bait," Jordan explains.

He thinks it best that he be very transparent with Delgado on his intent. It wouldn't be right if this whole plan goes bottoms up and Jimmy loses his boat. It would be a lot more difficult to reacquire the boat than to keep Arbuckle from seizing it in the first place.

"What do you have in mind?" Delgado is inquisitive about Jordan's plan.

Jordan is ready to lay out his strategy as to how he plans to get Delgado off the hook for the entire tax debt that the IRS has assessed on him. "Based on your audit, let's assume that most of the cash calculations that the IRS examiner utilized were way overestimated. They have no receipts nor paper trail. You tell me that your accountant is very meticulous on collecting receipts from you for expenses, correct?"

"Drives me crazy sometimes. But yes, he is very picky about that."

"In addition to those facts, they overappraised the amount of the sale on the Catalina, so we can throw out that excise tax. Most of the rest of the $160K will be penalties and interest." Jordan is laying this out in a particular order to make his point.

"So sounds like we can get me off free and clear, huh, amigo?" Delgado says with a hopeful tone. He is listening intently.

"Even better than that, Jimmy." Jordan has a confident gleam in his eye. "I say we let Arbuckle chase after this boat for a while. I will protect your other assets, and you keep your boat hidden. Act very concerned about him finding the boat. Show him some fear. That will cause him to think he is getting close, and if I know Jack, he will get obsessed with hurting you through the boat seizure."

Delgado nods and Jordan continues, "I will submit an offer in compromise doubt as to liability, which means that we are contesting what you owe, not your ability to pay it. It will take time to examine and negotiate those financial numbers. Jack will get more and more determined to find and seize your boat as long as the tax debt is still on the books. We will document all of his harassing phone calls, threats, and whatever other means he tries to employ to get that boat.

We will be building a case of taxpayer abuse. I haven't told anyone in this office, so this stays between you and me, Jimmy. But with help from some colleagues, we are going to expose the IRS for their abusive methods of collecting taxes from people like you."

Delgado follows his new compadre's eyes to the plaque on his desk as Jordan says, "We will dodge him for a bit, then we will ram him!" Jordan punches his fist into his palm.

"*Caramba!* You want me to be part of a scheme to beat the IRS at their own game? Turn the tables on those cabrones... *Claro que sí*, I want to be part of that!" Jimmy is smiling from ear to ear again.

"All right!" Jordan exclaims. "Remember, this strategy stays between us. We need to play a game of cat and mouse with Jack Arbuckle."

"He started this war, vato! We will finish it our way and make him know that he is messing with the wrong hombres!"

Arthur contacted Shelley Davis, who seemed genuinely delighted to hear from him. She said that she would be glad to meet him for lunch and catch up. They decide on the Woodmont Grill, located between Woodmont Avenue and Old Georgetown Road in Bethesda, Maryland, in October of 1995.

Arthur listens patiently to Shelley describe the frustration she encounters, particularly in trying to retrieve what little records exist within the IRS. She has, as she says, hit a brick wall even when she turned to the National Archives to locate records of IRS dealings.

"My gosh, Arthur, they don't even cooperate with the National Archives. The amount of arrogance and above-the-law attitude within this federal agency is incredible to me." Arthur can see that she is at her wits' end. "I have lost faith in this branch of the government. I've always approached my position as a historian within the federal government as a public servant. I can no longer do that within the IRS," she concludes, shaking her head as she takes a sip of her club soda.

Arthur absorbs what she shared with him, and both are silent for several moments. Finally, he responds, "I feel your pain, and I'm sorry for what you have endured. It surprises me, too, that they would have the audacity to ignore your efforts of transparency and integrity. As you know, I worked within the service for thirty years. For most of that period of time, I was managing people and not really working much in administration. For the past three years, I have been working as a consultant for a CPA firm that also has a division that specializes in tax resolution."

"Yes, I remember you working on the revision of the offer in compromise program before you left. I thought that was a wonderful idea," Shelley replies.

"It has worked out well for the service and the taxpayers for the most part. Of course, the firm has made a pretty penny bringing delinquent taxpayers to the negotiating table. Just recently, it was brought to my attention that there could very well be instances wherein the CPA firm is working in cahoots with the IRS in targeting corporate audits."

"Those are serious allegations, Arthur. Do you have any evidence of such activity?" Shelley inquires with a furrowed brow.

"Some, but not enough to bring it forth. Obviously, I could not bring this to the IRS commissioner, as we both know I would be facing complete and total denial. Therefore, any allegations of illegal activity within the IRS would have to be brought up through Congress. You know as well as I do that it would be a very delicate proposition to broach. It would take extreme selectivity as to whom in particular within Congress would be willing to hear such accusations."

"I agree with you on that!"

"My thought was to share this with you in hopes of perhaps discovering some data and documents that might substantiate these allegations—for instance, a list of corporate audits over the past few years. I don't suppose, based on what you are telling me today, that you would have access to such information?" Arthur has a hopeful but doubtful tone in his voice.

"Believe me, Arthur, there is nothing I would love to do more than help you as a parting shot on my way out the door. But I have made up my mind to resign from my position. I will be giving notice on November 30, and December 31 will be my last day with the IRS."

"What are you going to do next?" Arthur asks.

"I'm not sure at this time, but I can't stay working for an organization that doesn't trust me nor allow me to do my job," she says as if she can't even believe how accurate that statement is. "There's an election year coming up. I will see how that plays out. It seems as though tax reform is going to be a major issue."

"I think you are right on that. Any ideas on whom I might go to in order to obtain information on audits?"

"No one with an official title. They are incredibly hush-hush on anything administrative. Maybe an assistant or even a clerk. Of course, it would be illegal to divulge any taxpayer information. However, let me ask around a bit as it pertains to a list of corporate audits. It would be illegal to share any taxpayer data," she says with a weak smile.

"I understand. I'm simply looking for info on who was audited."

"You never know. As a historian, I always say, 'You'll never know if you don't ask.'" Shelley smiles.

"One last question. To your knowledge, are there any records of interactions between IRS officials and the CPA firm of Epstein, Levin & Ohlman Tax Consultants?" Arthur figures, like Shelley said, "You'll never know if you don't ask."

She smiles and responds, "I highly doubt it. However, I will look into it."

"Best of luck to you, Shelley. It is nice to see you again."

"Likewise, Arthur," Shelley says as they both stand and shake hands before departing. "I will contact you if I find anything pertinent. Good luck on your quest to find the truth. I hope you are more successful inside the IRS than I have been."

The official announcement of Steve Forbes for president campaign comes on September 22, 1995, although he and his crack staff had been working feverishly on the campaign the entire year. In September through November, the team makes stops in Iowa, Delaware, New Hampshire, and the entire northeast region. Forbes speaks incessantly about his message of growth and opportunity. He preaches of smaller government controls and regulations. Of course, the main entrée of his campaign is the implementation of a flat tax.

The flat tax that is at the core of Forbes's campaign would cap individuals' taxes at 17 percent of their income above $13,000 while eliminating deductions for such things as home mortgages and property taxes. Deductions of $5,000 would be granted for each child in a household. The flat tax is, in essence, a tax on what people consume. The Forbes flat tax would apply to wages but not on capital gains. Dividends interest, rents, and most royalties would be tax exempt. Corporate profits would be taxed, but dividends, interest, and capital gains would flow untaxed to individuals. Corporations would be allowed to expense all capital expenditures, such as for new factories and equipment instead of capitalizing them over a period of years.

At the same time, Forbes's social views seem far more libertarian than the conservative Republican mainstream. He favors open immigration: "This country has the capacity to absorb more immigrants than we are absorbing now." On the campaign trail, Forbes has promised to implement GAO reports on government waste that he says are gathering dust. Forbes has surprised critics both in the media and opposing political camps by his laser-like ability to keep to his message.

Janne is learning a lot and able to contribute to the effectiveness of the campaign efforts. She is involved in marketing the message, interacting with donors, scheduling events, and responding to questions and inquiries. The more she gets to know Steve Forbes and his family, the more her respect for them grows. She is onboard with his political message. She also believes that when the time is right, he will be quite interested in what Jordan is working on in exposing the IRS. In her opinion, he will be able to point them in the right direction within Congress to conduct a formal investigation and make necessary reprimands and changes.

At 10:00 p.m. on Wednesday, November 22, Jordan surveys the underground parking lot at the Sherman Oaks office of Jacobs & Goodman. As soon as he is certain that all is clear, he parks the Bronco, and with Little Al, they ascend the stairs to the back entrance of the suite, where Jordan uses a flashlight to open the door with his set of keys. Without turning on any lights, he leads Al down the hallway to the far end, where his office is adjacent to Marlin's. The plan is that Al will practice first on Jordan's door so he can get a feel for the lock mechanism. They don't want to leave any markings of forced entry. If Al needs to experiment a bit, it's best to use Jordan's door to perfect the movement before attempting the "real McCoy" on Marlin's office door.

Al has brought his tools, which consist of an Allen wrench and a medium-sized paperclip. Remembering John Sawyer's discourse on "Two is one, one is none," he has two of each in two different sizes. It only takes Al a few tries to get Jordan's door open without leaving any forced marks. They proceed next door to Marlin's office. Al slides the Allen wrench into the lower edge of the keyhole. Applying a bit of pressure but not so much as to break or jam the lock, he turns it slightly in the direction that the key would turn. Keeping the pressure steady, he inserts an unbent paperclip with a small crook at the end to pick the lock. It works to perfection, as these office door locks are not built with heavy security against breaking and entering as their main feature.

Al turns to Jordan and smiles. Without saying a word, they both slide on full-face stocking caps with holes for their eyes and mouth. Jordan does not believe that Marlin and David have gone to the trouble of installing cameras in their respective offices, but they might as well take precautions. They also wear tight scuba gloves that will prevent fingerprints from being discovered if searched. These gloves allow them the dexterity of handling paper files as they search Marlin's filing cabinets. Once inside, they are pleased to find that the filing cabinets, which have two full-length cabinets with four drawers each, are not locked. They move quickly without speaking.

Jordan has instructed Al as to what they are looking for. With their small flashlights in hand, they examine the files, which are sorted by name alphabetically and type of tax debt. They pull files that are marked "Payroll Tax" or "Trust Fund Recovery." It doesn't surprise Jordan that the majority of the files are marked as such. They stack the appropriate files in a pile on the floor near the door. Once they have finished going through both cabinets, they take the stacks down the hall to where the main copier is located. Even though Marlin has a smaller copier / fax machine in his office, Jordan thinks it is more prudent to use the larger one in case of any paper jams or other issues. Jordan brought extra copy paper to work and stashed it in his office so as to not deplete the office supply.

They make copies of the information page, which lists the source of the lead, the taxpayer identification information, and notes, which could be very instrumental in identifying the evidence that Jordan searches, including other possible "responsible" persons. It also lists the amount of the debt and dates. Jordan doesn't bother making copies of the financial and IRS forms. Primarily, he is trying to ascertain whether these clients come directly from the IRS databanks to J&G or possibly through E, L & O. Once that is determined, they can delve into the details of the cases. The entire process takes a little over one hour, and they are ready to return everything to its proper place and get out of there. Jordan brought two backpacks, and they fill them with the copied files.

They drive away and head to LAX, where they have reservations for a redeye flight at 2:00 a.m. to Newark, New Jersey. They will have Thanksgiving dinner later that day with their respective families. They use the long-term parking lot, grab their carry-on bags, along with the backpacks, and catch the shuttle to the terminal.

Having spent much time in the northeast campaigning this fall, it was natural for Steve Forbes and his family to spend Thanksgiving at their enormous ranch-style home in Far Hills, New Jersey. He invited those on his campaign team that did not have family nearby to accompany his family for the holiday. That included Janne Sawyer. Graciously, she passed on the invite, as Jordan had invited her to spend Thanksgiving with him and his family in Short Hills, New Jersey. They timed their flights so that they could meet at the Newark airport, and they were picked up by Gabriela. Thanksgiving is traditionally a day of high school football in New Jersey, so Big Al has been busy preparing for his traditional rivalry game with Madison High School. Jordan, Little Al, and Janne will attend the game.

Gabriela is delighted to see Jordan. She gives Al a warm hug and a smile and is almost just as excited to meet Janne. After dropping off Al, they arrive home and get some sleep. Teri is bursting with energy and excitement when they wake. Dominating the conversation, she tells Jordan all about her AYSO championship soccer game that will be played on Saturday. Teri wants to make sure that Janne will be there too. Jordan introduces Janne to Phil. He is quite impressed that she works on the Steve Forbes campaign. Phil is a big supporter of Forbes and makes sure to tell Janne all that he knows about the political platform and how he endorses the flat tax that Mr. Forbes is presenting. Luckily, Jordan has warned Janne about Phil and his grandstanding.

In her typical classy manner, Janne handles Phil's ego smoothly, and Jordan once again is amazed at how well she interacts with anyone and everyone. It is no wonder to him that she excels in the political arena, as she seems to be a natural at appeasing all types of personalities that she encounters. Jordan excuses himself to take a shower, feeling confident that Janne will be fine without him.

The football game is in the early afternoon, so they go before the Thanksgiving meal. Teri begs to go with them. Jordan and Janne don't object, so when Little Al arrives, the four of them drive over to Millburn High School together. The stands are packed, and Jordan is surprised and a little embarrassed as to how many people remember him and Al as they climb the steps to their reserved seats just below the press box. Of course, Al, being Coach Bockman's son, has certain seat privileges. Jordan is astounded at how they receive a standing ovation from the Milburn faithful as they proceed to their seats. People of all ages reach out to shake their hands, pat them on the back, and call them by name as they pass. They represent the first and only state championship football team that Millburn High School has ever produced.

Jordan recognizes some faces and even some former classmates, but many seem to be complete strangers. He graciously accepts their applause and glad handling. He thinks about how sports and winning can bring a community together with lasting memories. Janne is impressed with the reception the boys receive as Jordan holds her hand. Teri is so proud of her brother that she grabs his other hand while sporting a huge smile as they walk. The temperature is considerably cooler here than SoCal; however, they are bundled together and enjoy the game as Millburn defeats Madison 21–20. Jordan promises Al that he will come by tomorrow to say hi to his mother and sit down to chat with Big Al.

Thanksgiving dinner is wonderful. The food is excellent and very filling. The company is delightful, and Janne fits in quite well. Jordan is actually content to let most of the conversation go through her. After dinner and dessert, they all pitch in to help clean up. They enjoy some TV, and then Teri scurries off to bed. Phil senses that mother and son would like some alone time to chat, so he excuses himself to the den to work on a project. Jordan is grateful that Phil leaves them some time to themselves. Janne also senses they might want some alone time, and she tries to excuse herself to go take a shower and get ready for bed. Jordan asks her to stay. She obliges without any debate.

Jordan proceeds to tell Gabriela about his encounter with John Sawyer and Pete Marshall. Upon hearing the story of the Battle of Hamburger Hill and how the two former soldiers had described the conditions in Vietnam and how sure they were of the bravery and valor of Edward Duncan, Gabriela can't help but let the tears flow unabashedly down her cheeks. Jordan moves over to the couch next to his mother, puts his arm around her, and expresses his love for her. She turns to him and puts both arms around him and begins sobbing with her head on his chest. Janne is crying in her chair across from them as she witnesses this outpour of love between mother and son.

Jordan has a lump in his throat. After a few minutes, he begins to tell his mother about his newly discovered love and appreciation for his father. He speaks slowly and quietly, but his words are measured and profound. It becomes a moment in their history that they will never forget. They each in their minds and hearts reminisce about all they have been through together—the early days in San Diego, running with each other every morning, struggling together with his homework, long working hours at her job in the restaurant, trying to stay financially solvent while Jordan was playing sports and learning to surf, Gabriela attending every game and important event in his life, the difficulties they confronted when she made the decision to marry Phil and move across the country.

She knew her son didn't understand why she made that decision and that she had his well-being in mind more than her own. She endured his initial complaints and struggles but also admired his strength to never complain again once they made the move. She thinks of his determination to become an outstanding athlete, earn a college scholarship, and be a great role model for his younger sister.

Jordan never doubted his mother's love for him nor for his father. He didn't understand how his father could not be with them, but he admired his mother's strength and vowed that he would be just as strong emotionally, mentally, and physically as his amazing mother. Now finally they can share in the love for and be proud of Gabriela's first and only true romantic love and Jordan's biological father, Edward Duncan. She will no longer have to suppress her feelings when she recognizes the character traits of her lover in their son. Jordan can now talk openly about all the press clippings that his mom kept of his dad's athletic accomplishments without suppressing his pride and admiration.

Janne is thankful to be here at this moment and thinks of the blessings she has experienced to have spent time with her mother and the close relationship she has with her father. It truly is the best Thanksgiving that each of them has ever experienced. Janne calls her father to tell him about the entire day and express her love and gratitude for him. John Sawyer is delighted to hear from his beloved daughter on Thanksgiving and tells her to please invite Jordan and his family to come spend Christmas with them at the cabin in Yosemite Valley.

It is agreed that a good run in the brisk morning air on the day after the Thanksgiving feast is just what each of them needs and desires. Teri, who metabolizes her meals almost as fast as she digests them, insists on joining them. Gabriela, Janne, Jordan, and Teri all engage in a quick-paced five-mile run up and down the hills encompassing the Short Hills neighborhood where the Conley family resides. Jordan knows what a superb runner Janne is, and he is equally impressed that his mom, who is now forty-six years old, can still keep pace. Teri is impressive as well. This little girl is full of grit and determination, Jordan observes.

After their invigorating run, they have breakfast with Phil, who has showered and dressed to go into his office in New York. Jordan has to admire, as he thinks to himself, Phil's work ethic. While growing up, he didn't really appreciate the fact that Phil never seems to miss a day of work and has done an admirable job of providing nicely for his family even if he was brought up with the proverbial silver spoon and handed an excellent opportunity right out of school. He could have dropped the ball but has made the most of his opportunity. The longer they remain together, the more Jordan realizes that Mr. Arrogant, Phillip Conley, does love his wife and daughter and provides them with a quite comfortable living. So what if he is totally nonathletic and somewhat narcissistic? The world is made up of a diverse mix of characters and personalities.

It would be boring, uneventful, and without challenges if we were all the same, Jordan concludes. *Wow, this is an interesting holiday weekend! I'm even gaining an appreciation for Phil!* The thought causes him to smile.

Janne gets clearance to join the campaign staff on Sunday evening in Buffalo. After showering and getting dressed, she accompanies Jordan to the Bockman residence. She is surprised at how close they live to each other. It is only a few blocks away, and they decide to walk. Janne notices and comments about the lovely neighborhood they live in. The streets are wide and lined with trees. Most of the homes sit on well-manicured, spacious lots with various landscaping diversity. Though the cold winter months are announcing their arrival, there still exists colorful life in these very beautiful hills and large custom homes.

Mrs. Bockman, Elaine, is a stout woman also of German descent and has a kind heart inside of her stern exterior. It took a good year and a half before they developed a mutual respect and could converse comfortably with each other. Jordan established a good amicable relationship with her during his high school years.

"Well, hi, Jordan," says Elaine as she gives him a hug with a smile at the door when he enters. "You are looking as handsome and fit as ever."

"Thanks, Mrs. B. You look good too. This is my friend Janne Sawyer. She went to UCLA also. However, we met later after both graduating. She currently is working on the campaign team of Steve Forbes."

"Oh, how nice. It is a pleasure to meet you."

"The pleasure is mine. I have heard wonderful things about you and your husband from both Al Jr. and Jordan," Janne says with a smile as she shakes Mrs. Bockman's hand. "You have a lovely home. I adore the coloring of your flooring and walls. It is so inviting and comfortable looking."

"Why, thank you, dear. Come on in and make yourselves comfortable. I will let the men know you are here and fix you some warm tea if you'd like."

"Thank you. That would wonderful, Mrs. Bockman," Janne responds while still smiling genuinely.

"Please call me Elaine."

Mrs. B has become the most recent fan of Janne Sawyer, Jordan thinks to himself as he, too, smiles.

Big and Little Al come up from the basement, where they were shooting pool, to greet them. Big Al gives Jordan a hearty handshake and hug.

"You look great, Jordan!" says Al Sr. with a big grin.

"Thanks, Coach. I want you to meet my girlfriend, Janne Sawyer. As I was telling Mrs. B, Janne is working on the Steve Forbes campaign. She is from California and graduated from UCLA."

"Nice to meet you, Janne." Big Al shakes her hand gently. "My son has told me quite a bit about you and Mr. Forbes. I've never met him personally, but he is well known in these parts with a stellar reputation as a fine, ethical businessman."

"He speaks very highly of you and your reputation in the community as well. I think it is about time the two of you meet!" Janne comments enthusiastically.

"I'd like that," says Al.

Add Big Al to the Janne Sawyer Admiration Society.

The four of them are joined by Elaine, and while sipping on warm tea, they get caught up in one another's lives. As the subject gets around to the dilemma that Jordan faces at work with the questionable ethics and possible illegal activities of the CPA firm with the IRS, Big Al listens intently. Little Al describes Alexander Epstein to his father as an arrogant jerk and goes into detail about their encounter at the Final Four.

Big Al shakes his head and with a half-smile says, "Why does it not surprise me that my son stoked the fire rather than pacify it?"

"If you were there, Pop, you would have decked him and his bodyguard."

"If I've taught you boys anything, it is to know your competition before you engage. I don't think I would haul off and belt a former Navy SEAL prior to sizing up the situation thoroughly and leveraging an advantage. Remember the rules of engagement from Sun Tzu." Big Al never stops teaching.

> Know the enemy and know yourself; in a hundred battles you will never be in peril.
> When you are ignorant of the enemy but know yourself, your chances of winning or losing are equal.
> If ignorant both of your enemy and yourself, you are certain in every battle to be in peril.

I like this guy already, thinks Janne.

Little Al smiles and nods his head.

"So you have decided to go to battle against the IRS and this bully from the CPA firm, huh?" Al Sr. questions Jordan.

"Yes, that's the plan." Jordan proceeds to lay out everything that they know so far and how they plan on acquiring more information. He concludes by adding that once they feel they have sufficient evidence, they will try to present it to a member of Congress. That is where Janne's connection with Steve Forbes could help.

Big Al looks at Janne and says, "Be careful, young lady, about to whom you say what in the US Congress. No offense, but politicians in general have a reputation of being snakes if it seems to be in their best interest. Mr. Forbes seems like a stand-up man, but he is not a true politician. You never know who is connected to whom in federal agencies."

"That is so true, Mr. Bockman. I do know that Mr. Forbes is extremely close to Mr. Jack Kemp, who has been a proponent of tax reform for a long time and not a fan of the IRS."

"This girl has done her homework," Big Al says with a smile. Janne returns the smile. "Jack Kemp sounds like an excellent advocate to your cause. However, both Forbes and Kemp are up to their necks in the presidential elections currently. I suggest that you continue to gather as much information as possible and be patient in presenting your case."

"I agree 100 percent," says Jordan. "Hey, Coach, this guy Epstein will play dirty, no doubt, if he feels threatened. But I'm pretty sure he will hide behind others when push comes to shove, as most bullies do. How do you propose we flush him out from behind his protection?"

"Very astute observation, Jordan. Do you boys remember what I taught you in football about getting an opponent to break from the game plan?"

Little Al smiles and says, "Make it personal. Get in his head that you are challenging him man to man."

"That's right, son. Win your one-on-one battles, but get your opponent to make it personal by getting into his head. He will deviate from the overall game plan. To a degree, you have begun that process by winning his basketball tournament two years in a row. Be careful, though. This guy sounds dangerous, especially if he has connections within the IRS."

They spend a little more time together talking about their glory days of winning the state championship, and then Jordan asks Big Al about this year's team. Coach Bockman never shies away from talking about his team and his boys. Before they leave, Jordan asks to have a few minutes in private with the coach. They go downstairs, while Little Al and Janne visit with Elaine and she shows Janne the rest of her home.

Jordan relates the story that he heard about his father up in Yosemite from the former soldiers, one of whom actually fought in the Battle of Hamburger Hill alongside his dad. Knowing that Al Sr. is a history teacher and has a special interest in US military history, Jordan believes Big Al will appreciate this first-person rendition that he heard. He is correct in that assessment. Alvin Bockman Sr. is misty-eyed as Jordan finishes the story, and he puts his big arm around Jordan's shoulder.

"I always felt that your father was a special kind of soldier that would make you proud if you knew the truth. I felt that because he produced, along with your mother, such a fine young man. I have seen you as a fearless competitor out on the football field who also sticks up for the less fortunate. I knew that fire within you comes from good, strong stock. I'm very happy that now you also know that, Jordan. Thank you for sharing the story with me."

"Thanks, Coach. I appreciate all that you have taught me and for being there when I needed someone in high school to discuss personal things."

"I'm always here. Good luck with the challenge ahead of you. Let me know if you need any help," Big Al reassures Jordan.

On Friday afternoon, Little Al has organized a game of pick-up basketball for him and Jordan down at Taylor Park with some of their old classmates and teammates who are in town. Though most are not in the same shape they were in high school, they have a nice run and engage in great conversation with their former friends. They discover that Miles Jackson has moved to NYC and is working on Wall Street. Teddy "Ballgame" Balcom played football four years at UNC, got married, and stayed in North Carolina. He is now a supervisor for a large building contractor firm in Charlotte. Paul Hoage sheepishly confesses that he lives in his parents' basement and works as a day trader. He has become quite adept with his computer skills as he loses both Al and Jordan with his technology talk. Little Al brags about the contract he got for Gambo. It is a fun time, and they promise to stay in touch upon departing once again.

On Saturday morning, Teri is the first to rise. She eats a small breakfast and is totally stoked for her soccer match. She explains to Jordan and Janne that this is the championship game. Her team is undefeated and untied. The team they will be playing is also undefeated but has one tie game. The winners will be awarded individual trophies and bragging rights as Section 3 AYSO champions.

Knowing that even in the midday, the temperature will be in the low forties, Teri wears compression leggings under her uniform shorts and a dry-fit pullover under her jersey. She wears jersey number 9 and asks Jordan if he has ever heard of Mia Hamm. Jordan smiles and tells her yes, that he knows who Mia Hamm is. Mia played at the University of North Carolina, where she was a two-time NCAA national player of the year and a three-time national champion. She has become perhaps the greatest female soccer player in the world representing the USA national team. Teri tells Jordan a little apologetically that Hamm is her new role model in sports and that she is now considering trying to get a scholarship to play at UNC rather than UCLA. Jordan assures his sister that he will be extremely proud of her no matter where she goes to college and in whatever she pursues.

Both Jordan and Janne, who are joined by Gabriela and Phil in watching Teri play, are amazed at how fast and precise she is on the field. She is by far the best player out there for either team. They win the game 5–2, and Teresa Conley has scored four goals! Walking off the field toward the car, Jordan has his arm around his sister's shoulder, and it is now he who is proud to be her sibling.

She looks up to him and says almost in a whisper, "If I do go to UCLA, I'm thinking of playing under the name of Teresa Duncan. So that people will know I am your little sister. Someday maybe I will have my photo on the Wall of Fame next to yours."

Jordan smiles and says, "You should be proud of being Teresa Conley. We will always be brother and sister and connected through our mom's bloodline. You have a fine father and a great name!"

"Okay. But will you help me set up my offseason training? I want to start on Monday."

This girl is dedicated, Jordan thinks.

"Just keep running with Mom, do a lot of stretching exercises, and work on your footwork and ball skills when you can get outside or in the gym."

Teri motions for Jordan to lean down so she can whisper in his ear. "I want to get killer abs like Janne has."

Jordan laughs and says, "You will have to ask Janne about her secret formula for that."

Teri converses with Janne about an ab routine and seems anxious to implement it into her life as soon as possible. The ab routine will have to wait until after the family enjoys pizza at Teri's favorite pizzeria to celebrate her win.

On Sunday morning, after a nice breakfast, Gabriela tells Jordan and Janne goodbye with a hug for each. Phil shakes hands with both of them, wishing them each well. Teri is practically in tears as she says goodbye to them, giving a heartfelt hug to Jordan and a sweet hug and kiss on the cheek to Janne. Big Al has agreed to take them all to the airport.

Jordan and Janne exchange hugs and kisses at Newark airport before departing for their respective gates. Both Little Al and Jordan will sleep most of the way on the flight across country to LAX. They agree that it was a wonderful holiday and time well spent with family and friends.

Jordan never even looked at the files stashed in the backpacks but is glad that he brought them along so that he knows the information therein is secure. His mind is now locked in on what is ahead. He looks forward to reviewing these documents and making a determination as to what will transpire next. He glances over at Al, who seems to be in a deep sleep without a worry in the world. He knows he can count on his big friend in any way necessary. He feels comforted as he puts his seat back and closes his eyes.

CHAPTER TWELVE

Battle Lines

After reviewing the documents that were retrieved from Marlin's files and after much thought and deliberation, Jordan comes to the decision that it would be best to share this information with Tonja and Brookes. He has two reasons for this: (1) As they are dedicated employees and close personal associates, he feels as though they have a right to know what is going on behind the scenes as their respective careers are at risk. (2) He feels as though perhaps they can help him in deciding how to move forward with the damning evidence. He thinks they may be able to assist him in tying E, L & O to J&G and the IRS.

Considering the sensitive subject matter, Jordan has asked them to meet him outside of the office. They agree to have dinner after work hours at P. F. Chang's located in the Galleria. As they arrive, they order their meals and engage in some office small talk.

Tonja shares this recap: "Ever since the OJ acquittal, David has been in such a cranky mood. He keeps mumbling about how 'only in LA' could O. J. Simpson get away with murder. I have heard him and Marlin argue and complain very loudly about how it could happen. Marlin is convinced that the case was lost when the prosecutors allowed the trial to be conducted in downtown LA instead of Santa Monica. That led to having nine Blacks and one Hispanic on the jury. He insists that lost the case before they heard any testimony. David, on the other hand, is convinced that the ineptitude of the LA

Police Department in planting evidence and botching the investigation created enough doubt that ultimately lost the case for the prosecution. They both agree that OJ is guilty, but the verdict probably saved the city from some more major riots!"

Jordan and Brookes are equally surprised but not shocked with the outcome of the trial nor with the fact that David and Marlin are still arguing and upset about the verdict two months after the trial concluded.

"Being that he is an SC guy, I never really liked him anyway," Jordan says, speaking of OJ, with a slight grin. "But in all seriousness, I do find it odd that there were zero other suspects. It was either convict OJ or throw it away into the unsolved-murder files."

Brookes shakes his head and says, "Yeah, I guess now only time will tell if the case will ever be solved."

Jordan begins the conversation on why he wanted to chat with them by explaining that it is imperative that they swear secrecy on the things that will be discussed. Tonja and Brookes agree, and it only adds to their curiosity as to why Jordan wanted to meet outside the office.

He proceeds to explain the identity of Royce Dawkins, the allegations that he made concerning E, L & O, and the subsequent confirmation of suspicious activity by Arthur Gibson. He then talks about how the declaration from JoJo at the Sportmen's Lodge piqued his personal interest to discover the truth, as it pertains to the involvement of David and Marlin in the dealings with the IRS. Jordan definitely has their undivided attention as he further details how he recovered files from Marlin's office in the attempt to discover the origin of the trust fund recovery cases. Tonja reassures him that even though Marlin sees the majority of his clients in Beverly Hills, he keeps all his files in the Sherman Oaks office except for some of the cases he is currently working on in Beverly Hills. Jordan tells them that each one of those cases have come to Marlin via fax from the main office of E, L & O. Since he is almost 100 percent sure they don't do any active outside marketing for tax resolution clients, his only logical conclusion is that these cases are originating directly from the IRS. Jordan pauses to get a response from his colleagues.

Brookes responds first. "This is incredible news to me. I'm shocked by what you are telling us."

Jordan interjects this question, "Have you written any ads for E, L & O or for David on the subject of payroll taxes or trust fund recovery tax debts?"

"No, I have never been asked to. You have seen all the ads that I have written and have been placed in the various newspapers," Brookes replies. "Do you think this means that the work we do is not legit?"

"No, I don't think that at all. And neither does Arthur. Everything we do is legit. Your ads entice delinquent taxpayers to call our office. Jo's team screens the calls and sets appointments. The TDAs bring them on board with the POA and collect fees. Tonja and her team gather the financial information, and the tax managers negotiate settlements. I am totally convinced that the process is legitimate and has been quite successful. Arthur confers that feeling," Jordan states emphatically.

"Whew, that is good to know. I'd hate to think otherwise," Brookes says with some relief.

Tonja finally responds, "I have to say this does not shock me."

Both Jordan and Brookes look at her inquisitively.

She further explains, "What I mean is, I am completely caught off guard in what they are allegedly doing with the IRS in getting leads. However, as much as I love David and the way he has always treated me, the man is haunted by demons. Nothing is ever enough for him—in his marriage, in his business, in his bank account... He is haunted by *greed!*"

"That is really sad," Brookes concludes. "David has always treated me well, and I know he cares about his family and those that work for him. But I must admit, Tonja, I see the same affliction in him."

"The question is, what are we going to do about it?" Jordan asks. He doesn't disagree with what his friends are saying about David; however, at this point, he is not feeling any sympathy for him.

"I think it is important to know for sure that these leads are coming from the IRS," Tonja says.

"The only way to do that is to get confirmation from within E, L & O. I don't think we can go to David and Marlin to ask them," Jordan replies.

"I am really torn," says Tonja. "The thought of going behind David's back and then throwing him under the bus is just something I cannot get myself to do. We go way back." Tonja's loyalty to David obviously is causing her to be quite perplexed by the situation.

"How about this idea?" Jordan starts to present a plan that he has been thinking about. "We infiltrate E, L & O to get the source of the leads. Tonja, you used to work for them, so you probably know how they work and who might be able to guide us down the trail of leads. Then with that information and the files that show Marlin on the POA, we pin the blame on Marlin. David would be an accomplice. Someone is setting the appointments for Marlin, as I think we can all agree that he is not calling potential clients to set appointments. I highly doubt that the IRS is involved in scheduling. That means it is probably someone from within E, L & O." Jordan is trying to soften the impact of the ramifications directed toward David. He knows neither of them have warm feelings toward Marlin.

Brookes is shaking his head. "This is sounding pretty dicey to me. Perhaps I should just resign."

"I understand how you feel, Brookes, and believe me, I've had the same thoughts. But if we can hang in there a little longer, we can establish that the leads come directly from the IRS through E, L & O, which is illegal. Right now, none of us have done anything wrong, and there is no proof that Jacobs & Goodman has done anything illegal."

Tonja is in deep thought. She has this to say: "I will look at the copies of Marlin's files that you have and determine who sends the leads to him from E, L & O. From there, I can figure out from where they get the leads. That is where I will have to draw the line as far as my involvement. I don't want to implicate David in any illegal activities. I'm sorry, Jordan, but that is the best I can offer. I promise I won't let anyone, including David, know what you are doing."

"No problem, Tonja. I appreciate that. If I get confirmation that Marlin is being fed leads that come directly from the IRS, I will let you know before I act on it. That way, you can jump ship or even let David know by then. Brookes, if you can wait until I know for sure, then I will support you also." Jordan wants their cooperation but realizes that it is important to give them the opportunity to get out before things get ugly.

"Okay, thanks," says Tonja. "But I will probably go down with the ship. I'm pretty sure David will go down fighting, and I feel like I have done nothing wrong nor was I in the loop of having information that anything illegal was happening. I will stay with him until the end."

"I can hang in there until you know for sure, Jordan," Brookes confirms.

Jordan nods his head in appreciation to both of them. It is with heavy hearts and a sad demeanor that Tonja and Brookes leave their meeting with Jordan.

During the Christmas holidays of 1995, John Sawyer invited his daughter, Janne, her boyfriend, Jordan, and his family to spend time at his Yosemite Valley cabin home. The Conley family had to respectfully decline due to other commitments. John and his partner, Peter Marshall, thought it might be a good time to invite Arthur Gibson and his wife, Donna, to the cabin for a nice holiday. It's time to review in person the progress that Arthur, Jordan, and Janne have made in the past few months in carrying out the plan to expose the IRS. Jordan confirms there will be enough room to accommodate Al to the rendezvous as well.

As Jordan and Al chill out in Jordan's apartment after playing hoops at the Venice Beach courts, Al proposes an extended invitation to his girlfriend, April, to join them in Yosemite. Before Jordan agrees to that plan, he questions Al's relationship status with April and the level of trust he has with her as it pertains to keeping everything she sees and hears confidential.

Al smiles, puts his arm around Jordan's shoulder, and says, "You know, D-Can, you have been so wrapped up in this espionage work that we haven't had a chance to chat much lately about our personal lives. The fact is, April and I have been working on our relationship ever since the Final Four and have become very serious. My plan is to ask her to marry me up there at the cabin on Christmas Eve." Al's smile now extends from ear to ear. "I am going to shoot for a late April wedding. Yes, that is intentional based on her name and timing, being just after the NFL draft and tax day. I would like you to be my best man!"

Jordan is stunned for a moment. He didn't see this developing, but he is genuinely thrilled for his best friend. "It would be my honor to be your best man, Little Al."

They do the bro hug and laugh as Jordan looks for something to use for a toast. The best he can come up with is a couple of bottles of Corona in the fridge.

"That will do perfectly!" says Al.

"To everlasting joy and marital bliss for Alvin and April Bockman!" Jordan toasts, and they clink their bottles of beer and chug them down.

Jordan, Janne, Al, and April all drive up from SoCal together in Jordan's Bronco. The forecast is for a white Christmas in Yosemite this year, so having the four-wheel drive Bronco with chains is most appropriate. Pete flies the chopper to the Sacramento airport to pick up Arthur and Donna, who fly in from Virginia on Friday, December 22.

Donna Gibson is sixty years old and quite attractive. Her gray hair is cut short, and she has a slender build on her five-foot-six-inch frame. She has a most pleasant-looking smile and a beautiful caramel-colored complexion. Like her husband, she dresses impeccably. She received her college degree in English literature from Georgetown University, where she met Arthur when he was in law school there. She taught high school English for several years before giving birth to their first daughter. Two years later, the Gibsons brought another daughter into the world. Donna remained a stay-at-home mom until both girls were in junior high. Then she took up teaching at the high school level once again. She is now retired and is looking forward to Arthur also retiring so they can travel more frequently and visit their extended family, which now includes three grandchildren.

After introductions, the group enjoys a nice dinner together on Friday evening. On Saturday morning, John takes them on a horseback excursion through the snow-draped mountain range. They spend the entire day immersed in the beauty of nature and are blessed with a crystal-clear day of midforty-degree temperatures. They arrive back at the cabin before sunset and once again are the beneficiaries of a superbly cooked meal by John and Pete—smoked venison with baked potatoes and fresh asparagus accompanied by an exquisite Cabernet Sauvignon red wine from Napa Valley. After dinner, all of them change into comfortable attire and retire out on the back deck to gaze at the magnificent view of various star formations in the sky.

The younger generation of Jordan, Janne, Al, and April brave the cool air and dip into the warm bubbly water of the spa. The others within earshot on the bench surrounding the spa, they decide to begin their discussion concerning their respective activities over the past few months.

Arthur begins by recounting his visits with Shelley Davis, the IRS historian. He recounts her description of how secretive the IRS is about its history. She shared with him that the IRS keeps lists of American citizens for no other reason than that their political activities might have offended someone at the IRS. She explained also about how the IRS believes that anyone who offers even legitimate criticism of the tax collector is a tax protester. She told him how the IRS shreds its paper trail, which means that there is no history, no evidence, and ultimately, no accountability. The IRS destroys its own records, which is against the law, breaking the Federal Records Act. As she escalated her findings and complaints up the ladder of authority within the agency, she was met with apathy and was ultimately stonewalled. Arthur tells his colleagues about Shelley Davis resigning as IRS historian, effective December 31.

Arthur surmises that the IRS Special Service was created for the sole purpose of gathering information and targeting certain individuals and groups for the political gain of their rivals. There is sufficient evidence to prove these accusations. The challenge, as he sees it, is to gather evidence proving that the IRS has also worked in collaboration with CPA firms such as Epstein, Levin & Ohlman Tax Consultants. Arthur points out that the IRS has recently spent hundreds of millions of dollars installing new computer systems. His belief is that an infiltration of this compilation of data might present the most effective manner to breach the necessary evidence indicating irregular and illegal activities between the IRS and the CPA firm in targeting audits for financial gain.

When Arthur suggests this strategy, Jordan and Little Al look at each other in the hot tub as if the same thought is crossing their respective minds.

Al is the one who voices the idea. "Jordan and I have a friend and former classmate whom we recently discovered has become very adept in his computer skills. He calls himself a day trader; however, he also indicated that he has learned to hack many computer systems." Al continues with the thought, "Perhaps since the IRS has recently transferred all this data to a new system, they haven't yet perfected their firewall for security purposes."

John Sawyer chimes in immediately, "I like it. Pete and I haven't shown you as of yet, but we have quite an elaborate high-tech 'bunker' set up. Dave Lackey, whom we mentioned is our third partner, worked closely with the Pentagon when he was in the CIA. He was able to reach out to his contacts and get the most advanced sophisticated computer system equipment. One of Pete's clients is the founder and CEO of a telecommunications firm based in the Silicon Valley. He has donated a highly sophisticated satellite system from which we have international access across the globe. What we lack is someone with the skills to run the system. Maybe your buddy could be that person."

"Wouldn't hurt to ask and see if he would be interested," Jordan says. "He can certainly be counted on for confidentiality. His name is Paul Hoage, if you want to check him out."

"I say let's give it a shot. Pete is more familiar with our setup than I am, so he can work on scheduling a visit from Paul and train him on our equipment," John responds.

Arthur and Pete both agree with the plan.

Next is Jordan's turn to recap his activities. "Al and I were able to retrieve files from Marlin's office in Sherman Oaks, where he stores all of his caseloads. We hit the jackpot, so to speak. We focused on the payroll tax and trust fund recovery client files. There were close to a hundred files, and every one of them was transmitted to him via fax from Epstein's CPA firm. Knowing that E, L & O doesn't do any marketing for tax resolution cases, that indicates that they receive the leads from an alternative source. Based on the financial and personal data listed, we can be confident that it originates from the IRS database." Jordan turns to look at Al and continues, "Next, I met outside of the office with my two most trusted colleagues, Tonja Farley, the office manager, and Brookes Peterson, the marketing specialist."

Arthur cuts in, "I have met both of them, and they are quite competent. But I know that Tonja goes back several years with David Jacobs, to when he was a partner with Epstein. Not sure how deep her loyalty is."

Jordan continues, "That's right, Arthur. However, Tonja and I have a strong, trusted relationship as well. Even though this information about Royce Dawkins and the subsequent allegations surprised her, as she indicated, she was not shocked. In her words, 'David has demons,' most notably the affliction of greed."

Al lets out a little laugh.

"I waited until I had reviewed the files from Marlin's office before sharing any of this with them. Here is the plan we laid out moving forward. As Arthur mentioned, Tonja has connections within E, L & O. She is going to trace the faxed files back to whomever is sending them. Interestingly, many of these clients come from all across the US, which is another indicator that this is a national operation that has the smell of IRS influence." Jordan takes his wet hands and rubs his face and hair with the warm water. "Once it is confirmed from whence these leads originated, we can prove the relationship between E, L & O and J&G with the IRS. From there, we can present our findings to the appropriate members of the US Congress." With that statement, he looks to Janne.

Janne explains, "I was able to mention some of these allegations to Mr. Forbes, and though he seems interested in hearing more, we have been so focused on the campaign. He advised that you continue to collect evidence and at some point, we will be able to present our case. I think he will help us get in front of the right people. We have the Republican Party debates starting in just a few weeks."

John speaks next. "I think everyone is making great headway. We are definitely building a case on plan A. How is plan B progressing? Jordan?"

"I have two specific cases that scream taxpayer abuse. I have established a strategy to document abusive action by the revenue officer. There are more general episodes that I can present. However, I believe these two cases are illustrations of continuous abuse throughout the history of the case, and one also involves the Criminal Investigation Division."

Arthur adds, "Excellent! I have reached out as an informational gathering tactic to other tax professionals, asking them to document taxpayer abuse episodes from the IRS Investigative and Collection Divisions."

"Very good!" John replies. "Pete, should we give these folks the grand tour of the 'bunker'?"

"Sure thing." Pete sounds anxious to show off this crown jewel of their impressive complex.

Upon showering and changing clothes, the younger group joins the others in the basement sitting at the bar. They enter the laundry room, which is a good-sized room measuring 12' × 12'. It has a commercial-size washer, dryer, deep double sink, ample cupboard space, and a 3' × 6' folding table. The back wall to where the washer and dryer butt up against is concrete. Behind the washer, there is a faucet for hot and cold water and a lever, which appears to be the master on/off mechanism for the water supply. Behind the dryer is a ventilation system. The lever is actually a mechanism to operate a "false" trap door. Once it is engaged by way of a combination code, the door, which is hidden by an area rug, is opened and exposes a stairwell.

The group follows Pete down the stairs, holding on to a rail on the side. The bottom of the stairs opens into the computer bunker room. Pete flips on an overhead light. There is a rather large computer hardware mainframe with a monitor and keyboard on a desktop. There are two other smaller desks with slightly smaller monitors and one more monitor mounted high on the wall. A printer is sitting on top of an adjacent desktop. Pete explains that they have a satellite receptor attached to the roof of the cabin, which appears to coincide with the TV antennae. The monitor up on the wall is set up to show current and forecasted weather conditions throughout the world. Pete explains that not only do they have worldwide access to the Web but that they also have capabilities to infiltrate other hardware systems across the country and in some other parts of the world. They just lack the know-how in computer technology.

Pete smiles as he says, "I'm anxious to see if Paul Hoage can help us overcome that liability."

At the back of the room, there is a rather inconspicuous-looking small door.

"Are you interested in where that leads?" Pete asks while pointing at the door.

After a unanimous nodding of the heads, Al says, "If this is a replica of the bat cave, I am going to say I've seen it all."

There is some laughter, and Pete responds, "Not exactly, but you may find it quite interesting."

He works the combination to the door and flips a switch, which illuminates a lighting system along the walls. He leads the group through a tunnel just wide and high enough to comfortably allow each of them, including the 6'5" Al and Arthur, to walk single file behind him about thirty yards to where there is another door. They always bring flashlights with them as well. A second door opens to a similarly sized room. However, it is stacked with a various arsenal of weapons hanging on brackets against the walls—many AR brand rifles, hunting rifles (some with scopes attached), AK brand automatic weapons, handguns, shotguns, knives, machetes, silencers, hand grenades, even a couple of rocket launchers. There are different types of head gear hanging on the wall as well. John points out a small door at the far end of this room, which he explains gives access to a ladder that leads to an opening in the barn and is well camouflaged behind the horse stalls. On the other side of the ladder is a small room, which is filled with condensed food storage and gallon water containers.

Arthur speaks first. "Most impressive indeed. You have obviously taken a lot of time and preparation in designing this entire complex."

Pete responds, "Can never be too cautious. By the way, all these doors are fireproof." He points to a bench, which has boots on it, against the sidewall. "Inside that bench box is camouflaged gear, with night goggles, infrared lasers, body armor vests, and insulated clothing. Behind the bench, there is a locked crawl hole, which leads to an alternative escape route. It surfaces in the forest near the chopper pad."

"Like I said, this is my plan C exit strategy, if you don't mind," says Al as April grins, tightly holding his hand.

On Christmas Eve day, Al takes April for a walk out to the snow-covered meadow. At the edge of the opening, just as it converges with the path into the forest, Little Al turns toward April, drops onto one knee, and proposes marriage to her while presenting her with a beautiful diamond ring. Jordan and Janne, who are sitting on the back deck at the cabin and out of the line of sight, can hear April's scream as she accepts. They laugh in unison while holding hands.

Christmas Eve and Christmas Day are filled with happiness and gratitude as the small group mingle and enjoy one another's company while engaging in various games of billiards, poker, and table board and card games. Jordan and Al discuss what Al has planned over the next few months before the NFL draft. April and Janne discuss wedding plans. Arthur and Donna thank John and Pete for hosting such a wonderful holiday. John is insistent they bring their daughters, their spouses, and three grandchildren to the cabin. The Gibsons most graciously agree to extend the invitation.

On Christmas night, the eight of them sit on the back deck. Dressed in warm clothing while drinking various beverages, they gaze at the stars this clear night and reflect verbally on how blessed and grateful they are for the magnificent event that took place in a small manger halfway across the world nearly two thousand years ago and is the reason for this celebratory day. Their lives are precious gifts, they all agree.

Meanwhile, in Southern California, the weekend is enjoyed by Alexander Epstein, Barry Levin, and their respective spouses at the Beverly Wilshire Hotel. It provides a nice break from the dismal

East Coast weather for a few days. As the women enjoy a day shopping on Saturday, December 23, the men have set up a meeting with David and Marlin in the Sherman Oaks office, which is closed for the Christmas holiday.

David has provided each with his beverage of choice from his office bar as they sit to discuss the uncomfortable situation in which they find themselves in terms of business activities of late.

Epstein begins speaking. "I was hoping that exposing Royce Dawkins simply as a disgruntled ex-employee would be sufficient to keep Arthur Gibson and Jordan Duncan at bay. Apparently, that is not the case, at least not with Arthur. I will explain in detail what we have discovered about his recent activities, and then I would like to hear what you know about Duncan's most recent operations."

"Please proceed," David says.

"During my conversation with Arthur, he agreed to not meet with nor speak to Dawkins again. It was a condition of his continued association with the firm as a consultant. To the best of my knowledge, he has abided by that agreement." Alex demonstrates a serious and concerned demeanor, which is typical in his business meetings. "However, he proceeded to meet in public with the IRS historian, a woman by the name of Shelley Davis. Although there is evidence that they had previously met, there was no indication of any kind of friendship or relationship during or after his time at the IRS."

David interrupts with a question, "Is there a possibility of an affair?"

Epstein looks at him annoyingly. "No. Please let me finish, and then I will entertain questions."

David nods his head and reaches for his drink.

Epstein continues, "After meeting for over an hour, they departed shaking hands, and Arthur handed her a business card. A week later, they met briefly again, and she handed him a file." Epstein pauses to take a sip of his drink before continuing. "The information she provided was some IRS historical data pertaining to allegations against the Kennedy administration of directing IRS audits against a right-winged group called Young Americans for Freedom." Again, Epstein pauses for a moment before continuing. "There must be a compelling reason why, at this time, Arthur Gibson is so interested in meeting with Shelley Davis. My assumption is that he is trying to gather information about target auditing within the IRS. And I don't think it has to do with his politics." Alex seems to be through with his discourse and ready to entertain questions. There is a significant period of silence due in part for each of the others to contemplate on what they just heard and also to make sure he is finished so that he doesn't reprimand anyone as he did David.

Once again, it is David who breaks the silence. "How were you able to get this information? By tailing Arthur, how would he know what they discussed? I highly doubt that Davis would speak openly to Turlock."

"The IRS has been investigating Ms. Davis. There are two agents assigned to her. I have my own sources within the agency from whom I receive information. This is verifiable information." Alexander Epstein never shies away from trying to make sure everyone in the room knows how important he is.

"So Turlock is not following Gibson?" David inquires.

"No. Kurt is working on some other things for me, which is not relevant to this conversation," replies Epstein in his condescending manner.

Marlin speaks next. "What are your thoughts on what Gibson is up to?"

"May I?" asks Barry Levin, looking toward Epstein, who is seated across from him. He is essentially Epstein's "right-hand man."

"By all means." Epstein relinquishes the narrative.

Levin is rather small in stature, his height being between that of Epstein and Jacobs, about 5'8". He is small boned and thin and soft in build. He probably hasn't done anything athletic in decades, if ever. He is on the fading end of a long career in accounting and statistics, which is his forte. In addition to being a partner at Epstein, Levin & Ohlman Tax Consultants, he has taught courses in statistics at the University of Maryland, his alma mater, where he received an MBA with an emphasis in statistical finance. He is definitely the numbers guy within the firm, a certified public accountant, and even though he is in his late sixties, he thoroughly enjoys developing algorithms and doing statistical analysis on E, L & O clients' financial business models.

Levin addresses the small group. "Statistically speaking, the risk of Arthur Gibson connecting a parallel that would indicate a correlation between IRS corporate audits and our CPA firm is low—due mainly to the sheer volume of IRS audits. However, the risk is much greater if he continues to probe into the IRS seeking some kind of collaboration that a leak will occur to someone on Capitol Hill." Levin pauses to gaze at Epstein, who gives him a nod to continue.

"This poses a much greater statistical risk of investigation aimed toward the IRS that could impact E, L & O particularly due to the fact that we are entering an election year and those within the Republican Party are building a platform largely based upon tax reform. If there are allegations or even suspicions of any inappropriate activity occurring between the IRS and a public CPA firm, the issue could get blown up into a major scandal by those wishing to overhaul the entire tax system." Again, Levin turns to make eye contact with Epstein, who nods his head of approval.

Epstein says, "Thank you, Barry. That was very well explained."

"So I think it is evident that we cannot allow Arthur to continue searching for information regarding target auditing. So far, his probing has not infiltrated our auditing documents. We have firewalls to prevent that from occurring. But he must be stopped from questioning IRS personnel."

"How do you propose handling that, Alex?" David inquires. "The man worked there for thirty years at a high level."

Epstein responds, "He obviously doesn't know enough to go directly to high-ranking IRS officials. My guess is that he is well aware of the hierarchy that exists in the agency and knows that anything in the nature of what he suspects would be covered up. Therefore, he is looking to attain records that might implicate the illicit action of target auditing."

"So how do we stop him?" David asks directly.

"We can terminate his association with the firm as a consultant and remind him of the NDA that he signed. If that doesn't work, we can be more forthright in the severe consequences of his continued actions."

"You mean threaten him?" asks Marlin.

"With legal action, yes," replies Alex.

"Can we legally keep him from speaking to employees of the IRS or members of Congress?" Marlin continues his questioning.

"As it pertains to the nondisclosure agreement, yes. He is not allowed to discuss any business activities from within E, L & O."

Epstein abruptly changes the subject. "Tell us what Duncan has been up to." He is looking directly at David.

"Business as usual. He is signing up new cases, bringing in top revenue, and doesn't seem to be fazed by the new IRS national and local standards. Hasn't said anything to anyone about Dawkins and, to the best of my knowledge, hasn't communicated with Arthur." David is not exactly sure of these declarations, but he is wishing and hoping them to be true.

"Marlin, what are your observations?" Epstein knows that Marlin shares in his distrust and dislike of Jordan Duncan.

Marlin hesitates momentarily as he gathers his thoughts. He wants to measure his response, as he knows of David's support for the kid and Alexander's disdain for him. "There is no doubt that the kid can sell our services. However, he scares me with the way he does things his own way. I don't have any evidence that he is working with Arthur and/or Dawkins, but it wouldn't surprise me if he were."

David shakes his head. "What has he done that makes you distrust him?"

Marlin looks directly at David and responds, "You know what he did with the Delgado case." He looks back to Epstein. "He signed up a client who is being investigated by the CID. He got a $10,000 fee, but we need to be extremely careful about the cases we represent. He didn't bother consulting with David before taking the case and didn't mention the investigation until David received a call from the LA IRS district director."

"What do you propose we do about him?" Epstein asks, looking at Marlin.

David interjects before Marlin can speak, "There is nothing to do, because he has not violated the terms we set concerning Dawkins. Perhaps I could set the same terms in reference to Arthur—"

Epstein interrupts before David can finish his sentence, neglecting to even look at him. "Let's hear what Marlin thinks."

Again, Marlin is careful to measure his words. "I believe he represents a real threat to our operations. We can replace the revenue, but he is uncontrollable. He marches to his own tune. He's smart, confident, and everyone likes him, including staff members and clients. Worst of all, he can't be intimidated. I can see where he would start a rebellion that could escalate out of our control in a hurry if he ever suspects that our operations might not be completely kosher with IRS regulations."

Epstein rubs his chin with his hand. He has a furrowed brow as he replies, "Everyone has their breaking point of intimidation. Has he asked any questions about the cases you work? Trust fund recovery cases?"

David is fuming just under the surface of his calm demeanor as Epstein focuses his inquiries and attention to Marlin. "No, surprisingly, he never has. I gave him the Delgado case, which was probably a mistake," Marlin responds without looking in David's direction. "In spite of the $10,000 fee, he also might bring the CID to our doorstep, which we all agree is not what we want."

"Do you think we should fire him?" Epstein asks Marlin directly.

David jumps back into the conversation. "We don't need to fire him. I will explain that Arthur is no longer with the company and that we need him to sign an NDA that includes not speaking to Arthur. I will continue to keep him on a short leash, as I have been doing with the Delgado case."

Epstein looks at Marlin. "Would that be acceptable to you, Marlin?"

Marlin looks at David, who glares back. "I suppose we could try that approach. Is there a way to monitor whether he contacts Arthur?"

"Through the office phones, yes. We could bug his office. Outside of the office, the best we could do is put a tail on him. I doubt if we could get access to his cell phone and listen in on his calls," Epstein answers.

Marlin again looks at David and says, "Let's bug his office and monitor his office calls."

David nods his head and says, "We can do that."

The group concludes their meeting by discussing the overall welfare of the business, future plans of action, and how they will implement their strategy as it pertains to Arthur Gibson and Jordan Duncan. Epstein instructs David and Marlin to not speak to Jordan about Arthur until he gives the okay. He does authorize them to set up the bug in Jordan's office and monitor his office calls.

In January, the first of five successive Republican presidential primary debates are held in Des Moines, Iowa. There were eight candidates for the first debate, and by the end of February, the field had essentially been whittled down to three viable candidates—Senate majority leader Bob Dole, conservative talk host Pat Buchanan, and businessman Steve Forbes. Forbes had done a formidable job of presenting his message of growth and opportunity during the debates. His primary focus was to return economic control of the country to the people. The message is being well received by Republican constituents. However, Senator Dole entered the field as a huge favorite to carry the party nomination come August of 1996 at the Republican Party Convention.

Forbes won primaries in Arizona and Delaware. In a last-ditch effort to make a legitimate run at the nomination, Steve Forbes receives a huge endorsement on March 6 from Jack Kemp. Mr. Kemp's endorsement was highly sought after by all candidates as he is a popular, supply side economics, tax reform advocate, a la Ronald Reagan. In fact, he worked closely with President Reagan on his 1986 tax reform bill. Kemp and Forbes worked together on the Empower American Project in 1993, which formed a conservative think tank and advocated low taxes and deregulation as a means to stimulate economic growth. While endorsing Steve Forbes, Jack Kemp promotes the flat tax platform.

Janne is super excited about the Kemp endorsement and calls Jordan to enthusiastically share the news with him.

As Jordan is working in his office in early March, he gets buzzed by Vanessa that he has a call on line 2 from a Mr. Fernandez of the Drug Enforcement Agency. He had reached out and left a message for the DEA in an attempt to discover the details of the Delgado investigation.

"Hello, this is Jordan Duncan."

"Hello, Mr. Duncan, this is Gabe Fernandez of the DEA." There is a pause after the introduction. "You don't remember me, do you?" Fernandez says in a pleasant tone.

"Should I?" Jordan asks, obviously not being able to place the name nor recollect having ever spoken to a DEA agent.

There is laughter coming from the other end of the call. "1982 Chula Vista South Bay Little League All-Star team."

"Oh my gosh, Gabe Fernando Valenzuela! Wow, what a surprise name from the past." Jordan is now smiling ear to ear as he remembers Gabe's nickname. "How are you, man?"

"I'm great. Married with a son, Gabriel Jr., who is one year old. Still living in San Diego County, and as you just heard, I am working for the Drug Enforcement Agency. What's up with you?"

"That's fantastic, Gabe. I'm happy for you."

"Thanks."

"I'm working as an enrolled agent for a tax resolution company up here in LA. Still single."

Back in 1982, when Jordan was twelve years old, before his August birthday, he played shortstop in Little League and was selected to the All-Star team. Gabe Fernandez was a catcher on an opposing team in the league and was also chosen for the All-Star team. It was truly a magical summer for the boys as they won four consecutive games to win the San Diego County Championship and advance to the West Regional Tournament in San Bernardino, California. The winner would advance to the Little League World Series in Williamsport, Pennsylvania. Chula Vista South Bay swept through their first three games by outscoring their opponents by an aggregate score of 44–3. For the championship game, they faced the team from Kirkland, Washington. There was a kid on Kirkland named Cody Webster who at twelve years old was already 5'7" and 175 lb. He was their pitcher and could throw the ball 75 miles per hour. Kirtland beat Chula Vista 3–1 and went on to win the Little League World Series by snapping Taiwan's thirty-one-game winning streak.

"I remember in college I heard you were playing football at UCLA. I played baseball at San Diego State. It was fun, but I was never good enough to go pro. My claim to fame is taking batting practice with Tony Gwynn, who came back to campus while playing for the Padres."

"That's cool. My claim to fame is that I caught some passes from Troy Aikman once in a while in practice during my freshman year. I wasn't good enough for the pros either. But college was a blast and got me a diploma without having to pay tuition."

They both agree on that point.

"So I saw your name pop up in regard to an investigation on Jaime Delgado. You had some questions. Are you representing his attorney?"

"I am representing him to the IRS. They, too, have been investigating him. In his words, he has done nothing illegal, and I just wanted to find out what is going on in the investigation with the DEA."

"Well, before I called you, I pulled his file. Apparently, some Mexican gangbangers got busted in the US for possession of some serious quantities of weed, and crack cocaine. They rolled on your boy Delgado as their gateway to the US. After a thorough investigation, we couldn't find any connection between Delgado and the Sinaloa Cartel from where he grew up. In fact, he came up clean on all cartel connections and hasn't even been pulled over for smoking a joint. The companies he works with in the US all spoke very highly of him. As far as I can tell, the investigation is dead," Gabe explains quite thoroughly from Jordan's viewpoint.

"Why did the DEA contact the IRS if there was no evidence of any drug connection on the part of Delgado?" Jordan asks curiously.

"Actually, it was the other way around. The IRS contacts us at times, looking for potential tax cheats whom we might be investigating. I guess it's the ole adage 'Follow the money.' They think that if someone is bringing drugs or is even being suspected of bringing drugs across the border, there must be a lot of cash involved. Obviously, these cash transactions aren't showing up on any tax returns."

"So what you're telling me is that the CID of the IRS inquires from the DEA as to whom they are investigating and then opens their own investigation without any due process or even any evidence?"

"Sounds that way. One thing that is evident about Delgado is that he makes a ton of trips across the border each year, usually with passengers. We found his paperwork to be impeccable. Never had a problem with any illegals as far as we can tell. The border patrol confirms that analysis. I think the IRS is just sniffing the money trail."

"Yeah, you are probably right. Hey, Gabe, I'm glad things have turned out well for you. Congratulations on the little one. Maybe next time I'm down in San Diego, we can meet, have a couple beers, and get caught up!"

"That would be great, Jordan," Gabe says with enthusiasm as he gives him his cell number.

Jordan leans back in his chair with his hands behind his head and smiles. That was a great time in his life. He was just learning to surf and playing baseball almost every day with his buddies in the California sunshine without a worry in the world.

Then he starts to think of the implications of what Gabe revealed to him about the DEA, the IRS, and Delgado. They had nothing on him other than that they discovered the DEA was investigating him. It wasn't the DEA who was trying to use the IRS to nail him like Capone. This is a very interesting twist and abusive action on the part of the IRS! Jordan smiles again.

CHAPTER THIRTEEN

Deadly Intentions

On Friday afternoon, March 8, 1996, Jordan gets a call from Little Al on his cell phone while at his office. He answers, "What's up?"

"Hey, I need a *huge* favor. Can't discuss over the phone. Chez Jay's tonight, 10:00 p.m.?"

"Yeah, no problem. You okay?"

"Yeah, but something urgent came up that I need to discuss with you."

"Sure. See ya then."

Jordan and Al have agreed to not discuss anything of importance over the phone. Jordan also has told Tonja and Brookes not to converse about the subject of their P. F. Chang powwow at the office. They have collectively agreed to only discuss cases that are current. Jordan didn't explain to them the angle he is working with Delgado but asks them to not ask questions about it in the office. His trust meter with David is at an all-time low, and he has never trusted Marlin and thus doesn't speak to him. He is also measuring his words carefully with JoJo, just in case. The stakes are high, and the ramifications could be severe if his actions and intentions are discovered by the wrong people.

Just before walking out of the office, Tonja pokes her head into his office and says, "David would like to see you before you leave."

"Any idea why?"

"Not a clue. He has been kind of quiet all day. Very unusual for him."

"Okay. I'll go see him now." Jordan accompanies Tonja down the hall.

"You wanted to see me?" Jordan inquires as he stops at the entrance of David's office.

"Yes. Come on in, Jordan." David stops reading the papers on his desk and reaches to grab an envelope from the top drawer as Jordan sits down. "I received this. It is an invitation for you to participate in the annual Final Four two-on-two tournament sponsored by Alexander Epstein." David hands the envelope to Jordan without a trace of emotion on his face.

Jordan smiles. "He won't quit until he gets his revenge, will he?"

"With Epstein, payback is more important than winning in the first place," David replies dryly.

Jordan nods his head. "Are you going to the Final Four this year?"

"I think I am going to pass this year. It is in East Brunswick, New Jersey, and I could go see family in New York. But I have a lot of work here. You know, it is right in the middle of tax season. You're welcome to go. I know you have family in Jersey, and Alex is expecting you." David looks at Jordan, anticipating a confirmation of his participation.

"I'll think about it. Anything else?"

"How is the Delgado case developing?"

"Good. Still working it. Nothing from the CID."

"Okay. Have a good weekend," David says with the slight hint of a smile.

Friday night at Chez Jay's in March is busy but not filled to capacity. Al is able to secure a booth in the far corner just beyond the end of the bar. Jordan walks over from his apartment and greets Al, who is seated.

"Hey, how are you?" Jordan asks as they shake hands.

"Okay. I told April that I needed to talk some business with you tonight, so she gave me some space."

"This must be pretty serious. What's going on?"

"Here's the deal," Al starts to explain. Their server, who sets their mugs of beer on the table, is told they don't need menus. He continues, "You know I've been working on signing Devin Joseph, right?"

Joseph is an All-American quarterback who has just finished his college playing career at Penn State.

"Yeah, sure. You mentioned it when we watched Penn State demolish Auburn on New Year's Day," Jordan confirms.

"Well, he just told me an incredible developing story that could seal the deal of him signing with me, depending on the outcome." Al seems more serious than Jordan can remember seeing him.

"I'm all ears. Go on."

"He told me how his dad, Del Joseph, played in the NFL back in the '70s. Seems he was teammates with a linebacker named Calvin Hayes. He considers Hayes a huge inspiration in teaching him how to be a professional athlete. You remember the name?" Al pauses.

"Yeah, didn't he play for the Niners in the '70s and early '80s?"

"Exactly. Apparently, he was an inspirational locker room influence on the young '82 team that won their first Super Bowl," Al recounts.

"Yep, I remember the team—Joe Montana, Dwight Clark, Ronnie Lott."

"That's right. Joseph was on the team, and it was Hayes's swan song as he retired after winning the only Super Bowl ring of his fourteen-year career."

Al continues after taking a swig from his mug, "He suffered quite a few injuries in his career, including three knee surgeries, a couple of separated shoulders, a pinched nerve, a debilitating back injury, and several concussions. He moved down to LA after he retired but was too beat up to really find any work. He and his wife lived off his NFL pension and savings, which, back in his time, was a fraction of what they receive now. He played his entire career before free agency hit the market."

Jordan is interested in where the story is going and how it affects Al signing Devin. "So how does this relate to you signing Joseph?"

"I'm getting there. Believe me, you are going to freak out when you hear the rest of the story." Al is being deliberate in relaying the story. He continues, "After a decade, in the early '90s, Calvin was invited to a ten-year reunion gathering of the first Super Bowl team in Forty-Niner history. They had a celebratory party and were introduced at halftime at a Niner game. At the party, some teammates told Hayes about football card and memorabilia signing opportunities. Hurting for money and afraid he would probably outlive his retirement income, Calvin thought it sounded like a great deal. He always loved interacting with fans, and it would also be a way in which he could, in some way, reconnect with the game he loved. He started attending organized functions at malls, shopping centers, health expos, sporting goods store openings, even showing up at some tailgate parties. The problem was, he was paid in cash or check for his appearances and signings. You can probably guess where this is going now," Al says as he pauses.

Jordan shakes his head slowly as he says, "The tax man cometh."

"Yep. But it doesn't end there. Of course, they audit him a few years later, and they exaggerate the estimates on the amount of money he took in—"

Jordan finishes his sentence, "Adding penalties and interest to the sum."

"Exactly. But it gets worse. After months, an IRS representative contacts him and tells him that he might qualify for a settlement."

"Offer in compromise. But more than likely a bait and switch to find out what he has in the way of assets." Jordan is right on the mark, knowing only too well how the IRS works.

"Bingo!" Al is now leaning forward with both elbows and arms on the table between them. "The agent invites him to come into the IRS office in downtown LA, even tells him which 'special lot' to park in so he won't have to pay a meter. Calvin follows the instructions and parks his truck in the designated lot. After their meeting, in which they discuss Calvin's financial situation, he returns to fetch his car, but it is gone!"

"You're kidding! Fear tactic, no doubt. But that is extreme." Even Jordan, who works with these slime balls every day, is shocked at the gall of that maneuver. "What happened next?"

"Hayes went back into the office, but the agent he met with was unavailable. He was given a phone number for a cab and was shown a consent-to-seize form that was signed by a manager. He called his wife from a payphone. He doesn't even own a cell phone. She had his nephew come pick him up and take him home."

"Incredible." Jordan is now sensing what the favor is. Get Calvin Hayes's truck back for him and settle his tax debt.

"But the truck isn't the real issue. You see, before walking in to meet this IRS agent, Calvin decides that it might not be a good idea to wear his Super Bowl ring, thinking they might confiscate it to help pay the tax. So he takes it off and places it in the glove box." Al is adding a twist to the story that Jordan didn't see coming.

"Oh no. They got the ring when they seized the vehicle and searched it," Jordan says sadly as he buries his face into his hands.

"Yep. When Calvin finally talked to the dude whom he met with, he asked for permission to get personal property from the truck. The agent says he has good news. Since the truck is the only source of transportation that he owns, they are going to let him retain it upon working out a payment plan on the taxes owed."

"Did the revenue officer give any mention of the ring?" Jordan asks.

"Not at that time. When Calvin went to pick up the truck, nobody at the lot had any knowledge of the personal property that was taken into custody. He was told to contact—I guess you call them the revenue officer in charge. So now they have his one prized possession that represents the success of all the hard work and effort in his football career. Just for kicks, guess who the revenue officer in charge is?" Al asks with a rather sadistic, sick-looking expression on his face.

"Oh no. There is only one RO in the LA District that I know of that would be so low as to pull this off...Jack Arbuckle!" Jordan's hands continue to cradle his face.

"Yup. The one and only, of whom you have told me horror stories."

Jordan shakes his head as he looks down at the table.

Al takes a long swallow of beer and says, "You help me get his ring back, I get Joseph as a client. Hayes has peace of mind and memory for the rest of his days, and you get more dirt on Arbuckle and the IRS for abusive behavior."

Jordan looks up. "Quite a story, Lil Al. Of course, I will do what I can. I will need Mr. Hayes to sign a power of attorney."

"Absolutely, and I will pay his fees to your firm," Al states confidently.

"Let's hold off on that. I will take power of attorney solo and contact Jack, leaving Jacobs & Goodman out of the mix, at least until I get a feel for what Jack is up to. His tactics have been very unorthodox so far. I'm wondering if he has something up his sleeve on this case."

"Okay, however you want to handle it. I just appreciate your help, buddy. This means a lot to many people."

"Yes, it could have an impact on many levels," Jordan agrees. "Set up a rendezvous for me to meet Calvin Hayes as soon as possible."

"Will do. This weekend?" Al asks.

"Perfect," Jordan replies.

Before they leave, Jordan says, "By the way, David handed me an invitation to Epstein's two-on-two tourney as I was leaving the office today."

"We going this year? It's in East Brunswick, you know."

"I've been thinking about what Big Al said concerning getting Epstein off his game plan. I think if we refuse his invitation, it will piss him off even more than if we showed up and won again. This way, he will have never beat us and can't get his revenge," Jordan says with a sly grin. "Besides, I'm tired of his crap, and I really don't even want to see him. The thought of watching the championship game in his suite gives me kind of a sick feeling. We are going back to Jersey for your wedding later in April. I say we skip the Final Four this year. We both have a lot to work on between now and then anyway."

Al smiles, raises his mug, and as Jordan clinks it, Al declares, "Here's to screwing Alexander Epstein one more time!" They finish off their beers, lay down cash for the tab with a tip on the table, and exit Chez Jay's.

"Hoops in the morning, 9:00 a.m.!" Jordan says as they head opposite directions out the door.

Saturday morning is a brilliant, sunny, blue sky spring day at Venice Beach, with the temperature already approaching seventy degrees at 9:00 a.m. The players are warming up, and the boom box is blaring:

> *Party people!*
> *Tag Team music in full effect!*
> *That's me, DC, the Brain Supreme, and my*
> *man Steve Roll'n!*
> *We're kickin' the flow!*

As Jordan and Little Al are warming up shooting, Tio comes flying up on his bike. He jumps off, barely letting it come to a halt and says, "Yo, Taxman, my folks wanted me to share some good news with ya."

"Hey, Tio. What's up?" Jordan responds.

"The Caterpillar Company finally reached a settlement on the strike. Even though the workers didn't get all they wanted, the company agreed to hire back those they let go during the strike. So pop's back workin'! He gonna do a desk job until he can get back into his rig. But they gonna pay for his rehab, give him full pay and benefits in the meantime." Tio has a huge smile. "And we got no tax debt over our head neither!" He gives Jordan the handshake routine and bro hug.

"That is *awesome*, man. Tell 'em I'm really happy for them."

"You can tell 'em yourself. They want you to come to dinner tomorrow. You can bring your lady you been hangin' with too."

"Hahaha, Janne is out on the campaign trail, but I will be there!"

"Let's ball, bruhs!" Tio declares as he fist-bumps Lil Al.

Tag Team, back again
Check it to wreck it, let's begin
Party on, party people, let me hear some noise
DC's in the house, jump, jump, rejoice
Says there's a party over here, a party over there
Wave your hands in the air, shake your derriere
These three words mean you're gettin' busy,
Whoomp, there it is! Hit me!
Whoomp, there it is!
Whoomp, there it is!

"Ah, look who's here, my boss man!" Tommy Paranucci walks up dribbling his b-ball. "Let's show these bruthas some TnT, Tommy 'n' Da Tank! Whoomp, there it is. Thought you knew!" Tio is fired up for some serious ballin' during the next two hours.

On Sunday morning, Jordan meets with Calvin Hayes, who turns out to be an extremely humble and respectable man. He is in his early fifties. It is sad, Jordan thinks, how Calvin walks with a cane and physically is a shell of the menacing terror on the football field he once was. The self-pride and dignity of his leadership qualities still exist, Jordan observes. He really wants to help this man. Mr. Hayes signs the POA, and Jordan promises to do all he can to reclaim his Super Bowl ring while getting his tax debt resolved.

On Sunday evening, Jordan goes to the Williamson family apartment where everyone is in a joyous mood. After a delicious dinner, dessert and some wine that Jordan brought as a congratulatory gesture, they promise to stay in touch and wish each other the very best moving forward. Jordan is thoroughly satisfied with how their case turned out and the friendship he has developed with Tio's family.

By the end of March, rather unexpectedly, Steve Forbes announces his withdrawal from the Republican Party presidential primary nomination. He cites the fact that every candidate that has dropped out has endorsed Bob Dole and that the path to victory for him is no longer a possibility. He thanks his campaign team, his supporters, and Jack Kemp. He pledges his support to the party moving forward. He will continue to campaign for pro-growth and tax reform. He endorses Bob Dole and is delighted that Dole has asked Jack Kemp to be his vice-presidential running mate. Mr. Kemp makes it clear that he will continue to promote the flat tax platform that Forbes has presented. Senator Dole welcomes the addition of Steve Forbes to back his campaign along with his constituents.

Janne calls Jordan. She is sad yet feels as though they did the best they could. She's still enthusiastic about promoting the message that Steve Forbes was advocating. She tells Jordan that she likes Jack Kemp a lot and thinks he is their best bet in getting heard in Congress about the misdeeds of the IRS by way of her connection with Mr. Forbes. Jordan looks forward to meeting him when the time is right. Janne says the silver lining to Forbes withdrawing is that she will be able to attend Al and April's wedding in New Jersey with him.

Before contacting Jack Arbuckle, Jordan has decided to give Tonja a heads-up about looking into the case. He won't mention that he has personally taken POA yet. However, if Arbuckle calls the office, wanting to discuss the case with Jordan when he is not there, Tonja should have some clue as to what is going on. His thought process in taking personal POA is that he does not want David looking over his shoulder on this and would prefer to do it pro bono.

Jordan calls Tonja at the office on her cell from his cell as he is commuting to the office. He briefly explains the situation about the seizure and that he will be contacting the RO on the case, Jack Arbuckle, to gather the details.

Tonja says, "No problem. Let me know if I can help."

Jordan realizes how fortunate he, David, and the entire staff at J&G are to have Tonja running the show. She is incredibly efficient and doesn't bother with the nonsense that can bog down operations in an office setting.

From the parking structure at the Galleria, Jordan calls the IRS LA District office. He faxed the POA from a Kinkos earlier this morning.

"Arbuckle."

"Jordan Duncan here, calling on behalf of my client Calvin Hayes."

A laughter erupts from the other end of the connection. "How did I know that somehow this case would find you? Well, guess what, Superstar. I have something that you have dreamed about since you were a little kid in Pop Warner football all the way through your miserable career at UCLA. Yep, a Super Bowl ring! Something that you will *never* have!" Jack then describes the ring in detail.

"I'm sure you are immensely satisfied with the manner in which you obtained the ring. However, Calvin Hayes legitimately earned it on the field of play. To me, you just stole it from him."

"Bullshit! He stole from the federal government, and I am just doing my job to enforce repayment. I can tell you right now, Superstar—any negotiations between us will not include him getting the ring back. That ship has sailed. Now I am willing to negotiate a possible OIC with you."

Jordan pauses as he is stunned that Jack wants to begin the negotiations with an OIC. This is totally out of character for him. Quickly Jordan pivots in his mind and responds, "Have you filled out a 433a and b?" Those are the financial forms necessary to ascertain ability to pay.

Jack doesn't hesitate. "Yes, I have. However, I will allow you to resubmit on behalf of your client so that we can begin discussions on an offer."

"I understand that his liability, with penalties and interest, is $125K. That seems excessive for card show income. I want to see the audit, and I also want to see a written assessed value of the ring." Jordan is presenting his case in a very professional manner as he is following his gut instinct.

"I'll tell you what, Duncan. He owes a buck and a quarter. Owns his home although I understand he has taken a second on it. Owns his truck but has some other debts. You offer $12,500, 10 percent of the debt, plus the ring, and I can guarantee you an accepted offer," Jack responds confidently.

This is incredible, thinks Jordan. Jack Arbuckle is *so* by the book on OICs that it normally takes months of haggling over asset value and allowable expenses to ever reach an agreement on an offer amount. Jordan definitely knows Jack has something up his sleeve.

"What if the ring is worth $100K?" he says.

"No way! Forty grand, tops. I don't even think it will be that high. It just has sentimental value for your client, but that does not factor into monetary value." Jack is sounding like his usual cocky self.

Jordan has an idea that he wants to explore. "Okay. Let me discuss it with my client, and I will get back to you."

"Make it quick. You know me. I close cases!"

Jack is such an ass, Jordan thinks, but if his instincts are right, he is going to regret this negotiation for a long time!

After hanging up, Jordan goes directly to the office. Upon arriving, he finds Tonja and says, "Have you had lunch?"

"No, too busy. I was going to skip it today."

"Come on, let's go. My treat," he insists.

They sit outside at the Stand, which is a deli on Ventura Boulevard. Hedges protect the patrons on the patio from the traffic view and noise. There is a grass area with picnic tables that provide ample privacy from others.

Jordan begins speaking between bites of his Reuben sandwich. "Do you know the protocol within the IRS LA District office on seized property?"

"No, not exactly, but I can find out from Bobbi." Tonja has a curious look on her face. "Why? What's up?" She takes a bite of her Caesar salad.

"I told you I was looking into a case for a friend that is being handled by Jack Arbuckle. Well, I have a gut feeling Jack is not following proper protocol of a seizure he enforced."

"What makes you think that?"

"Let's just say he is not acting like himself, and we both know what a creature of habit he is."

"That's for sure. So what do you want me to ask Bobbi specifically?"

"Don't mention any names—"

Tonja cuts him off, "You haven't told me any names." She chuckles.

"Yeah, but don't even mention Jack's name. Just ask that, for future reference, you would like to know exactly how seized property is handled and, most importantly, if there are any timelines attached to these protocols. I know they eventually go to auction, but try to get the entire timeline from the moment the seizure takes place." Jordan knows Tonja can obtain this information without drawing any suspicion. If he went directly to Bobbi, she would suspect that he was referring to a specific case and ask about it.

"I can do that. By the way, I have a name for you on who sends the leads to Marlin from E, L & O," Tonja says with a sly grin. "But that will cost you a dinner. It is a little complex, and I have to get back to the office. We are in tax season, you know!" Tonja stands.

"Absolutely. Let's get on this seizure info ASAP. Then we can discuss your espionage work over a nice dinner and wine." Jordan returns her smile.

"Jordan Duncan, you sure know how to draw favors out of me."

Back at the office, David summons Jordan to his office. As he enters, David says, "Alex says he hasn't received an RSVP from you on the invitation to his basketball tournament at the Final Four."

"I talked to my buddy, and we have decided to skip it this year," Jordan says, doing his best to suppress a smile.

"No, that's not good. Epstein has gone to a lot of trouble and expense to line this up. He has brought in 'ringers' to ensure that you and your buddy don't win for the third year in a row." David has a furrowed brow as he does not want to inform Alexander that Jordan won't be there.

"Well, he won't have to worry about us upsetting his tourney this year. We're not going." Jordan is calm but unrelenting.

"Is it because of the cost? I will pay for your plane fare. I know you have family in Jersey, so you will have a place to stay." David is sounding a bit irritated and desperate, in Jordan's opinion.

"No, it's not the money. It's really timing more than anything. Al is getting married in New Jersey in late April, so we will already be going there."

"Epstein won't like to hear that. It might affect how he feels about your work status here," David says.

"Seriously? This guy needs to reset his priorities. It's just recreational basketball. Honestly, I have better games and tougher competition here locally at the Venice Beach courts every Saturday morning. I'm done playing in his tournament. Frankly, the guy irritates me with his superior attitude." Jordan doesn't hold back expressing his feelings.

David pauses, then says, "I think you are making a big mistake, son." There he goes again with his lame father-to-son advice routine. "We have a great business model that is working well for all of us here. As you know, Alexander Epstein is the CEO. It is his final say as to whom we hire and fire. I genuinely want to work with you. You know that, Marlin knows that, and Alex knows that. However, the man has a big ego and a lot of pride. I would hate to see you get terminated over something as silly as insulting him by not playing in his basketball tournament."

"He would fire me for not playing? If we go, and I say this not boastfully but realistically, we will probably win again. Then what? He fires me for *winning* his tournament and hurting his pride? Unbelievable! He can do whatever he wants. We won't be at his tournament this year." Jordan walks out of David's office.

David is beginning to think that perhaps Marlin is correct in his assessment that this kid can't be controlled or manipulated. He shakes his head as he regretfully is going to have to make a most unpleasant phone call to Epstein.

Before the end of the day, Tonja reports to Jordan everything Bobbi explained about the IRS protocol for personal property seizures. Essentially, the property needs to be appraised by a property appraisal and liquidation specialist within the IRS (PALS). A revenue officer is required to record the transaction into a seizure log with the date of seizure, which is then assigned a seizure number. They must transfer the property to PALS ASAP but no later than thirty days after the date of seizure. The property will be appraised and placed into the next scheduled IRS auction. The taxpayer is notified and can retain the property only if they pay their tax debt in full.

Jordan knows that the seizure took place well over thirty days ago. Now he needs to know if and when Jack recorded it and subsequently transferred it to PALS. The way Jack was describing the ring to him on the phone, Jordan is quite confident that Jack never turned it over. In actuality, the ring was found by accident when Jack had the vehicle seized, kind of like found money. Jordan surmises that Jack got so excited when the guys at the tow shop turned over what they found in the glove box that he couldn't help himself but derive a plan to keep the ring. It's probably a one-time occurrence for Arbuckle. He would return the vehicle and go straight to an OIC to let Hayes off the hook on the tax debt. Little at that time did he know that Jordan Duncan would get involved. When Jordan called, representing Calvin, the temptation to rub it in Jordan's face about having a precious Super Bowl ring was too great to pass up for Jack.

That mistake is going to be very costly for ole Jack, Jordan thinks to himself.

Jordan gets Tonja to ask for a copy of the seizure log over the past sixty days, which she has a right to view. As he expected, the Super Bowl ring of Calvin Hayes is nowhere to be found. Next, he will call Jack, and the nature of their negotiation will have a much different complexion.

Jack Arbuckle is in his normal obnoxious mood at the IRS LA District office on Tuesday morning, March 18, 1996. He is flirting with the female clerical staff, boasting about his number of case closures and seizures to other revenue officers, which once again will lead the district by the close of the first quarter in '96. For the most part, Bobbi simply tolerates Jack but doesn't appreciate his methods of taxpayer intimidation nor his office demeanor. He is a little surprised to receive a call from Jordan Duncan this early in the day but is anxious to get closure on the Calvin Hayes case. He is even willing to drop the OIC number down if he needs to, but it is important for him to get a deal done today if possible.

He answers the call enthusiastically, "Jack Arbuckle, how may I help you?"

"Jack, Jordan Duncan here."

"Hey, Superstar, how are you? Did you talk to your client? Are we going to wrap up this OIC?" Jack says with an uncommon friendly tone.

"I'm going to cut to the chase, Jack. I know all about how you confiscated Mr. Hayes's Super Bowl ring and neglected to list it on the seizure log. Then you never turned it over to PALS. You are in deep shit, Jack." Jordan states these facts with a calm but stern demeanor.

After a brief hesitation, Jack responds, "What are you talking about? You don't know anything about how we operate here!" He is obviously somewhere between terrified and angry.

"If you try and deny this just one time, I am going to hang up and call Bobbi, followed by Woodruff." Jordan is not messing around nor acting as though he is fishing for information.

"There…there must be some kind of mistake. I will check into it and get back to you as soon as possible." Jack is reeling fast.

"You hang up, and our dealings are done. I make my calls to your superiors and lay out the facts. If you want to negotiate, then you need to listen to me very closely and not give me any excuses. Are we clear?"

"I'm listening," Jack says with a shaky voice.

"You are going to meet me face-to-face today, 1:00 p.m. at Carney's in Studio City. You know where it is?" Jordan is speaking with authority.

"Yes, I know the place. I will see you then," Jack responds.

"And bring the ring, Jack!" Jordan demands.

Carney's Restaurant is on Ventura Boulevard in Studio City. The uniqueness is that the entire restaurant, which seems to resemble more of a large diner, is within a former Southern Pacific railroad car. They are known to have the best hamburgers and hot dogs in LA County.

Jordan is waiting when Jack shows up. They have never met in person, but when Arbuckle walks in and starts looking around, Jordan is certain who he is. Jack is 5'8" and weighs no more than 155 lb. He has medium-length brown hair and fair, almost chalky white, skin. He is wearing khakis with a striped button-up shirt covered by a red windbreaker with a USC monogram. He spots Jordan and walks over to his booth.

He extends his hand with a nervous smile and says, "You still look like your *Sports Illustrated* photo."

Jordan refuses to shake his hand and says, "Sit down, Jack."

As Arbuckle sits, he asks, "Are we going to get something to eat? Their burgers are the best in town." Again, he is trying to be friendly.

"I'm not hungry. We need to discuss the situation we find ourselves in."

Jack has green beady eyes and about a three-day growth of sparsely separated whiskers on his chin and upper lip. "I know you think I was trying to steal this ring, but you are wrong. I only wanted to keep it for a while. I am a big NFL fan. My buddies and I bet on games every week during the season and watch together at a sports bar. I knew they would go crazy over seeing a genuine authentic Super Bowl ring."

"Cut the crap, Jack. If that were the case, you would have shown it to them and logged it in maybe a week later. It has been over forty-five days since the seizure. You're busted, and I told you I don't want to hear any excuses." Jordan is sticking to his guns.

Jack's eyes narrow. "What do you want, Duncan?"

"First, I want the ring." He sticks his hand out.

"What do I get in return?" Jack asks as though he wants to negotiate.

"You get to keep your ass out of jail. And if you follow the rest of my instructions, you might keep your job." Jordan is not letting up.

"What else do you want?" Jack realizes Jordan is not going to negotiate.

"You will write off the Calvin Hayes liability. I don't mean 53 it. It needs to disappear. Paid in full or offer accepted. Zero balance."

"I can't just write it off." Jack seems disjointed.

"How long have you been with the IRS?" Jordan asks.

"I am forty-two years old, and I started when I was twenty-five in the ACS. I have been in the service for seventeen years and a revenue officer for twelve years. You know I am the top producer in the LA District," Jack boasts.

"This isn't an interview, Jack. If you have been in the service for that long, I'm sure you can figure out a way to zero out Hayes's balance. My understanding is that the IRS isn't real good about record keeping and your computer systems leave a lot to be desired. Just make it happen. That is nonnegotiable." Jordan is speaking from a position of power.

"Okay. Is that it?" Jack does not like the position he finds himself in.

"No. One more thing. Take Alice Johnston out of the 53 status, and get her innocent spouse relief accepted." Jordan is staring directly into Arbuckle's shifty eyes.

"If I do that, I will still be able to go after her deadbeat ex," Jack says as if he is trying to gain some footage.

"Do whatever you want with him. I don't care." Jordan is not relinquishing anything because he genuinely doesn't care what happens to Donald Johnston. It was because of his foolish, irresponsible, greedy errors that Alice's life was turned upside down. The woman and her children have suffered enough. "This also is nonnegotiable."

Jack pauses before responding as if he is trying to determine what kind of leverage he can grasp.

"The tables are reversed now, Jack. I am the one in power. You screwed up big time and got busted. Actually, I am letting you off easy. The way in which you treat delinquent taxpayers, I should get you canned. But I'm not like you, Jack. I believe people deserve second chances. This is yours now. But it is a one-time offer, and I need to walk out of here with the ring in my possession and your commitment on the other two issues. Both of those items need to be completed by week's end." Jordan is right. He does have the power now, and Jack knows it.

Jack is matching Jordan's stare. "You know, Duncan. I have never hated you. In fact, I admire you for the way you represent your clients. I hope that we have a mutual respect. I am going to accept your terms." Jack reaches into his windbreaker pocket and pulls out the ring.

Jordan looks over the ring closely and determines that it is authentic. "You will close the Hayes case and accept Johnston's innocent spouse offer by week's end." Jordan seeks confirmation, though he knows he still maintains all the leverage.

Jack nods his head while saying, "Yes."

As Jordan gets up to leave, Jack stands and abruptly asks another question. "Jordan, do you at least respect me for the job I do? I seized Hayes's vehicle to use it as leverage for an OIC that would include his Super Bowl ring. I had no idea the ring would be in the vehicle. I just got carried away... This is not the way I do things."

Jordan shakes his head as he looks down at the smaller man and says, "Jack, tomorrow we will be back in the trenches, battling over our cases. Respect is something earned through honor and integrity. You have shown neither in this case. Keep working on that, and I won't hold this over you." With that, he turns and walks out.

Before heading back east to attend the NFL draft in New York and prepare for his wedding in New Jersey, Little Al accompanies Jordan to the home of Calvin Hayes. Upon returning his Super Bowl ring, Jordan also explains to Mr. Hayes that his tax debt has been relieved with the stipulation that he remains current in paying taxes for the next five years. Calvin graciously thanks them and assures Jordan that he won't make the same mistake again with his tax filings. His wife is overcome with tears of joy, knowing how much that ring means to Calvin and what a tremendous stress and burden the tax debt has been on each of them.

Al tried to insist on paying the fees for Jordan's help in the matter, but Jordan is more insistent that he did it out of their friendship and to correct a wrong done to Calvin. He reminds Al of all the help he is providing him in the collaboration scheme that Epstein and Jacobs are pulling with the IRS. He tells Al that he won't be paying him for his efforts. They both laugh, and it is agreed that friends help friends in need with no regard to fees for their time and effort. Al takes off for the East Coast excitedly as Devin Joseph is both delighted and impressed at how quickly and thoroughly Al had resolved the problem with Calvin Hayes. He has agreed to sign with Alvin Bockman as his agent as soon as he arrives.

Jordan and Tonja have dinner at Ruth's Chris Steak House on Topanga Canyon Boulevard in Los Angeles. After sharing some deliciously plump shrimp, they order their respective entrees. Tonja selects the petite fillet, and Jordan goes with the fully marbled ribeye. They enjoy a bottle of Cabernet Sauvignon direct from Chateau Montelena in Napa Valley.

Tonja is thirty-two years old and a divorced mother of two small children—Alex, seven, and Angelina, five. They live in N. Hollywood, which is about an eleven-minute commute to the Sherman Oaks office. She has been single for the past four years, and it is not easy for her to raise small children while working full-time. She is a very resilient and resourceful woman with strong work ethics and sense of loyalty. She is an attractive woman standing 5'4" and has dark-brown hair and hazel eyes. She is rather large breasted, which solicits unwanted and certainly unwarranted attraction and comments from the male gender. She and Jordan have always had a great working relationship. After he had been with J&G for almost a year, they had a brief fling, which was consensual and enjoyable for both. They decided for the sake of the working relationship that it would be best to curtail any physical relationship. That decision, which has been adhered to without any conflict, turned out to be a wise choice. Their mutual respect and dedication to the success of the business has jelled well in the office. They share in their belief and actions toward resolving tax problems with the utmost commitment to finding the best possible solution for their clients. That attitude has served Jacobs & Goodman Tax Resolution immensely.

"So give me the lowdown on what you found out from within E, L & O," Jordan asks as he sips from his wine glass.

"I must say you picked the perfect setting to discuss this. There is a twist that is going to complicate things and being relaxed as we talk about it, will help in our decision moving forward, I believe," Tonja says while smiling and enjoying the wine at a slow enjoyable pace.

Jordan nods, and his curiosity is piqued as Tonja continues, "A girl by the name of Alessandra DeBosa works in their main office in Maryland and receives the leads directly from the IRS database in real time, meaning that they have it programmed to generate a list of all taxpayer's debts categorized by name, amount of the liability, and type of tax, such as payroll, trust fund recovery, and responsible parties. From that list, she copies and pastes the leads into the E, L &

O computer. Then she prints the list and faxes it directly to Marlin's office in Sherman Oaks."

"That means there is no one specifically at the IRS sending the leads to E, L & O. But they do give them access to their database, which I'm sure is irregular and illegal, right?" Jordan asks.

"Yes. The list by itself of tax debtors is actually public information once a tax lien is filed. However, it is the list of 'responsible persons' and their contact info that gives E, L & O and subsequently J&G an unfair competitive advantage. That is where the illegality comes in."

"Does the IRS actually send this list, or do they just make it available for them to access it?" Jordan is trying to determine the trail.

"Sounds to me as though they simply give them access to the database."

"So the IRS could claim that E, L, & O hacked into the database if the heat gets too hot by way of investigation."

"I think you're right. But here is where it gets complicated for us. My source insists that no one at E, L & O does any scheduling for Marlin. In fact, they have received numerous inquires from one JoJo Montanez."

"So Jo does Marlin's scheduling!" Jordan is not so shocked but is still surprised.

"It appears that way. I think you should obtain proof of that before making concrete allegations. But it makes sense to me." Tonja doesn't act too surprised over this declaration; after all, Jo is sleeping with David.

"Yes, I agree. I am going back east for my buddy's wedding. Let's hold off on doing anything until I return, okay?"

"Absolutely. I told you that I am not comfortable with doing anything within the office that might implicate David in this mess."

Upon receiving written confirmation on Alice Johnston's innocent spouse relief offer acceptance from the IRS, Jordan calls her to share the news. "Hi, Alice. This is Jordan, and I have some good news. We have received the acceptance of your innocent spouse relief offer."

"Oh my gosh! We won?" Alice says almost in disbelief.

Jordan can't suppress his joy and lets out a laugh as he confirms, "Yes, we won!"

"Oh, Jordan, I can't even tell you how much of a relief it is to hear that." She is now crying. "Going to bed every night for the past two years, literally not knowing if my house would be taken away, fearing and praying to God every night that my children would not be taken away from me! Oh, Lord, I am *so* happy and relieved right now—you have no idea." Alice is overcome with emotion and cannot speak any longer.

"Alice, I know what an extreme burden this has been on you. I am very happy as well that it is now settled." Jordan genuinely feels a great sense of satisfaction in helping Alice out of this mess.

"Honey, if you were here right now, I would smother you with hugs and kisses! You told me we were going to win. I was a little disappointed when we were put on hold with no payment but no settlement for almost a year. It was a relief to not have to pay and allowed me to stay in business for sure. But the fear of that creepy Jack Arbuckle showing up one day and taking possession of my house was always in the back of my mind. Thank you *so* much, Jordan, for sticking with my case and seeing it through to the end. WE WON, YIPEEE!" Alice is overjoyed.

"My pleasure. Thank you for believing in me and doing everything that I asked of you. You are a strong woman, Alice. Your children are blessed to have you as their mother. If I may, I would like to ask a favor of you."

"Of course, anything." Alice is quick to respond.

"At some point, maybe later this year, I would like you to a sign a statement about how you were abused by the IRS in the collection process. I will have the statement prepared. There is a chance that I might ask you to testify in front of congressmen. I am in the process of building a case of taxpayer abuse by the IRS," Jordan explains.

"Oh, absolutely! You can count on me for that whenever and wherever!"

"Thank you, Alice. But please don't mention this to anyone until I give you the word. Then you can tell anyone and everyone!"

"Deal," Alice agrees enthusiastically.

"I will send you the official statement from the IRS releasing you from all tax liability. Take care, Alice," Jordan says with satisfaction.

"Thank you again, Jordan. I am going take my kids to Chucky Cheese and celebrate!"

They both laugh as they conclude the call.

On Saturday, April 27, 1996, Alvin Bockman Jr. and April Stone meet at the Lake Valhalla Club in Montville, New Jersey, to exchange vows in holy matrimony.

April is from Parsippany, New Jersey, which is a small community just south of Montville and fifteen miles northwest of Short Hills. They never met each other in New Jersey. She attended and graduated from the University of Tennessee in Knoxville, Tennessee, before heading west to take a position as a paralegal with a law firm in Los Angeles, California. She was doing some freelance contract work when she met Al Bockman. She was intrigued with working on NFL player contracts as she was a huge UT college football fan. The two of them formed a congenial relationship almost immediately. They have much in common, both being from Jersey and both loving to follow college football. They often engage in friendly bantering over superior college football conferences.

Al and April discovered they also enjoyed each other's company away from work and developed a chemistry that neither could deny. Ultimately, they have come to the realization life is much better for each them when they are together. So despite the potential conflict of working together, they have concluded marriage is what they both desire.

Being in the spring, the setting at the club venue is spectacular with flowers blooming, the grass green, the trees in blossom, and the sun shining over the ninety-acre lake. The wedding is taking place on a small section of sandy beach with a waterfront view of the Pyramid Mountain range. The chairs for spectators are on a grassy area just before you reach the sand and is accessible from a walkway that extends from the club, with willow trees adorning both sides of the path.

Al is looking sharp in a white tuxedo to match April's beautiful white wedding gown. The men in Al's line—which include Jordan as the best man, Sal Gambadoro, Miles Jackson, Paul Hoage, and Ted Balcolm—are dressed in light blue tuxes. April's bridesmaids are dressed in canary yellow dresses in keeping with the springtime theme. The ceremony is marvelous. The reception is held in the Tudor-style house at the club and features dinner, dancing with live music, and a full bar.

Arthur and Donna Gibson received invitations and are in attendance. At the reception, Arthur approaches Jordan when they can be alone.

"Beautiful wedding. I'm very happy for your friend, Al. I really enjoy his wit and sharp mind."

"Yeah, Al and I go back to the beginning of high school together. In fact, everyone in his line played together on our high school state football championship team." Jordan fondly recollects.

"That's wonderful. I wanted to give you a quick update if it is not inappropriate in this setting," Arthur says almost as a question.

"Of course, what is it?" Jordan inquires.

"I have been able to acquire some additional information on firms that have been represented by E, L & O. I told you how there is definitive evidence that the IRS has participated in audits that were politically directed. Well, I believe there are political links that may be in play with the Epstein and IRS collaboration of target audits," Arthur reveals.

"That is amazing, and it makes sense. It seems as though politicians have always had their finger in the pie of IRS activities."

"Exactly. This could be the tie-in I've been looking for to blow this thing wide open. I will keep you informed as I get confirmation." Arthur sounds excited about the possibility of being near the time to expose the IRS and Epstein, Levin & Ohlman Tax Consultants in fraudulent activities.

"Great. Keep me in the loop. I have concrete evidence on our plan B of taxpayer abuse. As soon as we can communicate with some other tax pros around the country with specific cases, I think we will be ready to present a case to Janne's contacts in Congress."

"Outstanding. Enjoy your friend's wedding reception, and we shall talk again soon."

"Thanks, Arthur, I look forward to it."

Janne is looking beautiful in a light blue dress with black trim. She wanted to try and match Jordan's attire. She is chatting with Gabriela and Teri as Jordan approaches.

"What an extraordinary wedding, huh?" Janne says with a big smile as Jordan joins in the conversation.

"Absolutely. Never seen Lil Al look so dapper and happy at the same time before," Jordan says while greeting and kissing his mom on the cheek.

"Hey, Jordan, maybe you and Janne can be next. And I can be a bridesmaid and sister of the groom at the same time," says Teri with her usual enthusiasm.

Nervous laughter ensues as Jordan says, "You stick to your soccer regime for now and don't worry about things like that." He and Janne are both smiling, a bit embarrassed.

Jordan spots Paul Hoage standing alone with a drink in his hand. He walks up to him with Janne, introduces them, and explains to Paul Janne's role in their investigative activities.

"I met your father and Pete as they were kind enough to fly me out to their cabin in Yosemite. That is quite a setup." He turns to Jordan. "I've decided to take them up on their generous offer to move in and help hack the IRS computer system."

"Well, it's about time. We are moving forward quickly, Paul, and we need some more evidence as to what the IRS is up to. Apparently, they destroy all written trails. When can you leave?"

"As early as next week if we can make arrangements."

"Good. I will contact John and have him or Pete get in touch with you," Jordan says as they shake hands.

Jordan spends some time conversing with his old buddies Gambo, Jacks, and Teddy Ballgame. Janne enjoys listening to their high school recollections and easily segues into the conversation along with their wives and girlfriends. The men toss around the idea of getting up early on Sunday for a game of hoops at Taylor Park, but their respective significant others nix that plan. They stop by to say hello to Big Al and Elaine, who seem delighted to see them.

Jordan and Janne also seek out Donna and Arthur Gibson to chat with them socially. Donna comments on what a lovely time they've had at Christmas in the cabin at Yosemite Valley and how much they look forward to returning with more of their family.

After having fun dancing, eating, drinking, enjoying the live music, conversing, and laughing with friends, Jordan and Janne say goodbye while wishing Al and April a happy honeymoon. They look forward to seeing them again in SoCal. On Sunday, they depart their separate ways at the Newark airport. Janne returning to the campaign trail endorsing the Dole/Kemp ticket with Steve Forbes. Jordan back to work in LA.

Back in Maryland, Alexander Epstein rethinks the circumstances regarding Arthur Gibson and his interactions within the IRS. He decides to follow the political theory of "Keep your friends close and your enemies closer." Interpreted to mean that he would portray confidence outwardly to Arthur as a consultant on tax issues, all the while keeping a keen eye on his activities with whom he speaks within the framework of the IRS and anyone within the realm of the CPA firm's business associates. Not entirely sure if Arthur represents a friend or enemy, although his perception is favoring the latter as time passes.

In May of 1996, the incident that makes up his mind definitively occurs. Epstein has his connections within the ranks of the IRS, and it seems as though Arthur's inquiries are not getting him anywhere near any connection between E, L & O and the IRS Examination Division. Then a business client that is represented by Epstein's firm contacts him and asks why their tax consultant, Arthur Gibson, is speaking to their CFO, inquiring about their IRS corporate audit. That is crossing the line of no return according to Epstein. Further action must be taken.

Arthur knows he is sticking his neck out a bit by reaching out to E, L & O's audit clients but believes that he has legitimate reason to contact them as a tax consultant to the CPA firm that represents them in their audit. He receives a phone call from a Mitchell

Shumway, the CFO of Findlay Electronics Inc. located in New York. After several minutes of discussing the details of his firm and dates of the audit, he convinces Arthur to meet him in person to share his concerns about the audit. He claims to have information that implicates political motives behind the audit and actual ramifications not only within Findlay Electronics but also links to the entire electrical manufacturing industry. After his due diligence in confirming the existence and position of Mr. Shumway, Arthur agrees to meet him on Friday evening, May 24, at the Embassy Suites Hotel's lounge and bar, located at the Chevy Chase Pavilion in Washington, DC.

Arthur informs Donna of his business meeting in DC without going into much detail but does tell her it has something important to do with his investigative efforts. She wishes him luck and advises him to be careful about whom and what he believes.

Engaging in small talk while sitting in the lounge adjacent to the bar on the main level of the Embassy Suites and while nursing their respective alcoholic beverages, Arthur and Mitchell begin discussing details of Shumway's allegations. Mitchell Shumway has a stocky build and appears to be in his early forties. He is wearing slacks, a button-up shirt, and a blazer. He has medium-length brown hair and wears glasses. As he speaks, it is sounding much like what Arthur had heard from Dawkins, however, with political parties, offices, and even specific names being brought into play.

As the evening crowd begins to become denser in the lounge area, Shumway looks around and suggests they go up to his suite to continue the confidential conversation. He informs Arthur that his room has a living room outside of the bedroom and would allow them the privacy they need. Arthur agrees and Mitchell offers to re-up their drinks before heading to the elevator. He confirms that Arthur is drinking Scotch on the rocks and walks over to the bar. He hands Arthur his drink and they go to the elevator. As they enter the room on the seventh floor, they proceed to make themselves comfortable by removing their respective jackets. Arthur asks permission to take notes, and Shumway agrees as Arthur sits in the armchair across from Mitchell, who sits on the couch. There is a coffee table between them. Shumway begins to recap what he said downstairs and then starts spitting out more names and facts. He is very methodical as he speaks, with Arthur writing everything down. Within twenty minutes, Arthur begins to feel dizzy and somewhat nauseated. He excuses himself to use the bathroom. As he stands, the room starts spinning in his head, and he tumbles to the floor. Shumway remains seated and watches without offering any assistance. Arthur tries to stand, but his efforts are futile. He collapses and loses consciousness.

Shumway scurries over to where Arthur is lying to make sure he is unconscious. As he burst through the bedroom door, he is startled as he finds himself staring directly into the barrel of a Glock 19 9mm handgun, suppressor attached, pointed at his face in a double-handed grip by a former soldier wearing surgical gloves. The man is clearly ready to end his life in an instant if his next move isn't abrupt in a submissive attitude.

Shumway immediately stops in his tracks, throws up his hands, and exclaims, "Whoa! Easy, T! It's just me!"

"Being ex-military, you should know better than busting in here," Kurt Turlock retorts, and he slowly lowers his weapon but doesn't completely relax to a noncombative posture. "What's happening with the subject?"

"He's out cold. Time to move!"

"Let's check it out," Turlock says as he shoves the weapon into his waistband and grabs the gym bag next to him on the floor, at the base of the closet in the bedroom.

They proceed to the living area, where the subject is lying unconscious on his side on the floor a few feet away from the armchair but in front of the coffee table.

"You sure he won't wake while we are doing this?"

"Not a chance. I used enough to knock out a horse! He's a big dude. No sense on taking any chances."

"Yeah, let's be quick and precise."

Turlock opens his bag and pulls out another pair of surgical gloves, handing them to his partner along with a surgical mask. They both apply masks, and Turlock methodically rolls up the victim's sleeve.

As he removes a syringe from the bag, Sean Callison (Shumway's true identity), asks, "Tell me again why we are offing this guy. For some kind of IRS tax issues?"

"Too late to question things, man. Concentrate. This is worth a lot of money for my client and will allow us to follow our plan to get out of this shit."

"Just seems like a real straight shooter. A death sentence might be a little extreme, don't you think?"

"We are not being paid to overthink this. We just need to make sure our tracks are covered. We complete this, see the rest of the job through, and we're done! Now quit talking, and let's finish this."

"Okay, good. I really don't like this dude you're working for. Sooner or later, I have a strong feeling he'll screw you too."

Without another word, Callison tightens a rubber surgical hose around the victim's upper arm with a knot. As the vein in the crook of the victim's left elbow bulges, Turlock inserts a two-inch needle into the vein and slams a "Hot Dose" mixture of heroin and battery acid into his bloodstream.

They take Arthur's right hand and place his fingers onto the syringe, making sure his prints will be the only ones detectable. They empty the glass of scotch on the coffee table down the sink and replace it with a quarter full of the same, but uncontaminated, beverage.

Next, they remove his billfold and confiscate the $225 cash it contains, tossing it into the bag while leaving the wallet on the floor next to his body. They remove their masks and all evidence of either of their existence in the room, and Callison takes off his toupee, glasses, and gloves, tossing them into the bag.

"Where's the girl?" asks Turlock.

"Just outside in the hallway, making sure the coast is clear."

"Is she still unrecognizable? Looking like the woman who checked into this room?"

"Oh, yeah, Cas is real good with makeup, and that wig makes her look like an entirely different person."

"Call her and make sure we are clear to leave."

Callison pulls out his cellphone, makes the call, and hangs up. "Good to go," he says to Turlock.

After shutting the door behind him, Turlock removes his surgical gloves, shoving them into his pocket. With the gym bag in tow, the three of them move quickly toward the stairwell.

It is 9:15 p.m. as they enter the parking garage. They get into two separate cars—Turlock in one, Callison and Cassie in the other.

Turlock places a quick call to Epstein as he drives away. "It's done," he says and then hangs up. And with his two words, a life gone, just like that.

May 24, 1996—the last day of Arthur Gibson's life.

CHAPTER FOURTEEN

Solo Aggression

On Saturday morning, May 25, as he is getting ready to walk out the door to ride his bike down the beach path to Venice and play hoops, Jordan's cell phone rings. The number is from the same area code as Arthur's; however, he does not recognize it. He answers, thinking that Arthur may be using a burner phone to contact him.

"Hello?"

"Is this Jordan?" The woman's voice on the other end sounds distraught.

"Yes. Who is this?"

"Jordan, this is Donna Gibson." She pauses momentarily to take a deep breath but continues before Jordan can respond. "Arthur is dead."

Jordan is completely caught off guard by that statement. "What? How could that be?"

Donna tries to keep her composure as she describes the situation. "Arthur went to meet a man from a company that hired Epstein's firm. Apparently, he had some dirt on them. He was from New York, so they were meeting at a hotel in DC." Again, Donna pauses to take a deep breath. "By 10:00 p.m., when I hadn't heard from him, I called his cell phone. He didn't answer, and I left a brief message asking him to call me when he could. By 11:00 p.m., I was very worried, because it is not like Arthur to fail to contact me. I called the police. They wouldn't do anything that night as it wasn't considered a missing person until twenty-four hours had gone by. I called the hotel. They knew nothing. Early this morning, someone at the hotel discovered his body while cleaning a room." Now Donna breaks down and starts crying.

"Donna, I am so sorry. Any idea as to the cause of death?"

She sounds as though she is panting trying to recompose herself and catch her breath. "That is the crazy thing. After the police came, they say it appears to be a self-inflicted drug overdose. Jordan, I have known that man for over thirty-five years, and he has never taken a drug. He is the straightest arrow, the most noble man I have ever known in my life. Something is not right with this. Someone set my man up and killed him!" Donna's grief is turning to anger.

"I agree with you 100 percent, Donna. I don't believe for one second that Arthur OD'd on drugs. Are the police going to investigate?"

"They say they will wait for an autopsy to determine the cause of death and then make a decision on an investigation."

"Well, we both know that Arthur was looking into the IRS and Epstein's firm. Sounds to me, like you said, he was set up. We will not stop following Arthur's quest for the truth. I will find out what happened, Donna. You deserve that... I'm so sorry."

"Thank you, Jordan. He told me several times how highly he thought of you and that you were a good, honest man caught up with some shady characters. I appreciate your condolences. I will keep you in the loop when I find out more."

"Thank you, Donna, and please let me know when you make arrangements for whatever services will be held. Are your daughters with you?" Jordan asks compassionately.

"They are on their way. We are all just shocked. I will let you know what we decide." She is sniffling, trying to hold back another burst of tears.

"Yes, please do. I want to be there. Call me anytime."

As they conclude the call, Jordan walks out onto his patio and looks across the beach into the ocean while resting his elbows on the railing. He shakes his head in disbelief over the news he just received. Donna was correct in her assessment of Arthur's nobility. Jordan sensed that from the first time he ever met the man. After several minutes of grieving the loss of his friend and mentor, Jordan feels a surge of anger mounting from within himself. This has gone too far. Someone killed Arthur to cover up whatever is going on. It is either the IRS, some politician, or Alexander Epstein. Jordan's guess is strongly leaning toward the latter. He swears to himself that he will find out and someone will pay the price for this evil action.

Jordan calls Janne, Al, and John Sawyer in that order to share the terribly sad news. Janne is so extremely sad as she always liked Arthur as a gentle giant of a man. Her heart goes out to Donna. Al immediately is convinced that Arthur was murdered.

John, while sincerely expressing his sorrow, takes a more intellectual approach in deciding what to do next. He, like Jordan and Al, strongly believes that foul play is involved. He suggests they wait for the autopsy and practice extreme caution in their efforts moving forward. He doesn't even consider aborting their efforts. In fact, he insists they now have added incentive to find the truth and bring those responsible to justice. But he states that Arthur's death must be avenged in a separate manner from the IRS–Epstein collusion allegations.

Monday, May 27, is Memorial Day. Jordan decides to go surfing up the coast in Malibu. He takes his Kory Edmunds longboard to Latigo Beach, which is three miles north of the Malibu Pier. It is less crowded as it is only accessible down a steep staircase. Not many can carry a longboard to the beach from the parking area. Jordan wants as much solitude as possible today. Latigo has consistently long waves that are not too big, which are perfect for extended smooth rides.

He needs time to think, and he can't imagine a better setting than out in the ocean on his surfboard. After a couple of hours of long rides, the waves hit a lull, and calmness abounds in the great Pacific.

Jordan is not wearing a wetsuit today as he wants to feel the coolness of the ocean currents in late May. The fog has receded, and Jordan sits atop his board, straddling it. The sun is glistening off his tan back, and the warmth feels good. As he waits for the next set of waves to form, he contemplates how surfing can emulate life in the way that you approach it. He thinks of surfing his longboard as being similar to his time at UCLA playing wide receiver. He learned to run precise routes, staying in constant balance with his body. Control and discipline were the keys to success. Conversely, when he played free safety in high school, it was more like surfing a short board—total aggression and speed, react and hit! It was much like a fast ride, duck and dive, turns and cutbacks. Aggression and attacking mode, shredding the wave. He realizes that his life since giving up football has been more like a beautiful long, smooth ride on a stable, secure longboard. Now with Arthur's untimely death, he must adjust his way of thinking if he is going to avenge his friend's murder and bring those responsible to justice.

Arthur wanted the truth and to make the IRS accountable while stopping the illegal financial advantages that have been given to E, L & O. Jordan concludes in his mind that he needs to be more aggressive, attacking his life like he would a big wave!

Having finished with his mindful metaphor just in time for the next set of waves, he waits for the largest one he can find and surfs it aggressively as if on his short board, cutting back, turning, and getting every inch out of riding the line into the beach. He grabs his board and starts jogging toward the staircase. He knows what he needs to do!

On Tuesday morning, May 28, just after 10:00 a.m., Jordan is in the office, working on some cases. Jack Arbuckle has been relatively quiet regarding the Delgado boat chase since the Calvin Hayes debacle. He does not believe that Jack will rollover on the Delgado case. Jordan still has not heard anything from the CID. He has not filed the OIC doubt as to liability as he patiently waits for Karen to complete reviewing the audit. So far, she has chopped it up pretty well. There has been no evidence to indicate that Delgado's accountant had made any errors on his original tax return. The office is quiet today as Marlin is in Beverly Hills, and David is meeting with Jeffrey Woodruff in downtown Los Angeles.

Vanessa summons him over the intercom. "Jordan, please come to the reception area." She doesn't wait for a response before cutting out. This seems a little odd to him as she generally announces if someone has dropped in to visit and he doesn't have an appointment scheduled.

Upon entering the reception area, Jordan sees Alexander Epstein standing in front of the desk with a grim look on his face. He is flanked by Kurt Turlock.

This can't be good, Jordan thinks to himself but remains calm as he approaches Epstein.

"I understand that you have taken on a client that is under investigation with the Criminal Investigation Division." Epstein has fire in his eyes.

"That is old news. I have discussed it and been transparent with David. The CID has not contacted me since I've been on the POA," Jordan responds without hesitation.

"That is against company policy to take such a case without prior consent from Mr. Jacobs or Mr. Goodman."

Epstein didn't come out here to threaten me, Jordan thinks. He feels inclined to defend his actions.

"Marlin handed me the case and asked me to take it," he said.

"According to him, neither he nor David knew of an ongoing investigation. You took it upon yourself to have the client sign the power of attorney without authorization, putting the company at risk for the liability costs of defending him. My understanding is that this is not a one-time occurrence. You continually act as you see fit, full of disrespect for your superiors. The way you showed up unannounced and uninvited to my basketball tournament a couple years ago and stole the glory from a well-deserving team is just one example. Then you were too cowardly to show up this year to allow the other contestants to rightfully defeat and humiliate you on the court as you deserve." Epstein continues in his accusations, his voice level rising that he is practically shouting.

"You are wrong. This was a one-time occurrence, and I collected a $10,000 fee to represent him." Jordan is just as intent in his defense. "I think it is the frustration of you not getting your revenge on the basketball court with your ringers that is behind this outrage."

The volume level of their respective voices has escalated with each sentence to the point where Tonja has appeared on the scene.

"It is insubordination regardless of the fees collected. As the chief executive officer of this firm, I hereby terminate your employment, effective immediately. You need to leave the office now!" Epstein uses his most powerful commanding voice in firing Jordan.

There is silence as the two men stare at each other. However, you cannot stare that mutual hatred down.

Jordan speaks next. "You know in football when someone shoots off their mouth like you, we have a saying for that: 'Your mouth is writing checks that your body can't cover.'"

Just then, Turlock says, "I can cover anything he says." He instantly balls up his fist and fires out a straight right punch directed at Jordan's solar plexus. Jordan is fifteen years younger than Turlock and is very athletically built with superb instincts and quick hands. He deflects the punch, drops one foot back, bends his knees, and lowers his shoulder while thrusting forward. His shoulder collides with Turlock just below the chest in a perfect-form tackle technique. As Kurt is driven back, his former military instincts kick in, and he shifts his left leg to absorb the hit and maintain balance. However, the heel of his left foot gets caught on the foot of a chair, and the momentum of Jordan's inertia causes the two men to veer to the side. They crash into the glass wall that separates the reception area from the conference room. Glass shatters as Turlock's back and head take the brunt of the contact. As they fall to the floor, Jordan has Kurt's left arm pinned to his side, but his right arm is free, punching Jordan on the side of the head. Jordan tries to stay on top of him as Turlock kicks his legs in an attempt to get free.

"Stop it!" screams Tonja as she runs over to grab Jordan and attempt to end the fracas.

Without moving to help, Epstein commands, "That is enough!"

Jordan hops up to his feet, and as Turlock is getting up to charge at him, Epstein barks, "Kurt, that is enough!"

Turlock has both fists clenched, and his face is an angry shade of crimson as he succumbs to his boss's command. "I will kill him!" he growls, seething.

"There is a time and place for everything, and this is neither," Epstein half-whispers to him. "You have glass stuck in your back, head, and neck. We need to get you to an urgent care."

"I'm fine. Just let me finish this punk." Turlock still has his fists clenched and is staring at Jordan, who is separated from him by Tonja. Jordan has a small cut on the side of his neck, just under his right ear.

"You need to leave *now*!" demands Epstein to Jordan.

"I have to get my things from my office," Jordan says as he starts walking toward the hallway to his office.

"Tonja will mail your things to you. Leave now!" Epstein insists.

Jordan shakes his head as he continues to walk. Turlock offers to force Jordan out, but Epstein declines, knowing that Kurt had initiated the physical incident and there were witnesses—Tonja and Vanessa.

The entire staff has come out of their offices after hearing the glass break. They are all dumbfounded, including JoJo and Brookes, as Jordan passes them on his way to his office without saying a word. He enters his office; gets his phone, plaques, photos; and has the presence of mind to grab all the paperwork from the Delgado file. He exits from the hallway stairs that leads to the underground parking. Tonja tells him that she will call him later. He thanks her and says goodbye.

As Tonja returns to the reception area, Epstein is leaving out the front door with Turlock. He demands that David call him as soon as he gets in.

"Believe me, I won't have to tell him to call you," Tonja replies in anger.

"Get that mess cleaned up" are the last words that Epstein orders as the door closes behind him.

Tonja turns and looks at the wide-eyed staff behind her and says, "What an ass... Unbelievable!"

After going for a run along the beach and a workout at Gold's Gym to burn off his anger, Jordan returns home only to see thirteen messages on his cell phone, which he left behind—Tonja twice, David three times, Brookes, JoJo, Delgado, Janne (she couldn't possibly know yet that he is unemployed). There was even a message from Karen and a couple of clients.

He decides to call Janne back first. He explains what happened and downplays the altercation with Turlock. Her main concern is whether he is okay. He assures her that he is fine physically and the predominate emotion he feels is anger. He is more determined than ever to see this through! She is glad to hear that and offers her support and help. He tells her that he would like to come join her out on the campaign trail after he talks to Delgado and figures out what they will do with his case. His other case files will be fine with Karen handling them. Delgado is a special case on many levels. Janne is thrilled of the prospect of having him come see her.

Next, Jordan calls Tonja and discovers that David was not aware that Epstein was even in town, much less there to fire him. She says David wants to see him as soon as possible. He asks her to thank Brookes, Karen, and JoJo for their kind messages and to assure them that he is all right but that he needs some space right now before reaching out to them. Tonja, as always, will handle things with class and efficiency.

As he prepares to call Delgado, Jordan pauses to make sure he knows how he would like to proceed with his case. Jimmy paid $10,000 to J&G, and they are officially on his power of attorney. He is confident that Delgado will want him to continue to work his case, but they will have to figure out how they will proceed. He wants to win the OIC doubt as to liability case for Jimmy but also continue to build the tax abuse evidence. At least he won't have David Jacobs hounding him about tiptoeing around the CID. Jordan is confident that the CID has no case and is keeping the investigation open simply as an intimating factor until collections can close the case. Another abusive action!

Jimmy Delgado agrees to meet Jordan at Carney's. Upon telling him of his dismissal from Jacobs & Goodman Tax Resolutions, Jordan doesn't even need to express his desire to continue working the case for Jimmy, as Delgado immediately responds, *"Pendejos*! I will fire them immediately. I want you to represent me solo."

"I appreciate your support and confidence, Jimmy. I believe we can win this battle, but as I mentioned before, there is more that I want to accomplish with your case," Jordan begins to explain.

"I feel strongly that Arthur Gibson struck a nerve within the IRS and Epstein's CPA firm. Ultimately, it cost him his life..."

Jimmy cuts him off, "You think those cabrones murdered him?"

"Yes, I do. We need to deal with that separately. First, I have evidence that the illegal collaboration between them extends to Jacobs & Goodman. If they didn't let me go, I would have resigned before too long. I am building a connection to present to the US Congress through my girlfriend, who works in politics. With a small group of others, which included Arthur, we are going to prove that the IRS target audits corporations for political purposes and to generate revenue. Part of our plan to expose them is to present multiple cases of taxpayer abuse. Your case is one of the key components of my personal experiences with taxpayer abuse, as I've told you before. So if we continue to work together, it may extend beyond liberating you from this tax liability. The stakes are now higher, but if you are still willing, I could use your help."

"Like I told you before, vato, count me in," Jimmy says, remaining wide-eyed and fully engaged in the conversation. "More now than ever!"

"Okay, great. I told you about the fiasco concerning the Super Bowl ring."

"Si. I love it!"

"Well, since then Arbuckle has been very quiet. Has not even inquired about your boat. However, I know Jack is biding his time. My guess is he will eventually try and get the CID to pressure you about criminal intent in hiding the boat. But it will just be a smoke screen. I'm convinced they have nothing on you. So my advice is, keep the boat hidden, and don't pay heed to their threats. I will deal with Jack, and now that I don't have David looking over my shoulder on this case, I can contact CID directly and find out more about this so-called investigation."

"*Tu eres jefe*... You are the boss!" Jimmy flashes his smile.

"I need you to sign a power of attorney with me." Jordan pulls out the form. "Then contact Jacobs & Goodman to tell them you no longer need their services. Let me know as soon as you do because I can't file until they are off."

Delgado signs it and says, "I will go do it right now. It's not far from here. I want to give them a piece of my mind."

"Don't tell them anything about what we're up to."

"*No hay manera, amigo...* No way."

They rise and say goodbye.

Delgado walks into the Sherman Oaks office, kindly greets Vanessa, and tells her that he needs to see David Jacobs.

Vanessa calls David on the office line and tells Jimmy, "He said that Marlin will meet with you in a few minutes, if you will kindly wait."

"*No bueno.* I already met with him. I need to speak to the jefe this time." He is not smiling now.

David comes out to the lobby to greet Delgado with a smile. The conference room glass wall is under repair, but the hole is patched up, so David escorts him into the room.

"I'm glad you stopped by, Mr. Delgado. Marlin Goodman had it on his calendar to contact you. Not sure if you are aware, but Mr. Duncan is no longer employed by our firm. Marlin is my partner and will give you excellent representation."

"Yeah, I met him once and got a taste of his representation. No thanks. I am here to terminate your services," Delgado says in a direct manner.

"I understand that you had a good working relationship with Jordan. Most people do, myself included. However, unfortunately, he is no longer with us. I can assure you that we will give your case top priority moving forward. I have a personal relationship with Jeffrey Woodruff, who is the district director of the IRS Los Angeles District. I will contact him about the CID investigation and get your case resolved in the most efficient manner," David says confidently with a smile.

"It is none of my business whom you have personal relationships with or what you do with them. I don't care. But I came to see you guys for help, and the only one who would help me and whom I trust is Jordan Duncan." Delgado gazes straight into David's eyes without a trace of a smile.

The smile has vanished from David's visage.

"I want you guys off my power of attorney today. I'm hiring someone else, so if I need to sign a form, that is why I am here."

"I will have Tonja bring the form out." David stands and exits without even offering a handshake.

Upon filing the POA for Delgado, Jordan calls Jack Arbuckle.

"Well, look who has surfaced from the cellar...Mr. Jordan Duncan, disgraced former Superstar. Looks like the tables have turned. Karma's a bitch, huh?" Jack begins the conversation with his condescending, sarcastic attempt at humor. He is getting back his obnoxious mojo.

"As usual, you are way off base, Jack, but I don't have the time nor interest in straightening you out. I'm calling because I am now on the POA for James Delgado, solo." Jordan will not use the Hayes episode to intimidate Jack. He wants Arbuckle on the job when he presents his case.

Jack laughs out loud. "I don't know who is more foolish, you or Jaime. Maybe he is paying you a lot because he feels sorry for your state of unemployment. But you are definitely on the losing team here. Oh yeah, I forgot, you are used to that, having played football at UCLA." Jack laughs, obviously amusing himself.

"I need the entire audit results sent to me. I will leave a fax number."

"Look, former Superstar, I am going to instruct the CID to lower the boom on Delgado. He is hiding assets from me, and I intend to find and seize his boat, to begin collection activity. We need to discuss a payment plan ASAP." Jack is no longer laughing.

"You listen to me, Arbuckle. Don't think it is a sign of weakness that I am no longer with Jacobs & Goodman. They were holding me back! As Delgado's representative, I have the right to review his audit before negotiating a settlement or payment plan. And stop bluffing with the CID. That trick and pony show is getting stale. I will be contacting the CID myself, and I will get to the bottom of this fictitious investigation. There will be no seizure before I can finish the review of the audit and resubmit my client's financials. Things change, Jack. Delgado now has new representation!" Jordan hangs up the phone. He has met the enemy, and the enemy is weak. Jack Arbuckle is going down. He is too foolish to know how and when yet.

Jordan meets with Tonja and Brookes at the Stand for lunch.

After expressing sorrow for the loss of Arthur, they discuss the state of affairs, and Brookes wants to know if he is clear to resign. Jordan suggests that he stay put until he has something else definitively lined up. He reminds them both that everything they have done and continue to do at J&G is on the up and up. They both agree. Tonja tells Jordan how sad Sunshine was to hear that he is no longer employed at J&G. She wanted Tonja to extend an invitation to him to attend her high school graduation later in the week. She says Sunshine admonished her to *please* make him say yes. Jordan smiles and confirms that he will attend with Tonja. He asks her to set up a lunch for him to meet with David tomorrow, if possible.

"Oh, he will make it possible, believe me. Just plan on Fromin's at eleven forty-five."

Jordan arrives fifteen minutes early and gets a booth across the dining hall from David's favorite spot and orders an iced tea. He wants to keep him out of his comfort zone as much as possible during this exit meeting. David arrives and, with a somewhat sad-looking smile, greets Jordan and sits across from him.

"I appreciate you meeting with me under these stressful and awkward circumstances." David tries to set the tone.

"I'm not feeling stressed, nor do I feel awkward," Jordan responds with his usual cool mannerism.

"Glad to hear that. First, I want you to know that I had no idea Alex was going to show up and terminate your employment. I let him know in no uncertain terms that I am quite distraught with the manner in which he acted." David is offering an olive branch.

"So are you here to offer me my job back? No thanks." Jordan is keeping an emotional wall between them.

"I wish it were that easy. I want to help you, Jordan. When I first met you, I was impressed with the way you conducted yourself on the football field. Such a cool character and an obvious high achiever. However, I had no idea if that would translate into success in the tax resolution business. I took a gamble on you, and it paid off big time. Your success has exceeded even my highest expectations. You picked up the business side quickly and became an enrolled agent, and your rapport with your clients is, quite frankly, the best I have ever witnessed in all my years in the tax business. People gravitate to your personality, compassionate care for them, and your sharp business acumen. Your future in this business is without a ceiling. I would just hate to see you throw it away at such a young age." His assessment sounds genuine.

"I appreciate your kind words, but I feel there is more that you want to tell me. How would I throw away my career, in your opinion?" Jordan knows David well.

"I don't know what you think you know or suspect is going on with Epstein and the IRS, but I can assure you that you are going down a slippery path. There will be nothing to discover if you continue to search for answers. Alexander Epstein is an extremely cautious and meticulous businessman. He is also a dangerous man to cross." David sounds like he is trying to warn Jordan more than intimidate him.

"I know that Arthur is dead." Jordan stares directly into David's bloodshot eyes.

David removes his glasses and rubs his eyes. "Yeah, that is a terrible tragedy. Who knew Arthur messed around with drugs?"

"Cut the crap, David. We both know Arthur didn't do drugs. He was set up. The question is, by whom and for what reason?"

David sits up straighter. "Those are strong accusations, young man. You best be extremely careful to whom you voice that, and I advise you to not try to pursue your hunches. It would be a most grave mistake by you. I say this as a friend, Jordan." David displays a stern demeanor.

"Or what? I will end up like Arthur?" Jordan is getting agitated with this conversation.

"Look, I am not involved with Epstein's operations. I run the tax resolution business and will continue to do so. I don't know all that was said or done between Arthur Gibson and Alexander Epstein, but I assure you that Alex did not kill him. Arthur was asking a lot of questions within the IRS. Maybe he messed around with the wrong people. I really don't know. My concern right now in meeting with you is to thank you for your hard work and wish you well in the future. I strongly advise you once again, for the last time, keep your nose out of Epstein's business. I would hate to see your career end so abruptly!" David seems to be finished talking about the subject of Epstein and Arthur.

Jordan lets the silence permeate for a few moments. He speaks very slowly as he leans forward with his arms on the table between them and hands clasped. "Okay, I hear your advice. Here is some for you. Watch your back, David. Do you really trust that Epstein is your friend? Seems to me that the guy's loyalties stop after he looks into the mirror." Jordan stands and says, "Take care, David, and thank you for the opportunity. I really enjoyed it and learned a lot."

David begins to stand, but Jordan has already walked away without ordering lunch or paying for his iced tea.

David sits back down and removes his glasses. Rubbing his eyes, he mutters, "Damn!"

Jordan attends Sunshine's graduation with Tonja before taking the redeye back east to attend Arthur's funeral services. David is seated with the Kessler family.

After the caps are thrown into the air and a large chorus of "Hooray!" is shouted by the graduating seniors, Jordan and Tonja make their way down to the football field to personally congratulate Sunshine. She is all smiles and laughs with her fellow graduates. When she sees Jordan, she sprints over to him. He kisses her on the cheek and congratulates her with a polite hug and smile. She excitedly informs him about an academic scholarship she has accepted to attend UC Berkeley in the fall. He offers her his best wishes. She promises to keep him informed of her progress.

The funeral service for Arthur Gibson is held at the Presbyterian Church in Fredericksburg, Virginia, where Arthur and Donna reside. Janne flew in from campaigning in the Midwest to join him. It is a solemn occasion, but they appreciate the opportunity to meet

Arthur's family and friends. The service includes several speakers who each recount positive experiences encountered through the years with Arthur. There is a speaker that worked closely with him at the IRS, another speaks of his involvement in community affairs, a former teammate from the University of Michigan recounts that experience, and finally, his pastor gives a heartfelt tribute to an amazing man, husband, father, and grandfather. The church choir sings beautifully.

Donna expresses her gratitude to Jordan and Janne for coming. She updates Jordan on the autopsy and tells him that the police have opened an investigation. She relays the name and contact person within the DC Police Department. Jordan assures Donna that he will not let Arthur's good name stay tarnished. She smiles and thanks him for that.

Jordan accompanies Janne to Ohio to continue the campaign in one of the critical swing states. He fills her in on all that has happened since they were last together. She does likewise. There is some time for Jordan to meet with Steve Forbes. He lays out what they have discovered and the game plan that they have derived to expose the IRS in wrongdoing and illegal activity. Mr. Forbes is quite impressed and encourages him to continue gathering information and evidence. He tells Jordan that when the time is right, he will introduce him to Jack Kemp. He is confident that Mr. Kemp will be able to get Jordan, his team, and their collective evidence in front of the proper authorities within Congress. Jordan is well pleased with the meeting and thanks Janne. They enjoy a couple of weeks together, and he is amazed at how much work and coordination goes into a presidential campaign.

As he is preparing to return to SoCal, he gets a call from John Sawyer informing him that Paul Hoage is making good progress. They are procuring more information. Jordan thinks to himself that all cylinders are now in motion with plans A and B. They have the added incentive to avenge Arthur's death. He knows that everyone must have their head on a swivel—on both sides! He has transitioned into his aggressive mode.

CHAPTER FIFTEEN

Republican Convention 1996

Janne invites Jordan to join her in attending the Republican National Convention on August 12–15, which is held at the San Diego Convention Center. Since it's conveniently located for both, they drive down the coast from LA and stay at a Marriott in Mission Bay to avoid the cluster of people converging on downtown San Diego from across the country. The festivities are entertaining, and the positive vibes reverberate within the Republican Party as even though he's trailing in the polls, Bob Dole remains optimistic in his battle with President Clinton.

The theme "Sail to Victory in '96" is consistent with the venue as the convention center is located on the waterfront of the San Diego Harbor. Hundreds of boats fill the harbor, including a contingent of the US Coast Guard. Dole and Kemp make a grand entrance to the convention aboard a large yacht, waving furiously to the throngs of cheering constituents lining the coastline.

It is nice for Jordan to return to the city of his childhood as he and Janne arrive a day early, on Sunday, August 11. He takes her to his old neighborhood in Chula Vista, which is only about a fifteen-minute drive from downtown. On Sunday night, he and Janne are accompanied by Al and April as they meet Gabe Fernandez and his wife, Sylvia, at Casa Guadalajara, a Mexican restaurant located on the corner of the Old Town State Park in San Diego. They are seated out on the expansive patio, and after introductions, Jordan and Gabe share stories of their youth. Then Al recounts stories with Jordan during their high school football playing days. Though it would be easy for the women to lose interest quickly in the subject manner, the skill of both Al and Gabe to "spin the yarn" in storytelling keeps everyone amused and entertained.

At the recommendation and almost insistence of Gabe, each of them orders the cucumber jalapeno margarita. None are disappointed, and the buzz they feel adds to the enjoyment of the evening. The ladies share how they met their respective partners, which perpetuates the fun and laughter. At the end of the evening, they all agree they should stay in touch and meet up again. As they separate, Gabe pulls Jordan aside and tells him privately that he looked into the Delgado file and that it has been officially closed. Jordan smiles and thanks Gabe for his help as they shake hands.

The convention is full of energy. Janne and Jordan enjoy the speeches. Bob Dole formally accepts the nomination to represent the party in the upcoming presidential election. He introduces the immensely popular and talented Jack Kemp as his running mate to a large cheer from the congregation. Dole promises a 15 percent across-the-board reduction in income tax rates, which receives another standing ovation. Curiously, there are no promises made concerning the flat tax platform proposed by Steve Forbes and endorsed by Jack Kemp, which had gained considerable momentum during the Republican primaries.

On Wednesday evening, the last night of the convention that will adjourn on Thursday, Janne is able to seize a moment to have Mr. Forbes introduce Mr. Kemp to Jordan. The short conversation is pleasant, and Kemp seems genuinely interested in the content of Jordan's allegations against the IRS. As Jordan briefly articulates, in short order, the evidence they have accumulated, Kemp notes that he is duly impressed with their efforts. He jokingly mentions that he is a little preoccupied by attempting to win an election but encourages Jordan to reconnect with him afterward. He hands him his personal business card. Jordan is excited about the meeting as he and Janne realize that this could be a critical breakthrough in their efforts to get in front of Congress!

Prior to leaving the hotel for the conclusion of the convention on Thursday morning, August 15, Jordan receives a phone call from Gabriela. She wishes him a happy twenty-seventh birthday! He thanks her, and as she asks about his experience at the convention, he mentions that he met Jack Kemp last night.

"Is that the same Jack Kemp who played professional football?"

"Yes, a long time ago, I believe he did play in the old AFL," Jordan replies.

"Oh my gosh, your dad met him when he was twelve years old. He was your father's first football idol as quarterback for the San Diego Chargers. He presented Eddie a trophy for winning the Punt, Pass, and Kick Competition of San Diego County in 1961. Of course, that was before I met your dad, but he told me all about it. In fact, he got an autographed football card from Mr. Kemp, and it was a prized possession." Gabriela sounds extremely excited to relay this story to her son.

"No kidding. That's amazing! Mom, is there any chance you still have that card?" Jordan is equally excited.

"I believe so. I remember packing it with the newspaper articles, trophies, and awards that your father received before we moved to New Jersey. Let me see if I can find it."

"Yes, and if you find it, please send it to me if you don't mind."

"Sure. I would love for you to have it." Gabriela is pleased to talk to her son about an experience of his father's.

"Thanks, Mom. I've got to go to the conference now. Tell Teri hi for me. Take care. I love you!"

"Love you, too, son, and please pass my well wishes to Janne and Al."

Jordan tells Janne about the irony of his dad having met Jack Kemp when he was a kid and how his father idolized him. They both believe it could be more than just a coincidence. Perhaps it's karma!

While Janne has another two and a half months left of strenuous campaigning, Jordan decides to make another trip back east. He contacted Shelley Davis, the now former IRS historian of whom Arthur spoke. Upon referencing Arthur, Shelley expressed her sorrow in hearing of his death and agreed to meet with Jordan.

They meet at the Embassy Suites at the Chevy Chase Pavilion in DC. The location where Arthur died is not coincidental. Jordan has stacked a meeting with the police detective investigating Arthur's death upon finishing his conversation with Ms. Davis. In the bar lounge area, Jordan and Shelley have an appetizer and club sodas while chatting. Jordan proceeds to fill her in on the progress he and his team have made in their attempt to connect the IRS with E, L & O. He mentions that Arthur had indicated he was making inroads within E, L & O that implicated political overthrows in their auditing schemes. Shelley listens intently and seems very interested as Jordan details their plan B of exposing the IRS Examination and Collection Division of taxpayer abuse. As he wraps up his summation of evidence and continuance of probing for information, he inquires of Shelley her thoughts and suggestions.

She begins by referring to the IRS headquarters as the temple of doom as she explains how the agency routinely destroys its own records. She reemphasizes how frustrated she was in trying to discover and document the historical references within the IRS. Much to her initial shock and dismay, she recounts that she is convinced of the unethical behavior that thrives in the highest ranks of the IRS bureaucracy. She shares with Jordan that, in her time there, she witnessed how the IRS runs from its past, lies to Congress, evades responsibility, retaliates against whistleblowers and squanders billions of dollars of taxpayers' funds on a computer system that doesn't work.

Jordan asks her if she believes they could eventually find evidence from within the system or through connections within the agency to implicate an alliance with a private CPA firm, participating in target auditing. She has little doubt that it is not only possible but more than likely occurring.

However, she points out that there are several instances that have been exposed that show audits have been targeted, initiated from within the bowels of Congress and even from the Executive Office, and go unpunished. She refers to a congressional oversight committee that was formed in 1988 that was focused on unethical practices within the IRS bureaucracy, including target auditing. The investigators had lined up witnesses from within the ranks of the agency, but at the eleventh hour, the IRS disclosure attorneys had sent out a briefing to the witnesses, reminding them of the penalties associated with unauthorized disclosure of confidential taxpayer information. Each of them rescinded their willingness to testify. She explains how the broad interpretation of the Internal Revenue Code 6103, which includes the "misuse of taxpayer information" is used by the IRS to withhold any information that they don't want to let out. So she points out that the downside to testifying is losing your job and even possible prosecution. The point she is making is that Congress was stonewalled because they couldn't penetrate the wall of agency loyalty, which is based on fear.

"Sound familiar to you as you deal with the Collection Division?"

He nods his head. "So how can we proceed, in your opinion?"

She rubs her chin as she looks at him and her eyes widen. "You attack them with your plan B. Formulate a coalition of tax professionals, like yourself, who have first-hand examples of taxpayer abuse. Offer taxpayer witnesses to your connections in Congress to testify of their experiences. Section 6103 obviously can't be used as a shield against taxpayers relating their own personal tax information! Then Congress may probe into the auditing issues. I think that is your best chance."

Shelley is smiling as she thinks of the prospect of Congress hearing example after example from around the country of IRS taxpayer bullying and abusive actions. Perhaps IRS arrogance and intimidation methods can be brought down a notch or two after all.

"Who is your contact within Congress, if I may ask?" she inquires.

"Well, he is not actually in Congress now, but when I presented my theory of abuse and that I had taxpayer evidence, he seemed quite interested and asked me to contact him after the election… Jack Kemp."

"Oh my, this could be fun! He certainly has all the necessary connections and clout within Congress. You know, I had a close friend within the agency that acted as a mentor to me. He died in a car accident last year. He called me the conscience of the IRS, and I referred to him as its soul. Arthur Gibson was of that same ilk, in my opinion. I only wish they were able to witness the execution of what you are initiating." She pauses for a second. As Jordan remains silent, she continues, "Somehow, I think they will!" Shelley smiles.

Jordan nods his head in agreement. "The spirit of Arthur's perseverance in seeking truth inspires me."

"I applaud your efforts!"

They shake hands, and she departs, telling Jordan to contact her if he has any questions that she might help him with.

Jordan feels encouraged after his meeting with Ms. Davis and goes to the bar to order a beer while waiting for the detective. He is approached by two men, who identify themselves as police detectives from the Metropolitan Police Department of the District of Columbia. Upon sitting down in a semiprivate location in the lounge, the detective whom Jordan contacted and who oversees the investigation asks why he requested the meeting and what pertinent information he can offer. Detective Dwayne Douglass is an African American in his early forties. He is a tall handsome man and has what Jordan deems as an athletic-looking build. He seems serious but not intimidating as Jordan explains his relationship with Arthur and tells him about their inquiries within Epstein, Levin & Ohlman Tax Consultants and the Internal Revenue Service. Jordan does not go into detail about the allegations.

"What do you think that has to do with Mr. Gibson's death?"

"Well, both Arthur and I were asked not to pursue any further information regarding the relationship between the CPA firm and the IRS. Mr. Gibson felt as though he needed to know if there was any inappropriate activity going on. I know Arthur well, and I have a very hard time believing that he would be reckless in a way that would endanger his life or his relationship with his wife by taking drugs. I talked to Donna Gibson, and she said Arthur told her he was meeting with a whistleblower from a client of Epstein's that night at this hotel. I believe Mr. Epstein has something to hide and felt that perhaps Arthur was getting close to exposing it. Epstein recently came out to California and personally terminated my employment from an affiliate company without giving notice to the president of the company. Something out of the ordinary is going on within their firm," Jordan responds.

Detective Douglass studies Jordan's face before responding. "I spoke to Mrs. Gibson, and she gave permission for me to give you details if I feel as though it might help with the investigation. The report from the medical examiner's office indicates that the drug Rohypnol was evident in Arthur's blood in addition to the bad heroin." Douglass ascertains that Jordan does not know what that is. "Ruffy."

"Oh, so he was drugged before he was infected with the contaminated heroin?" Jordan asks.

"It looks like that is a distinct possibility. I don't think Mr. Gibson would be foolish enough to mix those drugs. The 'ruffy' could have been used to render him unconscious in order to infect him with the 'hot dose' of heroin–battery acid mix. The room was registered to a woman, and Arthur's wallet was left with no cash. That could be a front." Douglass asks Jordan another question. "What is the full name of this Epstein CPA?"

"Alexander Epstein. You might want to check out a guy by the name of Kurt Turlock also. He is Epstein's 'head of security,' who seems to act as his henchman or bodyguard. Former Navy SEAL, I believe."

"Anything else you can tell us?" Douglass asks.

"Not at the moment. I just think those two guys had motive to keep Arthur quiet."

"Okay, we appreciate you coming forward, and we will contact you if we have any other questions." The two detectives rise. Jordan follows suit, and they shake hands before departing.

Next on his list to contact is Royce Dawkins. He no longer needs to abide with his no-further-contact agreement. He dials the cell phone number Dawkins gave him.

"Hello?"

"Is this Royce Dawkins?"

"Who is this?"

"Jordan Duncan."

"Hello, Jordan. I heard about Arthur Gibson, and I feel sick about his passing. But it has been made abundantly clear to me that for the safety of myself and my family, I can't discuss anything with you or anyone else pertaining to my previous employment. I'm sorry, Jordan, but I just can't talk to you. Please don't contact me again." Dawkins hangs up before Jordan can ask for any details about his safety warning.

Jordan sits and ponders about what he heard. First, he feels anger about Dawkins' choice of words. Arthur didn't "pass away." He was murdered! He thinks Dawkins knows that. Then he realizes that Royce Dawkins has obviously been threatened to stay quiet. He probably is living in fear every time he leaves the house or gets a phone call. He concludes that it is best to not try to contact him anymore and not pass his name to Detective Douglass.

Jordan flies nonstop from Dulles to San Francisco International Airport, which is located in Burlingame, just south of downtown San Francisco. There he is escorted to an outside airstrip where Pete is waiting with his chopper.

At the cabin, it is midweek in September, and there are no clients arriving until the weekend. He is welcomed by John and Paul. He recaps with them his experience in speaking with the police detective.

John and Pete look at each other, and John says, "We agree that Arthur did not die from a self-inflicted drug overdose. We will help you settle that score when the time is right." Upon descending into the bunker, they review what they have found thus far in the IRS computers.

Paul, sounding a little discouraged, summarizes what he has discovered. "There are several systems within the IRS, and ironically, very few of them are connected. That slows things down a bit but isn't a deal breaker in deciphering information. The bigger problem is that when I found the system that contains audit information, I found an incredible lack of organization. There are literally millions of audits with little in the way of categorization. It would take months, maybe years, to try to find specific audits that connect to the corporate accounts of E, L & O. The proverbial 'needle in a haystack' comes to mind." He is shaking his head as he stares at the computer monitor in front of him.

Jordan speaks up with an enthusiastic tone. "Forget that idea. I spoke with the former IRS historian that Arthur met. She said that even if we found a connection, the chances of getting Congress to do anything about it is slim at best. However, she was quite excited about our plan B strategy."

John, in particular, is intrigued with this development. "How's that? Does she recommend that we scrap plan A and proceed with plan B?" he asks.

"Not entirely. But her point is that the IRS has a stipulation in the Internal Revenue Code, Section 6103—ironically implemented by Congress back in the '70s—that prohibits any disclosure of tax-payer information. Subsequently, they hide behind that whenever they are questioned about audits and taxpayer returns. Her thought is that if we gather a coalition of tax pros with specific cases and witnesses of taxpayer abuse, Section 6103 would not come into play. Taxpayers can willfully discuss their own tax returns or interactions with the Examination Division by way of audits and with the Collection Division by way of payment enforcement. If there are a substantial amount of case witnesses presented, she believes that is our best bet to get the attention of Congress in exposing taxpayer abuse. It would lead to an internal investigation that may or may not lead down the trail of target auditing."

John smiles as he says, "I like it. You already have some specific cases with witnesses, correct?"

"Absolutely. I also received a list that Donna printed from Arthur's computer of tax professionals that he contacted. I propose that we construct a form letter and contact each of them to build this coalition."

He continues as he turns his eyes toward Paul, "I say we change our focus of computer hacking to E, L & O. Should be a lot easier to find their list of clients, right?"

"Sure. Then we can make connections to their audits and look for common ground, tendencies, and irregularities." Paul is catching on fast.

"Exactly! If we can expose E, L & O in misrepresenting their clients by showing an inordinate number of audits and maybe even some bad tax advice, we can nail them separately from the IRS," Jordan says with a fervent tone of voice.

John sums it up, "So Paul cracks the E, L & O system and downloads files on their clients. We then decipher a percentage of them that were audited and look for tax shelters, executive compensation adjustments, and midmanagement layoffs that affect the bottom line as well as their corporate taxes. In the meantime, we can send out a recruiting letter to tax pros from Arthur's list, enticing them to join our coalition of taxpayer abuse. In essence, we are simply adjusting plan A to go after E, L & O without necessarily connecting them to the IRS while moving ahead on plan B."

"Yes, with one other caveat. I have definitive proof that J&G has been contacting Trust Fund Recovery cases that originate from the IRS. I am going to follow-up on that to bring them down along with E, L & O. I just need to confirm what they are saying to these clients."

"Sounds like a winner. You okay with that, Paul?" John asks.

"No problem."

"I do have one request from you," John says to Jordan.

"As we build this coalition of taxpayer abuse clients and witnesses, I believe it is imperative that we have a keen understanding of tax protocols as it pertains to the Examination and Collection Divisions. I have acquired a law degree in taxation as you know, but it is more about theory and tax law. You have worked literally hundreds of actual cases in negotiating settlements. However, we no longer have Arthur's knowledge of tax codes. Don't you think it might behoove us to have a team member that is a tax attorney with Collection Division hands-on experience? Perhaps we can solicit someone from Arthur's list."

Jordan thinks for a moment, smiles, and says, "No need for that. I have the perfect person for the job. I will make the phone call from here."

In his next move, Jordan calls Tricia Sherman. After he briefly explains why he no longer works for J&G, she expresses that it doesn't surprise her that David got overruled by Epstein. Jordan asks if she would be interested in a side job that would require her to come meet him at a cabin in Yosemite Valley. The intrigue and mystery of this side job immediately has her interest, which he had anticipated. She agrees to meet with him. He tells her that he will have Peter Marshall contact her to plan to pick her up at the San Francisco airport in his helicopter.

"Jordan Duncan, what are you up to?" Tricia is definitely intrigued.

Jordan reviews Tricia's background with John, Pete, and Paul, and they all agree that she certainly has the credentials for what they are looking for as a consultant. John expresses concern about the confidentiality aspect considering that it would be a conflict of interest for her as an employee of Jacobs & Goodman Tax Resolution. Jordan suggests that they have her sign an NDA before presenting their plan. They can seek for consultation strictly on cases that are not connected to J&G in any form. Then she can decide if she wants to work with them. John and Pete agree with that scenario, and Pete makes the call to arrange the transportation.

As they await her arrival, Jordan and Paul go into the meadow area and throw a football around, while John draws up an NDA for Tricia. Paul tells Jordan that even though he has never said anything, he believes that Jordan helped immeasurably with his self-confidence in life. Jordan doesn't know what he is referring to, so Paul explains.

Most of their senior year, the championship season, Paul felt as though Coach Bockman had somewhat abandoned him on offense by relegating all the best players to defense, including Jordan, who was Paul's number one receiver as juniors. The coach constantly emphasized the strength of the team was on defense. Their offensive game plan had a rather vanilla flavor to it. Paul was explicitly instructed to not take chances and to not turn the ball over— to let the defense win the game.

Then in the championship game, they faced a team from south Jersey that featured a D-I quarterback prospect that had signed a letter of intent to play at Florida State. He surprised them with three touchdown passes in the first half alone. That was more than they had allowed all season! They trailed 21–3 at half, the defense made adjustments, but the team needed to score at least three times against a stout defense to pull out a win. Jordan made an interception to set up the first touchdown and cut the lead to 21–10 entering the fourth quarter. Jordan and Miles Jackson pleaded with Coach Bockman to let them play offense to try to win the championship.

The coach refused and said, "We will stick with what got us here." He looked at Paul. "Go win this."

He huddled his defense and told them they would need turn-overs to help the offense. Jordan approached Paul, who was obviously quite nervous. He hadn't needed to pull out a game all season.

"Paul, you have the best arm on this field today. I know that guy over there is good. I have been playing against him all day. But I have caught passes from you and faced you on defense all year in practice. I'm telling you right now, you are a better passer than he is. Trust your arm, and tell your receivers what you want them to do. There is no doubt in my mind that you can lead us to two touchdowns this quarter."

As Paul is reminding him of this history between them, Jordan is amazed at the detailed accuracy of Paul's memory.

"When you told me that, I knew you were right. I had practiced making every kind of throw and knew that I could lead the team to victory." He smiles. "I just needed to hear it from someone else!"

The rest, of course, is history. Paul led the team down the field for a seventy-yard scoring drive. The defense held, and with a lit-tle over three minutes left, with the ball at their own twenty-three-yard line, Paul got the chance he had been waiting for since his Pop Warner days. He methodically marched them down the field. With nine seconds on the clock, he threw a perfect pass on a crossing route in the end zone for the game-winning touchdown. The undefeated championship season was complete. Though everyone remembers what a dominant defense had done all year and that it certainly was the signature card of the team, Jordan has always privately told Paul it would all be for naught if it weren't for his stepping up when they needed him.

As Pete delivers Tricia to the cabin, she stands in the entryway as she is approached by the three men.

"Oh my gosh, this is place is amazing!" She displays her gorgeous smile while looking at Jordan. She says, "You never cease to surprise me, Jordan. What is going on?"

He gives her a polite hug and introduces her to John Sawyer and Paul Hoage. They go into the living room area and get comfortable. Jordan proceeds to explain how they are in the process of building a coalition of tax professionals to present real-life case witnesses of taxpayer abuse from the IRS to members of the US Congress.

Tricia looks at each of them curiously, directs her attention to Jordan, and says, "I believe there is merit to your endeavor. However, there must be more to the story. Why are you attempting this colossal project? What is your motivation?"

Jordan looks at John, who doesn't respond, and says, "Yes, there is more to it. We are glad to share it with you as we believe you could be an important piece of the team. But you will need to sign an NDA before we reveal any more info."

She again scans the participants in the room and says, "Okay… Let me read what I am signing first."

No doubt she is an attorney, John thinks.

After she signs the NDA, Jordan goes into some detail about their suspicions concerning E, L & O and the IRS. He then tells her about what he suspects concerning the trust fund recovery cases within J&G. He omits the part about breaking into Marlin's office. After all, he is speaking to an attorney and an employee of J&G. He concludes by telling her that he is certain that Arthur was murdered and that he intends to find out who killed him.

"Wow, that is quite a story. Doesn't surprise me terribly. As you know, Jordan, I have always had my doubts as to the integrity of David Jacobs and Marlin Goodman. I have been extremely careful not to cross any ethical lines in my work. I'm sure your work is on the up and up as well. We have discussed the big mystery as it pertains to Marlin's activities within the firm. As far as Arthur's death, I would really like to know what happened too. So what is it you would like me to do?"

John takes up the conversation and explains his background in obtaining a law degree in taxation but that he has limited experience with the Examination and Collection Divisions. He admits that he could use some consulting in dealing with cases that will be brought forth to testify before Congress. He feels—and Jordan agrees—that they need to screen the cases and maintain control over the process of solicitation of tax pro clients. Tricia agrees wholeheartedly.

When John completes his oracle and answers her questions along with Jordan, she stands and extends her hand toward John first. He takes her hand, and as they shake hands, she smiles and says, "It will be a pleasure to work with you, John Sawyer."

He smiles in return and says, "I look forward to it, Tricia Sherman."

Tricia turns to Jordan, shakes his hand, and says, "You are something else, my friend. But I love your ingenuity and assertiveness. You remind me of me when I was your age."

They all laugh as Tricia proceeds to shake hands with Pete and Paul.

Back in Maryland, at the Epstein, Levin & Ohlman Tax Consultant executive office of Alexander Epstein, he is seated with Barry Levin. The third partner, Joseph Ohlman, is the head attorney of the firm and has little to do with operations. His name is on the firm's title because Epstein thought it added prestige to have an attorney as a partner. They rarely include him in any operational or strategic meetings. He is consulted with strictly on legal matters.

Barry Levin is sitting across from Epstein at the small table in the room adjacent to the office suite. "We have effectively eliminated risks 1 and 2. However, risk 3 seems to remain at large. What is your intention on its elimination?" He speaks as though the "risks" are inanimate objects.

"It has proven to be more complex than I anticipated. He doesn't scare easily, so I don't think threats will work as they have with Dawkins. Gibson was a more eminent risk to our security that required more drastic measures. To try to stage a similar occurrence with Duncan would create too much attention. Too coincidental. We have a tail on him and his girlfriend. I've thought about abducting the girl to use as leverage, but she is constantly in groups of people. Her involvement with the presidential election campaign eliminates that idea for now," Epstein responds in a calm, coldhearted manner.

"Do you believe Duncan is getting close like Gibson was to finding incriminating evidence?" Levin asks.

"No. That is the short answer. However, he is harder to follow than Arthur. Number one, I can't get into his head and predict his moves. I have never encountered anyone that I detest as much as this kid!" Epstein is seething under his skin.

"You know, Alex, you have always said it is business first. Don't ever let it get personal. That will cause emotions to dictate actions and result in mistakes," Levin reminds him of his own counsel.

Epstein looks directly into Levin's eyes, and his voice rises. "I know that, Barry! He is not going to get the best of me. I will *not* allow that punk to bring me down! I will personally see to it."

Sure does sound like it has gotten personal, thinks Levin.

"Have you talked to your insider at the IRS?" Barry decides to change the subject.

"Yes. That is frustrating as well. There are no audits scheduled, and he can't predict when we can continue the scheduling. He is giving some BS about the election, but I'm not buying it. I don't know exactly what Gibson said to whom. However, it seems as though he might have raised a red flag." Epstein loosens his tie and the collar of his dress shirt.

"Do we still have access to their computers to retrieve the trust fund recovery cases?" Levin is doing his typical risk assessment.

"Yes. They don't worry too much about that. If it is ever exposed, they will undoubtedly claim we hacked into their system. There is little risk on their part. It is a revenue generator for us, and Marlin continues to snare a good percentage of cases. We will continue with that program." Epstein rarely asks Levin or anybody really, for their thoughts or advice.

"Do we have any new clients on the horizon?" Levin is covering all bases.

"Not that I am aware of. The marketing team is not performing up to expectations. I will have to make some changes in personnel if things don't turn around quickly."

"Are you worried about any whistleblowers with Duncan?"

"Duncan does not have credibility like Gibson. He won't be able to penetrate our client base. He wouldn't even know what questions to ask!" Epstein scoffs at the idea of Jordan Duncan conversing with management-level personnel within the ranks of his clients.

Levin pauses for a moment as if he isn't sure he wants to comment, but then he challenges Epstein's remark with "You said yourself he doesn't scare easily and you can't predict his moves."

Epstein glares at Levin and says with his most hateful tone, "Barry, I will *not* let this kid beat me! He got lucky to win my basketball tournament, then cowardly ducked the rematch. I will personally destroy the punk before he can get close to my business empire! He is *way* out of his league with me in the business world!"

Barry Levin shakes his head and raises his hands as if surrendering. "Okay, just please keep me in the loop. I am at risk as much as you are with our business empire."

He now knows that Alexander Epstein is obsessed with defeating Jordan Duncan on a personal level. That spells trouble, with the risk quotient extremely high!

CHAPTER SIXTEEN

Presidential Election 1996

Jimmy Delgado agrees to drive up north from his home in Torrance to meet Jordan at Chez Jay's in Santa Monica. They are seated in a booth on this Thursday night, October 10, 1996.

"I like this place, amigo. Peanuts and beer with some good vibes. I can smell the ocean from here."

"Close to home for me. I wanted to get you caught up on your case and discuss our strategy moving forward."

"I completed reviewing your audit and have concluded that we have grounds for an offer in compromise in doubt as to liability. I submitted the forms today. I'm sure I will get a call from Arbuckle."

Jordan takes a healthy gulp of beer and continues, "Jack will reject the offer and will once again use the threat of the CID investigation. What he doesn't know is that I also contacted the CID agent in charge and set up a meeting with him and his partner on Monday. I'm pretty confident to get the investigation put to rest as I will demand that they either file charges or dismiss the case. They would have filed by now if they had anything solid against you. They have contacted your business connections, your clients, and your accountant. Curiously, they haven't contacted me nor tried to set up a meeting with you. That tells me they have nothing of substance. I did some research on the CID and found that when they recommend prosecution, the chances for conviction is about 90 percent. However, they are selective on who they recommend, thus maintaining their high rate of conviction. I suspect that they have not already closed the investigation simply at the urging of the revenue officer, Jack Arbuckle, to aid in the intimidation for collections. That fact will be brought before Congress when we get on the stand to testify," Jordan assures him.

"Jack could not levy your bank account while I was in the process of reviewing your audit. As you know, he is ready to pounce on your funds and in seizing your boat, if he could locate it. Now that we have officially submitted the OIC, his hands are tied until the hearing takes place. He will try and expedite it, and I will stall it until after the first of next year. In the meantime, keep the boat hidden, and continue to keep as small amount of money in the bank as possible."

"*Muy bien*, amigo." Delgado is nodding his head as he continues to crack peanut shells and shove the nuts in his mouth, with an occasional swig of beer.

"I been thinkin', Jordan. You only been workin' my case for the past four months, right?"

"Yeah, that's right."

"What have you been doing for dinero, *mi amigo?*" Jimmy asks with a serious expression.

"I have a savings account stashed. Been living off that for the time being."

"No *bueno*. Can't work for nothin'. I want to offer you a job…"

Jordan counters, "I'm already working for you, and you paid J&G ten grand. I got a commission for that."

"Screw that and screw them! Hear me out." Delgado looks around to make sure no one can overhear their conversation. When satisfied he leans forward with his arms on the table and says in a barely audible tone, "I am willing to pay you 20 percent of the money you save me. I believe the IRS has jacked up my debt to $180K now with penalties and interest. But there is more." He wipes his mouth. "Remember the gold bars I told you about down in Mexico?"

Jordan replies quickly, "I told you not to mention that until we are free and clear of this case."

"Relax. I have a plan you need to hear. When this is all over—and I mean, after the testifying, *everything*—when the slate is wiped clean, I am going to sail my boat down to Baja and retrieve my gold. I want you to come with me." He hesitates to get a reaction.

"Why?" Jordan has always been a bit curious about these gold bars but hasn't wanted to complicate the case nor risk them coming into play with the DEA or the CID.

"*Porque*, I have no idea how to convert gold into cash and get it back to El Norte or even into an offshore account. I don't trust no one in Mexico to help. I only trust you, vato. You have proven to me that you are a problem solver. I like that. I need that!" Jimmy has his full-toothed smile flashing now.

"I really don't know anything about converting gold bars."

"Trust me, you will figure it out. That's what you do!" Delgado lets out a laugh. "I am offering you 50 percent of the value of whatever the conversion is on top of the 20 percent commission for my case. And I will start paying you now in advance to finish my case. Just shake my hand and tell me that we are partners." Jimmy extends his hand.

Jordan stares back as he ponders what he was just offered. The exhilaration of this proposition captures his interest. Frankly, he hasn't taken the time to think about what he will do next. He hasn't discussed the future with Janne, Al, Tonja, or anyone. He will need to generate some income before too long, and who knows how long this gig could play out once they present their case to Congress? How difficult could it be to convert gold to cash? Just a matter of shopping conversion rates and trying not to get screwed or robbed down in Mexico. He enjoys working with Jimmy Delgado and appreciates his trust in him. Besides, he has always coveted surfing in Baja!

He extends his hand, smiles, and says, "Deal!"

"*Excelente!*" Delgado shakes his hand robustly and then raises his beer mug. "Here's to the extended partnership of the Aztec and the Taxman!"

They clink and take a big swallow.

Jordan says, "I'm not doing your taxes on the conversion."

"Don't worry. I have an accountant for that—if we bring it to El Norte!" They both laugh. Delgado reaches into his pocket and pulls out a thick roll of $100 bills and hands it to Jordan with a wink and a smile.

Just before getting up to leave, Jordan says, "I have a favor to ask you."

"What's that?"

"Are you still interested in contacting JoJo?"

"*Si claro*…of course!" Jimmy's voice perks up.

"Since I don't work for David anymore, she is on the open market for you as far as I am concerned. They are not married or engaged," Jordan says with a sly grin. "However, I would like you to get some information from her, if possible."

Delgado is excited and curious at the same time. "Que es eso?"

"She is making appointments for Marlin, which has been very secretive in the office. I need you to find out what she is saying to the clients to book the appointment. I want to discover if she claims that they obtain the client name from the IRS?"

This info would nail them, Jordan thinks.

"Hmmm, okay, I think I should be able to do that. I will tell her that I didn't like the dude at all and ask how she likes working for him. That will break the ice. Then I will get your answer." Delgado flashes his smile.

"I discovered at a company retreat that when she drinks, she talks openly," Jordan declares.

"Haha, don't they all, amigo?" They both chuckle.

On Friday morning, Jordan gets a call from John. He explains that, much to his and Tricia's surprise, the response from tax pros they have contacted has not been overwhelmingly positive. It seems that, more often than not, the pros view the IRS fear tactics instilled into the taxpayers as an asset because it creates a greater need for their services. The majority conclude that they don't want to rock the boat by providing witnesses to testify of taxpayer abuse. They have procured some willing participants that view the publicity as a positive but not nearly the volume nor depth of what they anticipated.

Jordan ponders this dilemma and suggests a possible solution. He will contact his friend and marketing guru, Brookes Peterson, to create an ad directed toward the taxpayer. It will solicit them with an opportunity to voice their personal stories of taxpayer abuse from the IRS. There must be hundreds of frustrated taxpayers that would jump at the chance to get back at the IRS. They will offer anonymity to thwart the fear of retaliation. John runs it by Tricia to ensure the legality of the process, and they confer that it could work out.

Jordan meets with Brookes at the Galleria for lunch to present the plan. Brookes is fine with it as long as he doesn't market in California, where he believes it would create a conflict of interest. Jordan assures him that won't be necessary. Brookes enthusiastically creates a power-packed ad that generates more phone calls than they even hoped for. John and Tricia begin the process of screening potential clients, listening to their personal stories, and starting to accumulate ideal candidates to testify of taxpayer abuse to members of the US Congress.

The meeting with the CID special agents plays out exactly the way Jordan anticipated. He rents an executive suite office in Santa Monica for a couple of hours wherein they meet, and he listens to them trying to posture an act of intimidation. He cuts to the chase and explains that he has reviewed the audit and has submitted an OIC in doubt as to liability. He also mentions that he contacted the DEA and that they have closed the case on Delgado after having found no evidence of any wrongdoing. He asks them directly if they are filing charges or dropping the case. He indicates that those are the only two options.

Prolonging their investigation any further would constitute taxpayer abuse and would be noted in tax court while discussing the OIC. The agents obviously are not thrilled to be threatened in this manner. However, they abruptly end the meeting and instruct him that they will render their decision within the week. On Wednesday, October 16, Jordan receives a faxed copy of the decision from the Criminal Investigation Division to close the case of Jaime Delgado and not recommend prosecution. He calls Jimmy to let him know that it now has come down to a standoff with Jack Arbuckle without an investigation of the CID looming in the background.

The 1996 United States presidential election is held on Tuesday, November 5. Incumbent Democratic president Bill Clinton defeats former majority Senate leader Bob Dole, the Republican nominee, and Ross Perot, the Reform Party nominee.

Clinton's chances of winning were initially considered slim in the middle of his term as his party had lost both the House of Representatives and the Senate in 1994 for the first time in decades. He was able to regain ground as the economy began to recover from the early 1990s recession. Despite Dole's defeat, the Republican Party is able to maintain a majority in both the House of Representatives and the Senate. Thus, the inspired governmental infrastructure created by the founding fathers to maintain checks and balances remains intact.

Janne is disappointed and indicates to Jordan that she believes Dole's reluctance to promote the flat tax platform initiated during the Republican primaries by Steve Forbes and endorsed by Jack Kemp hurt the Dole/Kemp campaign. However, she is quick to point out that it still would have been extremely difficult to unseat the charismatic Clinton since the economy is on an upward trend.

With Republican majority power in Congress and the party's predominant disconnect with the IRS, Janne feels that it is a perfect time for Jordan to contact Jack Kemp to discuss initiating a congressional investigation of the policies and procedures of the Internal Revenue Service. He makes the call and is delighted to discover that Mr. Kemp will be in San Diego during the holidays, where he still maintains family relations. They set up a meeting during the week between Christmas and New Year's Day on Saturday, December 28.

Hotel Del Coronado, also known as the Del, is a historic beachfront hotel in the city of Coronado, just across the San Diego Bay from downtown. Jack Kemp is seated by himself as Jordan and Janne arrive. He stands to greet them with a hearty handshake. He is dressed casually in khakis, a light-blue polo shirt, and tan sports coat with beachside loafers. He still looks trim and fit at sixty-one years old. His silver hair is parted on the side, and he now dons eyeglasses.

He still has the engaging smile that has endeared him to so many constituents through the years as a professional football quarterback and as a member of the House of Representatives from Buffalo, New York, where his football playing career concluded. Kemp played professional football for thirteen years with the San Diego Chargers and Buffalo Bills. He was a seven-time All-Star two-time champion and the 1965 American Football League MVP. He co-founded the AFL Players Association, for which he served five terms as president.

As an economic conservative, Kemp advocates low taxes and supply side policies. He was a strong influence on the Reagan administration and the architect of the Economic Recovery Act of 1981, which is known as the Kemp-Roth tax cut. Among other features, it allowed all working taxpayers to establish individual retirement accounts (IRAs).

By 1996, Kemp has been named a director of six corporate boards, and in addition to those esteem positions, he serves on several advisory boards such as the UCLA Public School Policy Board. A busy and well accomplished man indeed!

As they are seated, Mr. Kemp is quick to acknowledge Janne's positive contribution to the Steve Forbes Republican primary campaign and, subsequently, the Bob Dole presidential campaign. He graciously gives thanks for her hard work. Upon learning that she graduated from UCLA with a masters' degree in political science, he suggests that she has a bright future in politics and offers his assistance in connecting her to several projects with which he is affiliated. Janne is delighted and thanks him for his support and endorsement. As he turns his attention to Jordan, he is surprised as Jordan hands him a 1961 football card with his image and autograph.

"Goodness gracious! Where did you find that?" he asks with a smile and small chuckle as he examines the card.

"Ironically, it has been in my family ever since you personally signed it in San Diego in 1961," Jordan answers with a glean in his eyes.

"No kidding. Tell me about it." Jack seems genuinely interested.

"My mother told me how my father met you at the San Diego County Punt, Pass, and Kick competition finals in '61. Apparently, my father, Edward Duncan, won the twelve-year-old age group, and you presented him with the trophy. You happened to be his football idol at the time and were kind enough to sign this card for him."

"Isn't that something? Boy, those were fun and exciting times for me back then. I remember that Charger team in '61. We went 12–2 and made it to the AFL championship game, where we lost to the Houston Oilers. I loved San Diego then, as I do now. I had a great coach in Sid Gillman and fantastic teammates!" Kemp is still studying the card as he reminisces aloud his fond memories of the time. "Where are your parents now?" he inquires of Jordan as he hands the card back to him.

"My mom is living in Short Hills, New Jersey, with her husband and my little sister. My father, after starring on the Chula Vista High School football team as the quarterback during their CIF Championship season, had aspirations of going to UCLA. However, he was drafted into the army in 1967. He was killed in action in 1969 a few months after I was born. I never knew him," Jordan says without the angry tone in his voice that he formerly expressed on the rare occasions that he spoke of his father's demise.

"I'm really sorry to hear that, Jordan. That's a tough break. It was a most difficult and dark time of political history in our country. Thank you for sharing your story. I feel that this connects us in a special way. I will do whatever I can to help you in your quest to challenge the authoritative abusive actions of the IRS."

Janne reaches over to hold Jordan's hand, and they smile at each other.

"What would you like to know about the things we have discovered?" he asks Kemp.

"Well, you laid it out for me at the convention. What we need is written documentation of several taxpayer abuse examples. If you could include dates and specific incidents of experiences that have occurred within the past several years from around the country, that would be most helpful. If called upon, you can produce witnesses to testify in front of Congress, that would definitely strengthen the case. Also, if there are specific problems within the policies of the

IRS Collection Division that you would like addressed, please clarify them in your report."

Jordan nods his head for a moment before commenting, "One thing that I find particularly disturbing is how the IRS piles on penalties to a delinquent taxpayer—filing late, paying late, paying too little, making math errors in their returns. They seem to have a carte blanche agenda when it comes to auditing and then assessing penalties and interest that cause a nearly impossible situation for the taxpayer to become current. Two of my partners are tax attorneys, and they will document cases pertaining to the practice of levies and seizures without due process."

Jack nods his head with a troubled expression and furrowed brow. "Our tax system was designed in a bygone era. It worked reasonably well for a national, industrial, wage-based economy. However, we have moved to a global, services-based economy. Our tax system needs more than adjusting. It needs complete overhaul."

He continues, "The constant changing of tax laws, which have amounted to thirty-two times in the past forty years, is one of the main reasons why Congress has such a bad reputation. As the great former president Ronald Reagan once said, 'The government is not the solution to our problem. The government is the problem.'" He pauses to let that statement hang for a moment. Then he finishes his thought, "There are currently over 2 million federal employees, who cost $161 billion a year. The Office of Management studies show that for 1995, the overhead is $234 billion. Each federal employee costs the taxpayers $200,000 a year. That, my friends, is the excessive cost of 'big government.'"

Jack exhales. "Perhaps if we can knock the Internal Revenue Service down a couple of notches and cause a downsizing, it will help reign in the government a bit. It is worth looking into for sure. I appreciate the thought and effort you have put into this, Jordan. I will have a member of the House of Representatives by the name of Charles McKean contact you. He is a member of the House Ways and Means Committee. Upon his investigation, we can push it forward to Representative Bill Archer of Texas, who is the chairman of the committee and a good friend of mine. He will make the determination on the merits of holding formal congressional hearings on the matter." Jack smiles and says, "I believe we have a pretty good shot at it if your witnesses are willing to testify in a consistent manner with your allegations."

Jordan and Janne thank Mr. Kemp for his time and his interest in helping them get connected to a member of Congress.

As they stand and shake hands, Kemp says, "I remember seeing you play football at UCLA. I would have loved to throw some touchdown passes to you." All three of them laugh. "You know, I am on the advisory board at the UCLA School of Public Policy. That is another connection the three of us have."

As they depart, Jordan and Janne are feeling really good about their meeting with Jack Kemp.

Jordan and Janne are planning a drive up to Yosemite to celebrate the dawning of a new year and invite Al and April to join them. It will give them a chance to get caught up with one another as well as collaborate with the team members in NorCal. Al tells Jordan that Devin Joseph is the odds-on favorite to win NFL Rookie of the Year with the Philadelphia Eagles. This will be huge for Devin and for Al's ability to leverage a more lucrative next contract. It certainly won't hurt his chances of landing more high-profile players as clients.

Al can't leave until after the games on Sunday, so he and April fly into SFO on Monday, December 30. Pete picks them up along with Tricia Sherman. On Tuesday morning, the men, which includes John, Pete, Paul, Jordan, Al, and Dave Lackey, whose wife has accompanied him to the cabin for the New Year's Eve celebration, all engage in a game of touch football out in the meadow. There are remnants of snow on the ground, but the field is clear for the most part. Instead of teaming the old guys against the youngsters, they split up the teams as follows: Paul (the best arm), Al (the biggest and strongest), and Dave (quick and shifty as a former running back at West Point back in the early '60s), versus John (the tactician), Pete (cagey and tougher than he appears), and Jordan (fastest, best athlete). Even though they are playing two-hand touch, the game gets physical as it is football and half of them have NCAA D-1 experience. Other than some bumps and bruises, there are no sustained injuries, and though each of them is highly competitive, the tone and mood of good sportsmanship is maintained.

With the game tied and a mutual agreement that the next team to score wins, John designs a play wherein he as the QB takes the snap from Pete, and instead of the usual strategy of passing the ball to Jordan as quickly as possible and letting him try to outrun or outmaneuver the other team, Jordan comes around behind him for a lateral. Upon receiving the ball, Jordan stops prior to turning the corner toward the goal line and throws a backward pass to Pete, who has broken off his block on Al and retreated to the other side of the field. Pete gathers the pass and, being still several yards behind the original line of scrimmage, takes a couple of strides as though he will run the ball, then abruptly stops, and launches a long pass to John, who had lackadaisically thrown a block on Paul before sprinting down the sidelines several yards ahead of a fooled and trailing Paul Hoage. John takes in the pass and strolls past the imaginary goal line they created to effectively end the game.

Jordan, Pete, and John are whooping it up while the others are moaning about the gall of them having to resort to a trick play to beat them. They all walk off the field tired and hungry and in good spirits.

Cold beers and hot venison burgers await them as they reenter the cabin. While eating, relaxing, and still talking some trash, Janne leans over to whisper in Jordan's ear, "Do you always win?"

He laughs and whispers back, "Hey, your dad pulled that one out for us. I was just lucky to be on his team."

She has always admired and appreciated his humble attitude. She knows that in reality he is extremely competitive and in actuality does almost always win in his endeavors.

Before they begin their partying on New Year's Eve, they discuss the progress of their plan. Tricia informs Jordan and the others that she has resigned from Jacobs & Goodman Tax Resolution.

Jordan is surprised and asks, "How did David take that news?"

She replies, "Not well and tried to convince me to stay. Even offered me more money now that you are gone. Thank you very much." She smiles, and he nods. "I told him I'm bored with the work, and with the new IRS standards, there aren't as many opportunities for OICs. Of course, he disagreed and offered to send me *all* of the big liability cases from Marlin's workload, leaving him only with trust fund recovery cases." She laughs. "When I turned that down, he asked if I had been talking to you. That was when I told him that it is none of his business with whom I speak. Then I ended the conversation."

Little Al asks, "From one attorney to another, what are you going do when this is all over? My business is booming, and I could use some help from a sharp contract lawyer like yourself." He is smiling but gets a subtle elbow to the ribs from April.

"Thank you, Alvin, but I have decided to work in partnership with John in forming a business to take on tax court cases as well as criminal investigation cases that generate from the IRS."

Jordan looks somewhat surprised but remains silent as Janne looks at her dad with eyebrows raised.

John breaks out into a wide grin and begins speaking. "Tricia and I have found that we work very well together and have also connected on a personal level. She is going to move into the cabin with us full-time. The business model will be fine-tuned after we conclude our dealings with exposing the IRS in taxpayer abuse and target auditing."

"That's great, Dad. I'm happy for you!" Janne walks over and gives John a hug. She turns to Tricia, whom she doesn't know, and shakes her hand. "I am looking forward to getting to know you, Tricia."

Tricia returns her smile and says, "Likewise, Janne. Your father has told me so many wonderful things about you."

Jordan smiles and nods his head toward Tricia as if in approval of the good news.

Jordan gives a recap of his and Janne's successful meeting with Jack Kemp. Everyone is quite excited at this development as there is now a clear path into Congress to make their case.

Next, John shares the progress they have been making in procuring witnesses, both through tax professionals and individual taxpayers that have responded to Brookes's ads. He believes that they will have a list of confirmed participants within the next couple of weeks.

Paul is up next, and he relays the information he has discovered inside the E, L & O computer system. He explains that there is a definite trend in how they conduct their business. Nearly all their clients have been audited by the IRS Examination Division and have gone through changes in their business models to ensure more deferred stock options for executives and layoffs of midmanagement personnel. He also has picked up on tax shelters that they incorporate to lower the corporate tax rates of their clients.

He briefly describes how, as a stock trader, he learned of various tax shelters that a majority of top 250 corporations in America have been implementing to effectively lower their tax rates to substantially less than the 35 percent of corporate tax rates. Nearly a third of them are paying less than half of that. Overall, the effective tax rate on large corporations for the past year has been 22.9 percent. There are certain industries that are able to attain the lowest rates. Among those are electronic companies (13.1 percent), transportation companies (14.1 percent) and auto companies (17.1 percent). He points out that almost 90 percent of E, L & O clients fall into these categories. It appears, in his opinion, that they are taking on smaller versions of the top 250 corporations within the same industries and trying to mimic their methods of lowering their effective tax rates after having represented them in IRS audits. Though he points out that he doesn't know exactly how, based on internal correspondence, he believes they are using the IRS audit to trigger their aggressive methods of fraudulent accelerated depreciation and abusive tax shelters, all because they are betting on the odds that the risk of another IRS audit is miniscule. In effect, Paul has recognized a mechanism with which E, L & O is working with the IRS to target audit their clients that benefits the IRS as well as E, L & O. Then they set up shelters that in turn benefit the clients and screw the IRS. In other words, they are playing both sides! In addition, he was able to confirm that they are getting leads from the IRS on trust fund recovery cases, including names of responsible parties.

"Wow, that is great work, Paul," Jordan exclaims. He looks toward John and asks, "How do you propose we proceed with this information?"

John stands in front of the group that is seated in various comfortable positions in the living room. "It appears that Arthur may have spooked the IRS with his probing questions because Paul has also discovered that there are no audits scheduled into the foreseeable future for the E, L & O clients nor have they been pulling any trust fund recovery cases from the IRS computers for the past few months. That leads me to believe that perhaps the IRS is distancing themselves from E, L & O."

He continues, "Because of what Jordan pointed out from his conversation with Shelley Davis, it might be an insurmountable challenge to infiltrate the IRS to prove target auditing in collaboration with E, L & O. I think it might be best to attack the CPA firm through their own clientele and perhaps entice one or more of them to bring forth a lawsuit of misrepresentation on them. That could effectively bring them down or, at a minimum, expose their operations and create a large financial liability. We can continue to proceed with our plan B with the IRS, which is moving in a positive direction. When we are in front of Congress, we can expose all that we know in terms of IRS misdeeds and see how that plays out."

Jordan is first to respond. "I like that, as it is in the same vein that Arthur was investigating. But with that said, we have seen what Epstein is capable of when *he* is spooked. We need to be careful. How do we entice the E, L & O clients to sue them?"

"Good point and good question. That is going to take some risk. Paul has procured a list of contacts from within the firms that they represent. I suggest that we come up with a script that creates some fear in the ethical manner in which their CPA firm is operating. We contact them by way of a third-party law firm. Confidentiality is critical to maintain throughout this process. We then proceed to interrogate the contact person to gather incriminating evidence of misrepresentation by E, L & O while sharing with them what we know on the operational methods of their CPA firm. Last, we threaten to go to the Securities Exchange Commission, who, we explain, will no doubt open an investigation. My thought is that they will either terminate their contract with E, L & O or file a lawsuit against them—or maybe both."

"Any ideas for a third-party law firm?" Jordan asks.

Al jumps into the conversation. "I might be able to help with that. I could set up a shell corporation that specializes in tax shelter investigations. My staff could then begin contacting these companies. I will work with my old buddy Hoagie, who apparently is smarter than the average bear!" He slaps Paul on the back with a grin on his face.

"You sure you want to risk that?" Jordan asks his friend.

"I don't see anything illegal with asking questions. I will make sure there aren't any regulations broken as far as setting up the company. If John and Tricia can create the script template to follow, I will simply hire some people to make the calls. We won't be involved with lawsuits. Seems like we only need one company to bite to ignite the whistleblowing process on Epstein's firm." Al looks toward John for confirmation on his statement, who in turn looks to Tricia.

"I will look into that and make sure we don't step out of bounds," responds Tricia.

"Okay, let's proceed with that plan of attack. Jordan, when do you speak to the Congressman?" John asks.

"He will contact me after Mr. Kemp explains the situation to him. I'm hoping soon."

"Great. There is one more item that I would like to discuss. Dave Lackey, whom I have introduced as a partner with Pete and me, has a rather unique skill set and business operation. I would like to have him explain some things to you."

All eyes turn toward Dave, who stands from his seated position next to his wife on the floor leaning against the wall.

"Thank you, John. I won't bother you with a full explanation of my business operation. Suffice it to say, my company performs security functions for various clients. John and Pete informed me some time back of the activities in which you have all engaged regarding the exposure of the IRS working in collaboration with a private CPA firm. John felt as though there was potential of a dangerous environment based on the emotional instability of the CEO of the CPA firm. He asked me to keep an eye on things as it pertains to his daughter, Janne, and her companion, Jordan. Without being intrusive in any way, my team has been observing from a distance to ascertain whether these individuals were being followed or harassed in any matter. What we have discovered is that both Janne and Jordan have been followed at times during their activities. It seems as though, whenever the two of you go on the road, there are eyes on you. I'm assuming that the perpetrators are interested in with whom you are meeting. This operation started right after the death of Arthur Gibson and the termination of Jordan's employ. At this point, we can intercept the perpetrators and put a stop to their activities, or we can continue to watch them and remain close enough to protect you from harm. We did cut them off without their knowledge to prevent them from following you here." He is looking directly at Janne and Jordan, who are seated together on the couch.

Janne is wide-eyed as Jordan speaks first. "I had no idea. I appreciate your concern and interest in protecting us." His eyes drift from Dave to John. "I think it might be best to keep an eye on them without disclosing anything. That way, we don't alarm Epstein that we are on to him. We will be very careful with whom and where we meet. What do you think?" He turns to look at Janne.

"Yeah, I mean I feel kind of violated… I guess we can just be careful like Jordan said." Janne is obviously a little shaken.

"Now that the election is over and we are in our slow winter months up here, you can both move into the cabin until this is over," offers John.

"I appreciate that, but I am still working with a client on a case in LA, and he is a critical witness of taxpayer abuse. I will be careful. What about you, sweetie? Do you want to stay here?" Jordan asks Janne.

Janne tries to force a smile and says, "No, I think I will stay in LA. But I appreciate your help, Dave. Is there any way we can contact your team in case of need?"

"No, that is not a good idea, but you can contact your father at any time. He has direct communication with me and I in turn with my team members. It is only a matter of minutes before the lines of communication can be transmitted," Dave replies, and Janne nods her head in acknowledgment.

That evening, the group engage in some games of billiards, poker, and various other table games as they eat, drink, and enjoy one another's company. At midnight, they boisterously welcome in the new year, 1997.

On Wednesday, they go for a hike in the morning in the brisk cool temperature of the mountains and decide after hiking about three miles to turn back toward the cabin when light snow flurries begin to descend upon them. The beauty and quietness create a most serene setting.

On Thursday morning after breakfast, they all pack up and say goodbye. The feelings of cohesiveness between them have strengthened through the process of working as a team for a common goal. There remains the underlying commitment to avenge Arthur's death by completing his quest for truth within the IRS operations and bringing to justice Epstein, Levin & Ohlman CPA Tax Consultants.

On the drive back to Los Angeles, Jordan invites Janne to move in with him as a matter of safety, and he feels their relationship is at the level of that type of commitment. She accepts his invitation, and they decide to complete the move as soon as possible. Jordan is somewhat surprised to receive a call from Representative McKean so soon just as he and Janne are descending down the grapevine on I-5, heading to LA County. Mr. McKean expresses a strong interest in the information Jordan has to present based on what he has heard from Jack Kemp. Jordan agrees to meet with him in Washington, DC, next week. Representative McKean offers to pick up the tab for his and Janne's airfare and hotel accommodations.

On the weekend, Jordan receives a call from Donna Gibson. She states that Detective Douglass has informed her that he has additional information and some questions concerning Arthur's case. She tells Jordan that it is too painful for her to speak to him directly and asks him if he would accommodate the detective on her behalf. She has given him permission to discuss the case with Jordan. Without hesitation, he agrees to speak to Douglass.

Jordan and Janne are now much more aware of their surroundings and who may be watching them as they proceed in their daily activities.

CHAPTER SEVENTEEN

Congressional Oversight and Hearing 1997

Considering all that has transpired and the fact that the presidential election is over, Jordan and Janne decide to dedicate their full-time efforts to finishing the task of presenting their evidence of misconduct of the IRS to Congress and bringing Epstein, Levin & Ohlman Tax Consultants to justice. In doing so, they agree for precautionary reasons and to maintain continuity, they will stay together wherever they go and with whomever they meet. They have become an unbreakable team.

Before flying back east to meet with Representative McKean, Jordan takes Janne with him to meet Delgado. Jimmy is his charming self, and Janne takes an immediate liking to his personality and his obvious dedication to Jordan and their cause. He wholeheartedly is ready to testify in front of Congress when called upon. He informs Jordan that JoJo "sang like a bird" on only their second date together. Jordan's suspicions were realized when she explained to Jimmy how she so expertly convinces over 90 percent of the perspective clients having trust fund recovery liabilities with the IRS to be represented by Marlin. She coaxes them by stating she has received their names from the IRS to present the best possible solution to their tax problem. She also tried to convince Delgado that he should hire Marlin to resolve his case.

"What did you say?" asks Jordan.

"I told her that she should probably stop drinking!" Jimmy chuckles.

Jordan tells Delgado that Jack Arbuckle is extremely upset that the CID is no longer investigating him and is trying to expedite his hearing on the OIC in doubt as to liability.

"It wouldn't surprise me at all if he initiates a bank levy since he can't locate your boat and has no grounds to get a court order," says Jordan.

"He already did, but I am a step ahead of him. He only got a couple hundred dollars. I moved everything but the minimum from the account he knows about," Jimmy says with his customary grin.

"You catch on fast, amigo," Jordan replies. "Just beware until I get back from DC."

Jordan and Janne leave the next morning on a United Airlines flight from LAX to Dulles International.

Representative Charles McKean of Maryland offers to meet them at the Old Ebbitt Grill, which is an ancient Washington, DC, saloon originally established as a boarding house in 1856. The long-time guest list includes such dignitaries as several former US presidents. Today it has been converted into an excellent grill with a five-star rating for American-style cuisine.

McKean is in his late fifties, has a round Irish-looking face, and a ruddy complexion. He seems quite congenial as he meets Jordan and Janne in his customary dark suit, white shirt, and narrow tie. His physique is rather robust. He has a full head of gray hair. After the pleasantries and ordering their meals with the obligatory drinks, McKean expresses an enthusiasm and excitement on the prospects of formulating an oversight committee to investigate the activities of the Internal Revenue Service.

He explains to them a brief history of Congressional interest in the dealings of the IRS. He tells them of the hearings in the late eighties that Shelley Davis had brought up previously to Jordan. It is McKean's belief that the failure to initiate change from those hearings was caused by the lack of foresight from Congress on the power that the leadership of the IRS maintains over their employees. It was clear, he points out, that witness after witness declined to follow through in any negative testimony of their working conditions and the cover-up tactics from the service in fear of losing their jobs by violating their sworn allegiance to the tax code statute section 6103. It is the same scenario that Ms. Davis had described.

McKean continues with his dialogue, stating that he believes using taxpayer witnesses to testify of IRS abuse is a brilliant plan. He tells them that, with the assurance of anonymity, he is convinced that they can also procure testimony from within the IRS ranks. Finally, he asks Jordan if he has any ideas on that front.

After thinking for a few moments, Jordan confirms that he believes he can entice cooperation from a branch chief within the Los Angeles District of the IRS Collection Division. He is thinking of Bobbi Sinclair—the most and, quite frankly, the only straight shooter he knows in the Collection Division. He also suggests that Representative McKean contact Shelley Davis, the recently resigned IRS historian. She will present a wealth of knowledge from within the inner workings of the Internal Revenue Service. McKean literally slaps his knee with glee at that suggestion. It is as if certain members of Congress have been searching and waiting for the proper time and mechanism to re-attack the IRS. He expresses his gratitude to their courage and patriotism in designing this plan. Jordan agrees to submit the list of witnesses, including one or more members from the ranks of IRS personnel.

Upon finishing an excellent lunch and a productive conversation, they shake hands with the congressman and leave the premises of Old Ebbitt Grill. Jordan smiles at Janne as they happily realize their hopes and efforts are being fulfilled beyond expectations in the progressive manner in which Representative McKean is taking up their quest for Congressional intervention.

Jordan comments, "I'm not so sure this is out of patriotism on my behalf, but whatever they want to call it, bringing the IRS to a state of accountability is worthwhile and satisfying to me." Janne tells him that she thinks he has more patriotism than he wants to admit. He laughs as he knows that Janne is the true patriot between them.

Before going to meet Detective Douglass at the Embassy Suites, Jordan calls Tonja. He asks her to discreetly talk to Bobbi about the prospects of her discussing with Jordan some procedural functions she has been required to oversee as a branch chief in the Collection Division. He instructs her to make sure she offers complete anonymity. Tonja agrees.

As they enter the lounge area off the lobby at the Embassy Suites, Jordan and Janne are both pleasantly surprised to see Donna Gibson sitting at a table with Detective Douglass and his partner. After a warm greeting, she explains her presence.

"Arthur was the strongest, toughest-minded person I have ever known. He used to tell me that he recognized that trait in me as well, and he thought that was one reason why we made such a good team." She smiles. "I know he would want me to be involved in solving his murder. I can't let him down."

Janne reaches over and squeezes Donna's arm and says, "I'm sure he is extremely proud of you, Donna, for the way you are handling everything and especially how you have stepped up with your daughters families."

"Thank you, Janne, that is very kind. I'm glad you came with Jordan. You both are a great comfort and support to me. I believe Jordan has inside information that will help those responsible for my husband's death get what they deserve. Let's get to the details of this case, Detective."

Detective Douglass proceeds to explain that he has questioned both Alexander Epstein and Kurt Turlock. It seems both have alibis as to their whereabouts on the night in question. They have produced a flight manifest, stating that they were each on a chartered flight to Los Angeles on the morning of the night Arthur was killed. In fact, he tells Jordan, they stated that they met with him the following Monday morning and described verbal abuse toward Epstein and a physical confrontation that he initiated with Turlock. He notes that they didn't press any charges in LA, so it is of no concern to him.

Hearsay…

Jordan just shakes his head and continues to listen to Douglass.

The detective goes on to reveal that the room wherein Arthur was discovered was registered to a female who was scantily dressed and had paid cash earlier that day. She showed an ID, but they have not been able to track down the name. Probably fake, he states. The glass that had Arthur's fingerprints came from the bar, which is in the lounge where they are currently seated. He points out that the bartender that night was a guy that had a past prison record and was fairly new to the job.

Donna had given the name of Mitchell Shumway of Findlay Electronics to Detective Douglass as the person with whom Arthur was scheduled to meet. Douglass recounts his discussion with Mr. Shumway in New York and tells the group that he has a rock-solid alibi for the evening of May 23. In speaking to others at the firm, it is believed that whoever met with Arthur was an imposter. Fortunately, Arthur was a large man with a professional demeanor who often stood out in a crowd. His photo was identified by a witness at the lounge that evening, having been accompanied with another man, who has yet to be identified. It certainly looks like a setup according to Douglass. He explains that their next step is to interview and, if necessary, interrogate the bartender to find out what he knows about Arthur's drink and who was with him.

Jordan tells the detectives about the possible shady dealings within E, L & O and that they have discovered more evidence that Arthur was on the right track in his suspicions. He agrees to keep the detective in the loop as they move forward. Douglass advises Jordan and Janne to be careful and to watch their backs. They appreciate his concern, and he promises to inform them when he learns more about the bartender, the girl, and the mystery imposter that met with Arthur.

Before saying goodbye to Jordan and Janne, Donna tells them that, in a strange way, she feels better having the detective convinced that it was a homicide that took the life of her husband. She expresses her confidence in Detective Douglass and again thanks them both for their help and support. Jordan assures her that they will find the truth in what happened to Arthur and will make sure Arthur's quest for truth from within the IRS and E, L & O be realized. Donna smiles weakly but warmly, hugs each of them, and promises to stay in touch.

Back in Los Angeles, Tonja informs Jordan that Bobbi has agreed to speak to him. They choose a coffee house wherein to meet, and Tonja comes along. Although it is the first time Bobbi has met either of them in person, they each feel as though they know one another quite well. The meeting is cordial. Jordan and Tonja are somewhat surprised as Bobbi tells them that she feels a huge relief in being able to share this information with them. She relates how there is pressure from her superiors to constantly increase collections. Although they don't use specific dollar amounts as criteria of job security, it is made abundantly clear that it is expected that her group of revenue officers collect as much as possible and close cases. She explains that even though she continually receives complaints from taxpayers about the tactics of Jack Arbuckle and others, she cannot escalate any disciplinary action as those who "feed the beast" are revered by the district director.

She also mentions that her counterpart in the San Francisco District, Sharon Bennett, the SF branch chief, who works with Tricia Sherman and Sterling Frey from Jacobs & Goodman, has told her that she actually has dollar quotas set on her performance in collections. Jordan asks Bobbi if she thinks Sharon would be willing to testify. Bobbi says that if they can assure anonymity, she believes Sharon will do it. He tells her that he has documented evidence of taxpayer abuse by Jack and that he and his clients are going to testify to members of Congress to that affect.

Bobbi grins and says, "I can't wait to see the results of that!"

They agree on the confidential nature of the matter, and Bobbi will wait for further instructions on how they will proceed.

The following week, Tonja confirms to Jordan that Sharon Bennett has agreed to add her name to the list of IRS witnesses of taxpayer abuse. Jordan relays the information to Representative McKean, who is delighted and informs Jordan that he has received a commitment from Shelley Davis among others from within the ranks of the IRS, including individual agents who conduct audits, to testify. The oversight committee has been selected, the venues to conduct questioning have been established, and the proceedings are ready to begin.

The oversight committee is headed by Representative Bill Archer from Texas. He has been the chairman of the House Ways and Means Committee since 1995 and has known and worked with Jack Kemp for a long time. Jordan has the opportunity to meet Mr. Archer prior to the cross-country investigative tour. They develop an almost immediate mutual admiration in their respective resolve to uncover misdeeds and inappropriate behavior within the IRS.

One of Archer's first acts as chairman was to focus attention on reining in the IRS. He seeks to downsize Washington by reducing the abusive manner in which the agency takes away from the people by way of tax collection. His strategy was referred to as "starving the beast"! In 1996, he enacted the Taxpayer Bill of Rights, which created the Taxpayer Advocate Service within the IRS. Unfortunately, as currently constituted, the advocacy platform lacks the teeth necessary to make much impact. When he was approached by Representative McKean with the plan to hear testimony from various taxpayers from across the country on the abuse they have endured from the IRS, it didn't take much convincing to obtain his endorsement. By adding testimony from tax practitioners and employees from within the service itself, Archer's enthusiasm and commitment to the endeavor of bringing accountability to the leadership of the Internal Revenue Service soared!

The committee starts a barnstorming trek across the country in March of 1997. They encounter a long parade of witnesses that are largely part of the coalition of tax professionals and individual taxpayers and were initiated and organized by John Sawyer and Tricia Sherman. Hearings are held in numerous venues during the months of April through August. In selected districts, testimony of IRS revenue officers from the Collection Division and revenue agents from the Examination Division are included with strict provisions of anonymity in place. Jordan participates by setting up the California hearings, which include testimony from Alice Johnston, Bobbi Sinclair, and Sharon Bennett, among others. The concept of collection quotas being set by IRS district management is revealed. Witness testimony is being recorded and documented. Jordan is told by McKean to save his best witness for Senate hearings on Capitol Hill, which he is confident will occur at the conclusion of this tour. Jordan is preserving Jimmy Delgado for that opportunity.

Testimony of taxpayers are brought forth, including cases such as the following:

- A $26K capital tax gain assessment caused a taxpayer to downsize, only to have their new home seized for failure to pay the liability in full.
- A daycare business owner with an installment agreement was horrified when an IRS revenue officer and other employees showed up unannounced at the center and set up a table in front of the room where the children were located. They instructed the parents that they had to either pay the IRS directly or sign a promissory note in order to pick up their children.
- Another taxpayer who had a $9K liability and was paying an installment agreement of $300 a month saw his liability balloon up to $18K due to penalties and interest. When he was delinquent for two months on his payments, his bank account was levied, and the IRS garnished his wages.
- A woman's house burned down and destroyed her tax paperwork. The IRS Examination Division cut her no slack in auditing her and assessing her a $20K liability because she didn't have the proper documentation to substantiate her expense write-offs.
- A Youth Soccer Association filed referees as independent contractors because they paid them on a per-match basis. The IRS auditors disallowed that classification, refiled them as employees, and assessed taxes to the tune of $330K for payroll taxes, penalties, and interest.
- One taxpayer was audited eighteen months after the fact for a two-year period, which is stressful enough. However, the IRS revenue agent went beyond the ordinary and demanded receipts for every expense for the past two years,

even relatively minor expenses. When the taxpayer couldn't produce all the receipts, they were assessed penalties, which when compounded by interest, accounted for a past due liability of nearly twice the original assessed tax bill.

- After an audit claiming improper business expenses, a tax-paying married couple contacted the Taxpayer Advocate Service (TAS), the independent service within the IRS to ensure taxpayers' fair treatment. The IRS agent who conducted the audit became enraged by this action, ignored the TAS, and charged additional penalties and interest. Thus, the concept of taxpayer advocacy backfired.

Sharon Bennett, branch chief in San Francisco, testifies that it is getting more difficult all the time to distinguish ignorance from bullying tactics. She has discovered in many instances that revenue officers are promised secret bonuses and promotions based on their total dollars collected and number of cases closed. This promotes overzealousness and seizure activities rather than reasonable payment plans.

A whistle blower within the IRS Collection Division rats out a fellow revenue officer, who, upon placing a tax lien on his clients, offers to get the lien subordinated through a local mortgage broker in order to pay off or pay down the tax liability. The revenue officer has a side deal in place with the broker and received kickbacks on the loan transactions.

Several innocent spouse incidents similar to Alice Johnston's are uncovered and brought to light. It is evident to those members of Congress hearing the testimony that the current innocent spouse relief program is not sufficient in protecting the victims.

Concurrent with the oversight committee embarking on their quest to interview taxpayers, tax practitioners, and IRS employees, a bipartisan congressional group of the Joint Committee on Taxation is formed to investigate allegations of target auditing by the IRS for political purposes. The investigation is directed by Senator William Roth of Delaware, chairman of the Senate Finance Committee and another close Kemp ally. The primary interests in the investigation includes the following:

- Tax-exempt organizations
- IRS "hit lists"
- Executive and congressional "enemies list"
- CPA firm "targets"

After several attempts to thoroughly investigate the auditing trends of target groups and organizations, due to lack of comprehensive data within the IRS computer systems, the Joint Committee is unable to evaluate systematically whether there is sufficient evidence of IRS misconduct.

Although there is not enough credible evidence of political bias in the IRS's auditing selection to conclude target auditing, the Joint Committee did identify certain procedural and substantive problems within the IRS auditing process that have contributed to a perception of unfairness and have hampered the IRS's ability to demonstrate unbiased treatment. All IRS "hit lists" of potential audit targets are ordered to be abolished.

They find that no standardized requirements are in place regarding the tracking, retention, or evaluation of audit referrals. In response, the committee has regulated the IRS to implement a new system whereby all information is tracked, evaluated, and retained in a standardized manner throughout every IRS district office with audit responsibilities.

In addition, the IRS must heretofore improve communications with and the training of IRS employees about the importance of ensuring that accurate information is maintained in the IRS database. The IRS is instructed to improve communications with taxpayers to ensure that they are aware of the reason for and the timing of audit examinations.

Meanwhile, as the investigations are in full swing, the IRS commissioner, Margaret Richardson, resigns from her post, effective May 31, 1997. Richardson sites her frustration by the ongoing congressional committee admonishment of the IRS for not collecting more revenue and then, at the same time, berating them for not being kinder to their customers.

"They want us to collect every nickel, but they want us to be warm and fuzzy too. It is schizophrenic!" she is quoted to have said.

It is discovered that, in fiscal 1996, the IRS collected nearly $29 billion in delinquencies and issued 750,000 liens—all without due process, without a judgment, and without the taxpayer having a day in court. Over 10,000 properties were seized during this time frame. IRS revenue officers in various geographical locations across the country testify that they were given a quota of taxes collected. The easiest way to meet these goals, they confess, is to target the poor and small business owners because they are less likely and financially able to fight back. Audit rates for the past seven years for people with incomes over $100K declined from nearly 12 percent to just under 3 percent, whereas the audit rates for people with less than $25K income nearly doubled. That constitutes a form of targeting in its own right!

Michael Dolan, who was Richardson's next in command, is slated as the interim commissioner of the Internal Revenue Service. Chaos has definitely infiltrated the normal tightly buttoned up IRS hierarchy.

A formal congressional hearing investigation of the procedures and activities of the Internal Revenue Service by the Senate Finance Committee is held from September 23 through September 25, 1997, at the Senate Office Building in Washington, DC. Presiding is Senator William Roth, the Finance Committee chairman.

Having read the transcripts from the interviews conducted by the House Ways and Means Committee contingent, several bipartisan senators speak on day one of the hearings. They express grave concern over the methods of audit examination and collection methods incorporated by the IRS. James Woehlke, the director of the New York Society of CPAs regarding tax policy, and Joseph Lowe, the chief officer of the National Association of Enrolled Agents, also address the floor. There is an air of astonishment, embarrassment, and a resolve to find a medium ground of resolution between the respective political parties as well as the professional associations that are represented. The members of the Senate present are informed that they will be hearing direct testimony over the next two days from various taxpayers, tax professionals, current and former IRS employees, the former IRS historian, and renowned authors and university professors who specialize in tax law. All the witnesses are sworn in to tell the truth before being allowed to address the senators. Everyone except the taxpaying citizens are subject to questioning from the floor.

Shelley Davis is first up on day two. She testifies that the IRS keep lists of American citizens for no other reason than that their political activities may have offended someone within the IRS. She recounts her experience in discovering that the IRS shreds its paper trail, which means there is no history, no evidence, and ultimately, no accountability. Congressmen are appalled at such a revelation of negligence.

Robert Schriebman, a tax professor at the University of Southern California, criticizes the agency's ability to ignore citizen's due process protections. He states that some IRS auditors and tax collectors have taken the position that congressional directives set forth in the Internal Revenue Code are simply guidelines that they may accept or reject at will. His experience has shown that their conduct is often condoned by their superiors, including those at high levels of authority.

David Burnham, author of *A Law Unto Itself: The IRS and the Abuse of Power*, tells the finance panel that one of the basic problems is that the IRS has come to think of itself as a law enforcement agency rather than a service agency. His statement is reciprocated by many head nods and several head shakes, not in disagreement but more in amazement at how off-track things have gotten. He continues by stating that the IRS's problems are dangerous to the nation for two reasons. First, he notes, a poorly managed agency does not collect as much as might be expected of federal taxes that are owed by noncomplying taxpayers. The second cost is harder to measure but probably more important. He explains that a poorly managed agency is unfair. Substantial numbers of individual citizens are radically subject to wrongful actions. Such treatment contributes to a corrosive public cynicism that undermines public confidence in the government in a dangerous way.

Following a recess for lunch, Jordan and Delgado are part of the group that testifies in the afternoon. Jordan sets the scene for Delgado by explaining his function in representing delinquent taxpayers before the IRS. He goes through the interview process that he had with Delgado and how it was evident to him that James was presumed guilty before any hearing or even any evidence of wrongdoing was brought forth. He also points out how the IRS CID initiated the contact with the DEA without any indication that Delgado had committed a crime. He walks them through his audit review and the fact that he has filed an offer in compromise in doubt as to liability because he found no merit in the IRS audit. He testifies that Delgado's accountant had presented verifiable documentation supporting his tax returns. He also testifies as to the severe and inconsistent collection activity that he encounters on a regular basis. He relays his frustration in never knowing what type of collection action the revenue officer will try to enforce. It varies from RO to RO and from day to day.

Following Jordan's testimony, Delgado takes the stand. He is his usual, outgoing self, not intimidated in the least by the moment nor the setting. He explains how the aggressive actions and the presumption of his guilt literally cost him thousands of dollars in revenue. He comments on the harassment he continually received from the assigned revenue officer. He states that if it weren't for the outstanding representation that he has received from Mr. Duncan, he would probably have lost everything he owns by now. Both Jordan and Delgado are given thanks by the committee for their testimony and commended for their perseverance in working through the broken system. Just before stepping down from the witness chair, Delgado is given assurance that his case will be dismissed immediately upon the conclusion of the hearings, with no further liability.

Five more taxpayers from across the country testify under oath as to abusive treatment they have received in their personal tax situations. They include an innocent spouse case, another bogus audit, and an OIC that was accepted but then collection activity continued. The common thread between all testimonies is the disregard of respect and the nonconformity of IRS collection procedures. All the taxpayer participants are thanked for their willingness to come forward and are given assurances that their respective cases will receive special attention. Retribution is promised where warranted.

On day three, the proverbial "shit hits the fan," as veteran IRS employees testify. To assure that they will receive the anonymity that they've been promised, each of them testifies behind a black curtain, with their voices altered electronically to protect their identity. Their testimonies depict an organization run amok, with claims of biased examiners and lurid tales of overaggressive collectors.

One witness states, "I can personally attest to the use of egregious tactics used by the IRS revenue agents, which are encouraged by members of the IRS management. These tactics, which appear nowhere in the IRS manual, are used to extract unfairly assessed taxes from taxpayers—sometimes illegally."

Another testifies, "I am only one representative across the country, but I have seen dozens of taxpayers severely damaged and even made homeless by the IRS Collection Division."

A thirty-five-year collection officer says, "Its original mission of collecting tax revenues has now become incidental to the production of statistics."

A long-time criminal investigator in the CID has this to say: "I am not here today to hurt or bash this agency or the vast majority of hard-working dedicated career public servants… But I have seen the efforts of IRS management to try to heal itself, and they are just window-dressing to appease you in Congress, while behind the shield of taxpayer secrecy, they shun public accountability and oversight."

Comments from the group of IRS employees include topics such as the following:

- Revealing IRS cover-ups
- Taxpayers being portrayed as crooks
- No consequences for improper IRS actions
- Talks of retaliation within the agency
- An "us versus them" mentality

- Allegations of listening devices used to monitor employee conversations

All agree that the IRS is incapable of reforming itself and requires intervention. The culture of the IRS must change, and it will not change on its own.

Michael Dolan appears dumbfounded at the conclusion of these testimonies. "These three days have been very painful," says Dolan, "painful because it distresses me greatly seeing the mistakes we've made and seeing the impact of those mistakes."

Dolan admonishes the senators to put the hearings in the context of millions and millions of successful taxpayer interactions that the IRS has each year. His statements sound as hollow as a beaten fighter begging the referee to let him go one more round. Roth thanks all participants and promises swift responsive action by the committee, and the hearings conclude. TKO!

Jordan, Janne, and Delgado fly back to LA and don't even need the plane to maintain their place in the clouds. They are "flying high" literally and figuratively. They can't stop laughing, giggling, and high-fiving as they reflect and reenact the days of testimony. It was quite an enriching experience to witness the IRS upper management, including the commissioner, sweating bullets for three days straight. They enjoyed the camaraderie with other tax representatives and taxpayers. It was a sweet time of redemption and accomplishment indeed.

To the surprise of almost no one in attendance, both the House of Representatives and the Senate construct their versions of reform as it pertains to the IRS Examination and Collection Divisions Policy and Procedures.

By early November, the Senate Finance Committee nominates Charles Rosotti, chairman of American Management Systems Inc., to be the commissioner of the IRS. It is imperative under the circumstances, they conclude, to bring in an outside person of vast, successful business experience and a sterling record of excellent customer service. Mr. Rossotti is sworn in on November 12, 1997.

Almost immediately thereafter, Congress presents a sweeping overhaul of the agency, limiting the IRS's collection powers and independence while giving taxpayers new protections.

The Internal Revenue Service Restructuring and Reform Act of 1998—the bill directs the IRS to review and restate its mission to place a greater emphasis on serving the public and meeting taxpayers' needs. Some of the key points include the following:

1. Internal Revenue Service Oversight Board, which shall have nine members (appointed for five-year terms), consisting of (a) six nonfederal employees appointed by the president; (b) the secretary of the Treasury or the deputy secretary of the Treasury; (c) the commissioner of the IRS; and (d) a full-time federal employee or a representative of employees who is appointed by the president, by and with the advice and consent of the Senate

2. For taxpayer protection and rights, the Taxpayer Bill of Rights, which places the burden of proof in any court proceeding with respect to any factual issue relevant to ascertaining the income tax liability of a taxpayer and shifts the burden of proof from the taxpayer to the IRS

3. Provisions set to regulate more reasonable interest and penalty amounts and from whence they may begin

4. Permits for a taxpayer with employees to designate the period for which each payroll tax deposit is to apply, thereby mitigating the current penalty for missing a deposit

5. Protections for taxpayers subject to audit or collections activities

6. Congressional accountability for the Internal Revenue Service, which directs the Joint Committee on Taxation to review all requests for investigations of the IRS by the General Accounting Office

7. Significant changes in respect to the appointment of the taxpayer advocate and in the operation and management of the IRS's problem-resolution program

8. Due process in IRS collection activities

9. IRS procedures relating to appeals of examinations and collections
10. The act imposing new roadblocks to the IRS's use of levies
11. Innocent spouse rules easing retroactively

It is the consensus that these are significant but necessary changes to ensure a more efficient and effective tax managing system. There is simply no magic cure for what troubles the IRS. However, the key element in the Restructuring and Reform Act is that the IRS and its employees must be held accountable. It is unanimously agreed upon that for the IRS reform to be successful, the agency must address training, operations, technology, culture, transparency, and taxpayer education.

The task confronting the IRS is daunting to say the least—enforcing tax laws, processing 200 million tax returns annually, and collecting the $1.5 trillion necessary to run the federal government, all in an efficient, fair, and evenhanded manner. The time and circumstances are right for this restructuring and reform. In the Senate, the reform bill passes 97–0.

In Santa Monica at Chez Jay's, Jordan and Janne are joined by Al and April in celebration of the new tax reform bill passed by Congress. Not as a surprise to any of them, Little Al was quite successful in penetrating the client base of Epstein, Levin & Ohlman Tax Consultants. They have procured several of E, L & O clients that have discontinued their working relationship with the CPA firm and are threatening lawsuits. They won't be able to prove the illegal activities of E, L & O with the IRS; however, the IRS has completely cut ties with the CPA firm. In addition to losing clients and having a class action lawsuit looming, their revenues are down significantly, and they are currently operating in the red.

Needless to say, Epstein is enraged. They do not believe he has made the connection to Jordan and his team. Being major players in the downfall of Epstein's firm is almost as satisfying as having a major impact on the IRS restructuring and reform.

"All we need is for President Clinton to sign the bill, and it is a done deal," says Janne.

"Do you think he might fight it?" asks Jordan. "It passed 97–0 in the Senate!"

"Well, it is a Republican majority House and Senate. He might try and stall it or seek revisions." Janne knows her politics.

Lil Al speaks up next. "Slick Willy is not in a position to fight anything right now." He has a mischievous grin on his face.

"How so?" inquires Janne.

"Haven't you heard? It has now become public that Big Willy's been having a hard time keeping Little Willy home." He breaks into song as he raises his beer mug to the center of the table.

> *'Cause little Willy, Willy won't go home*
> *But you can't push Willy 'round*
> *Willy won't go!*

All four of them clink their mugs, laughing out loud. "You're right, Al. Bill Clinton is in no position to fight Congress on anything right about now," Janne says with a big smile.

"Here's to Arthur! The orchestrator of this movement… Without his lead, none of this would have happened." Jordan offers the final salute.

They all agree and toast their friend and Jordan's mentor, Arthur Gibson.

CHAPTER EIGHTEEN

End Game

A two-week vacation at the Yosemite Valley cabin over the Christmas and New Year's holiday sounds heavenly to Jordan and Janne. They leave Santa Monica on Friday, December 19, in the Bronco.

Saturday morning, since it is only the two of them, they brave the freezing temperatures and go trail running. One thing Jordan appreciates about Janne is the way she trains. He doesn't have to slow his normal quick pace so that she can keep up. In fact, he finds himself having to push hard at times to keep pace with her. Although he is definitely the faster runner, she exhibits amazing stamina and never seems to slow her steady stride. Mile upon mile, up and down hills. He conjectures that all those HIIT workouts on the elliptical have turned her into an endurance machine! He thoroughly enjoys working out with her.

Jordan shares with Janne his plan to help Delgado retain his treasure in Baja. He assures her that he believes it will be somewhat of a quick transaction and he will be back in the states probably within a few months. She concludes that he has a fascination for adventure!

Upon returning to the cabin in time to enjoy breakfast with John, Tricia, and Peter. Paul had returned to New Jersey to enjoy the holidays with family and friends on the East Coast. They discuss the incredible past year as their plan B worked to perfection. Jordan and Janne go into detail about many of the witness testimonies. John and Tricia are delighted to hear it as they coached many of the delinquent taxpayers on how to deliver their messages. It was indeed a team effort wherein the outcome was even better than they had anticipated. The Tax Restructuring and Reform Bill is a significant accomplishment in helping curtail the out of control Internal Revenue Service.

Almost as if right on cue, Jordan receives a personal phone call from Jack Kemp while he is conversing with the others. He thanks Jordan for coming forth with such a well-thought-out and executed plan to expose the IRS. Jordan is quick to give his partners their due. Mr. Kemp asks what he and Janne have planned for the future. Jordan responds that they are currently exploring their options. Kemp offers to help them find positions in whatever realm they see fit. Jordan thanks him. He turns to Janne after hanging up and relays the context of the call.

"You know, I really like Jack Kemp. He seems so much more down to earth than most politicians. He is someone I think we should not forget," Jordan says, and Janne agrees that he might be an excellent resource.

His phone rings again. "Hi, Mom," he answers as he recognizes her number.

Right away he hears the distress in her voice as she speaks through intermittent crying. She is trying to hold her emotions in check to make sure she can accurately articulate the situation to her son.

"They took Teri…"

"What? Who took Teri? What happened?" Jordan asks anxiously. The others can overhear his side of the conversation, and Janne immediately gasps.

"She never came home after school yesterday. It was the last day before Christmas vacation. She asked if she could go over to her friend Jo Anne's after school and spend the night…" Gabriela is having a hard time holding back tears and completing the story. "She didn't come home this morning, and I tried calling her… No answer." She is sobbing.

"Mom, how do you know someone took her?"

"They called me. They said if I call the police, I will never see her again. They said you are the only one that can save her—" Gabriela can't continue.

"Jordan, I don't know what the hell you have been up to or whom you have been jerking around with, but you damn well better get my daughter back!" Phil has taken the phone from Gabriela and is ranting uncontrollably at Jordan at a very loud volume.

"Settle down, Phil, and tell me who called—"

Phil cuts him off, "How the hell should I know who it was? You think they're going to give me their name and whereabouts? Boy, you better fix this and get my little girl back. If they hurt her in any way, you are in big trouble, mister!"

"Shut up, Phil! Get a grip on yourself so I *can* fix this." Jordan sees that he has another call coming in from an unrecognizable number. Without saying anything more to Phil, he switches lines. "Hello, this is Jordan."

"If you want to see your little sister alive and well again, you will listen and do exactly as you are told."

Jordan doesn't recognize the voice.

"I'm listening."

"You screwed the wrong people, punk. You need to fix it. Now!"

"Who is this?"

"Listen…don't talk! Epstein, Levin & Ohlman will prepare a letter that you will sign that states you were mistaken about the intent of the firm's intentions. You will also sign a nondisclosure agreement that states you will never contact any of their clients nor will you proceed with any court action against the firm. Alexander Epstein will meet you in person in Los Angeles to attain these two documents. You are to tell no one of this transaction. The meeting will take place on December 24 at a location that will be given you on that date. Do you understand?"

"If I agree, when will my sister be released?"

"When Epstein has the signed letters, he will release your sister."

"How do I know she is okay and no harm has been done to her?"

"She is fine. She will remain that way unless you do not do as you have been told. If you deviate at all, all bets are off on her well-being."

"I want to talk to Epstein directly."

"He will contact you. In the meantime, do not contact any legal authorities, and you better make sure your mother and her husband abide by that rule as well." With that, the call is dropped.

"Damn!" Jordan is fuming as he starts pacing.

"Tell us what is going on," Janne asks frantically.

"Epstein had Teri kidnapped. He wants me to sign a letter that will go out to his clients saying everything was a hoax about their misrepresentation."

"Was that Epstein you spoke to?" John inquires.

"No. I don't know who called me. Wasn't Epstein nor his partner Levin. Too young. And I'm pretty sure it wasn't Turlock. I think I would recognize his voice." Jordan is still pacing as he is trying to figure out what to do. "I don't even have Epstein's contact info. I can call David Jacobs. I know he can give me Epstein's number."

"Hold on, Jordan. Let's think this out before reacting." John is staying calm. "Pete, get in touch with Dave, and let him know what's going on."

"He told me, to ensure Teri's safety, not to contact anyone."

"Believe me, Dave Lackey won't contact the authorities. That is not the way he operates."

"Okay. I've got to call my mom back, though." Jordan brings his phone up to dial her number.

John grabs his hand and says, "You handled that call very well, Jordan. It is imperative that you convince your mother—and I suppose that was her husband you spoke to—that they must not contact the authorities. Make sure to tell them that if they are contacted again, they should tell the perpetrators to only speak to you. I'm sure that is their intent, but it must be said to your mom."

"Okay. Good idea." Jordan speed-dials Gabriela.

"Jordan, what happened? Why did you hang up on Phil?"

"They called me, and they have told me what they want."

"Is it money? Do you need help in paying a ransom?"

"No, Mom. It is not money they want. I just need to sign some paperwork. I will be meeting with them in person to take care of it. You guys just need to stay calm, and everything will work out. Do not contact the police or tell anyone else about this, okay?"

"Jordan, when will we get Teri back? Is she all right?"

"They assured me that she is fine. They are going to call back, and I am going to insist that they let me talk to her before I complete the deal. It will happen on Christmas Eve."

"That is four days away. My poor baby… How will I know that she is okay? I won't be able to sleep until I get her back… Please, Jordan, get her back to me…" Gabriela is crying again.

"I will, Mom. I promise."

"Jordan, this is Phil. I'm sorry I threatened you. But you must do whatever they say to get Teri back. If you need some money, let me know. Anything—you understand?"

"Yes, Phil, but this isn't about money. This guy wants me to sign some papers to not contact his clients. I will take care of it in person. Just stay with my mom, and please don't tell anyone about this. It will all be over on Christmas Eve. I will get Teri back, Phil. I promise!"

"Don't let them fool you, Jordan. It's always about money in the end. Be careful."

"I will, Phil. Thanks. Take care of Mom. Goodbye." Jordan hangs up and just shakes his head as he bites his lower lip.

Janne puts her arm around him as they sit down on the couch. "We will get her back, honey." Janne tries to soothe him.

John returns from stepping out in the entryway to speak with Pete, who then rushed out the door. "Pete is on his way to pick up Dave. They will be back later tonight. We will put together a plan. What did they tell you will happen next?"

"He said Epstein will contact me directly on Christmas Eve. When I see him in person, as soon as I know Teri is okay, I am going to kick his ass."

"We just need to make sure that, whatever we do, it is with the end game in mind. We don't want to leave any way of retaliation." John has that steely look in his eyes.

Janne has seen it only a handful of times in her life—Jordan, only once, when they discussed Arthur's death. This is the first time Tricia has witnessed the determined, unwavering demeanor in John Sawyer.

On Sunday morning, December 21, Alexander Epstein conducts a meeting at the empty office building of Epstein, Levin & Ohlman Tax Consultants. Present are Epstein, Barry Levin, Kurt Turlock, Sean Callison, and Cassie O'Brien. Callison is Turlock's cohort, whom he has known since their time in the Navy. Cassie is his girlfriend. They were involved in the murder of Arthur Gibson. Callison impersonated Mitchell Shumway to lure Arthur to the hotel room. Cassie was the so-called hooker that booked and paid for the room. They are also the culprits that snatched Teresa Conley on Saturday. They drove from New Jersey to Maryland to attend this meeting.

"Where is the girl?" Epstein inquires of Callison.

"She is secure…and safe," Callison replies.

"I didn't ask about her state of being. I asked, where is she?"

"She is tied up and gagged in the van in the parking lot."

"Is she blindfolded? We can't afford to let her figure out anything about her whereabouts. You didn't have the radio on, did you?"

"Yes, she is blindfolded, and no, there is no way she has any idea where she is." Callison has known Turlock for a long time and trusts him, but he can't stand working directly with Epstein. Turlock has assured him that after they get their payday from this gig, they will have enough money to be done with Epstein for good.

"When we finish here today, I want you to drive her directly back to Jersey and wait there until Tuesday night."

This plan has been laid out with Turlock, but Epstein wants to make sure that there is no misunderstanding with the hired help. Callison nods his head.

"Okay, just to make sure everyone knows their role in how this is going down, let's review the details and timeline." Epstein, of course, is in charge.

"Barry, are all the tickets booked and paid for?"

"Yes, you and Kurt will be flying on a private charter to LA tomorrow, Monday, the 22nd, under the names of Barry Levin and Sean Callison. Sean, Cassie, and I have a one-way flight to Paris from Dulles on Wednesday morning, the 24th. We will be flying under the names of Alexander Epstein and Kurt and Katherine Turlock [Turlock's fictitious wife]. On Thursday, Christmas morning, you and Kurt will fly from LAX to Paris as Barry Levin and Sean Callison.

"Barry and Sean have a business meeting scheduled in Los Angeles on the afternoon of December 24 and will be staying at the Beverly Wilshire that evening. There is a Black Car Limo Service to take you to the airport Christmas morning. Once in Paris, you and I will take the train to Geneva, Switzerland. From there, we will follow our private plans to meet with your wife, who is already at a rented chalet in Neuchatel, Switzerland, and subsequently, my wife in two weeks. Kurt, Sean, and Cassie will go wherever they have decided to go," Levin states in his customary efficient manner.

"Okay, sounds good. Kurt, you have all the passports and IDs in order?"

"Yep. No problem." It helped that Epstein and Levin are close in age as are Turlock and Callison.

"Tell me about the location picked out for meeting with Duncan," Epstein inquires of Turlock.

Kurt Turlock explains the plan, "My guys in LA have scouted the area and picked Elysian Park, which is adjacent to Dodger Stadium. It is a sprawling area that consists of a wilderness area that overlooks the baseball stadium and includes several parks with grass and picnic areas. They are all connected by hiking trails. The particular area they chose is about one mile from the Dodger Stadium parking lot. Being Christmas Eve and the fact that the road going to Dodger Stadium is closed for construction, there is only a one road access to the park, and no one will be around. The homeless people in the area are not allowed to spend the nights in the grass park areas, so they tend to set up tarps in the trees of the wilderness area. Our location is not visible from the wilderness area. We will meet Duncan just after sunset. It will be dark, but the rendezvous spot is easily navigated. There is a small parking lot about three-quarters of a mile from Stadium Way on Academy Road. It's a dirt lot, and there is a hiking trail from the lot that separates the park to the south and a steep incline to the north. It is heavily lined with trees and shrubs on the park side, isolating the grassy area from the trail and pine trees on the hill side. About a quarter mile from the parking area, there is an opening into the park. It has six palm trees in an oblong circle that drops down at a gradual slope to a huge oak tree that is approximately fifty yards from the trail. Can't miss it… That is where you will meet Duncan. We will be there before they arrive. I will be situated in the trees just south of the trail and hidden from view. Jordan will be instructed to bring his girlfriend as a witness and no one else. I will be in a position to see them arrive to ensure he doesn't have any backup personnel. As they approach, you will order them to stop twelve feet from you. You will have the girl walk to you and hand you the paperwork. She will call Mrs. Conley and get confirmation that her daughter is safe. If Duncan tries to double-cross you or acts aggressively, you will pull the 9-millimeter Glock handgun from your overcoat and shoot him dead. I will take out the girl. We will ascend to the trail and proceed to the rental car, which will be provided by my LA guys. We can have them hidden, waiting for us, if you like." He looks at Epstein for his response.

"No. I want no witnesses. We will drive there well before Duncan arrives, and he will never see you. The only two witnesses will be dead, if necessary, by the time we leave. What about the sound of the shots?"

"I have silencers for each of us. I know you don't have much experience in shooting a firearm, but I will show you what you need to know. From twelve feet with a 9-millimeter, you can't miss, and he won't survive. If by chance he does, I will finish him off… You only get one shot. You are more exposed than I will be, and we can't afford you shooting more."

"I won't miss the son of a bitch." Epstein shows a menacing grin. He turns back to Levin. "Barry, are you sure Ohlman knows nothing about how we have transferred funds overseas and that we are going to shut down the business and declare bankruptcy?"

"He is clueless… But as an attorney of good standing and being well-connected, I am sure he will land on his feet."

As Levin sees the way Epstein is getting amped up about the prospect of killing Duncan, he adds, "Alexander, as your partner and friend, I strongly advise you to not shoot Duncan unless it is absolutely necessary."

"Don't worry about it, Barry. I know exactly what I'm doing." Epstein glares at his partner.

"Okay then, all that is left is what we do with the girl. You have a place picked out?" Epstein is speaking directly to Callison again.

"Yes. There is a Catholic church not far from their home. We will take the girl there Tuesday night and break in after everyone is gone. She will be blindfolded, gagged, and tied up. We will take her to the basement, where there is a janitor's closet. Leave her there and lock the door. The priest will come in during the afternoon on Wednesday to start preparing for the midnight mass that night, Christmas Eve. Once Duncan has arrived—and make sure to tell him no cell phone!" Callison points out, and Epstein nods his head in agreement. Callison continues, "You make the call to the mom, and she will make arrangements to get the girl at the church. By the time you get the papers from the girlfriend, they will have located the little girl and confirmed it. We will already be on our way to Paris by then."

"Good. I don't want the little girl hurt, unless Duncan tries to double-cross us. My beef is with him, not his family. Besides, I don't want the feds investigating a kidnapping murder!" Levin looks at Epstein and thinks to himself how obsessively distorted he has become over his hatred of Jordan Duncan. This nefarious scheme is completely overcooked and filled with high risk—and simply because Alex insists on getting revenge from Jordan Duncan… *Absurd!*

Meanwhile, on Sunday in Yosemite, Jordan brings Dave Lackey up to date on the events that have transpired. Lackey wants to know everything, including all that Jordan knows concerning the investigation of Arthur's death. According to Dave, most people in general, especially former military types, like to work with the same group of people. There is a trust factor that is critical when doing any kind of reconnaissance, espionage, or actual operations. He has ID'd those working with Turlock in LA and also his main connection on the East Coast. His men are watching Turlock's LA team round the clock. He is confident that Sean Callison, a known colleague of Turlock's from the Navy, was more than likely involved in Arthur's murder. He could also be a player in the kidnapping. He has photos of Callison and instructs Jordan to fax them to Detective Douglass right away. After receiving what Jordan details on the subject, Lackey excuses himself and takes John and Pete down to the bunker to discuss their strategy. Jordan and Janne are told that they will be informed once a plan is formulated.

After about an hour in the bunker, the three men ascend to the main floor and meet with Jordan, Janne, and Tricia. Dave, who is now the obvious leader of the pack in this operation, explains that Jordan and Janne are to remain in Yosemite until contacted by Epstein. Jordan questions on whether he should be in LA. Lackey tells him that he needs to keep the Bronco up north and when the time is right, Pete will transport him south in his chopper. He also explains that John and Tricia will be leaving in the morning for San Francisco in Jordan's Bronco to spend Christmas Eve in a hotel in the city under the names of Jordan Duncan and Janne Sawyer. Again, Jordan and Janne question that reasoning. No explanation is given other than that it is part of the plan. Lackey's men in LA will secure a taxi for Jordan's transportation, which one of his men will be driving. Now they wait for Epstein's call.

On Monday, a fax is sent to the executive suite where Jordan receives mail and faxes. It is the letters he is instructed to sign and bring to the rendezvous point. Jordan asks the secretary to send them to him. He reviews the paperwork and signs the letters.

The call comes early Wednesday. The location and time are disclosed. Jordan is told to only bring his girlfriend to ensure that he won't try anything stupid. The instructions as to the location are explicit, and he is told that when he gets to the oak tree, he is to stop twelve feet from Epstein. Janne will deliver the paperwork and then will call Gabriela to confirm that Teri has been recovered safely. Jordan is told that he and Janne should not bring a cell phone.

Immediately upon the end of the call, Lackey has his men checking the area. They discover a parking lot at the Grace E. Simons Lodge, located a mile east of the lot that Epstein recommended. There is a hiking trail that connects the two lots and continues on past the dirt lot, as the trail that Epstein described. One man is left there to scope out the area and report back to Lackey.

In the back of the helicopter pad behind Pete's trailer is a large shed. Pete had landed his chopper in the meadow, which Jordan and Janne find curious. As they open the shed, in the back, they see is another chopper. Military transport with plenty of cargo space. Pete explains that his biggest client, who is the CEO of the telecommunications company he had mentioned, has locations in SoCal and Pete transfers equipment from time to time in this military cargo chopper. It has retracting wheels on its rudders, and with an ATV, they pull it out onto the pad, extend the blades, and with Jordan, Janne, and Dave in tow, they take off on Wednesday, December 24, 1997. Dave Lackey is wearing all black and carrying a case that resembles a long, expanded briefcase…or a gun case. Jordan is told that he will be transported to the park in a cab driven by Lackey's man. They are told to hike to Epstein's lot and from there, follow his instructions. Lackey hopes that Epstein at least has the decency to not harm Teresa. Secretly, Lackey is counting on Epstein's lack of experience in this type of operation and Turlock's inability to persuade him to listen to more sound tactics in being a key component of their counterattack.

Dave's man on the ground at Elysian Park reports to him that just over the ridge of the steep hill to the north of the hiking trail, there is a flat open area conducive to landing the chopper. However, he points out that it is not accessible to any road for the cab. There is a vacant asphalt lot located a mile from the rendezvous area that serves as overflow parking for Dodger Stadium and would be more feasible for Pete to land and wait for the action to unfold. Although the road is closed for construction, a cab could maneuver into the lot. Lackey agrees and asks for the coordinates to give Pete. The man on the ground also describes that about 75 yards farther down the trail from the palm tree opening and approximately 30 yards up the steep incline, there sits a rather large tree stump. It is about 12 feet high and 5 feet in circumference. A man could easily hide behind it. There is a clear view from the stump's location through the palm trees to the oak tree, which is approximately 150 yards away.

"Perfect," Lackey responds. "If none of Turlock's men are lurking around, let's do my drop off on the ridge behind the hill you described. I will descend to the stump. You take care of Turlock, like we discussed. Pete will fly to the vacant asphalt lot, drop off Jordan and Janne, and wait until the mission is completed. Jason will transport them in the cab. Then we will pick up at the open area on the north hill, where he dropped me off."

"Roger that. Jason says Turlock's men look as though they are staying put. If not, we will take care of them. He thinks Epstein and Turlock are going alone. I will let you know when they are on their way."

"Thanks, Brian. Out."

En route, Lackey goes over the plan with Pete, Jordan, and Janne as far as landing and takeoff. Nothing is mentioned about the actual execution of their plan. That is intentional. The less Jordan and Janne know of what the others are doing, the better. They will not be overly anxious.

Sundown at the end of December in Los Angeles is officially listed at 4:50 p.m. With hills surrounding the park, it is dark by 5:15. Epstein told them to be there at 6:00 p.m. He wanted to make sure it is dark. He told them that they could bring one small flashlight.

At 2:30, Pete swoops down into the flat open area on the ridge that Brian had described. Without landing, he drops off Dave, who makes the short jump without falling, carrying his backpack and gun case. He jogs over the ridge and spots the stump on the hill. He makes it there by 3:00 p.m. He is well secluded behind the stump and removes his weapon from the case. He has selected a .300 Winchester Magnum. An excellent big-game hunting rifle, complete with a 12-power Browning scope. He inserts four Winchester Black Talon SXT hollow point bullets. It is a type of expansion bullet, meaning that it will explode outwardly upon impact with claw-like petals to maximize damage without passing through or the risk of a ricochet. He attaches the SIG Sauer suppressor that he picked up in

Norway years ago. Norway has no firearm and accessory registration requirements, and therefore, there is no tracing of the equipment purchased. It is a grade 5 titanium suppressor using a fast-attach muzzle device to attach to the rifle. He makes sure he uses nothing of military grade. Preparation. He will only take the shot if lives are at stake.

Epstein and Turlock arrive at 4:30 p.m. Epstein is wearing dark slacks with a black overcoat. In his right coat pocket is the loaded 9 mm with a silencer. Turlock is wearing camouflaged cargo pants, boots, and a pullover camo sweatshirt with a camo ball cap. He is carrying a British .308 caliber rifle with a strap over his shoulder. It has a suppressor on the end, and he elects to use a laser scope due to the darkening conditions. Epstein follows a path from the parking lot to the grass area and then hikes about a half a mile to the oak tree. He is there waiting by 5:15 p.m. Turlock finds his spot to descend into the trees twenty-five yards from the palm tree opening and within view of the parking area.

Just as he steps off the trail, he is hit with a dart in his neck. Never saw anyone or knew what hit him. Brian quickly jumps out from behind a pine tree on the hill side above the trail. He has what looks like a body bag and stuffs Turlock's unconscious body along with his rifle and butt pack into the bag. He drags the body bag up thirty feet on the hill and sits down next to it behind a pine tree.

Pete drops Jordan and Janne off in the vacant lot, where Jason is waiting with the cab, complete with fake ID and license. They wait to time their arrival at the Grace E. Simon Lodge parking lot at 5:20 p.m. Jason instructs them to wait five minutes before hiking along the trail to the rendezvous location. He jogs along the trail until Brian flags him down. Together they lift the body bag with Turlock inside and carry it up nearly a hundred yards to the top of the hill and just over the ridge. They will wait there for Pete.

Jordan and Janne are both wearing darks jeans, sweatshirts, and tennis shoes. For precautionary reasons, they each wear a bullet-resistant vest under their sweatshirts. Jordan dons a black stocking cap, and they both put on workout gloves that cover the fingers. He has the signed paperwork rolled up and kept in the pouch of his sweatshirt. They make the one-mile hike to the parking lot, see a parked car, and know that Epstein is waiting for them. They continue along the trail using the small flashlight. They spot the opening and leave the trail at 5:45 p.m. Epstein sees their light and makes his call to Callison. Jordan and Janne traverse through the palm trees and arrive in front of the huge oak tree at 5:58 p.m.

Epstein steps out from behind the tree. His voice sounds nervous from twelve feet away. "It didn't have to come to this, Duncan, if you could just follow orders."

"I don't take orders from crooks."

"Still trying to be a tough guy, huh? Your problem is that you don't know when you are out of your element and overmatched. On the basketball court, you might have an edge on me, but in the business world, you are no match for me, Duncan!" His voice strengthens.

Jordan stares at him and realizes this guy has lost his mind. He has gone way overboard in making this personal. "You still hung up about the basketball tournament?"

"That was just the beginning. But you never should have come back that second year. You should have just resigned. When you did and humiliated me again, you *never* should have ditched out the third year. I had a super team that would have embarrassed you and restored my dignity. But you denied me that!" Epstein is practically yelling now.

Not a good idea if you are trying to be discreet, Jordan thinks.

"Let's take care of business. I want to make sure my little sister is okay. I want to talk to her before you get anything from me."

"*No*, that is not how it is going to work. I am in charge, punk! Have your girlfriend bring me the paperwork. Then I will let *her* talk to your mother."

"Where is Turlock? I know you didn't come here alone."

"Don't worry about him. Just be glad I haven't turned him loose on you. He hates you almost as much as I do. But you can be sure he is watching. So don't be foolish and try anything stupid."

Jordan takes out the papers from his pouch and hands them to Janne. He whispers to her, "Don't get close enough that he can grab you." She nods her head and starts walking toward Epstein.

Janne stretches her arm out with the papers while she is still a couple of feet away. He snatches them out of her hand, looks very quickly at them with a small pin light, and pulls out a phone, obviously a burner. He hands it to Janne. She quickly dials Gabriela's number.

"Hello."

"Gabriela, this is Janne. Is Teri with you?"

"Yes, she is okay. The priest at the church has her, and we are on our way to pick her up... Where is Jordan? Is he all right?"

"Yes, he is fine and here with me. We will call you later."

Janne turns to Jordan and says, "Teri is with a priest, and your mom is picking her up now."

Jordan lets out a big sigh of relief. Epstein grabs the phone and tells Janne to get back. He is sweating profusely now, and Jordan senses that he is about to do something drastic. Janne hurries back to Jordan. When she arrives, Epstein looks toward the tree line but sees and hears nothing. Jordan and Janne start to slowly back away.

Just then Epstein yells, "Stop! I didn't tell you to leave." His hand is in his coat pocket but shaking. Jordan and Janne stop, and Jordan steps between Janne and Epstein.

"It's done, Epstein. You got your signed documents, and I give you my word, I will stop trying to prove you broke the law. We are going to walk away now."

"You stupid punk. You ruined my business! You are nothing. You are finished!"

He pulls his hand out of his pocket with the gun. The barrel of his handgun clears his pocket, but before he can raise it into a shooting position, his face explodes into a bloody mess. His body slams into the wide sturdy trunk of the tree and slithers down into a pile at the base of the mighty oak.

With his long-range night optics firmly fitted across his face and his body steadied against the large stump, Dave Lackey watched the entire drama unfold through his powerful scope as if it were midday at the park. With the patience of a trained sniper, which he is, he squeezed the trigger the second he spotted the gun in Epstein's hand.

With visual confirmation of Epstein flying backward, half of his face missing, he calmly speaks into his handheld radio to Pete, "It's a go." He packs his gear methodically with fast movements. He starts humping up the hill behind him.

Janne gasps but does not scream as Epstein's face blows up in front of them. Jordan immediately has the presence of mind to approach Epstein and carefully retrieve the signed papers and burner phone. He then takes Janne's hand, and they start sprinting back through the palm tree opening, across the trail, and up the hill. There couldn't be a better-conditioned man-and-woman team scampering up the steep hill.

As they approach the top, they hear the *whop, whop, whop* of the chopper blades just on the other side of the ridge. They clear the top of the ridge and sprint toward the chopper. Pete can't help but reminisce about how much they remind him of the encounter almost thirty years ago when he lifted Janne's future father and mother out of danger in the Vietnam jungle. They made a similar dash for his chopper, and he loaded them on board without proper authority because he respected their courage so much.

These two kids are very brave as well, he thinks as Dave, Brian, and Jason help them in just as Pete begins the ascent into the night sky.

On the flight back up north, it is dark and cold in the chopper. Not much is spoken, save for some updates on flight conditions. Dave is seated next to Pete. Janne remains cuddled up against Jordan on one of the side benches. They don't speak, but her face is against his chest, her eyes closed, and his arms are wrapped around her tightly. They don't even notice the body bag shoved up against the back wall as Brian and Jason sit in front of it. The two men will be taken to the Sacramento airport tomorrow, where they will catch a flight back to Los Angeles. It is late when they arrive in the Yosemite Valley. Pete calls John to report everything and assure him that Janne and Jordan are back safely.

Just before going upstairs to their room, Jordan stops and turns toward Dave and Pete. "Thanks...for everything. Because of you guys, we are alive, and my little sister is home safely."

"You both showed a lot of bravery. It was a pleasure to help you give Epstein the send-off he deserved," Dave replies.

Janne smiles weakly, and Pete says, "Tonight reminded me of picking up your parents so many years ago. I was proud to do it then and felt the same way tonight. You two get some rest... Merry Christmas!"

"Merry Christmas," Jordan and Janne repeat in unison.

The dart that penetrated Turlock's neck was laced with a strong tranquilizer and sedative that would begin wearing off after twelve hours. Pete, Dave, Brian, and Jason unload the body from the chopper and take Turlock down to the arsenal room in the bunker. He is placed on a chair with his arms tied together behind his back. The four men will rotate sitting in the room with him for a one-hour shift, while the others go upstairs to sleep in three-hour shifts.

At 4:00 a.m., Turlock begins to come around. By 5:00 a.m., he is awake enough to start yelling at Jason, who is in the room at the time. Jason ignores his demands of knowing where he is and to release him immediately. He even attempts to quote parts of the Geneva Convention prisoner-of-war regulations. He butchers that with his overall ignorance of the declaration.

Pete descends into the basement at 5:30 a.m. to relieve Jason and tells him to wake Dave. The interrogation begins calmly as Dave makes it clear to Turlock that he is in charge. He starts asking him questions concerning the death of Arthur Gibson. Kurt Turlock is not cooperating and repeatedly either ignores the questions or simply laughs and tells them both they are wasting their time.

"You know that nothing said here will ever be allowed in court." Turlock smirks.

Pete leans down and says directly into his ear, "This is your day in court, asshole. What you say here will determine your fate."

"Who are you guys?" Kurt inquires as he looks around the dimly lit room. "Former Army, no doubt. Typical grunts, always having to maneuver in packs. You don't have the balls to settle disputes man to man. A Navy SEAL can destroy an Army grunt any day, one on one."

Dave stands directly in front of Turlock and says, "Here is the deal jerk-off. You have one chance to tell us exactly what went down with the death of Arthur Gibson. We have Epstein's story also. Once we have both versions, we will decide who's story we believe. If you tell us it was Epstein's plan and you executed it, we will understand that, as a soldier, you were just following orders. You will live to see the light of day again. If we believe Epstein that you acted in a rogue manner and killed Arthur on your own, we will act as judge and jury to determine your fate here and now. What will it be?"

Turlock takes a minute to try to ascertain if these guys are for real and if they would really execute him on the spot. "Actually, you have it wrong. It wasn't Epstein who gave the order. It was that Poindexter-looking dude, Levin. Epstein wanted to set up Gibson to discredit him to the IRS and then fire him as a consultant. He figured that would take care of it. Mr. 'Risk Analyst' Levin said the risk was too great and he needed to be eliminated. So I carried out the order. Gibson was just collateral damage to their business model with the almighty IRS."

Lackey looks at Pete, who shrugs his shoulders. They both realize that they have attained the confession from Turlock that they were seeking. At this point, to them, it doesn't really matter who gave the order.

David Lackey stands 5'9" and weighs a tight 175 lb. He played running back at West Point for four years and then graduated from Ranger School at the top of his class. He became an expert in hand-to-hand combat as well as a fifth-degree black belt in martial arts. He continues to work out regularly and is an avid surfer. At fifty years old, he is in better shape than 98 percent of men half his age! He has also done some research on Kurt Turlock. As it turns out, Turlock never became a Navy SEAL. He was kicked out of the training school for an undisclosed reason, and although he completed his duty in the US Navy, he was never a certified SEAL.

Lackey tells Pete to escort Turlock down the tunnel and up the ladder to the helipad. He follows them. Upon ascending into the open air, the sun has risen. Pete cuts the ties binding Turlock's arms. Then he hands him the knife and steps back. Dave Lackey also has a similar weapon that he holds with tight scuba gloves.

"You wanted a chance for a fair fight. Here it is," Dave tells him with a calm, stern-looking stare.

Turlock looks around as they are standing on the helicopter pad. There is nothing but flat concrete and wide-open space. There couldn't be a more equal setting.

He nervously says, "If I beat you, he will just shoot me dead." He nods toward Pete.

"You have my word that if you defeat me, Pete will let you walk out of here. You will have to find your way, but you will be a free man."

"Yep. That's right," Pete confirms.

"You have gloves. I don't…" Kurt is trying to size up the shorter, lighter, older, but obviously confident warrior before him.

"Give the man some gloves, Pete."

Pete tosses an identical pair of scuba gloves to Turlock.

"Being a Navy SEAL, this should give you an edge…a one on one with an Army Ranger. You can 'destroy' him any day. Isn't that right, hotshot?" Pete says sarcastically.

Turlock puts on the gloves and takes his stance with his feet shoulder width apart, knees slightly bent and his right foot back. Lackey starts slowly moving to his left. He is going in a circular motion, knowing that it is more difficult for a right-handed fighter to cross over his feet in the defensive position that he is creating for his opponent. Dave continues his deliberate motion, waiting to see what kind of attack Turlock will initiate. Turlock gives a couple of feint movements to get a reaction from Lackey. Then suddenly Turlock lunges forward, thrusting the knife in his right hand in an upward motion toward Lackey's chest. As Dave steps back, causing the swipe to miss, Turlock swings his arm back in a backhanded motion aimed at Lackey's neck. It causes Turlock to become slightly off balance for a moment. That is the only opening Dave needs. He braces his right leg, and in an instant, he kicks his left foot directly into Turlock's chest. Pete can hear the wind depart from Kurt's lungs as he topples onto his butt. Lackey pounces on him like a hungry panther, slamming his left forearm into his prey's windpipe, further deleting oxygen from him.

Flat on his back, Turlock gives one last fling with his knife hand at the superior soldier, who now has a knee on his chest. Lackey lets the momentum of Turlock's effort pass harmlessly across his body striking nothing but air. He snatches his hand with his left hand and snaps his wrist back. Turlock winces in pain as the knife tumbles out of his hand onto the ground. With a swift upward thrust of his right arm, Lackey's knife penetrates Turlock's body just below the chest cavity and directly into his heart. Dave holds it in and gives it a sudden twist. Turlock's eyes are wide and bulging as the life is sucked out of him.

Dave slowly stands but leaves the knife inserted as he wants to minimize the outflow of blood. Brian immediately jogs over from the shed, where he watched the fight unfold, with a body bag. He and Pete quickly insert Turlock into the bag and zip it closed. Not a drop of blood on the concrete pad.

"Very neat," says Pete with a slight grin. "But that took a little longer than I expected."

"I wanted to see how much training he might have had with the SEALs before he flunked out" is Dave's response.

"Apparently, not much," says Pete sarcastically.

"Nope."

Pete and Brian load the body in the chopper and leave to dispose of it.

Dave walks back to the cabin, where Jason is cooking breakfast and Jordan and Janne are still sleeping.

"Merry Christmas, boss!" Jason says with a smile.

"Merry Christmas, Jason. We will get you guys home today. Thanks for your help. I'm going to call John and take a shower."

Dave calls John Sawyer and gives him an update on the morning's activities. "End game completed."

"Nice job, Dave. Thank you."

"That's what partners do. Merry Christmas, my friend."

Back in Maryland, Barry Levin had been scheming to double-cross his partner for several weeks. He knew that Alexander Epstein had lost his wits with his obsession on defeating Jordan Duncan. He now represented a high-risk liability and couldn't be reasoned with. Levin arranged for a confidential meeting with Joseph Ohlman. He explained the business situation, of course, placing the bulk of the blame on Epstein. Ohlman, like most people, was not endeared by Alexander Epstein's overbearing personality. It didn't take much convincing for him to believe Levin's allegations. However, he was outraged that Barry could let this happen to their company. Levin explained that they siphoned millions of dollars into offshore accounts and that he was prepared to share it with him and let Epstein take the fall for the company's misdeeds. The company would file bankruptcy, Ohlman would be able to successfully claim he had no knowledge of operations, pay some fines, and come out clean. Levin would be living out of the country and managing the offshore accounts. After weighing his options, Ohlman agreed to the plan.

Levin then met with his twenty-four-year-old son, Saul, who recently graduated from the University of Maryland with a degree in chemical engineering. Saul has a live-in male partner who is a student at Georgetown. His sexual orientation has been a bone of contention between father and son in the past, but they have moved beyond their differences of lifestyle choices and have been maintaining a cordial relationship. Barry offers to gift his late-model Lexus to his son as a belated graduation gift. To show that there are no hard feelings toward Saul's roommate, Barry suggests that he gift his 1993 Dodge Challenger to him in exchange for the pink slip to his 1986 Chevy Tahoe. Levin explains to his son that he wants to use it as a donation at a charity event. He tells Saul not to mention it to anyone, including the roommate, as he doesn't want to involve them in the tax ramifications. Saul is delighted with the deal! Maybe his father is beginning to understand and respect him after all.

On Tuesday, December 23, the day before he is to meet Sean Callison and Cassie O'Brien at the Washington, DC, airport, Barry Levin and his wife take what they can fit into the Tahoe and drive southwest toward the Mexican border. His broker is to sell their house. They drive all night and in the early morning, Wednesday, December 24, they cross the border into Mexico at Laredo, Texas.

They spend the night in Monterrey, Mexico. Their destination is Acapulco, where he has made arrangements to rent a spacious villa.

After leaving Teresa Conley at the church in Short Hills, New Jersey, on Tuesday night, December 23, Sean Callison and his girlfriend, Cassie, drive to Washington, DC. They are scheduled to meet Levin at the airport Wednesday morning, December 24, for a 9:00 a.m. flight to Paris, France. When they get there and can't locate Levin, who is not answering his phone, they decide to check in for the flight. As soon as they do, they are detained by airport security. Detective Douglass arrives soon thereafter, reads them their Miranda Rights, and informs them that they are under arrest for suspicion of the murder of Arthur Gibson.

Douglass had used his interrogating skills to convince the bartender to give up the identity of the person who paid him $5,000 to slip a ruffy into a drink on the night of May 24, 1996. In exchange for the confession, he would not be charged with being an accessory to murder but would plead guilty to the lesser charges of accepting a bribe and violating liquor laws. When Douglass received the photo of Sean Callison, the bartender made the ID. Cassie O'Brien's photo could not be ID'd by the check-in clerk as she had obviously altered her look and it was so long ago. Douglass arrested Cassie based on her association with Callison and is hoping to entice a confession on a lesser charge as a cooperating witness. Of course, at this point, he is unaware of the kidnapping.

The detective had been trying to get in touch with Jordan all day on Christmas Eve to inform him of the arrest of Callison and the girl. Jordan had not been able to take calls on the flight to LA from Yosemite.

On Christmas morning, Jordan first calls his mother and speaks with Teri as well. All are relieved that each is healthy and safe. He promises them a visit when he and Janne fly to New Jersey next week. Next, he calls Detective Douglass. The detective explains the arrests of Callison and his girlfriend. He has just been informed that Epstein was found dead in a Los Angeles park. He asks Jordan if he knows anything about it. Jordan tells him that he is up in northern California, spending the holidays with his girlfriend.

At that moment, Jordan realizes he never did hear what happened to Turlock. More than likely, he thinks, Turlock suffered the same fate as Epstein and is lying dead somewhere in the park, soon to be discovered. The former soldiers never told him the details of Turlock's demise, only that he no longer poses a threat.

Jordan calls Donna Gibson. He gives her the details of the arrests made and the fact that Alexander Epstein is dead. She thanks him for his help in solving Arthur's murder. She will rest better now. They wish each other well.

After a nice reunion of a few days with Gabriela and Teri at their home, Jordan and Janne join Al, April, and Paul at a local pub in Short Hills.

"I have an announcement to make," declares Al. "Since most of my clients are on East Coast teams and I have an excellent pipeline with the Penn State football program, April and I have decided to move back here to Jersey. We will be closer to each of our extended families, and…" He opens the palm of his hand toward his lovely wife.

April has a wide grin as she announces, "We are expecting our first child!"

"How wonderful!" shrieks Janne. "Congratulations!" She hugs April.

Jordan shakes Al's hand with equal enthusiasm. "Congratulations, man." He slaps his big friend on the back. Paul extends his congrats as well.

"What's next for you guys?" asks Lil Al to the group collectively.

"Well, with the recommendation of Jack Kemp, I have been offered a full-time position on the staff of Representative Charles McKean. I will be working in Washington, DC," Janne says with a big grin.

"That's great. Congratulations, Janne," says April.

Paul is next. "I am going to stay in Yosemite and work with John and Tricia, representing taxpayers in tax court. They have also commissioned me to make some stock trades for them." Paul is happy.

All eyes turn to Jordan, who sits silently, taking a big swig from his beer mug.

Janne says, "You know, sweetie, the IRS will be making whole-sale changes. I'll bet they could use someone like you to keep them on the straight and narrow. You could work in DC too!" She smiles and nudges him with her shoulder, already knowing what his response will be.

Jordan laughs out loud. "I'm taking a break from taxes. Delgado has hired me to help him with a project in Mexico. I am going to surf Baja and begin a new adventure, but I should be back in a few months."

"Whatever, man." Al is grinning ear to ear as he raises his mug. "Here's to our friendship—forever, wherever!"

They all reach toward the heavens with that toast. They bid one another goodbye for now.

At the Newark airport, sitting and waiting for their flight back to California, Janne leans into Jordan and says, "You know, you were a king."

He smiles. "And you were a queen."

"We were heroes…"

He finishes the line, "Just for one day…"

They laugh.

"We've been through a lot together, and I'd like to continue our relationship. How do you feel, Mr. Duncan?"

Jordan has his arm around her shoulder. "We are young. You will follow your dream of working on Capitol Hill, and I will follow my adventurous spirit for a while. You're right. We have been through a lot together, and things would not have turned out so well without you involved. I feel very close to you, Janne. I love you, Ms. Sawyer, for the person you are and for the experiences we've shared. I want our journey together to be continued." He leans over and kisses her on the forehead.

"I hope so." She kisses him on the mouth.

EPILOGUE

After the typical posturing and negotiating of any congressional bill, the $12.88 billion measure, officially called the Internal Revenue Service Restructuring and Reform Act of 1998, is signed by President Clinton and became public law on July 22, 1998.

The recently appointed commissioner of the IRS, Charles Rossotti, vows to lead the agency away from its heavy emphasis on enforcement to a more balanced policy where enforcement will be complemented with a systematic effort to make the IRS more hospitable to the taxpayer. The idea is that if it is easier for taxpayers to meet their obligations, voluntary compliance will significantly improve.

As Arthur had so appropriately pointed out to Jordan, we should remember that the IRS is the Frankenstein monster of the United States Congress. As has been the case for several decades, the tax code doesn't get smaller or less complex from one administration to the next. To the contrary, there will continue to be issues within the enforcement agency of the tax system. However, the reform act is a tremendous improvement as far as taxpayer rights are concerned. It will prove to be a significant step in reining in the absolute abusive power the Internal Revenue Service has taken upon itself in assessing and collecting taxes from US citizens.

The ramifications of the bill within the IRS infrastructure are profound. Before it became law, there were over nine thousand revenue officers in the Collection Division. The necessary cuts in personnel effectively has brought that number down to just over three thousand. The pressure to collect dollars ("feed the beast"), conduct seizures, and close cases has subsided drastically. Old school ROs, such as Jack Arbuckle, have become obsolete. Jack is expendable and does not survive the cut.

Bobbi Sinclair thrives in the new, friendlier version of tax collectors. In fact, after meeting in person, she has become personal friends with Tonja Farley as they discover much in common. Both are single moms, in their thirties, have outgoing personalities, and a get-the-job-done mentality.

Jordan meets with David Jacobs and Marlin Goodman to discuss the future of Jacobs and Goodman Tax Resolutions. Jordan lays out the evidence he has procured on their inappropriate dealings with the IRS through E, L & O. He agrees to not turn the evidence over to authorities in exchange for their commitment to close their business and no longer practice representing taxpayers to the IRS. After some heated debate with David in particular, they both consent and sign an agreement.

Ironically, Marlin seems more at ease about retiring and demonstrates a newfound respect for Jordan. He comments and does not appear too distraught in the fact that lifelong NY Yankees supporter Alexander Epstein met his demise in the shadows of Dodger Stadium. David, in a strange way, finds humor in the irony of that occurrence as well.

Tonja Farley and Brookes Peterson, with the assistance of a strong recommendation from Jordan Duncan, take positions in the newly formed firm of tax resolution and tax court experts founded by John Sawyer and Tricia Sherman. Brookes is the marketing director, and Tonja will manage the SoCal office and build sales and customer service teams. John and Tricia try to convince Jordan to join them as a partner, but he respectfully declines. Jordan has lunch with Tonja and Brookes. They all wish one another well until their paths cross again.

Jordan gives Tonja a heartfelt hug and thanks her for all her help.

"Take care of this new business. They are good people!"

She smiles and nods. "Absolutely! Take care of yourself."

Sunshine calls Jordan to tell him that, being in her second year at UC Berkeley, she has decided to pursue a law degree. She comments that an alumnus of Cal, Tricia Sherman, has become somewhat of a mentor for her.

She adds, "Guess what! I have a boyfriend!"

"No kidding? That's great. Who is he?" asks Jordan.

"He reminds me *so* much of you—only younger, of course. He's twenty-one."

Jordan laughs. He has finally crossed the threshold of being compared to younger guys instead of always being the young guy.

"His name is Michael. He is good-looking, athletic, plays water polo at CAL, and loves to surf. I told him about how you and I used to surf at Malibu."

Jordan chuckles. "Where is he from?"

"His family lives in Santa Cruz now, but his dad used to be in the military, so they have moved around a lot."

Jordan is very curious… "What is his last name?"

"Lackey. Why? Do you think you know him?"

"I think I might know his dad. Sounds like a great guy, Sunshine. Have fun. And be careful." Jordan shakes his head. *What are the odds?* he thinks.

Jordan and Delgado set sail from Catalina Island on August 1, 1998. They traverse the choppy sea and sail into the calmness of the Pacific on Delgado's Catalina 42, which has a cabin below with a fully functional kitchen, bathroom, and two separate rooms for sleeping.

They finally have time to relax. Jordan has been busy preparing for this trip. He drove his Bronco up to the cabin in Yosemite Valley and handed the keys to his buddy Paul. He terminated his apartment lease, packed some clothes and his two surfboards, said his goodbyes to friends, and promised to stay in touch with Al and Janne.

He realizes that he doesn't know much about these gold bars that they are going to fetch.

"So tell me, Jimmy, where exactly did these gold bars come from?"

"Yeah, I was wondering when you were going to ask that question. Have a seat, amigo. Let me explain it to you."

Jimmy goes below and resurfaces with a couple bottles of Dos Equis. He hands one to Jordan, who is sprawled on a lounge chair. Delgado sits next to him in another lounge chair, as they gaze out into the light-blue endless sky and the deep-blue ocean, wearing nothing but board shorts and shades.

"Back in the mideighties," Jimmy begins, "you may or may not know this, but there was a civil war down in Central America. The government was run by a sort of police state. When people tried to protest in El Salvador, a group led by a church priest was gunned down by the army of police. A guerilla rebellion was formed. One of the leaders was captured, and before he was to be executed or sent to prison, he contacted his *compadre*s to help get his seventeen-year-old son out of the country. His son refused to go unless he could bring his sixteen-year-old girlfriend with him. She was like part of the family, so the leader agreed. They needed a trustworthy 'coyote' to help with the border crossing to El Norte. They found me, and the only means he had to compensate me were gold bars that they had acquired during the Iran-Contra affair in South America."

"Were they stolen?"

"I'm not sure, vato. But I think we are going to find out a whole lot more about their history when we get there!" Jimmy says with his signature grin.

"Great. Can't wait," Jordan says sarcastically.

They lounge silently, each contemplating on their new adventure while enjoying the sun, the sea, the salty breeze, and their beer.

Author's Notes and Acknowledgments

Writing a debut novel at a rather advanced age is not exactly how I planned my life. However, having lived the extraordinary experience of being a taxpayer advocate during the time frame on which *Taxman* is set, I've always known that there's a story to share. Life kind of got in the way as I was busy raising five children. They are currently all grown and doing very well. The time was right for me to research facts, create compelling characters, and write the story about how I perceived the turbulent '90s, especially with regard to the significant tax reform that transpired in this country.

I tried to maintain consistency with historical context, incorporating a real-life timeline, historical events, and persons that were pertinent to the facts of the Internal Revenue Service Restructuring and Reform Act of 1998. As a voracious reader and a particular lover of historical fiction novels, I chose a style of narration from a conglomeration of various great storytellers.

One of the joys of writing historical fiction is the latitude of creating compelling fictitious characters to tell a story based on true events. In writing *Taxman*, I was able to draw on personal experiences and those of others during the time frame to create characters and storylines. Each of the cases that Jordan Duncan takes on were derived from real-life events. Of course, some names were changed, and some facts were expounded upon. The purpose of telling the story through a tax resolution firm was to demonstrate the incredible environment that taxpayers endured during the nineties. Taxpayer abuse was rampant, but so was the "golden age" of the offer in compromise, wherein people were literally settling tax debts for pennies on the dollar! The CPA firm and the Alexander Epstein character are fictional to add drama to the story.

It is not my intention to depict all IRS employees as bullies or abusers. That certainly was not and is not the case. It was just a matter of revenue agents and officers being given the unenviable task of assessing and collecting as much tax revenue as quickly as possible with an overabundance of power and authority.

It has been an exciting and exhilarating process to research, create, outline, and write this story. I understand now how authors can say that their stories literally develop as they write. Certain twists and new characters come to mind during the storytelling process. I hope that you enjoyed reading the story, were able to somehow relate to the characters and historical events that transpired, and felt a sense of realism while reading.

This book is the first of a series of stories focusing on the adventures of the "Taxman," Jordan Duncan. You can only guess where the next book will take the journey as Jordan Duncan and Jimmy Delgado set sail to Mexico with the intent of recovering Delgado's gold bars! The story is outlined and will also be based on historical events. Watch for it in early 2022.

Before closing, I want to acknowledge the individuals who helped me in the process of creating and writing *Taxman*. I express tremendous gratitude to Tonja Thomas, who was a true inspiration and a phenomenal editorial soundboard during the entire process. Having experienced the tax resolution business of the '90s alongside me, she helped recreate many scenes and details of the story.

I want to thank Dave and Lori Morse, who patiently and enthusiastically read the manuscript as it was being written in the first draft and provided invaluable feedback and insight.

I thank my father, family members, friends, and associates who also contributed by giving constructive feedback and editorial advice.

I thank Jimmy Kemp for graciously allowing me to include his father, the great Jack Kemp, as a pertinent player in the storyline of congressional oversight in the process of tax restructuring and reform. He is currently the president of the Jack Kemp Foundation.

A special thanks goes to Shelley Davis, who as it turns out was the first and only IRS historian ever appointed. Her willingness upon reading the manuscript, to allow me to include her name and excerpts from her very well-written book *Unbridled Power; Inside the Secret Culture of the IRS*, helped inspire and add depth and authenticity to the storyline.

My thanks to the entire team at Fulton Books for an outstanding job of publishing my novel. A special shoutout to Ashley Tyler as my personal representative. Her prompt, professional, and accurate communication with me on the publication details throughout the process was greatly appreciated. May this be the beginning of a long, mutually enjoyable, and successful endeavor.

About the Author

John Ginos worked as a taxpayer advocate during the decade of the 1990s. *TAXMAN* is his debut novel and is based on his personal experiences and historical events during that period of time. He is a California native but has recently moved to Arizona to be closer to his grown children and grandchildren. He is currently writing the sequel to *TAXMAN* and will be working on a series of novels featuring the main protagonist, Jordan Duncan.

CPSIA information can be obtained
at www.ICGtesting.com
Printed in the USA
FSHW011320171121
86283FS